SPIRITS OF THE EARTH BOOK TWO
TOMORROW'S CHILDREN

MILO JAMES FOWLER

www.aethonbooks.com

TOMORROW'S CHILDREN
©2020 MILO JAMES FOWLER

This book is protected under the copyright laws of the United States of America. No part of this publication may be reproduced, stored in a retrieval system, or transmitted, in any form or by any means, without the prior permission in writing of the publisher, nor be otherwise circulated in any form of binding or cover other than that in which it is published and without a similar condition including this condition being imposed on the subsequent purchaser. Any reproduction or unauthorized use of the material or artwork contained herein is prohibited without the express written permission of the authors.

Aethon Books supports the right to free expression and the value of copyright. The purpose of copyright is to encourage writers and artists to produce the creative works that enrich our culture.

The scanning, uploading, and distribution of this book without permission is a theft of the author's intellectual property. If you would like to use material from the book (other than for review purposes), please contact editor@aethonbooks.com. Thank you for your support of the author's rights.

Aethon Books
PO Box 121515
Fort Worth TX, 76108
www.aethonbooks.com

Print and eBook formatting, and cover design by Steve Beaulieu.

Published by Aethon Books LLC.

Aethon Books is not responsible for websites (or their content) that are not owned by the publisher.

This book is a work of fiction. Names, characters, places, and incidents are the product of the author's imagination or are used fictitiously. Any resemblance to actual events, locales, or persons, living or dead is coincidental.

All rights reserved.

ALSO IN THE SERIES

After the Sky
You're reading: ***Tomorrow's Children***
City of Glass

For Sara

*"Generations come and generations go,
but the earth remains forever."*
Ecclesiastes 1:4

PART I

CONTACT

1. BISHOP

18 MONTHS AFTER ALL-CLEAR

I look into the mirror over the sink, but the face staring back at me is not my own. Maybe it was, once. Now I can't be sure. The eyes are wrong: dead in their red-rimmed sockets. Yet somewhere down deep, shoved under and held there by forces beyond my control, a heart still pumps. Fresh blood circulates. Lungs manage to squeeze oxygen out of the air.

So I'm alive. For what it's worth.

I close my eyes and pinch the bridge of my nose, inhaling, exhaling. Focusing on the moment. I allow my gaze to return to the mirror, drawn like a cold hand to flame. Somewhere, beneath the surface, I glimpse a ghost of the man I was: James Bishop. Husband. Father. Soldier. It's enough to press on with—that scrap of myself.

They haven't destroyed me completely.

Not yet.

I pull on the heavy-duty hazard suit over my combat armor and zip up the interior lining. Attendants seal the orange outer layer to lock me inside. Good thing I'm not claustrophobic, or I would be hyperventilating right now. O2 is circulating well enough via interior cooling vents. The oxygen supply smells okay, tastes all right, and will last six to twelve hours, depending on my exertion level. I don't plan on overdoing it. And I don't intend to take that long.

Get in, get out. Do the job. Do what they expect. Nothing more.

"Test, test," a voice comes through internal comms, loud and clear, as my head is encased within a triple-polymer helmet. "Sergeant Bishop, do you copy?"

I stare at the scrawny scientist in a white lab jacket—pencil neck, golf ball eyes. *Copy?* The geek seems to enjoy playing military.

"Yeah." I nod.

The scientist smiles with gums more prominent than teeth, his head bobbing in a quick series of jerks. "Your entire team will be wearing these next-gen environmental suits, Sergeant. They will provide complete protection against whatever viable contaminants you come across over there. Even if a toxin manages to penetrate the outer layer, you'll have enough time to radio the chopper and get out before your primary protective lining is compromised."

Comforting. And what makes it even better? These government geniuses don't have a clue what I'm going to find *over there*. They just know it's so messed up that nobody has dared come close to that continent for the past decade. A quarantine zone, blockaded by a fleet of well-armed battleships like the one where I find myself at the moment.

Nobody in or out. Until now.

I've won the lottery. Not the kind they had way back before D-Day, when the biggest news on the Link was the rising cost of fuel and the building fervor over climate change. Back then, lottery tickets were sold by the kilo to folks hoping to trade in their hard-earned credit for a big piece of the pie. Millions of dollars—billions, eventually, as inflation rose. Winning the lottery held a rare distinction in those days.

Maybe it still does, even without the monetary reward. Now when your name is picked by the military powers that be, you go wherever the United World government sends you. And in the case of Sergeant James Bishop, I sure have drawn the short straw.

But I won't be alone. A few others share my unlucky distinction. A team of real winners. They might have gladly let me carry the banner alone if they could, but they'll follow orders like good little soldiers.

We all will. Or face the consequences.

Rumors about the forbidden continent are ubiquitous. You'd have to be a total zombie not to hear the myths and legends. Some say what remains of the North American Sectors are haunted, that the ghosts of those souls nuked on D-Day still roam the earth, physically possessing anyone stupid enough to set foot on that godforsaken continent. Others take a less supernatural slant; they say there is still something in the topsoil, some kind of fast-acting mutagen that can turn you into a monster of freakish proportions. Supposedly, this mutagen has evolved as a result of nuclear radiation interacting with the rebels' toxic bioweapons released at the start of the war, and the residue somehow managed to remain viable over the decades that followed.

Locked in the dust. Contagious and lethal. Just waiting to infect somebody.

They sure knew how to kill people in those days.

How else can you explain it? some say. *What happened to those teams we sent over there two years ago? Why'd they never return?*

I don't try to explain it. There's no point. Besides, I have other things on my mind, more important things. Like my wife and kids, held for safekeeping in the bowels of a UW prison. As long as I play ball, my superiors will allow me to see them when this mission is over. Maybe even go home together. One big happy Eurasian family again, living out our days in one of the outlying self-sustained biospheres.

"Hey, Captain!" Granger the engineer—barely 150 centimeters tall but with enough muscle mass to make up for some of his missing stature—calls from across the sterile medical bay.

Captain? Not a bad promotion.

"How're we gonna move around in these things?" Granger swings his arms upward in the hazard suit, and the Kevlar-plated sleeves hardly shift.

I shrug and face the geek currently in charge.

"Right. Mobility." The scientist swallows, and his Adam's apple looks as large as one of his eyeballs, lodged in his throat. "It will require an increased amount of effort to maneuver in these suits, due to the added weight of the protective layers, but as with anything, you'll get the hang of it. Eventually."

His words are nothing if not inspiring.

"Put all those rippling muscles to work, Granger." I heave my arms upward despite the resistance. It feels like gravity in the bay has increased by fifty percent. "I'm sure you'll fare better than the rest of us."

Granger curses. Like me, he was picked for this mission because of his track record. One successful campaign after the next, always returning with a full crew, always with mission objectives met, recorded, and filed for the superiors to read while they're on the pot. As far as I can tell, my team members have one thing in common, despite their diversity: they're career military, serving the UW out of a sense of duty to the common good, an honor that runs deep despite the current regime's fascist tendencies. The team was handpicked for a singular purpose, one they'll be briefed on in detail while en route.

They don't have to like each other to get the job done. They're professionals.

"The Wastes are a level playing field." Sinclair the science officer, a woman who looks to be twice Granger's height and half his weight, strides into the medical bay in her bulky suit. Swiveling at the waist to give me a cursory glance, she returns her attention to our miniature engineer. "None of us will have an edge."

I force my arm upward and tap my helmet with a thick gloved finger. "We'll be breathing. That's all the edge we'll need."

She blinks at me, but that's about it as far as a response. She strikes me as one of those cold, intellectual types with a staggering IQ and a never-veiled disdain for the rest of the world's Neanderthals. I skimmed her datafile. As with Granger, there was nothing but a detailed log of successful missions, along with an extensive list of accolades I was quick to categorize as scientific mumbo-jumbo.

The other two members of the team show up eventually, staggering beneath the weight of their suits. The bug-eyed scientist responsible for our prep-talk welcomes them with a wide grin and wobbles his head like some kind of large, extinct bird.

"Great, looks like we're all here now." He stares at us and grins, touching the tips of his long fingers together. The silence drags on longer than necessary. "Right. So, any last-minute questions before we go topside?"

"Yeah," grunts one of the latecomers—Morley, the weapons officer, a shaggy-haired fellow with a lineage stretching all the way back to the Caribbean, the Old World's definition of paradise. According to his file, he prizes his guns over his own family. Fine by me; best to be well-armed on this trip. "What if we need to take a dump, man?"

"Just let 'er rip, pal." Granger chuckles.

The room explodes with raucous laughter, all present contributing—except for the distinguished science officer. She sighs instead, looking bored.

"It's really not that complicated," chortles the scientist in charge. He's the last one to overcome his giggles, and by the time he does, he's the only one enjoying himself. "There is a waste reservoir built into the suit. If you have an *excretory emergency*—" He grins like a five-year-old. "Go ahead and make your deposit. We'll retrieve it once you're back here, safe and sound."

"How can I sign up for that job?" asks Harris, the other latecomer—oldest member of the team by at least twenty years. He had quite the distinguished medical career both in the UW military and private sector prior to D-Day, publishing studies on genetics and such, the kind they studied in med schools. It's unclear why the elderly doctor has been included on this trip.

I haven't been told much. I know we're headed into forbidden territory, but that's about it. No one has set foot in the Wastes for years, not since those reports of something going horribly wrong with the search and rescue teams dropped onto the North American continent. No details, of course, only rumors that spread like a virus. The entire situation reeks of a government cover-up.

Have we been drafted for a suicide mission?

"What do you say, Sergeant?"

The bug-eyed scientist stares at me with an expectant grin.

"How's that?" I frown, lost.

"Our fearless leader," Sinclair mutters.

The scientist gestures toward the door, reaching out his spindly arm. "Shall we go?"

Like we have a choice. But I nod anyway, turning to lead the team in an awkward, exaggerated march out of the medical bay, down a long, narrow corridor, and into the ship's main storage area. The cargo lift awaits—a glorified freight elevator—and all of us somehow manage to cram inside the oily smelling thing.

"How many hazard suits can you fit in an elevator?" Adam's apple shuddering, the scientist giggles like it's a joke worthy of a spectacular punchline. Only he doesn't seem to have one prepared. Dipping his chin, he moves to follow us in.

"We're full." I stiff-arm him and punch the UP arrow. The cage doors slide shut. "Take the next one."

Granger chuckles at the hurt look on the scientist's face.

With a groan, the lift rises toward the flight deck, passing through levels one at a time and seeming to linger unnecessarily between each floor. It wasn't designed for cargo of the human variety. For the massive crates of foodstuffs, weapons, and supplies that usually come down through here, the passage of time is immaterial. But for me, every second counts—every moment I'm away from my family. There is no time to waste.

Get in, get out. That's the mantra. *Get the job done right.* Then I'll see my children again—before they forget me.

Assuming I make it back alive.

"So, Captain. You ready for this?" Granger nudges me.

I barely feel the gesture through this suit. "I doubt any of us are."

"It's true, yeah? The stuff they say?" Morley pipes up.

"The rumors?" Sinclair intones, affecting both disdain and disinterest in a single aloof expression, sharp nose angled upward. She succeeds in removing herself from the conversation while standing smack-dab in the middle of it, staring at the seam in the elevator doors. It looks like she's willing them to open and save her from what promises to be a wearisome discussion.

"They're more than that," Doc Harris says. "*Rumor* implies it might not be entirely true."

"And you think it is?" Granger tilts his helmet back to look up at the doctor. "Cuz I've heard plenty of crazy stories."

Harris nods, pursing his lips in thought. "There is a certain mythos to the continent, to be sure. An aura of secrecy, maintained by ships such as this one and the naval blockade. Its purpose being what exactly? To keep the rest of the world away from that wasted, inhospitable land?" He narrows his gaze. "Or to keep something already there contained?"

The rest of the world. As if it still exists as anything more than a domed megacity along the Mediterranean.

No one says anything for a few seconds. There's only the whine of the elevator cables and the creaking of the ship to punctuate the silence.

"What do you think, Captain?" Morley points his chin at me. "You believin' the ghost stories?"

Captain again. As far as this team is concerned, I guess I am the *Ubermensch*. I'll lead them straight through the gates of Hades with the UW's blessing. How far they follow me will depend on one thing: whatever their superiors are holding over their heads. Children are probably out of the question. As far as I know, I'm the only man in my cube complex with offspring under the Terminal Age. One in ten thousand, they say.

Mr. and Mrs. Bishop are special that way. Or we were—before we, too, found ourselves unable to conceive.

"I believe what I can see," I mutter.

Sinclair glances at me and quickly looks away.

"A realist," Harris says with half a grin, revealing a set of pristine, white dentures. "So you don't believe the reports of a highly contagious mutagen? Difficult to *see* something like that, I'd wager. Without a microscope, anyhow."

"You're thinking that's what it is, then?" Morley says. "Some sort of creepy crawly?"

"Well, duh!" Granger gestures at our suits. "Why do you think we're wearin' these things? What do *you* think's waiting for us over there?"

Morley's eyes are naturally wide, noticeably so when he neglects to blink. "I believe in the eternal soul. It cannot be destroyed by bombs. You may think of it as the spirit within us all." His gloved hand pats his chest twice. "A soul that has been taken against its will—as so many were on D-Day—remains on the earth for one reason only." He pauses dramatically, looking at each of the faces around him. *"Vengeance."*

Sinclair releases a petulant sigh.

Granger stares for a moment, his lips parted. Then something seems to click in his brain, and he guffaws abruptly. "What a load of crap! You hear this guy?" He nudges Morley with his elbow. "Talk about ghost stories!"

Morley shrugs, barely noticeable in the suit. "We shall see."

"Perhaps it would be prudent to withhold speculation until after the briefing," Sinclair suggests as the lift groans to a halt. She faces Granger.

"Prudent, yeah." Granger's line of sight travels down her suit out of habit, despite the fact that her figure remains completely obscured.

She graces him with a withering look.

The doors seem reluctant to open, but after a few moments of awkward silence, they part with a metallic squeal. We're met with a blast of blinding sunlight, our helmets darkening instantly to shield exposed faces from the harmful ultraviolet rays. A gangly silhouette approaches.

"What took you so long? This way, this way." With a sweep of his scrawny arm, the scientist from the medical bay beckons us out of the elevator and onto the flight deck. A chugging chopper sits fifty meters away, its rotors slicing neatly through the air.

"Hey, how'd you beat us here?" Granger says.

"Short cut." The scientist shrugs affably. He wears a white jumpsuit with a transparent face shield now, having somehow found time to change. "Gather your team, Sergeant Bishop, and follow me."

I blink away the white spots from my glimpse of the sun. My gaze wanders toward the rolling sea, grey ocean water stretching infinitely on all sides. Easy to imagine the breeze on my skin. I can almost feel it, fished from deep memory.

I step out of the lift and glance back. The others are tough to tell apart with their black bubble helmets, except for Granger and Sinclair, whose respective size differences make them easy to identify. They take a moment to collect themselves and then march after me, ducking slightly once in range of the chopper's rotors. A makeshift ramp has been set up to aid us in climbing aboard. No chance we'd be able to, otherwise.

The scientist jogs up the ramp and finds a seat inside. He quickly buckles himself in.

"He's coming with us?" Granger sounds disappointed, like a kid hoping to avoid being chaperoned.

"Briefing us en route." I heave myself onto the ramp. "I doubt he'll stick around after the drop."

"How 'bout we drop him instead and head home?"

"They might have something to say about that." I nod toward the row of well-armed soldiers with opaque face shields already seated inside. They wear jumpsuits over bulky body armor, but no hazard protection. Their purpose is clear: to ensure that my team makes the drop. Not to join us.

Granger falls silent.

The chopper lifts off once all five of us are locked into place with magnetic clamps fastened to our unwieldy suits, holding them upright and immobile. Sitting is not an option. The tinting on our helmets dissolves just enough for me to catch Sinclair's eye. I give her a wink. She stares me down, unimpressed. The woman has a real attitude. I like that.

"Test, test," chirps the scientist through our comms. "Can everyone hear all right? Let me know if you can hear me with a thumbs up. Hello? Everyone?"

We nod or mutter in the affirmative. Granger feigns technical difficulties with his helmet, but decides to give up the gag when nobody but me notices. Their attention remains elsewhere. The murky ocean depths pass swiftly below, and every meter takes us closer to the North American Wastes. It has a way of dampening the spirit and the sense of humor: the impending unknown.

"Good, good," the scientist bobs his head, again reminding me of an extinct angular waterfowl. Can't remember the species. "All right then. We're on our way. Your suits check out, your O2 reserves are stocked. We'll be in constant communication while you're over there. Remember, you run into any unexpected difficulties, you radio. Don't delay. That's what we're here for." He grins. "We're your backup."

Encouraging. I avoid Granger's sardonic gaze while Harris clears his throat.

"Yes, Doctor?" The scientist raises both eyebrows.

"Where will you be, exactly?"

"Back on board the *Argonaus*. We don't have enough fuel for the chopper to remain above your location. Once we make your drop, we'll return to the ship, refuel, and await your call."

"Ten minutes, then," Harris says.

The scientist frowns slightly. "How's that?"

"That's how long we'll be stranded, once we radio you. Ten minutes."

"I see what you mean. Unfortunately, the *Argonaus* cannot position itself closer to shore. UW mandate and all—government red tape, I'm afraid. And yes, it will take us ten minutes to reach your position."

"Where is that exactly?" Morley speaks up. He glances at the other members of our team. "Am I the only one who's got no idea where it is we're goin'?"

The scientist holds up his hands and closes his eyes for a moment. "We're getting ahead of ourselves." He licks his lips and fixes his bulbous eyes on me. "I thought you would have told them *something* by now, Sergeant."

Passing the buck. "Under orders." I can play the game as well as anybody. "They're supposed to hear it straight from you," I lie.

I'll be hearing it for the first time as well. Right here, right now. But of course I can't admit that in front of my team. I have to at least look like I know what I'm doing.

"Very well, then." The scientist straightens his posture and sweeps the five helmeted heads before him with his gaze. For a moment, it doesn't look like he knows where to begin. "The D-Day bunkers across what remains of the United Sectors were programmed to open on a designated date: All-Clear. We sent our search and rescue teams in early to survey the situation." He nods, fully aware this is common knowledge.

"Right. And they never came back," Granger says.

"Hundreds of 'em," Morley echoes.

"Two hundred seventy. Thirty squads, to be exact. We lost all radio contact within an hour of their landing. They were fully equipped with solar jeeps, supplies, weapons, and hydration suits, tasked to check on each of the bunkers and aid the survivors in their reentry and rebuilding. Salvage as much as they could." He pauses. "Twenty years after the bombs dropped, we assumed there would be nothing left on the surface."

We did a real number on them. I was only a kid at the time, but I remember well enough. How could anybody forget such a war? The Sector Patriots, or whatever they called themselves. Terrorists. Cowards. The biological weapons they released resulted in global catastrophe. For the planet and its people.

I blink, fighting to return to the moment—even as my thoughts drift back to my kids. Mara and Emmanuel, two of the last children born in Eurasia.

"I'm sure we'll never forget their final radio contact." The scientist nods with reverence.

It was all over the Link at the time: a squad leader screaming his guts out, sounding like he was being flayed alive. Choppers were sent en masse, but they couldn't get close. The dust storms were too massive, on a scale of the Saharan variety. They wouldn't quit—not until the choppers backed off. Uncanny, to say the least. Remote drones flew in next, and the footage they captured was even more horrific, also broadcast throughout the Eurasian domes.

"May we dispense with the nostalgia? I believe our memories remain completely intact," Sinclair says. "The issue is our current mission. We'll be landing in a matter of minutes. I, for one, would appreciate knowing what our orders are."

"Right on," Morley mutters.

The scientist clears his throat. "Very well. I guess it's all a matter of record—"

"And rehashing it doesn't do a whole lot for the ol' morale," Granger adds. "Every tour of duty's a one-way trip, like as not, but how about we accentuate the positive here? Last thing I want to be thinkin' about is all those boys and girls getting their skin ripped off by some freaky sandstorms." He shivers in his suit.

The scientist smiles, and it looks almost genuine. "Lucky for you, I do have some good news." He claps his gloved hands and rubs them together, glancing at each of us and seeming to expect an eager reaction. So we stare back at him until his grin falters. "Now, this is top-secret information here—"

"You don't have to tell us twice." Nobody on board is a security threat. The UW has made sure we won't be, has taken certain precautions. *Mara and Emmanuel.*

I dry-swallow and focus my attention on the rivets along the steel floor.

"Let's hope not." The scientist forges ahead. "A few months ago, we established contact with a group of survivors within the Forbidden Zone. Sector 31, to be exact—a trade sector, back before the war." He watches us, pleased now to have our undivided attention. "They have managed to keep themselves free from contamination by remaining beneath the surface since All-Clear. We have learned much about their current situation over the past months, and we believe the time has finally arrived for us to make contact. In the flesh." He leans forward. "That, my friends, is why you are here. You are the first UW team to meet the only survivors from the North American Sectors!"

Morley and Harris cast glances at me. I do my best to maintain a stoic expression—as much like Sinclair's as I can muster.

Granger clears his throat. "Am I the only one who thinks that's a load of bullcrap? Only half the story, if that?" He chuckles awkwardly. "I mean, don't get me wrong, I'm sure we're honored and all, but take a look at us. An engineer, a science officer, a weapons tech, a doctor, and—" He gestures at me. "Fearless Leader here. We're not exactly poster-ready ambassadors."

"Granted." The scientist nods. He doesn't smile, which is nice for a change. "But that's all I'm authorized to tell you right now. The particulars of your mission will appear on your heads-up displays once you've reached the drop site."

Morley forces an arm upward and raps on his helmet. "These things are equipped with HUD's?"

"State of the art, with night vision and thermographic scanning capabilities. No matter where you are, you'll be able to see where you're going." He glances outside. "Go ahead and try them out, if you can maneuver yourselves adequately. Practice using them long-range."

I'm the only one facing the open side of the chopper. I squint my eyes, straining to see beyond the whitecaps of the ocean below. The shore will soon be in sight, but it's still too far to make out any particulars.

"Voice commands," the scientist says. "What optical device do you normally use for long distances?"

"Binocs," I mutter.

Instantly, the HUD blinks on my transparent face shield, and my field of vision zooms toward the coast. My head lolls backward involuntarily at the sudden change in perspective.

"Cool, huh?" The scientist giggles, returning to obnoxious mode.

I mumble something in the affirmative. *Very cool*. I can see it all: the beach grey with ash, polluted by all manner of debris. The foul breakers rolling in with foam an unmistakable toxic yellow tint. Overturned ships lying scattered all along the shore like the massive bones of a disturbed nautical graveyard. No signs of life anywhere.

"How do you shut it off?"

"Just say the word."

"Off." The HUD vanishes. I return my gaze to the pronounced rivets along the floor.

"Does this thing have x-ray vision?" Granger faces Sinclair.

"What would be the point?" she counters. Then she notices his gaze, level with her chest. "Grow up."

"Afraid not," the scientist says. "No x-ray. But it'll *see* you through." He's the only one to find that pun humorous. "Keep an eye on the temperature gauge—it'll be on the bottom left of your HUD. Those suits can get up to thirty degrees warmer than the ambient temperature. Not a problem at night, but right now—during the heat of the day? It'll get pretty toasty in there. So when you see the gauge dip into the red zone, just give the voice command: cool down. The suit will take care of the rest."

Granger frowns. "Is there some kind of owner's manual we should be reading?"

The scientist laughs out loud. "Actually, if you say *manual*, it'll pop right up. Some in-flight reading material for you, how's that?"

Harris and Morley take his tip and start skimming over the text on their face shields. Granger is quick to follow suit, followed by Sinclair with another bored sigh. I refrain from activating the HUD manual. In my mind, I can still see the overturned ships, the obliterated shoreline, completely devoid of life. So much for the North American Sectors. The idea that anything other than death will be found on this continent is difficult to accept. Yet here I am, flying straight into a wasteland with one purpose in mind: first contact.

"Something wrong, Sergeant?" The scientist leans toward me. "Is there a glitch with your operations manual?"

I look at him, look through him. Something in my blank expression makes him sit back in his seat and keep to himself, fidgeting a little.

"I'll figure it out as I go," I tell him.

Like I always do.

2. CAIN

13 MONTHS AFTER ALL-CLEAR

A rusty, slow-revolving ceiling fan dangles from the deck above with a single spotted lightbulb. The sickly glow illuminates the top of a crate—a makeshift poker table. We sit in a tight circle around it, three men to my left, two to my right, using whatever is available for chairs. Smaller crates work for them, but not for the biggest one in their midst, the one with the hand to beat: me.

I have a sturdy folding chair all my own.

One by one, this motley bunch—sun-damaged, scarred, thickly muscled and glistening with sweat—folds, tossing down their tattered cards in disgust. I chew my cigar with relish in the hazy smoke and watch them, keeping my face an expressionless mask. A single opponent remains, and I stare hard at this one, the youngest at the table, reading him, sensing his heart rate quicken. Is he bluffing? Or merely excited at the prospect of holding a winning hand for once?

The stack of hydropacks in the middle of the crate is more than enough to last a body two weeks, maybe three. In the Old World, they might have been bars of solid gold.

"Think you can beat me, Lemuel?" I ask, my voice deep and husky.

Lemuel licks his lips. Now that is an obvious tell. He is uncertain. He perspires as we all do; it is always hot as hell this time of day. But his thermal energy output is twice that of anyone else at the table. My eyes miss nothing.

"You're going to lose, one of these days," Lemuel says. He fights to keep his features slack, his eyes free of emotion. A futile effort.

I chuckle, and the sound reverberates deep in my broad chest. "Not today, Lemuel. Make up your mind. Call or fold."

"Piss or get off the pot," snickers one of the others.

Lemuel glares at him.

The iron door clangs open, and with it blasts a flood of blinding white from outside. I look away while the men groan, wincing like rodents unaccustomed to sunlight. They hold up their hands to shield their eyes and curse. A dark figure enters, waddling with great effort.

"What is it, woman?" I demand with a scowl as the door slams shut.

She approaches my side without hesitation, far along in her pregnancy. Her protruding abdomen stretches her stained tank top.

"He's back. And he's got that cyborg with him."

"Gaia-dammit." I pound my fist on the crate, jostling the hydropacks. "I said we weren't to be disturbed!"

"Keep your voice down." She rests a hand on my bare shoulder, slick with sweat. "You'll wake the others."

I allow myself to seethe for a moment, nostrils flared. "You embarrass me in front of my chieftains," I warn her.

She shrugs, winking at Lemuel—who averts his eyes. "They already know who wears the pants in this family."

I grab her, and she nearly cries out at my strength and roughness. But I grin amiably as I set her down on my lap and hold her there like a child.

"Gentlemen, say hello to Lady Victoria." I playfully pinch her cheek, and she slaps my hand away. "My fourth wife. Obviously the youngest, as she has yet to learn her proper place."

The chieftains stir and nod, grunting about it being a pleasure to see her today. But they don't seem to know where to direct their eyes.

"Your fourth," Lemuel echoes. "How do you make time for so many women?" Now that he sits at a man's table, he seems to think he has the right to ask any impertinent question that pops into his head. "Are they on a rotating schedule or something?"

"Mind your idiot tongue!" The wizened old-timer at his side throws a hard punch into Lemuel's shoulder. The youth winces.

"A good guess, but no." I caress Victoria's giant melon that holds my child. "They come when I summon them. For now, they are where they belong: deep in the bowels of this ship, safe and sound. Just as ripe as my dear Victoria. I will be the father of four robust lads and lasses by this time next month." I pinch her again. She squirms, struggling to rise.

"Luther and the cyborg wait for you outside," she says. My hands drop from her, allowing her to stand. "They are patient men, but—"

"They are infidels. Gaia should drown them in sand and deliver us from their bothersome meddling. I would kill them myself, if only they were not human."

The chieftains watch me silently. One clears his throat, but none speak. They know better.

"Who are they? These visitors?" Lemuel asks. He grimaces as the old-timer punches him a second time.

"You're a guest here! You don't get to question Lord Cain—"

"It's all right, Justus. Lemuel sits at this table now. And rightly so." I narrow my gaze at the youth. Victoria stands by, watching the scene unfold with unguarded curiosity. "How many goblyn heads have you spiked along the wall, Lemuel?" I stroke my wide, stubble-covered chin.

"Thirty-four," Lemuel says without hesitation, proud of it.

"Thirty-four?" I nod, pursing my lips. "Not bad. Not bad at all." I direct my gaze to Justus. "You see? Because of this young man, there are now thirty-four fewer of those flesh-eaters out there on the loose. I'd say he's more than earned his place among us. Don't you agree?"

Not one to question authority, the old-timer bows slightly. "Of course, Lord Cain. As you say. Always."

"Regarding your question..." My eyes return to Lemuel. "These men, these desert nomads from the east, they are followers of a lesser god. They have no home, no land, nothing but what they carry with them. They have not carved out a place for themselves in this world, as we have here in the Shipyard."

"They seek our assistance, then," Lemuel says.

"Don't interrupt!" Justus lets fly with another punch.

"You would think so," I continue. "But that is not why they are here. They do not wish to join us." I pause. "They want us to join *them*."

Subdued laughter erupts among the chieftains, but it is quickly snuffed out by a stern glance from Lady Victoria. A reminder that the others are sleeping during the heat of the day, when the sun is at its strongest and most dangerous. It is time for rest in the shelter of this ship and the others like it, toppled along the seashore.

"But who are they? Where do they come from?" The eager, undying flame of curiosity burns in Lemuel's eyes.

I look to my wife. "How many times have they taken advantage of our hospitality?"

"This is the third."

"And always with the same song: Join us. Leave all that you have worked so hard for and follow. Like sheep." I curse mildly, shaking my head at the audacity of it. "Fools. That's what they are. It's all you need know."

I rise then, ducking my head to keep from hitting the whirling rotors of the fan above. I tower over everyone present. The top of Victoria's blonde head reaches only my sternum.

"I won't be long," I tell the chieftains, who nod, mumbling that they will await my return. Of course they will. They have nowhere else to go.

Victoria leads me to the room's iron exterior door and spins the hand wheel deftly, heaving it open. I squint in the glare of the sudden light outside and step over the lip of the doorframe, shielding my eyes with one hand.

"Where are they?" I reach for my goggles and dark cloak, dangling from one of many steel hooks beside the door. Similar garments left by the chieftains line the rusted wall.

"At the gate."

"You didn't let them in?" I glance at her as I pull on the cloak. It will shield me from the sun's merciless rays, even at their strongest. I tuck in my braid of coarse, black hair before tugging the hood over my head.

"Not this time. It's as you say. They have worn out their welcome."

I smile. Sometimes the woman actually speaks sense. "Just the two of them then. Unarmed."

"Yes. But the cyborg—"

"A weapon in and of himself. I know full well." I strap on the goggles and adjust my hood. "How do I look?" I take a step backward, out of the shadows and into sunlight, my protected skin instantly warmed by the relentless heat. I flex my muscles for her, and they strain against my garments.

"Go on and strut, you big rooster." She folds her arms across her belly, remaining in the shade of the ship's hull.

I lick my lips. "Mmmm. Chicken." My stomach growls at the memory of it. "Grilled. Fried. Or roasted?"

"Don't torture me," she pleads with a sudden wince and a hand to her stomach. "You have no idea what sorts of things I've been craving lately. But what do we have instead? Protein packs, vitaminerals, and let's not forget the stuff that passes for water. So much to choose from!"

"I could roast you a goblyn."

She almost vomits right there.

I chuckle. "Go back to bed. I will join you before sundown."

With a tolerant flutter of her hand, she turns away, waddling along the side of the ship's hull toward another door that opens into the women's sleeping quarters. I watch her until she vanishes from sight, shutting the door behind her.

I hope for a son. *I will name him Adam.* Fitting for the firstborn of a new generation. Unless Gaia chooses another, of course.

"Lord Cain," one of the guards greets me as I cross the meters of ashen sand between the overturned ships and the wall. "They're back."

With a grunt, I approach the rusted sheet metal driven deep into the ground, standing three meters high and topped with coils of barbed wire. I nod to the men at the gate.

"They're nothing if not persistent." I slow my pace, noting the rash of bullet holes piercing a large section of the east wall. "Those were to be plugged."

"On it," the guard says. He shoulders his rifle by its leather strap and beckons to a comrade farther down the wall.

I take a moment to survey the damage, cursing the goblyns and their bloodlust. While I am at it, I curse the nomads and their heretical beliefs. Under my breath, I also curse my men who neglected to do their assigned repairs. Dereliction of duty is not something I take lightly. It may as well have been outright insubordination. I will have to make an example of these two, scurrying about in their cloaks as they search for the bucket of tar necessary for the job.

Incompetent idiots.

I turn from the punctured metal and sweep my gaze along the shore, across the row of capsized ships rejected by the sea long ago, abandoned like a giant child's playthings. I watch the breakers roll in, the murky water, the yellow foam. I stare out into the distance.

My eyes gradually adjust, focusing a kilometer out, then two, three. My jaw muscles tighten as my gaze locks onto the United World warship sitting there, patrolling this Forbidden Zone as if it owns the waters. The UW soldiers aboard it have yet to venture ashore. What are they waiting for?

We are hemmed in before and behind. The wall the chieftains built months ago to protect us from the goblyn raids forms a semicircle around the overturned ships. The thick metal barrier does not extend far into the water. For some reason, the goblyns refuse to go near the crashing surf, as if it frightens them. Even so, I had the men plant the wall a hundred meters seaward so that, between the tides, there would be no absence of protection at our flanks. The ocean itself provides a line of defense behind us, one neither the goblyns nor the UW have dared to breach. Yet.

I scowl at the grey battleship. The *UW Argonaus*, according to its white lettering along the side. How long has it guarded the coast, ensuring that no one leaves this diseased continent? As far as we know, the naval blockade has been in place ever since All-Clear, when my men and I were released from our underground bunker. We left Sector 15 eleven months ago and headed due west to fulfill nothing less than a manifest destiny, guided by Gaia herself every step of the way.

Why do they watch us? I turn away from the sea.

"We meet again," the man outside the gate calls amicably. He is the leader of the nomad heretics, and his name is Luther. He wears light, sand-colored garments that wrap him like a mummy. With the black goggles, he also resembles the *Invisible Man*. Perhaps I spent too much time in the bunker watching old horror films.

I step forward to grip one of the gate's iron bars at eye level. "You don't take no for an answer. What is this—your final plea?"

"If you accept our offer." Luther nods.

My eyes flick to the figure beside him. Samson, the cyborg. A large man, close to my stature and well-developed musculature. In a fair fight, we might be evenly matched. But Samson has biomechatronic arms and legs, powerful prosthetics. From what I remember of such things, a cyborg can easily possess the strength of ten formidable men.

Blistering sunlight flashes from the cyborg's naked metal. He stands with his mechanical arms folded across a massive chest, only his head and torso covered, protected from the sun. *Luther's bodyguard. Why does he think he needs one? My warriors and I have been nothing but genial in all our interactions thus far with these misguided people.*

A wry grin twitches at the corner of my lips, hidden in shadow beneath my hood. *Perhaps not entirely genial.*

"The offer of which you speak," I feign a temporary memory lapse. "Could it be the same one that sent you out of our gates last time, chased by our laughter?"

"The same," Luther returns without pause.

"To join you. Wandering vagabonds of the desert. While we have everything we need right here. Protection. Food. Weapons. Company—strength in numbers. How many of you are there now?"

"Forty."

I laugh out loud. "Compared to our ninety strong! If anything, you should be asking *us* to welcome *you* into the fold."

The cyborg leans over to whisper something to Luther, keeping his goggles fixed on me. I would enjoy seeing what this Samson is made of. Pit him against two dozen goblyns and watch the blood fly.

Perhaps there will be time for that later. For now, I subdue my laughter, clear my throat. Wait with all the patience I can muster.

"It may appear that you are safe," Luther says as Samson leans back, resuming his silent stance. "You have done well for yourselves here, I grant you that. Better than we have, in many ways. But your people are in grave danger. They cannot remain in this place."

I exhale harshly, dropping my hand from the gate. "We've been over this already. You have no evidence—"

"That has changed."

I watch them for a moment. A cool breeze chills the already sweat-drenched cloak clinging to my back. "How so? There hasn't been anything new on the radio—just that quarantine message on an endless loop. Don't tell me you've got somebody who can overhear a conversation three kilometers away."

Luther tilts his head to one side. "Actually, we do. But even she would be unable to hear anything on board the *Argonaus* or the other ships out there—too much interference. Suffice it to say, we have learned that a special team of soldiers will soon be dispatched ashore."

"Finally decided to make contact, have they?" I cross my arms. "No idea why it's taken them this long."

"First contact, yes. But not with you." He pauses. "With Eden."

I glance from Luther to Samson. "Eden is not our concern." My tone is cool, detached, even as my heart rate surges. "From what you've told me, they should be able to fend for themselves well enough."

"It's not them we're worried about," the cyborg mutters in a low baritone.

"It speaks." I smirk, noticing my guards now hard at work with a tub of tar and a spatula. "Every last one," I order. "I don't want to see any daylight through there."

They nod, slapping thick gobs of the black muck onto the wall. Will they have enough? Damn those goblyns and their submachine guns.

"Eden's survivors are expendable. As are we," Luther says. "The UW is only interested in—"

"The children." I think of my own on the way, all four of them. The mothers I sleep alongside every day. *I should be with them now.* Not out under this hot sun, shooting the breeze with these infidels.

That is the truth of it. They worship a false god, one Luther calls *The Creator*. Ridiculous. Gaia is the earth spirit of creation itself, and she has no rivals. When asked for a sign of his god's power, Luther was unable to call forth a single one. Pathetic and impotent, this god he serves.

"Yes." Luther nods. "The children." His words hang in the air, unfinished.

I glance at my guards. If they are listening, they give no indication of it. They know that if they spread a word of what is spoken between Luther and me, they will die by my hand.

"And you know this how, exactly?"

"One of us, he is blessed, *gifted* with the ability to—" Luther falters. "To cross great distances with great speed, to—"

"Fly," Samson says bluntly.

That earns another laugh. I can't help it.

Gaia has given all of my people special powers which vary from my own ability to sense a body's heart rate and temperature to my superhuman vision that spans distances of five kilometers. Then there is Lady Victoria. Her prowess, prior to pregnancy, was diving into the depths of the sea in a fruitless search for ocean life —without the need to come up for a single breath. Old Justus is able to see clearly in the dead of night. One of the chieftains can make himself invisible to the naked eye. Another can leap over the wall with little effort; he doesn't even bother using the gate. There are many others like them, each blessed by Gaia with abilities no human has ever possessed before in the history of the world.

But to *fly*? It is ridiculous, even to think it. There have to be natural limits to what is possible, after all. Despite our plethora of supernatural blessings, not one of my people has managed to soar like an extinct eagle.

"Like a *superhero*, you mean?" I hurl my fists into the air and lock my elbows. I mimic the sound of rushing wind and guffaw. "Nope. Haven't seen him around lately."

There was a wide variety of films in the Sector 15 bunker, and I watched them all—repeatedly. Most seemed alien to me at the time, being from a world so unlike my own, created long before the Sectors existed. *Hollywood*, it was called, the city that made such films back in the days of the United States of North America. It must have been their only purpose at the time, no other function than to entertain the masses. So unlike the digital propaganda used solely for United World indoctrination. Many of the old Hollywood films were perhaps juvenile and crude, but I always found myself enjoying the hero tales. There was something in their essence I could easily relate to, being the alpha male of my bunker.

"Yeah." The cyborg watches my impression with no humor in his tone. "Just like that."

"Does he have a little red cape, as well?"

"He has been aboard the *Argonaus* and has heard their Captain Mutegi speaking via radio to his Eurasian commanders," Luther continues as if he hasn't been interrupted. "Eden is only their first stop. They have also discussed coming here, to your people, on their return trip. To forcibly take away every woman with child."

My hands curl into tight, broad-knuckled fists.

"Your *wives*," Samson drives the point home.

"Who is he, this man of yours? Why is he not here to tell me this himself?" I curse, growling, "You have no evidence. Only hearsay—from someone I have no reason to believe even exists." Gaia would have warned us, if any of this were true. She would not have left my people in danger, not after doing so much to aid in our survival. It is not her way. "This talk of a *flying* man does little to support the credibility of your claims, Luther."

"They are preparing a team in Eurasia to be sent aboard the *Argonaus*," Luther replies evenly. "It will be only a matter of time —weeks, perhaps—until they arrive." He pauses, his goggles staring without expression. "Please, Cain. Will you not reconsider our offer of friendship? There is indeed strength in numbers. Just as your people outnumber ours more than two to one, the UW troops who eventually land on these shores will greatly overpower you. You will not—"

"Gaia will help us." The words escape my lips before I have a chance to weigh them.

The cyborg snorts in derision. Luther clears his throat and

prepares to continue, but I will not allow it.

"You do not share our beliefs, and so you cannot know. But we serve a God who is alive and active, and she will not allow harm to come to us." *We are her chosen people.* I nod to myself; she has told me so. "While I appreciate your concerns, Luther, I cannot share them. We have nothing to fear. If we did—"

"Then she would have told you." Luther's voice is quiet, as though he is reliving a distant memory.

I regard him silently for a moment. "Yes."

The two guards finish their repair work. It should hold. They even have some tar left over for next time. And there will be a next time, I have no doubt. The goblyns are insatiable devils.

"Return to your posts." I dismiss them, and they move quickly to obey.

"Your word is law," Luther observes.

"I run a tight ship."

"They will follow you to their graves."

"We all die someday." I sniff and half-turn toward the massive vessel planted upside-down in the sand behind me. "Tell me, Luther, who is protecting you out there? In that barren wasteland you call home? Does the god you serve keep you from harm?"

"He does. In His way."

"He helps those who help themselves," the cyborg rumbles.

I glance at him with mild interest. "A platitude from your holy scriptures?"

"My mother," Samson retorts.

I chuckle at that. "Well, Gaia is our mother. She is the life force of this planet—what remains of it. So let the UW come. Let them try to breach this Forbidden Zone they've quarantined. If they set one foot on our soil, they will find Mother Earth is still a force to be reckoned with." I step back from the gate with a mock salute. "Tell your god he's welcome to switch sides if he wants. Because this, right here—" I stretch my arms out to the sides, taking in everything around me. "We're the winning team, Luther. Think it over. My counter-offer still stands: you're welcome to join us anytime. We can be friendly folk, believe it or not."

"As he keeps us locked outside," Samson mutters under his breath.

"Need an oil can? You've got some squeaking going on there. No?" I shrug. "You should be careful, my friend. This climate wreaks havoc on steel parts."

Before Luther can restrain him, the cyborg throws both mechanical arms into an unmistakable uppercut gesture. "Go to hell!" Turning to Luther, he growls, "Why do we keep wasting our breath on these people? They don't want our help!"

I wave broadly and back away across the sand. "Goodbye, gentlemen. We'll have to do this again sometime soon. I do so enjoy our conversations."

Luther steps forward suddenly and grasps one of the gate's iron bars. "Who gave you your name?"

I frown, my face still a hooded shadow. "What?" I despise being caught off guard like this.

"From the Book of Genesis, in the Holy Scriptures—Cain killed his brother Abel. You'll be doing the same if you remain here. Your people will die because of you!"

The guards stare at me, awaiting my command. The quick, whip-like motion of my arm sets them into action. They converge on the gate with rifles at the ready, laser sights targeting the two nomads outside in jittery red pinpoints.

"Back away!" they shout, almost in unison. "Move!"

Luther does so, his hands raised in reluctant surrender.

"Be on your way." One of the guards glances back at me for approval, which I provide with a nod. The guard adjusts his grip on the gun. "Go on. Clear out of here now. You are no longer welcome."

They have the situation under control. Luther and his bodyguard will leave. If they are wise, they won't bother to return.

I turn to face the ship's hull looming close to the lapping water's edge. How many souls sleep within the shelter it provides from the sun? I cross the grey sand, backtracking the trail I made earlier nearly stride for stride. It will be good to get this sweat-drenched cloak off. If only there were some way to reclaim the moisture, like those hydration suits before they started malfunctioning.

I shove open the door and hold it, keeping it from clanging against the hull. The chieftains' faces inside squint, wincing in the light. I throw off my cloak and grab hold of Lemuel's collar.

"Out."

The youth releases a short, garbled cry as he is thrown through the doorway, landing in the shaded sand outside. Before he can collect himself, I shut the door without a word and give the wheel a spin, locking it into place.

"What I am about to say will not leave this hold." I approach the poker table. Dumbstruck faces stare back, eyes gleaming in the yellow light. "Understood?"

The chieftains nod, glancing at one another first in bewilderment, then in a conspiratorial manner. They lean forward, listening. I plant my fists on the large crate, the muscles of my biceps twitching as I look at each man in turn.

"I need our best swimmers, those who can hold their breath and stay under, out of sight. I have an important mission for them."

"How many?" Justus speaks up.

"As many as you can spare."

"This wouldn't..." Theseus—a short, broad-necked fellow with a long beard—clears his throat. "Does this have something to do with those nomads? They—"

"Reconnaissance," I cut him short. "That is all."

"You mean to send our people out to sea? To one of those warships out there?"

I nod. Half-muted gasps answer me.

"What makes you think we will even get close?"

I narrow my gaze, sensing the man's racing heart, feeling his fear. But I do not share it. "They will not see us coming."

3. MARGO

15 MONTHS AFTER ALL-CLEAR

I watch over them like I'm a brooding hen and they are my own offspring, taken from my body and planted in these foggy incubation chambers to grow and mature. I move down the aisle between them with my hands out to the sides, fingertips drifting across the translucent glass hatches that bulge outward like pregnant bellies. Out of habit, my eyes scan the digital display at the head of each chamber. The steadily blinking lights tell me the vital signs are within acceptable parameters. Better than adequate; they are exceptional.

Six months since their inception, when ova from the two Sector 50 females in captivity—Daiyna and Shechara—were artificially fertilized by sperm from the Sector 51 males—Luther and Samson—the growth and development of these twenty fetuses have been inexplicably ahead of schedule. Perhaps it is due to the synthetic environment or because of the genetic makeup of their parents. Regardless, as I look down at one particular male beneath the glass, I find it completely reasonable to assume he will be ready to emerge from his chamber in a matter of days.

Three months ahead of time.

Willard won't be happy about that. I sigh at the thought, my fingers splayed across the warm glass. The miniature face engulfed in gelatinous nutrients, eyes closed, tiny fingers curled into wrinkled pink fists, turns slowly in its artificial uterus. Somehow, he seems to sense my presence. If necessary, the incubation chambers can keep the young ones in stasis long after they would rather be greeting the world.

"You don't care about timetables, do you, little one?" I whisper. My lips struggle to create a smile that is warm and nurturing. I hope I'm not frightening him—and immediately chide myself. He cannot possibly see me standing here. "You'll let us know when you're good and ready to come out of there."

It doesn't matter that the UW scientists aren't scheduled to arrive for another few months. These fetuses are ready to hatch.

Eden's only hope of survival.

How are we going to care for so many? My palm slides from the glass and drops heavily to my side. I stare at the face of this defenseless innocent. It is difficult to imagine the wails of young ones echoing throughout these catacomb-like chambers. There have never been children here before. These substructures were not designed with them in mind. Then again, they were not originally intended to house the thirty-odd engineers who now reside within their concrete walls.

Engineers-turned-soldiers. The men of Arthur Willard's Eden Guard.

They finally have something worth protecting. These unborn test-tube children, rows of them, oblivious to the world outside their incubation chambers. Ignorant of their own value. They will continue to develop until the time is right to harvest them from their secure cocoons.

Will the cold concrete welcome them?

I sweep my gaze over the perimeter of the room, across the large generators that hum a rhythm with no melody, and follow the plastic hoses piped along the low ceiling and plugged into the fetal chambers, providing nourishment and carrying away waste. I close my eyes for a moment. *This should be a nursery.* I can almost imagine the walls painted with smiling cartoon animals and mobiles dangling above cribs with fresh linens. Again, my lips want to smile. But as I open my eyes, I see the room for what it is.

A factory with one purpose: manufacturing the future.

"They're looking healthy, Margo."

I stiffen with a short gasp. But I recognize the voice.

"You've got to stop doing that." I exhale irritably and run my fingers through my tangled hair.

"What? Sneaking up on you?" Tucker sniffs. "Can't really help it, things being the way they are."

He is invisible—a weird side effect of his extended contact with the surface, breathing in the dust up there. But *invisible* does not mean he is transparent. From what I have been able to tell, his ability is similar to that of the chameleon, an animal extinct for over two decades. Somehow, his skin is able to blend into its surroundings. It seems to be an involuntary response; try as he might, he cannot revert to a visible form. And while the fluorescent bulbs cast no shadow from his figure, sunlight is a different story.

He can see his own shadow when he is on the surface. I am at a loss to explain that.

As for my own bizarre ability—

"What do you want?" My tone is sharp, perhaps more so than I intended. There was a time when I related better to others socially, knew how to employ vocal inflections to convey specific nuances of meaning. But that was long ago.

"Am I interrupting anything?"

Yes. He is. I treasure my time alone with them—these little ones. But I would never tell him this, nor anyone else. It is part of my secret inner life that I guard jealously, sharing with no one.

"Of course not." I take a step toward his voice. Blink. And in the moment it takes for my eyelids to meet and part, I have already probed his thoughts. "He has sent for me."

"Damn it, Margo." He chuckles. "I can't keep anything from you."

"No. You can't." My tone is matter-of-fact. "Where are they?"

He shuffles his feet. "The apartment."

I glance in his general direction without bothering to pretend I know where his face is. With a nod, I leave the room, calling back, "Keep an eye on them for me." I gesture toward the chambers.

"What should I be looking for?"

"You'll know." If anything goes wrong, the alarms will deafen us all.

The fetuses will be fine in my absence. But this way, it appears that I expect Tucker to assume my post. It gives me control of the situation. A power play, perhaps; but he will have to get used to following my orders.

I will need him to, without question, when the time comes.

The apartment is located across the main floor of Eden's central dome—a massive underground water reservoir once upon a time, but now the continent's last bastion of *all-natural* humanity, untainted by the mutagens running rampant on the earth's surface. For the thirty-odd men who remain just the way God made them, it is home. Willard's Eden Guard, resplendent in their blue fatigues, fetching black berets, and the best weaponry hard-earned credits would have been able to buy prior to D-Day.

Sometimes it is difficult to imagine what these men were before: a bunker-full of brainy engineers itching to get out and build things, to make the world on the surface better than it was before all the bombs started falling.

But that was prior to the *demon dust*. Before the *dogs* and the *sand freaks*. Now these engineers make a habit of playing soldier, and they've gotten pretty good at it. They defend Eden with their lives. And whether or not they like Willard's orders, they obey their commander without question. A few months back, they welcomed an invisible man and a mind-reading female into their ranks, despite serious reservations, despite the way of things at the time: a zero tolerance policy for *mutos*. Just because Captain Willard said so.

I climb the ladder to the steel catwalk above and the living quarters suspended from the dome's soaring concrete wall. Two armed guards stand outside the unit's door. They were talking, laughing even, before they saw me. Now they're more subdued, eyes set straight ahead, avoiding any chance of contact. They seem to cringe inward as I pass, as though I am somehow contagious. Maybe they're afraid I'm probing their minds.

Maybe I am.

"At ease," I mutter, but they pretend not to hear me. I stand before the solid steel door. Neither one of them moves to open it. "You mind?" I gesture at the guard who makes the mistake of glancing my way.

His eyes dart away, but he realizes too late that I've caught him. Something human beneath his soldier facade causes him to turn in resignation and heave the door open, shoving it aside.

"Thank you," I say icily, stepping into the apartment's plush interior.

"Shut up," the guard snaps at his snickering comrade as he hauls the door back into place.

I stop in the middle of a warm, simply decorated living room with thick carpet and comfortable sofas. An artificial fire flickers in the hearth, fueled by natural gas. I know this place well. It was my home, once.

Willard and I were lovers then.

"You got here fast." Willard paces in front of the bookshelves. He locks his beady eyes on me like he's some kind of predator who isn't finished playing with his food. "Did you know?" He catches himself. "Of course you did." His upper lip twitches, but he doesn't scratch at the narrow mustache. "You know everything, don't you?"

"Not everything." I stare back at him, my arms limp at my sides.

"What's she doing here?" The block-jawed man sprawled out on the sofa fixes me with a hideous glare. "Waltzing in like you own the place. Mutant *bitch*."

"Knock it off, Perch." The slender, sandy-haired fellow with a boyish face rises from the adjacent cushion. "Margo—" His intentions are noble as he offers me his seat, but he doesn't know what more to say. He stands there with a vacant look in his eyes.

"Sit down, Jamison." Willard leans back against the bookcase, folding his arms now and pinching the bridge of his nose. He grimaces with another headache. He's been having a lot of those lately. "You too, Margo. If you don't like it, Perch, you can leave."

"I just might."

"You want out?" Willard fixes him with a direct look. "Just say the word. You can spend the rest of your miserable life underground, while the rest of us are living it up in Eurasia. You like the sound of that?"

Perch crosses his arms and curses under his breath. "I'm good, Captain."

Willard shifts his line of sight to me, seated rigidly on the edge of Jamison's armrest. "How are they?"

I don't have to ask for clarification. I know his mind. "Healthy. Developing well."

"On schedule?"

Ahead of, actually. But I won't tell him this; it would spoil everything he's planned so carefully from the start. "Of course."

"No problems?"

I shake my head. "None."

"Five kids." Perch curses again. "You think that's enough for each of us?" He glances at me again, and there is nothing but disgust for me in his eyes.

"The UW isn't getting squat until we're guaranteed safe passage out of here. That's the deal." Willard nods resolutely. "Even if we have to lock up the incubation chambers and hand over the key code once we're well on our way into Eurasia." He strokes his stubble-covered chin. Neglecting to shave is a rare occurrence for him.

"This is the next generation," Jamison says. "*Our* next generation. But we're talking about them like they're chattel to be bartered. Like *currency!*" He throws his hands up as though he's the only sane person in the room. "Doesn't that bother any of you?"

Perch curses again. "Get off your high horse. Things have changed. We're not responsible for the survival of the human species anymore—that burden's been lifted off our backs." He shifts his weight. "The way I figure, all that fetal tissue we've got growing in those test tubes is a real godsend. It's sure as hell going to pay our way. The UW gets what they want, and we get off this diseased continent. Win-win for everybody."

Jamison shakes his head. "Human life. That's what we're talking about here. Valuable enough in its own right, particularly now. There haven't been many births in Eurasia lately." He faces Willard. "Isn't that what she told you, the Supreme Chancellor—?"

"Persephone Hawthorne." Willard nods once. He smooths down his mustache and stares glassy-eyed at a point midway down the far wall. I recognize the look and know he is deep in thought, barely listening to what's being said.

Before I realize what I'm doing, I've tuned-in to his mind, sensing each of his private thoughts:

Should I tell them? What difference would it make? Clones. Genetically engineered life forms. Take that route, and the UW wouldn't even need our infants. I should move up the timetable, say the incubation process has gone faster than anticipated, that the newborns will be ready for pickup within a matter of days, not months. They would have to scramble a team together and send them over here ASAP. We'd sure as hell get their attention, and they wouldn't need to pursue cloning—

"Is that what she told you?" I bring him back to the moment. He stares hard at me, his reverie broken, defiled by my intrusion. "They have other options now?"

"Did she just—?" Perch curses, knowing the truth. "Stay the hell out of *my* mind, freak!"

Nothing in there worth the trouble.

"What does she mean, Captain?" Jamison frowns at Willard. "What kind of options?"

Willard sighs, sliding both palms down his face as if trying to wipe away his exhaustion. He forces a taut grin. "I only know what Hawthorne tells me. I'm no mind-reader, and that's a fact." He casts a withering glance at me. "Chancellor Hawthorne has been candid regarding our arrangement from the start. Once she tabled the plan to nuke Eden, things between us have gone smoothly every step of the way, and I have no reason to believe that she—"

"Queen Bee of the UW," Perch mutters.

"Would you shut up?" Jamison snaps.

"Make me." Perch winks up at him, puckering his lips.

Willard looks briefly amused. "She's been under some pressure from her advisors—her cabinet. They want results. They're saying they might not need the tubers we've got. There's one genius in particular: Solomon Wong. He's pushing for genetic-cloning, says it's the best way to uphold the status quo over here while, at the same time, fixing the Eurasian infertility problem."

"He'd be dead *wong* about that." Perch glowers for a moment, then guffaws at his own stupid joke. He's the only one laughing, but he doesn't seem to mind.

"Status quo," Jamison clarifies. "The quarantine, you mean. Hawthorne's advisors don't like the idea of breaching the blockade."

"Can you blame them?" Willard raises an eyebrow.

Perch shares a few choice expletives. "Those UW mucky mucks won't be the ones getting their hands messy. They'll send expendables over to do the dirty work. It was the same before D-Day, and I sure as hell doubt it's changed any. I almost feel sorry for the poor bastards. They'll risk their lives picking up the tubers from us, and what'll they find waiting for them back home? A firing squad. No way their superiors would risk contaminating the rest of the population over there."

"If we don't kill them first," Willard mutters.

"*What?*" Jamison starts.

"Just thinking out loud is all."

Jamison shakes his head as if to clear it. "Will Hawthorne go for it? This cloning option?"

"She would be a fool." My fingers tuck loose strands of hair behind my ears. The three men stare at me. "The United World's population is sterile now. Their only hope of survival as a species is a new generation of offspring capable of reproduction. The concept of copying themselves and hoping the clones will be able to reproduce—" I shake my head. "It's a ridiculous solution to their problem."

Jamison's frown deepens. "How so?"

"You remember copy machines?" Perch butts in. "Back in the old days?"

"Make your point," Willard says.

"I'm no expert geneticist like our resident sand freak here," he points at me with his middle finger. "But I'd assume it's the same principle. You start making copies, right? Then all the originals are lost—they die. And all you've got left are the copies—clones —who are going to have to clone themselves if they want another generation. So, eventually, you've got copies of copies of copies— clones of clones—and I don't even want to speculate on the kind of mutants those sorry sons of bitches would produce." He coughs into his fist.

"You're assuming the clones wouldn't be able to reproduce. Sexually, that is," Jamison adds.

"No clone ever has." My shoulders rise and fall. "Unless this Dr. Wong has advanced the procedure beyond what was possible twenty years ago."

"Anything is possible." Willard laughs harshly. "I reckon that's something we should take into consideration. The rest of the planet didn't take a time-out while we were in deep hibernation. We're playing catch-up here, and that's a fact. Two decades behind the times. That about sums up our place in the world."

"So let's say Hawthorne goes for it—this cloning option. What then?" Jamison frowns. "She wouldn't abandon us, now that she knows we're down here."

"She says they can't wait anymore." Willard's eyes are glassy, staring vacantly at the carpet. "Sounds like things are not going well in paradise."

"The UW natives getting restless?" Perch quips.

Willard shrugs. He doesn't care about Eurasian problems. He has enough of his own. "I only know what she tells me. But it sounds like they've got their share of trouble across the ocean in that bubble-world of theirs."

Another string of obscenities erupts from Perch. "Bunch of crybabies, if you ask me."

"Nobody did," Jamison mutters.

Perch wrinkles his face and starts wailing. "Oh, we can't have children! We're gonna die out as a species!" He scoffs. "Screw 'em. We'll raise the tubers ourselves, have a whole generation of Edenites born here within these walls. And in a few decades, they'll be the dominant species. You just watch. They'll wipe out the UW's cloned clones and take over the world!"

I note Willard's reticent smile, the distant look in his eyes. He doesn't want to live here anymore. Ever since he learned of the United World's existence, this is all he's wanted: to be welcomed back into the land of the living. Even as he led the others into this subterranean Promised Land over a year ago, he always hoped for more. He might not have been aware of it himself at the time, but I've become familiar with his deepest desires as my telepathic ability has developed.

Eden was never meant to be a permanent solution.

"We're the only *uninfected* survivors from the North American Sectors. She can't abandon us." Jamison sounds like he's trying to convince himself. "She couldn't do that."

"She doesn't owe us anything," Willard says. "Not yet, anyway." He locks his eyes on me. "How long till we can start pulling those tubers out of their incubation units?" He doesn't wait for an answer. "That's all we need. Show Chancellor Hawthorne what we've got, right here and now. No clinical trials needed." He pauses. "With clones, there would have to be tests, right? To make sure they're a viable option. But with the tubers, we already know they're growing, and they're healthy. We've got exactly what we promised her." He stares hard at me, like he thinks he can read my thoughts.

I nod with some reservation. "But we don't know yet if they carry the same abnormal genetic properties as their parents."

"A sand freak gene?" Perch seems intrigued for the first time in the conversation. "Cuz that would sure solve a whole lot of problems." He mimes a pair of scissors with his fingers. "Snip-snip, right? Just cut it out of 'em. Try it out on you first, maybe. You and Tucker." He grins.

I direct my response to Willard. "We tried that with Luther and the others. Remember how that went?"

Willard averts his gaze. "Yeah. I remember."

"There was no way to identify any sort of genetic marker—"

"But the tubers have never been topside. That's the key." Willard gestures at me in a dismissive manner. "Both you and Tucker were out on the surface, breathing in that demon dust up there. But not us." He nods toward Perch and Jamison. "And not those tubers."

"Can we stop calling them that?" Jamison says. "They're humans, soon to be newborn babies."

"*Born?*" Perch raises an eyebrow. "Do we have some kind of artificial birth canal I don't know about? Something we're gonna hook up to those units when it's time for the tubers to pop?"

Willard seems oblivious to their banter. He faces me. "We've got no reason to believe these infants will show any signs of mutation, not as long as we keep them down here with us. Doesn't matter diddly-squat who their parents were—like you said, there are no genetic markers."

I nod slowly. "But there is so much we don't know yet."

"Once they start walking, moving around on their own," Jamison adds, his back turned to Perch, "then we'll be able to tell."

"Whether they'll grow up to be mutant freaks? Hell, by then

we'll all be enjoying the good life in Eurasia. Evening martinis on the Mediterranean, watching the palm trees sway in the artificial breeze." Willard claps his hands together. In his mind, everything is settled. "We'll give the UW those tubers and let them sort things out."

Jamison narrows his eyes. "You're saying you don't care if these babies turn out to be sand freaks." He glances at me. "No offense."

I don't respond. I haven't been merely human for a long time now.

"You don't care about the next generation on this planet." Jamison's voice pitches with incredulity. "Whatever happened to Eden being the last bastion for all-natural humankind—the way God made us? I thought that's what we stood for!"

You thought wrong.

I watch them, these men who will decide the fate of the little ones. Perch, the cynic. Jamison, the optimist. Willard, the survivalist. That's all it has ever been about for him: living to see another day. Nothing has changed. But Jamison is just realizing the truth.

"We're not the *last bastion*. We never were." Willard shakes his head and curses under his breath. "Haven't you been paying attention? While we were struggling to survive underground after All-Clear, they were still out there—the UW, Eurasia—pretending we didn't even exist. And if we hadn't stumbled across that shortwave radio, I'm damned sure they would have kept right on pretending." He curses again, tightening his hands into fists. "I won't be ignored by them anymore."

"So, anything goes. Paying for our passage to Eurasia with innocent lives. Whatever it takes, right?"

Willard grins, but there is no humor in his eyes. "You're welcome to stay here, Jamison. I'm not forcing any of you to come along with me." He chuckles. "But I sure as hell ain't sticking around, and that's a fact."

"That makes two of us." Perch rises, groaning with the effort.

"My bags are already packed, Captain."

"What will you tell her?" I watch Willard closely.

"The Chancellor?" He shrugs with a wink. "How about, *Come and get 'em, lady.*"

Jamison looks stunned. "Before they're even ready?"

"What she doesn't know won't hurt her." Perch nods with approval.

"You really think they'll take you with them—after you've *lied* to them?" Jamison's incredulous tone returns. "When they get down here, it'll be obvious the chambers aren't ready for transport."

Willard's expression darkens. "We're leaving this place. We're going where we belong, to the land of the living. I'm gonna feel sunshine on my face again, even if I have to get us there myself."

"How? Commandeer their chopper?"

"Whatever it takes. We're going to Eurasia."

"I can't believe I'm hearing this."

"Grow a pair, Jamison," Perch growls. "Don't you want to be out in the world again? Find yourself some little hottie who ain't an infected freak? *No offense.*" He smirks at me.

I'm barely aware of his presence as my mind reels from the sudden turn of events. *I won't be able to get them out in time.*

"How long will it take?"

Willard frowns at me. "What?"

"Until the UW envoy arrives. How long do we have?"

"Don't know. Guess it depends on how prepared they are. If it was me, I'd have a team on one of those ships out there patrolling the coast, ready to go. Soon as they got the word, they'd pack themselves into a chopper and head inland, straight for our coordinates."

What sort of welcome does he have planned for them? I glance at Perch, entering his mind.

"What kind of welcoming committee were you thinkin'?" Perch grins broadly as if the question is his own. "Sic some of the dogs on 'em?"

Dogs—the collared mutants Willard uses like an army of deformed automatons, wired to do his bidding.

I do my best to quell the unsettled feeling within me. I rarely force my ability on these men; I can't remember the last time I did. From the moment Willard removed my control collar and made me swear never to use my *ESP* (as he called it) against him, I knew it would be tempting to do so. But I promised myself I wouldn't become the puppet master of Eden's men who outnumbered me thirty to one. Not until the situation demanded it.

"I should check on them." I interrupt Willard's laughter.

He frowns at me. "Weren't you just down there?"

"I need to monitor their nutrient consumption. We may have to increase their intake if you're planning to release them ahead of schedule. There may be a way to have them ready just in time."

He stares at me as if trying to decipher something coded behind my eyes. They're vacant, I know. I've seen them in the mirror. But they haven't always been this way. Does Willard remember how they used to spark in the throes of our relentless passion?

"All right. Meet us at the radio room. You'll want to be there when I give Chancellor Hawthorne her marching orders."

I nod with an awkward jerk and back away, rapping on the steel door as I approach it. One of the soldiers outside hauls it open, averting his eyes as soon as he sees me. I leave the apartment, but not before Perch mutters something to Willard.

"Hell if I know what you see in that one. You're crazy to even think of taking her with us."

Willard may change his mind, after all, and decide to leave me behind. But it doesn't matter, either way. I won't be going with them, even if they somehow manage to convince the UW team to take them off this quarantined continent.

Clones. They must be at the end of their rope.

For the geniuses of the United World scientific community to consider cloning as their only chance at procreation, it would mean they have reached the very end of all viable options. Human cloning has always been illegal. Violating the UW constitution is not a matter they would have taken lightly.

Why are they giving up on the children of Eden?

Do they fear us?

They must. The fear of the unknown, that eons-old boogeyman from childhood who hides under beds and in dark closets. And even worse than the monster itself is the fear of becoming it, being transformed into the same kind of nightmarish creature.

So they will leave us here. They won't risk contamination to send a team for these children—not unless Willard is exceptionally eloquent in his persuasive tactics.

And I know he can be.

"Tucker," I call as I enter the room, my voice exploding in the silence.

"Yeah?" For once, the invisible man sounds startled.

"I need your help."

He sniffs and shuffles his feet toward me. "Okay?"

I can already feel the adrenaline accelerating my heart rate. For the first time in a very long time, I feel *alive*.

"We need to take them away from here." My hand rests on the chamber of the young male I watched earlier. Offspring of Shechara and Samson's seed.

"*All* of them?" At first, Tucker seems confused. But a moment later, he understands the situation completely—without a single word spoken between us, thanks to my gift. "I see. Just these two." He sounds awestruck.

"Yes." I place my other hand on the chamber where a young female sleeps peacefully, the daughter of Daiyna and Luther.

You two are the most special of them all. I can already perceive their shared ability.

The female's eyes blink open in the gelatinous artificial uterus. *Where are we going?* her mind asks.

I smile. *Home.*

4. BISHOP

18 MONTHS AFTER ALL-CLEAR

I taste stale ash and worry my suit has been compromised. My eyes dart, scouring the interior of my helmet for any cracks in the polymer. None that I can see. The heads-up display flashes OFFLINE in bold crimson letters along with showers of static, obstructing my view of the sandy landscape around me.

A high-pitched whine hums in my ears. I can't tell if it's from the suit or inside my skull. I try to swallow and cough instead against the dryness in my throat. I lie on my back like some kind of pathetic creature unable to turn itself over while the sun scorches its underbelly.

That scientist didn't exaggerate about the heat inside a hazard suit. I'm being cooked alive.

"Cool down," I murmur, remembering the voice command.

No response from the HUD.

I curse and strain to rise. Useless. The suit won't cooperate.

Clenching my teeth, I focus all my strength into one arm, forcing it upward. I groan and will it to rise, straining against the weight of the suit. As my arm slowly levitates and then bends at the elbow, my fingers curl into a fist. Gloved knuckles tap against my helmet, and I knock once, twice.

OFFLINE jitters on the display.

My knuckles crunch into a pocket of broken polymer. *That*

can't be good. I spread my fingers and slide them across the helmet's surface, probing as far as I can reach around the outer layer. The tips of my gloves discover three other fractures.

Not good at all.

Why am I holding my breath? It's futile. The damage has been done. I drop my arm back to the hard-packed earth in disgust. It's too early for despair.

"Anybody there?" I shout.

No response.

I squeeze my eyes shut and shake my head sharply. The ringing in my ears remains undiminished. *I've gotta get out of this thing.* But it's insane even to think it. Just because some ash has gotten into my helmet doesn't mean the entire system has been compromised. The suit still provides protection, even as it pins me to the ground, exposing me as easy prey for whoever shot down the chopper.

We were passing over the coast where rusted hulks of old sea vessels sat overturned, planted in the sand. No signs of life there —other than a security fence of some kind, topped with scrolls of barbed wire. Remnants from before D-Day, the scarecrow scientist told us. The pilot headed due east, straight into the interior of the continent. At the time, Granger, Sinclair, and the others were fully engrossed in their operations manuals, studying up on how everything worked. They didn't see the clouds of dust on the surface below or the trio of black solar jeeps tearing across the sand on an intercept course.

"Hostiles sighted—advise, *Argonaus*," the pilot barked into his headset.

"Our welcoming committee?" I strained against my suit for a better view.

The UW scientist sat frozen and unresponsive. His bulbous eyes stared out from behind his face shield, and his thin lips parted as if to speak. But no words came.

"Captain Mutegi is saying to turn back." One hand on his earpiece, the co-pilot turned in his seat to face us.

The scientist nodded quickly, mute. The jeeps beneath us halted.

"Binocs," I gave the voice command. My helmet's HUD zoomed to focus on the first of the three jeeps. There were four men, two seated, two standing in the back behind the roll bar. But they didn't look exactly...*human*. "What the—?"

One of them lifted a Stinger missile launcher to his deformed shoulder and swung the business end up toward the chopper. Chaos ensued as the pilot attempted to evade the heat-seeking rocket. The scientist hit a manual release lever, and the clamps on my hazard suit unlocked as the hull beneath me gave way. I was jettisoned from the chopper—and just in time. As I spiraled end over end to the earth below, the missile found its mark above me, exploding like a massive wildflower in reds, oranges, and black smoke. The concussion that followed plowed into my midsection like a two-fisted blow to the ribs.

"Captain—is that you?" Granger's voice comes over the comm channel in my helmet. Boots shuffle across the sand nearby.

"Give me a hand." I reach out blindly, unsure the short engineer will be able to help me up.

"What the hell happened?"

"I can't see a thing."

Granger takes hold of my arm and heaves, hoisting me into a seated position.

"HUD on the fritz?"

"Yeah. You?"

"Naw. Guess I landed on my feet." Granger sniffs. "You get a good look at 'em before?"

"No."

Hostiles—that's what the pilot called them. They hadn't moved like men. More like humanoid animals, garbed in sun-scorched skins. But that's impossible. The animal kingdom was obliterated years ago across the globe, on both land and sea.

"Something you're not telling me, Captain?"

"You know as much as I do." Determined to stand, I tip

myself forward and land on my padded palms, drawing up my knees. "And it's *Sergeant*."

"Either way, you're in charge of this godforsaken expedition."

I nod. "Where are the others?"

"Don't know. Found you first."

"No sign of...hostiles?"

"Not yet. Sure hope some firepower fell out of that chopper with us."

"Morley was in charge of the guns." Our weapons-tech officer.

Granger chuckles. "Then I suggest we find him next."

I grimace as I force the cumbersome suit to comply, arching my back and planting the soles of my boots in the sand. It takes some doing, but with a well-timed shove from Granger, I manage to stand.

"Offline—that's all this thing keeps saying." I rap on my helmet again. "Any chance you could turn it off?"

"The HUD? Not without opening up your suit. And I'm pretty sure you don't want me to do that out here." He pauses. "Looks like there's a fracture in your helmet's outer layer. Must have broken some of the optical transfer filaments—"

"You'll have to lead the way." I close my eyes to shut out the flashing display, but the red glare pierces through my eyelids.

"Where to, Captain?"

"We're out in the open, I take it?"

"We're sitting ducks, to use an antiquated phrase."

"So we find cover." In my mind's eye, I can see the overturned ships on the shore. Discarded playthings left by some monstrosity of a child. "How far to the coast?"

Granger's boots shuffle as he faces west—using his HUD compass, no doubt. "Distance," he uses a voice command from the owner's manual. "Distance to shore," he specifies.

I strain to hear approaching sounds of any kind. Footsteps. Humming solar engines. Those jeeps couldn't have vanished without a trace. The hostiles are still here, somewhere. And they're watching.

"It's saying five and a quarter kilometers. Quite a trek in these suits. In this heat."

"Describe the terrain."

"Well, uh—"

"Just tell me what you see. Sand dunes, rock formations—anything that would provide adequate cover?"

"Yeah, there's plenty of both. It's a desert wasteland out here, man. But I see a few outcroppings of rock that look promising."

I hold out my arm. "Lead on."

"How's your O2?" He guides me forward.

"Fine." Without the gauges on my HUD, there's no way to check pressure levels. "For now."

"Guess you'll know for sure when you start choking."

I clench my jaw.

Granger clears his throat, breaking the silence. "Just saying it like it is, man."

Again, I consider removing the helmet. Insane, sure, but I have only two options: suffocate as the suit's oxygen runs out, or breathe in the contaminated air outside. I try to swallow. The dryness is still there.

"We're here." Granger places the palm of my gloved hand against solid rock. "Granite boulders maybe four meters high. Should give us enough cover."

I sense a shift in gradient. "How steep is this hill?"

Granger chuckles. "You sure you can't see?"

If the hostiles abandoned their vehicles, they would have taken to higher ground in order to command a better vantage point. Which means my trusty engineer and I will remain exposed until we hold a similar position.

"We need to climb."

"You really are blind as a bat. Cuz there's no way you'd even think of hauling your ass up this hill if you could see what I'm seeing. One slip on the way up, and we'll be acquainting ourselves real intimately with a few jagged rocks below."

"We have to get to higher ground. We're not alone."

"I sure as hell hope not! The others made it—we've just got to find them."

"They're watching us." I keep my voice low, though I doubt it matters. Despite the fractured outer layer, my helmet is soundproof. But my ears are still ringing, and I don't want to overcompensate by shouting at the internal mic. "They haven't left."

Granger's breathing on the comm channel cuts out for a moment. His boots shuffle. "You mean—the hostiles? Where?"

"Can't say." The short hairs on the back of my neck are standing at attention right now. A marine always knows when he's being watched. I can't understand how Granger doesn't sense it too. How many tours of duty has he seen? You don't last long in the field without a second pair of eyes in the back of your head. But then again, the guy's an engineer—a whole different breed.

"Captain, I don't see anybody. But if you're right, then finding some firepower should be our top priority."

I tap my helmet and curse. I can move properly in the suit now, but I still can't see a damn thing. "Afraid I won't be much help."

"Fine. I'll go look around. Meet you back here."

"We stay together. That's an order."

"Listen, you just stay put, and I'll—"

"I gave you a direct order."

"Sorry, Captain. I hate to do this, but it looks like I'm assuming command here. You're in no condition to argue—not until your HUD's back online, anyhow." His boots trudge away. "Don't even think about court-martialing me later. You know I'm right." He takes off across the sandy hardpan.

I grunt in acknowledgment. There's no reason to believe we're not the only two survivors from the chopper. We stand a better chance sticking together. Apart, we'll be picked off easily—and without Granger's eyes, I'm completely lost.

I curse the hazard suit, the scientist who prepped it, the UW itself. What were they thinking, sending us into this war zone?

The particulars of your mission will appear on your heads-up displays, once you've reached the drop site. Well, that's not happening. *You run into any unexpected difficulties, you radio. Don't delay. That's what we're here for. We're your backup.* Also out of the question. Even if my HUD was functioning and I could contact the *Argonaus*, I don't recall seeing a second chopper on that flight deck. Captain Mutegi will have to send a bird inland from one of the other vessels in the naval blockade. But would he risk a second chopper after what happened to ours?

I have some trouble wrapping my mind around it. These *hostiles* are well-equipped. Their solar jeeps ran at full power, and that Stinger was obviously fully functional. It blew a LoneWolf UAX-38 out of the sky, for crying out loud. But who the hell are they—and what idiot armed them?

A gust of wind blasts against my back, throwing me into the rock. I groan out loud, surprised by the sudden force of the blow. I half-turn, as if to glance back. But that's pointless; the suit won't allow it, even if I were able to see.

Everything's still.

"Papa?"

A shock jolts through my system, but it has nothing to do with the hazard suit's power coming back online.

"Papa, is that you?"

I'm not hearing this. It can't be happening. The voice isn't coming through my headset on the comm channel. I can *hear* it with my ears. The ringing has stopped, and I hear the small voice as it approaches with footsteps shuffling toward me through the dust.

"What's wrong, Papa?"

I can *feel* the voice in the center of my chest. I squint against the red glare blinking OFFLINE on the HUD. My eyes sting. My lips part without sound.

It can't be Mara. Not my little girl. Not out here. It makes no sense. She's with her brother, with their mother in Eurasia—

I'm losing my mind.

I'm better than this. Trained better. UW marines are disciplined to withstand every brand of hardship. Nothing can break us.

"Papa?" The voice comes within reach.

"Stay back." I force an arm outward, palm extended. I'm cornered here with no retreat. I'll have to climb uphill in spite of Granger's warning if I plan on moving away from this voice. "Identify yourself."

"But you know who I am." Mara sounds hurt.

It's not Mara. It's some kind of trick. The hostiles—it has to be one of them with a bizarre telepathic ability that reaches into the subconscious, somehow able to pull out what I hold most precious and use it against me.

But that's insane. *I'm totally losing it now.*

"Did you fire on us?" I keep my tone steady, under control. It's a wonder she can hear me at all through my helmet.

"You're not safe here, Papa. They're going to be looking for you, and they are very hungry."

I hear her take another step toward me. "I said stay back!"

"I know you're scared, but you have to think. Where should you be right now?"

Up. That's my first thought.

"I can help you," she says. "If you let me."

"Who are you?" I demand.

"You know who I am."

I shake my head. "It's not—you're not—"

"You want to see me again, don't you, Papa?"

Of course I do. It's the only thing that gets me through every endless day apart from my family: the hope that when this tour of duty ends, we'll be reunited.

"You're not my daughter," I manage at last. "I don't know who or *what* you are, but you're not her."

Not my Mara.

Silence follows except for my own labored breathing.

"You're a smart man, James. But I guess that's why I married you," comes the voice of my wife.

Emma.

I feel a sudden chill despite the temperature inside my suit—well over seventy degrees centigrade by now. *This isn't real.* I squeeze my eyes shut and force a deep breath. My mind has snapped. That's all. I just need to remain calm and focus on something else. Anything.

But all I can think about is my family, and I can't push their faces out of my mind's eye.

"Do you remember the last thing you told me?" Emma asks.

Like it was yesterday. The UW soldiers in their crisp grey uniforms and black boots, escorting my wife and children from our home. The scene so diplomatic and orderly. Such a pretentious façade. My family taken hostage, the official government representatives acting as their captors—until I return.

"I'll be back before you know it," I offered at the time, seething, detained at my own front door by a high-ranking official.

Emma glanced over her shoulder at me as they were led away. She smiled. Not because she understood what was going on or because she was okay with it. She smiled at me because she loved me.

"You must stay alive, James. So much depends on you," she says now in this hot, alien place where neither one of us belongs.

I frown, back in the moment. "How do you know my name?"

"There will be time for questions later. For now, we must get you to safety. You cannot hear them, but they are coming."

"The hostiles." I strain to listen for the sound of their jeeps.

"You could call them that. To others, they are known as goblyns. Or daemons."

"And what are you, exactly? I'm not going anywhere until you tell me that." I take a bold step forward, reaching blindly. "Some kind of mind-reader?"

My gloved hand makes contact with a bare shoulder—my

wife's? I know its shape better than my own. But I draw back sharply, as if I've been burned. How could I feel such a thing with my glove on?

She takes my hand in hers, and I feel her skin against mine. "Come with me." Her grip is strong and sure as she pivots to lead me up the hill.

A hot tear spills over the corner of my eye and skids down my cheek. I resist, even as I yearn to go with her. *It's not her. It can't be!*

"What are you?" I don't pull away.

"You are here for a purpose, James Bishop."

My mission: first contact with the only D-Day survivors on the continent. Is this one of them? Did the biological weapons and nuclear fallout turn them into telepathic shape-shifters?

Science fiction. Get a grip!

"We cannot allow you to be harmed."

"We?" I let her pull me forward and upward, but I hold my other hand out to the side, remembering the rocks Granger was so concerned about. "There are others here like you?"

"Yes." Her voice drops near a whisper. Even so, I hear it as clearly as if she's brushing my earlobe with her lips. "But we are not the same."

You're telling me. "Not exactly human, are you?" A heat-induced hallucination. That has to be it. She isn't really here talking to me. I decided on my own to climb to higher ground. It only makes sense.

"We are spirits of the earth."

"Like ghosts?" I almost chuckle. Might as well enjoy the ride.

"Careful there—lift your right boot a little higher."

I raise it as high as I can, fighting the unwieldy suit for every centimeter. "So you're able to appear as people from my life? How does that work exactly?"

"We are able to see your memories."

"You can read my mind." *Figured as much.* A hallucination would obviously know my own thoughts. "Okay then. What am I thinking right now?"

Her grip on me does not falter. "You think I am a figment of your imagination, induced by hyperthermia. Your suit is offline, and you feel as if you're being cooked alive inside it."

Not bad.

Engines hum in the distance. They have to be real; no reason for me to hallucinate them into being. So even with my fractured helmet, I'm able to hear ambient noise. Good to know.

"Get down!" She pulls me to the ground, and I drop to my knees, feeling sand and gravel shift beneath me, slipping away. "Do not move."

I don't plan to. Gritting my teeth, I refrain from cursing the OFFLINE message glaring in my face. It's ridiculous to ask a hallucination such a thing, but I have to know: "Any chance you could fix this?" I bob my head a little to draw attention to the helmet. "I can't see a thing."

And it's driving me crazy!

"We are unable to interact with your technology," she whispers into my ear again—as impossible as that is. "We can only interfere with it."

Sweat dribbles down from my upper lip, and I spit against the inside of my face shield. "They're not ghosts, are they?"

"The daemons?"

Hostiles. "Whatever. Yeah."

"They were like you once. But they were...damaged."

I frown. How can these be my own thoughts? "What do you mean?"

"I must leave you now. But I will return. Remain here, and be still."

Winds gust with a sudden burst, and I flinch as gravel pings against the exterior of my helmet. I reach for her, patting at the ground. My gloved fingers collide with granite. I feel along the uneven surface and find that it reaches high above me. She's led me to safety, and now I'm trapped on three sides by igneous rock.

I shake my head. No one led me here. I found cover on my own.

Focus. I strain to listen.

One of the solar jeeps draws near, maybe five to ten meters below. Difficult to gauge exactly by the sound. It grinds to a halt as boots hit the sand, two, three pair, charging off in different directions. No verbal communication that I can hear.

The footsteps stop. Everything is still.

Then a guttural roar tears through the silence. A blast of wind howls past me, showering me with grit. I fight to raise my arms instinctively to shield myself. Something cracks nearby like a dry branch or a broken spine, and another feral wail erupts into the air.

Shots fired—automatic weapons. Submachine guns by the sound of them, standard-issue UW Uzi Type 4's or something similar.

Another scream and another crack, this time accompanied by the sound of a rib cage crunched, piercing the heart and lungs and muting the victim mid-shriek. What the hell is going on down there?

More shots, aimed now in my direction. I cower as the rounds chip the granite above me. My hazard suit sports some next-gen Kevlar, but my helmet is a different story. I don't know how much more abuse it can take, and I don't want to stick around to find out. But what choice do I have? Like Granger said, I'm blind as a bat.

Where is he now? And what about the others?

The machine gun below is silenced abruptly as a third and final scream takes its place. The wind returns, raging among the rocks and pelting me without mercy. I have never been in the middle of the Sahara or the Gobi during a sandstorm, but I imagine it to be something like this: powerful and wild, a ravenous beast.

Then everything is still once again.

I remain crouched as low as this cumbersome suit will allow, my arms out to the sides, braced against the granite. I listen, barely breathing. There is no sound.

I start to rise but rethink that idea. One well-aimed shot is all it would take to shatter my helmet in its current condition, and then I'll be at the mercy of the contaminated air. But I can't stay hidden indefinitely. I have to find Granger and contact Captain Mutegi. That's the priority.

"Captain—how the hell did you make it up there?"

I reel around in an awkward slow motion, fighting against the suit. "Granger?" I call down. "You're alive."

"Can't say the same for these guys." He clears his throat. "Or whatever they were."

"What do you see?"

"I thought you said his HUD was malfunctioning," says a familiar voice on comms.

"Sinclair?"

Granger chuckles. "Gang's all here, Fearless Leader."

"And the hostiles?"

"Scared off, man," Morley says. "Two jeeps took off due east, soon as that dust devil started up."

"They must have known." Harris sounds like he's investigating something, thinking out loud in the process. "They've seen such an occurrence before."

What the hell is he talking about?

"Help me get him down from there," Granger grumbles, his boots digging into the hillside below me.

"I'm fine." All I have to do is backtrack the trip I took with my hallucination-wife, recalling each step in reverse. "But feel free to catch me if I slip."

"Have you ever seen anything like it?" Harris says. "That whirlwind seemed to have a mind of its own, and what it did to these...*creatures*—"

"Describe them." I judge the placement of each boot before giving it my full weight.

"They're...unlike anything I've ever seen."

Granger curses. "You can say that again."

"Humanoid physiology, Sergeant," Harris continues, "but they have evolved to adapt to these harsh conditions. Their skin is..."

Morley groans and retreats a few steps. "Oh, don't go touchin' it like that!"

"I'd have to describe their flesh as charred, burned beyond repair due to extreme exposure to the sun. Or radiation, perhaps, from a nuclear blast. Impossible that they would still be alive, if that were the case." Harris clears his throat. "Their eyes are lidless, but with a yellow, free-flowing mucous that appears to coat and protect them. No nose to speak of, but the nasal cavity is coated as well. Viscous, but fluid. And quite pungent."

"You touch that stuff, I'll blow your hand off." It sounds like Morley has cocked back the hammer of a semiautomatic pistol.

So, he's armed.

"Stand down, soldier." I descend the bottom of the hillside and face the voices of the others, doing my best to exude the appearance of authority despite my inability to see any of them. "Give me that sidearm." I stretch out my gloved hand, palm upward. "Have you already outfitted the other members of our team?"

Morley is slow to answer. "This piece is all we've got, Sergeant."

How can that be? "Hand it over, weapons officer."

"*Weapon* officer." Granger chuckles. "You know, because there's just the one."

"All due respect, Sergeant. But is it true that your HUD is offline? You can't see?" Sinclair says.

Morley uncocks the hammer. "Perhaps it should remain with me."

"It should remain with someone who doesn't threaten to shoot his crewmate." I ignore Granger's snickering. "So hand it over before I take it from you."

"Look at these teeth!" Harris gasps.

Morley groans again. "Why does he insist on touching that

thing?" His boots pound the dust toward me, and he places the sidearm squarely in my hand.

"What is it, Doc?" I shuffle toward Harris's voice.

"They're—why, they're—"

"Fangs," Sinclair says. Both of them sound like they're kneeling by one of the corpses. "But they did not grow this way naturally."

"What do you mean?" Granger says.

"They have been filed to points. Intentionally."

"What the hell for?"

"What do you expect?" Morley keeps his distance. "They're flesh-eaters. Plain as daylight. I don't have to go poking and prodding the thing to see that."

"Flesh?" Granger's boots shuffle. "But animals haven't been around since before D-Day."

"No one said anything about animals," Sinclair retorts. "By all indications, they are pack hunters. The sandstorm frightened them, but they will return."

I nod. *We're the only game in town.* "Collect whatever weapons they left. Granger, check out that jeep. See if you can get it running." I step toward Morley. "The other jeeps took off toward the east, you said?"

"Yeah. Along the same heading we were given."

I blow out a sigh. Our orders haven't changed.

But if these fanged creatures are the survivors we were sent here to meet, then first contact has already occurred.

PART II
TURMOIL

5. CAIN

18 MONTHS AFTER ALL-CLEAR

A long time ago, in a world far different from this one, the ocean liner was queen of the seas. Magnificent, undoubtedly. But now, overturned and half-submerged in ashen sand, the rusted, charred hulk of this vessel isn't much to look at from the outside. Just something belched onto shore by an ocean-faring world that no longer exists.

Inside, with the grand ballroom's dance floor now serving as a ceiling for the arched, gold-plated floor, things are entirely different. If you were to stand on your head, you could almost imagine a big band on the stage and wealthy couples swinging to the music, hand in hand and hip to hip. But it seems almost sacrilegious to imagine such things now. This place is no longer meant for parties and frivolity. Here, the faithful gather to hear the words of Gaia through her son: Lord Cain, Chieftain of Chieftains.

This is Gaia's Temple. These are her chosen people.

Tonight the floor gleams like streets of gold. Candelabras hold green glowsticks which add to the otherworldly aura. The believers have gathered, sitting cross-legged and silent along the sloping floor. Every tribe is represented here, every chieftain accounted for. I stand before them, sweeping them with my gaze.

I do not bother to count. I know with a glance at each chieftain that all are present.

"My brothers and my sisters," I begin, extending my strong hand out over the heads of those assembled. "War is upon us."

There is no murmur from the gathering, no gasps of shock. For as long as they have lived here beneath the shelter of these derelict ocean-faring vessels, they have known it was only a matter of time before the UW ships patrolling our coast decided to do more than hold the blockade. Even those not blessed with far-sight have seen the *Argonaus* from shore; it is a familiar shape on the horizon. My water-breathers overheard the captain of this ship, a man named Mutegi, in radio communication with his superiors. There was no mistaking his orders. Since All-Clear, the UW has chosen to observe my people from a distance but not interfere. This will be the status quo no longer. The UW is sending soldiers to land, and it is only a matter of time before they arrive.

"The United World cowards have sent their first scouts inland, as we expected them to do," my voice echoes as all listen attentively. "They came in a helicopter. Most of us are old enough to remember what such vehicles of the air looked like."

Lemuel, standing near the back of the large room, frowns. Of course he is too young to remember. He was born months after his pregnant mother went underground, into one of those government-issued bunkers that protected us from the fallout.

"They came with their science and their weapons and their ignorance of Gaia's ways. They came in pride and arrogance." I pause, savoring the silence and the effect it has on the assembly. They hang on my words. "And mighty was their fall. Gaia used the goblyns to shoot them down from the sky!" I chuckle, baring my teeth, and everyone present echoes my laughter. "Gaia works in mysterious ways, and while we would sooner strike the head from a goblyn's shoulders than look twice at one, we are grateful for this act. They saved us the trouble of downing the aircraft ourselves."

More laughter erupts from the crowd.

"Why would they do this?" Lemuel speaks up, his young voice echoing. "The goblyns, I mean."

"Who are you to interrupt Lord Cain?" old Justus demands, striding toward the youth with a trembling fist raised to mete out punishment for this flagrant breach of etiquette.

"Let him be. It's an honest question—from one whose voice still cracks." I watch Lemuel redden and sink to a cross-legged position as raucous laughter fills the Temple. I hold up a hand, and they quiet down. "Why do the goblyns attack us without provocation? Why do they eat the living and desecrate the dead? Gaia has told us why. They were like us, once. The United World government sent them to this continent before it was ready for them, before it was safe. They thought it was only the radiation and the residue of biological weapons that they had to be concerned with. They did not know about Gaia or her rival, the false god worshiped by Luther and his nomads. They did not know of the gifts Gaia had given us. They sent troops here with weapons and vehicles, and their own hate devoured them. Gaia turned their flesh inside-out, fried their minds with the unforgiving sun's rays. Now they are nothing more than wild animals, acting on instinct."

I narrow my eyes at Lemuel. "You ask why they would blow that helicopter out of the sky. I ask you, why wouldn't they? It carried fresh meat!"

The throng nods and murmurs their assent. Lemuel sinks closer to the gilded floor. Old Justus seems pleased; the young pup may be learning his place.

"There were many UW scouts on that helicopter when it crashed," I continue. "Little remains of the hull or the engines, but the rotors somehow managed to remain intact." Another pause, for effect. "As did five of the crew."

Now excited whispers of surprise pass among all present. I draw myself up, my chest swelling. I wait for the fervor of their questions to settle.

"They are all that remain. The bodies of the others would be difficult to collect and identify, even with the most advanced retrieval systems. The goblyns hit them with a shoulder-launched missile."

"How did the five scouts survive?" Lady Victoria asks with mild interest from the front row, seated with my other pregnant wives.

"They wore heavy body armor and environmental suits that protected them from the fall. Someone must have told them our air is toxic." I chuckle and wink. Victoria smiles back at me. "But they are unarmed," I add. "Not a weapon to be found among them."

"Why would they come so ill-equipped?" asks a skeptic from the crowd.

"That is not our concern." I square my jaw. "We must decide what to do with them."

"Kill them!" cries Justus with an upraised fist.

Many join in his exuberance, but a few voice the word *retaliation* with concern.

I cannot help smirking. "Those United World warships have been bobbing impotently beyond our shore for as long as we've been out of the bunkers. Their scouts were shot out of the sky days ago, yet the *Argonaus* has done nothing to rescue them. What makes you think they give a damn?"

"Why were they sent ashore in the first place?" Justus asks with a frown. "Some kind of suicide mission?"

I wait for silence to reclaim the room before speaking. "Eden," I say in a calm, cool tone. "They came for Eden...and their *children*." I spit out the word.

A faint ripple of laughter sweeps through the masses. I face my people with both arms outstretched. "Gaia will decide what is to become of those scouts. If they are to be blessed as we are, then she will decide what gifts they are worthy to possess. If the vileness of their true nature is to be exposed to the ravenous sun, then she will turn them inside-out. They will become goblyns, added to the ranks of our enemies." I nod. "Gaia's will be done!"

"Gaia's will be done," the throng murmurs, nodding solemnly.

All except Lemuel, who leaps to his feet. "We should send them back."

Justus turns sharply on the lad, who cringes but remains standing.

I regard him coolly. "Come up here, Lemuel."

The young man swallows, uncertain.

"You heard Lord Cain," Justus hisses, striking his shoulder with a fist. "Get your ass up there!"

Subdued laughter courses through the crowd as Lemuel awkwardly makes his way forward to where I stand. Stepping over the people sitting cross-legged all around him, he stumbles headlong until he is caught by the scruff of the neck in my vice-like grip.

"What's that you say?" I hold him still. "Send them back? To their ship, is that it?"

Lemuel stiffens, looking like some kind of bizarre ventriloquist's dummy. "They'll leave us alone if we do. If we don't—"

"Are you afraid to die?" I growl.

"Their people will kill us all. We'll bring war on ourselves—"

"War is already upon us." I shove him down, and he sprawls into the front row of the assembly. Rough hands push him aside, but Lady Victoria makes a place for him beside her. She glares up at me defiantly as Lemuel folds his legs beneath him and hangs his head. I clench my jaw but say nothing to my young wife. "Their scouts crossed the border into our land! We who saw their helicopter rejoiced greatly when it burst into flames, exploding in pieces. They are the ones who have brought war—"

Come outside. Come to me.

I freeze mid-sentence, my mouth open. Puzzled frowns crease the brows of my people, and they glance at one another in the awkward silence.

I turn away without a parting word. A collective murmur of

disquiet reverberates against the walls as I bound up to a hatch and climb out.

Come, my son.

Gaia's voice beckons, and I go willingly, pausing only to throw on my cloak. The iron door clangs shut behind me as I stride out into the cool night, inhaling gusts of ocean air that chill my lungs and calm my spirit. The moon is out full and bright, casting a ghostly pallor across the bluffs and dunes of ashen sand around me.

She stands facing the sea. The breeze tosses her silk white garments about playfully. I approach her, striding toward the base of the dune where she stands. I wait to be beckoned closer.

She turns and graces me with a loving smile. *Gaia...*

"Mother," I manage, hoarse with emotion as I dig my boots into the shifting sand and climb.

"My son." She holds out a hand to me, not to help me up, but to be taken and kissed with the deep reverence that is due.

I kneel as I do so, bowing my head. She slips her hand free of my grasp and rests her palm on the back of my head.

"War is coming." Her voice is soft and tranquil. "You feel it."

I nod, staring at the ash between the toes of her bare feet, smooth and white as alabaster.

"It is inevitable." She sighs, sliding her cool hand down the side of my unshaven face, lingering under my chin. She lifts it with a strength I dare not resist. "Look at me, my son. Am I afraid?"

I blink as conflicting desires rage within me. To look upon the face of Gaia is more than I can bear, but it is truly all I want. I swallow reflexively, feeling just as awkward as young Lemuel looked in front of the assembly.

"No, Mother." I gaze up at her smile, her eyes radiating warmth as her fingers drift away from my face. How long has she been standing out here alone, exposed to the night's chill? Should I offer her my cloak? "Neither am I. You have blessed us with these gifts—our miraculous abilities make us a force to be reckoned with. We will be more than a match for the United World bastards they vomit onto our shore." I wait for her nod of approval.

"Will you destroy them?" She turns her gaze to the oily depths of the sea and the *Argonaus* in the distance.

"Yes. Every last one."

"They outnumber you, my son. You will risk the extermination of your people?"

I clench my jaw. "This is our land. They have no right to it. They chose to forsake us long ago, and they have quarantined us ever since. Let them come. Let them see how we have evolved in their absence."

"Do you remember your life before?"

"I..." *Shouldn't we discuss what to do with the UW scouts?*

"Before they sealed you up in those tombs, you weren't much older than that boy who irritates you. None of you were." She pauses. "They locked you under the earth while they destroyed everything you knew. And now the world will never be the same. Your world, as well as theirs." She faces me. "Did you know they cannot go outside freely?"

I nod, averting my gaze from her direct look. I lower my head again. "They fear our air. They believe it's contaminated."

She laughs softly. "Not only yours—their own air as well. The United World has been reduced to a series of domed cities on the banks of the Mediterranean Sea. They call the sprawling bubbles *Eurasia*. They hide behind thick walls of glass as the world goes on outside without them. They live in perpetual fear, afraid they will die out as a species without the children from this continent."

They do want our children. It is just as Luther said. I clench my fists, hating that the infidel was right about something.

"Luther has told you this."

I glance up in surprise.

"You cannot hide your thoughts from me, my son."

I should have known better. "Of course not, Mother." I scowl for a moment, then meet her gaze. *Is he right?* But I refuse to vocalize the question.

She graces me with a wan smile. "You would be stronger together, your people and his."

"But they serve a false god—"

"Not false," she reprimands me. "Another god, an ancient one no longer involved in the lives of his creation. But very real."

I do not understand. "You want us to join with those nomads against the United World? Is that what you ask of me?"

She returns her gaze to the sea. "Five from that ship are here now. On your land." She watches the warship bob upon the murky surface of the sea, far beyond the foaming breakers.

I nod. "They crashed down..." But she knows that already. She used the goblyns—

"Those creatures acted of their own accord. Hunger was their only motivation."

"Of course."

"The five survivors—what will you do with them?" she asks mildly.

"I have two men following them at a distance. They appear to be continuing with their mission, heading eastward. Toward Eden." I pause. "We await your word, Mother. We will do as you demand."

"Kill them."

I watch the sea breeze catch at her dress. Her skin glows in the moonlight. She is so beautiful, so serene. A goddess, but one who deigns to set the sole of her foot into the ashes of Hell.

I tremble before her power.

"Yes," is all I can articulate in a hoarse whisper.

"Bring them here and stake their bodies in plain sight. Leave them to roast in the sun."

I glance at the *Argonaus*, only a small buoy in the distance to the ungifted eye; but I can discern every detail of the vessel with my far-sight. "You want them to see—"

"Their children have grown up." She smiles down at me with

a mother's pride. "This is your land now. They have no claim to anything on it. If they were wise, they would leave you and your offspring alone."

I see the knowing look in her eyes. "But they won't."

"No. When they see you have killed their people, then there will be war. It will come as a tidal wave upon these shores. But you will not be alone."

"You will fight with us." I nod, gazing up at her.

"You will join Luther's people and go to Eden. There you will be safe—all who remain of this continent's people. There you will defend what is yours, in the concrete catacombs beneath what was once a great city." She pauses. "The UW troops will have to deal with the goblyns—your first line of defense."

As will we. I cringe inwardly, knowing my doubtful thoughts are far from private.

"Do not fear. I will go before you, blinding the goblyns' eyes to your movement across the desert. But I will not be so gracious to the United World soldiers. They will encounter the goblyns, and those who survive will press through to the city above Eden. There, the man named Willard will have his own line of defense: goblyns he has trained as pets to do his bidding." She smiles at the look on my face.

"How is such a thing...possible?"

"Willard and his people are masters of technology. They have reconstructed a life for themselves under the earth, one that you will find familiar: the world of your youth. Running water, lights and electricity. Very little is beyond them."

It sounds too incredible to believe; but I do not doubt Gaia's word.

"Have your men bring the five UW scouts to you. Before first light. Let the *Argonaus* see their skewered bodies greet the day."

I like the sound of that. "As you wish, Mother."

"Then gather all of your people and go into the desert. Move with great haste."

"How will we find Luther?" *He usually comes to us.* My abdomen tightens at the thought of joining forces with the infidels.

"I will guide you, my son. Through the desert, you will follow me as a pillar of dust in daylight, and at night you will see me as you do now." She touches my face, tracing the shape of my jaw with her fingertips. "You alone are blessed to see me in this form."

My heart swells beneath her gaze, and I lower my head, eyes stinging, suddenly overwhelmed. "I am unworthy."

She rests her hand on the back of my head. "I have chosen you to be a great leader among your people. You will be their Moses. They will follow you in victory against the United World and its evils." She wriggles her toes in the ash. "The old has passed away, burned in the fires of judgment. But now behold, all things will become new."

Twin streaks trail from my eyes as I turn my face up to her—

But she has vanished.

I cough self-consciously and scrub away the tears. Then I rise and turn to face the breeze, blinking my eyes at the barren moonscape beyond the barbed, bullet-notched fence of our compound. Not a single goblyn in sight.

Our first line of defense. I almost chuckle, shaking my head at the thought of it. Gaia surely moves in mysterious ways.

A confident excitement stirs within me as I return to the ocean liner and climb through the hatch, leaving the door to clang shut behind me. I shrug out of my cloak and make straight for the Temple where three guards stand at attention, more or less.

"Lord Cain!" one of them greets me, jerking into a rigid posture. The other two follow suit, their idle conversation dying at once.

"You—gather the chieftains. Go," I direct the one on the left who scurries to obey. "Dismiss the faithful from the Temple. The gathering is over," I command the second guard. "And you," I turn to the third, placing a fist against the young man's chest. "Summon Lady Victoria to my quarters. I require her presence."

The guard looks dumbfounded. He lingers, unwilling to enter the Temple as the other two have, unable to decide what to do with his eyes or his mouth.

"Why do you delay?" I scowl at him.

"My lord, I—"

"Do you have something to tell me?"

"Yes. I—that is, Lady Victoria—"

"Spit it out!"

The guard nods, a startled jerk of the head. "Lady Victoria is not in the Temple. She asked to be excused—"

"And you let her leave?" I narrow my eyes, glowering down at the youth. "Without my consent?" Such a thing is unheard of.

The guard swallows. "I—that is, with her condition, I assumed she must have needed to..." He cringes slightly. "Relieve herself."

I almost smile. This late in her pregnancy, there is little else she does as religiously. "Very well. Send her to my quarters when she returns."

The guard hesitates. He leans toward me, prepared to speak, but no words appear.

"What is it now?"

"My lord—Lady Victoria—she..."

I grab the front of his tunic and hoist him up onto his toes. "If you have something to say to me about my wife, then you had best say it now."

"Yes, my lord." The guard nods. "You see, Lady Victoria, she...was not alone."

"Explain." I will shake it out of him if I have to.

The guard seems to realize this. "She had an escort." He winces, predicting the reaction the news will elicit. "It was Lemuel."

I bare my teeth. "How long ago was this?"

"Just a few minutes after you left the assembly."

Long enough. I release the guard, sending him sprawling against the bulkhead. I jab a thick finger in his direction. "No one else hears a word of this."

The guard nods in a rapid succession of jerks.

"Go!"

My roar sends the young man floundering into the Temple. The faithful will wonder why the assembly has been cut so short, but I do not answer to any of them. Gaia's word is my command, and right now I need to be in communication with the two men I sent after those UW scouts. There is only one among my ranks gifted with far-speech, one who can send word to my men to capture the scouts and bring them back.

"Victoria!" I stiff-arm the hatch to her compartment, breaking the chain on the inside—a futile attempt at ensuring privacy.

A cry of alarm comes from the bed, but it is not from a woman's throat. Lemuel stands naked, gangly and pale, with both hands cupped over his crotch. His eyes bulge from their sockets and his mouth gapes open, having ceased to draw breath.

"Welcome, husband." Lady Victoria lies sprawled atop the sheets, her legs closed for now. Her abdomen swells outward, carrying my child. Her clothing has been discarded across what once was the ceiling of this room. "Did you miss me?" She gives me a broad smile and a wink.

"You dare to mock me in this moment?" Both of my hands have tightened into fists. My eyes dart from the youth to my wife, sizing up the situation as best as I can. So young, both of them. Young and foolish. I should have expected as much. "If it were not for my unborn child within you, I would break your neck without a thought, woman."

"That's likely so." She sighs, rubbing the palm of her hand across her belly. "Lucky for me then, isn't it?"

"*You*—" I face Lemuel. "Speak up! Whatever words you say will be your last."

He shudders mutely, staring at Victoria for help.

"Oh, let him be. My back aches all the time now, and he has

such *strong* hands." She slides her thighs against each other and gives me a direct look. "I have needs. And Lemuel is here for me when you are not."

"So this has happened before." I take a step toward the boy and watch him cower. *There will soon be nothing left of you but blood and broken bones!*

"No—Lord Cain—I didn't—!"

"Stop your babbling!" I roar.

Victoria laughs, tossing back her head.

I turn my seething gaze on her. "You disgust me. This many months with child, yet you cavort like a common whore."

"Didn't seem to bother you before you made me your wife."

My arm swoops down and strikes her hard across the mouth. Her head whips to the side, golden tresses flying. Fury kindles in her eyes, even as a thick line of blood trails from her broken lip.

"Hold your tongue, or I will cut it out," I whisper into her ear, clutching a handful of her hair at the scalp. "You don't have to be entirely in one piece when you birth my son. You just have to be alive." I throw her back onto the bed and bear down on the lad, cornering him. "Which is more than I can say for *you*."

Lemuel doesn't seem to know whether to cover himself or fend off the impending blows. More than likely, there will be only one. I will lay him out with a fist to the face, breaking his nose and shoving the fragments of it up into his brain. Or I will tear the youth's head from his shoulders and mount it on the gate outside. Or rip his limbs off, one at a time.

I have so many options.

"Please, Lord Cain—please, listen to me—" he begs.

"There is nothing I want to hear but your screams. I have been patient with you, no matter what others have said. Justus and the chieftains see you as a worthless pup, but I fed you at my table. And this is the thanks I get? You go behind my back to bed my pregnant wife?" I grimace, cursing. "It is obscene!"

I lunge for Lemuel then, pinning him easily by the throat and squeezing, lifting him up along the wall, raising him to eye level. He claws at my grip in vain, his legs dangling.

"You won't be needing these again." I grin, seizing hold of the lad's scrotum.

"Cain!" Victoria's cry rings out.

"I thought I told you—"

My voice dies in my throat. For there sits my wife upright on the bed, holding a blade to her own throat, the same weapon she once used to slay almost as many goblyns as any warrior. "What are you doing?"

My voice trembles as all the blood drains from my face. I release Lemuel's balls but maintain a choke-hold on his throat. He continues to grimace, but he's given up struggling. He too stares at Lady Victoria.

"Let him go." Is she holding herself hostage?

I release an uncertain chuckle. "Or what?"

"I said let him go." She presses the blade into her flesh. A thin trickle of crimson dribbles down onto her collarbone. "It was my doing. I forced myself upon him." The mirth has left her eyes. "Do not maim him."

"Maim him? I'm going to *kill* him!" I watch her. "Eventually."

Lemuel whimpers.

"Do it, and you'll lose the child within me as well." More blood trickles.

"You're insane. You would end your life for this worthless runt?" I shake Lemuel by the throat. It wouldn't take much to snap his neck and be done with him. "I don't believe it. Your life is too precious to you."

"Why should it be? You'll end it once the child is born. You've said as much already." She takes the hilt in both hands and hovers the point of the knife over her protruding belly. "Or would you rather—?"

"Stop this," I growl. "Right now."

"Let him go." She punctures the taut skin. Blood runs freely in rivulets from the apex.

"What the hell has gotten into you, woman?" With a curse, I hurl the lad to the floor where he lies choking, doubled over as he draws breath. "Put that weapon away!"

"When he is far away from here." She glances at Lemuel. She makes no movement to lower the blade.

"You ask me to banish him? That is his only punishment for making a cuckold of me?"

"You promised his mother you would guard his life. You granted her dying wish, Cain. Would you go back on your word?"

"Had I known he would become such an impudent libertine—"

"I told you it was not his doing." She gives the boy a direct look. "Leave us. Take what you need and be gone. He will not stop you."

Lemuel glances up at me. "I will die...out there."

"Or I can end you now." I reach for him.

"Go!" Victoria's eyes bulge as she shouts, drawing my attention. "Now!" She watches Lemuel scramble to gather his clothing, covering himself as he dashes out of the room.

I have yet to relax my fists. "You try my patience."

She brings the blade back to her throat, toying with it. "We'll give him plenty of time to escape. You won't go after him, nor will you send anyone else." She runs her eyes along my muscled frame, savoring the sight. Her appetites are insatiable. "Then we'll discuss what you need from me. Because you do need me, don't you, my love? There is no one else among your ranks gifted as I am."

I grind my teeth together, refusing to meet her gaze. Of course she is right. She is the only one who can contact my men tracking the UW scouts. Because of this, and because she carries my child, I need her.

For now.

6. MARGO

17 MONTHS AFTER ALL-CLEAR

I see it all—perceive it through the senses of the little ones Tucker carries across the wilderness, strapped to his back in the portable incubators I rigged for his journey. As soon as he touched them, they vanished from sight—as with anything that comes into contact with Tucker's flesh—but I knew they were all right. I could sense their thoughts, both the male and the female, and they were not afraid. Completely at peace, they floated in their artificial amniotic fluid, unaware that Tucker and I risked our own lives to see these two unborn children to safety.

"Sure you don't want to tag along?" Tucker asked, cinching the belts so they were nice and snug. He didn't want the canisters clinking against each other while he attempted his silent escape.

I shook my head. "Someone needs to stay behind to monitor the others." I gestured lamely at the rows of incubation units around us. "Besides, the mutos won't see you. If I were to come along, my presence would endanger your lives. Even as it is, you will have to be careful."

"I'll travel by night if I can. The mutos aren't nocturnal, far as I can tell. And I won't have to worry about my shadow without sunlight."

"What about the moon?"

"Shouldn't have another full one for a couple weeks. Plenty enough time for me to get where I'm goin'."

"Due west."

He sniffed. "That's what they said."

I nodded with some lingering reservation. "The *spirits of the earth.*"

"Yeah." He almost chuckled. "Crazy as that sounds."

It sounded far beyond the realms of sanity weeks before, when Tucker returned from one of his routine salvage runs on the surface. The city ruins above Eden were a virtual cornucopia when it came to useful items and well-preserved foodstuffs. Tucker along with Willard's *dogs*—collared, remote-controlled mutos—made regular scavenging excursions throughout the rubble, searching and rescuing all the goods that made Eden a subterranean paradise.

On this particular occasion, Tucker returned a bit shell-shocked. He said later it was a good thing Willard and Perch hadn't been able to see how pale he was. When he managed to get a moment alone with me, he shared about the encounter he had with his mother in the middle of a cracked and dusty street.

"Your mother?" I had been unable to contain my incredulity.

"Hear me out," Tucker said, keeping his voice low. "I know full well it wasn't really Momma. She died in the blasts on D-Day. But she was just how I remember her: standing there in her apron and her rose-print dress, like she was a hologram projected straight from my own mind. There she was in the middle of the street talking to me. None of the dogs gave her any notice—except for when she showed up in that dust devil."

"A what?"

"A little twister along the ground. It spiraled toward me down the middle of the street, and I held up my arms like this to shield myself from all the grit." He demonstrated. "When I brought 'em back down, there she was, standing right there as solid as you are right now."

"What did she say to you?"

He sniffed, shuffled his feet—the usual tics when he starts to feel uncomfortable. "Told me a lot of stuff about myself, stuff only she'd know. Sounded just like her, too. Her voice. But I knew it couldn't be, not out there like that. So I had her tell me straight out what was going on. And she sure did. Told me all about Milton and Daiyna and Luther and the others, about how they went west and met others of their kind—*our* kind—changed by the dust of this crazy new earth and made into something a hell of a lot more than human."

"Are you certain you weren't hallucinating? The temperature spikes can be extreme on the surface, not to mention—"

"No, I'm sure. Just hear me out." He took a quick breath and resumed, "She—it—this spirit manifestation or whatever it was, she went on to tell me that Luther was the leader of these folks, and they were all holed-up in caves out west, near the Pacific coast. And if we—you and me—ever wanted to join up with them, that's where we'd find 'em all."

"You and me," I mused. "Is there any particular reason why this spirit-projection cannot come down here and invite me herself?"

"Yeah, actually. It's got something to do with them being unable to co-exist with all these manmade materials we've got. They can only move through dust and air. If they're really the earth's spirits and whatnot, I suppose that makes some sense. Right?"

I hadn't been so sure. I'm still not.

"Let's just hope they know where they're sending you," I told him. "Did you get an accurate count of Luther's numbers? He will need to return in force if he is to reclaim what belongs to him."

Tucker sniffed. "I know it's kind of late in the game to be bringing this up, but... What if they aren't all that interested in coming back for these little ones? What if they're busy out there makin' a new life for themselves instead? Making their own children the natural way?"

I remember mulling this over like it was yesterday.

"Luther is a man of integrity—the last of a dying breed. Daiyna is much like him. You tell them what Willard plans to do with these children—using them as bargaining chips to get himself off this continent—and they'll come back. I know they will." I paused, staring at the empty space where Tucker stood. "As long as you get to them in time."

"I'll move as fast as these boots carry me. But remind me again: Why don't I just borrow one of the Hummers?"

I shook my head. "You do that, and Perch will have the dogs hot on your trail. This way, you sneak out quietly, and nobody knows you're missing until they find your shock collar without you attached. By the time they start hunting you down, you should have close to a day's head start." I paused. "Then I will tell Willard about the missing fetuses."

"Shouldn't you do that right off? Won't they suspect you had something to do with it, otherwise?"

"Let me worry about that." In the end, the timing was far from perfect, despite our best-laid plans. "You just get to where you need to be—as fast as you can."

"All right." Tucker's last words as he left.

But his voice has returned since then in garbled, gentle tones as heard by the neonates in their amniotic chambers. Somehow, I share the makings of a telepathic link with these two little ones that does not diminish over space or time. It's not something I am always conscious of, but I can tune in whenever I wish to check on their progress.

It has already been weeks, and they have yet to reach Luther and his people. Wild mutos along the way impeded Tucker's progress, as did the dogs Willard sent after them once the two fetuses were discovered missing. Much sooner than I anticipated.

Now I sit bound to an unforgiving steel chair in one of the bare rooms that was used for interrogating and dismembering *sand freaks* last year. Yet it doesn't seem like that much time has passed. This is the same room where I fitted Samson with his artificial arms and legs...after the gruesome amputations Perch performed during the interrogation process.

"Where'd he take 'em?" Perch demands for the umpteenth time, slugging me across the face with his brick of a fist.

My head whips to the side and I spit blood, see it splatter across the cold floor, feel it ooze thick and warm down my cheek. My daily beating. I'm almost numb to it by this point, but the blows still have a way of stinging, bringing me out of my thoughts.

He grabs a fistful of my hair and jerks my head back. Perspiration stands out on his upper lip and glistens across his flushed brow.

"You'll tell me. Oh yeah, one of these days. Once I start taking pieces of you." He chuckles. "Willard doesn't want me to go that far, and I'm sure you don't either. But we're getting awful close to a turning point, darlin'. Real close."

I close my eyes and focus on an image from my youth: a mighty torrent of rushing water cascading off the side of a cliff, down into a deep lagoon below. I project this scene into Perch's subconscious mind.

He releases me abruptly.

"I-uh—" There's a look of bewildered discomfort on his broad face. "I'll be back. You sit tight and think about how you're gonna start answering my questions."

He leaves the room, sliding the door shut behind him with a bang. I hope he fails to reach the restroom in time.

Alone now, I reach out to the young ones with my thoughts, closing the gap of endless barren kilometers between us.

Where are you?

I sense they are out in the open and on the move. There is an urgency to Tucker's movements, stronger than before. Is he drawing close to their destination? Or is he once again being pursued? Willard called off the dogs when a sandstorm cleared all traces of Tucker's tracks. It would have to be the wild mutos now who caught Tucker's scent and are tracking him through the day or night—I cannot determine which, trapped in this room. His plan was to travel only by cover of darkness, but perhaps the mutos are making that difficult for him. If it is daylight, and if his shadow is plain to see, they will close in on him easily. Gun him down and devour him, as well as the young ones he carries.

I have to banish the images from my mind. These are my own fears, nothing more. There is no reason to assume such things. Tucker's pulse is elevated; I can sense the neonates take notice of this, but he might be picking up the pace for no other reason than to reach Luther's people before another encounter with the wild mutos.

Be at peace, little ones, I project my thoughts. *Soon you will be safe.*

Then it will be time to rescue the remaining fetuses housed deep in Eden's core. As long as Luther and the others are courageous enough to return for the sakes of these innocents—

The door slams open, and Perch enters with Jamison on his heels.

"No more games!" Perch slaps me hard, streaking the blood across my face. "Keep your damn mind tricks to yourself!"

I wince, feeling the inside of my swollen cheek with my tongue. "You didn't have to go, after all?"

Jamison chuckles. "He ran over to the urinal like he was going to explode. Took him a while to realize it was all in his head."

"Bitch!" Perch brings back his fist to strike me again, but Jamison steps in the way with a frown.

"Enough. We've tried it your way. Willard wants results."

"Don't you think I know that?"

"Let me give it a shot. A little *good cop* routine might be all she needs."

"You do realize I'm sitting right here," I say, "hearing every word."

Jamison shrugs. "We can't keep our thoughts from you. So why bother?"

"She's not talkin'. Maybe once she starts losin' her fingers and toes, then she'll have something to say."

"Fine." Jamison extends his arm toward the door. "Give me five minutes. If I can't get her to tell me anything, then come back in here and do your thing. I just hope you get Willard's permission before you start taking her apart. For your sake."

Cursing under his breath, Perch stalks out of the room. Jamison shuts the door behind him and lingers there a moment before turning to face me.

"I understand why you did it," he says.

I keep my gaze on the floor, on the pattern made by my own blood spattered across the concrete.

"You know I was never a fan of Willard's plans. They're human lives, after all. Not bargaining chips." He presses his fingertips together, brings them to his chin. "But to put them in even greater danger, that's beyond negligent, Margo. It's insane. The mutos out there won't think twice about gobbling them up as an afternoon snack!"

I shake my head, just enough for him to notice, careful not to add to the excruciating pain slicing through my skull. "They're fine."

"And you know this how, exactly? Are you...in some kind of communication with Tucker? Are you people able to do that—speak telepathically?"

I cough, spitting out more blood. "I never said he had anything to do with it."

"He goes missing the same day we find two of the incubation chambers empty. It's easy to put two and two together here."

"I don't know where he is. He is not my concern. As far as Willard knows, two of the neonates unfortunately did not develop to term. I found them expired that morning, and I disposed of the remains in one of the trash incinerators. I was about to inform Willard, but then Tucker didn't return from scavenging. I assumed Willard wouldn't want all that bad news on the same day, so I waited to tell him about it."

Jamison approaches me. "You may be the only mind-reader in this room, Margo. But I recognize a load of crap when I hear it.

And so does Willard. He knows you removed Tucker's collar. Again."

I glare up at him through the sweat-drenched clumps of my bedraggled hair. "Send Perch back in here and let him have at it. Because that's all you're getting from me."

"You don't seem to realize that I'm on your side. Go ahead, read my thoughts and see if I'm wrong. I'm not lying to you." He pauses. "We want the same thing, you and me: to see these babies grow and develop into fully functioning adults. The first generation of humankind to be born in captivity."

He is speaking the truth, as he sees it. But he and I do not want the same thing. I want the young ones to live out in the open with their own people, their parents. Not here in Eden's sterile subterranean depths.

Jamison sighs and squeezes the bridge of his nose, closing his eyes briefly. "Listen, we don't have to play games. You know where Tucker took them. It's obvious." He watches me. "To Luther and the others. You know where they are."

I almost smirk. "I don't."

But someone else does—a *spirit of the earth*.

"The dogs followed Tucker's tracks as far as they could, south out of the city ruins. But they veered west before that sandstorm kicked in. We had to call the dogs back."

"I'm sure it had nothing to do with them almost being out of range by that point."

"That too. The collars aren't a perfect solution. Not yet, anyway."

I shake my head slowly. "Even if I knew where Tucker was, you wouldn't be able to bring him back. You can't go after him on the surface. Willard has you all so paranoid about the *demon dust* that—"

"The main thing on Willard's mind right now is whether he'll need to reinforce our defenses. He's got a feeling that if Luther and company decide to come back for their children, they won't be alone." He watches me. "Is there some enclave of sand freaks out there we should know about? Is that where Tucker's going?"

I look him in the eye. "Bring Perch back." I won't tell him anything.

"You're making this more difficult than it has to be. There was a time when I would have said you were more valuable to Willard in one piece, that you were necessary for the wellbeing of those little ones below. But that's not the case now."

"Do you plan to replace me?" Unlikely.

"You misunderstand, Margo. Willard isn't concerned about them anymore. They could all shrivel up and die in their incubation chambers for all he cares. All he wants is to get off this continent. When the UW arrives, he plans to barter the lives of those fetuses for his safe passage. And if that doesn't work, he'll strip the soldiers of their hazard suits at gunpoint and take their chopper. He won't think twice about abandoning those infants."

Willard is insane. I've known this for some time. "The warships patrolling the coast would shoot him down."

"Don't underestimate him. I'm sure he has some kind of contingency plan." He nods, gesturing lamely toward the door. "When Perch returns, he will hurt you. At that point, there will be nothing I can do for you. While he's cutting off your fingers one knuckle at a time, I want you to think back to this moment. When you shut down the only man in Eden willing to help you."

I close my eyes, imagining myself under Perch's knife. But I can also imagine the chambers in the nursery neglected, the neonates abandoned when they need me most.

Jamison spoke the truth regarding Willard. All that matters to him now is self-preservation. Escape. And which is more dangerous: a man fighting for a cause, or one fighting for his own survival?

Jamison turns away and approaches the door.

"Wait," I stop him. He half-turns toward me. "I need to bring them into this world—such that it is. I cannot allow them to be forgotten."

"Then give me something. I guarantee you'll be back in the nursery within the hour." He winces a little at the condition of my face, no doubt swollen and multi-colored. "After we get you cleaned up. Wouldn't want you to frighten those little guys."

"If you are truly on my side in this...then tell me exactly what Willard wants to know."

He nods. "Your get-out-of-jail-free card should be worth this much: Where is Tucker going? Do you know the exact location—longitude, latitude?"

"No." I frown. It is the truth.

"Is he going to find Luther and the others? To tell them about their children?"

I hesitate. How long has it been? Weeks now, brought here for daily questioning and beatings, then released to the nursery to continue my work. Every day, I've denied knowledge about Tucker's MIA status. But now?

Have they finally broken me? Or is it the fear that this time, they won't allow me to return to the little ones unless I give them what they want?

"Yes," I admit. Closing my eyes, I see with an evolving inner sight I can no more understand than explain, that Tucker has slowed to a walking pace. It may be the dead of night, but light shines from above. A full moon?

"Are you able to communicate with him?"

"No." As much as I wish I could, it is impossible.

"But he took them due west, as far as you know."

I nod. "Will that be enough to get me out of here?" I meet Jamison's gaze as he mulls it over.

"Enough to keep Perch's bloodthirsty paws off you, at any rate. I'll go to Willard myself and tell him what you told me. Just sit tight for now. He may want to come up here and question you himself."

Won't that be a treat. "I'm not going anywhere."

He offers a sad excuse for a smile and exits the room, sliding the door shut and locking it behind him. Not much of a deterrent to Perch if he's determined to get in here, but it's the thought that counts. Perhaps Jamison really has my best interest at heart. If not, I will know soon enough.

There are voices, faint murmurs as through the wall. But it can't be coming from next door; these rooms are soundproof, intentionally so. Willard didn't want the rest of Eden to hear the screams of the sand freaks as they were experimented on.

So it has to be—

I shut my eyes and focus on the link I share with the two unborn children Tucker carries. That is where the voices originated. It's like listening to a conversation while being submerged in a pool of water—the artificial amniotic fluid in the incubation pods. I can't hear exact words or phrases, only the tone of each voice, and I recognize Tucker's. I sense strong emotions, but it is unclear whether they belong to the speakers or to the two little ones who are listening.

How is this possible? I am floating far beyond the realms of science now, for this ability—much like my recent adeptness at telepathy—defies every scientific principle I know.

Regardless, Tucker seems to have met someone capable of speech, wherever he is. That rules out the mutos, too deformed to do anything but gargle, grunt, and ooze that foul-smelling yellow fluid that coats every facial orifice. It has to be Luther or one of his people. Either that, or the UW troops have already landed, and Tucker has inadvertently reached some kind of military checkpoint. There is no way for me to know.

If only I could hear what the voices are saying. How can I tell the little ones to focus their abilities on understanding what's said? I can receive information from them, but it is unclear whether I am able to send it. And even if I can, how would fetuses have any way of understanding adult speech?

The female spoke to me before.

Down in the nursery, in the incubation chamber, she and I shared an interchange of thoughts. Telepathy.

That's it.

If I tell the little ones, mind-to-mind via this incomprehensible metaphysical link we share, not to focus on the words themselves but instead on the thoughts behind the words—

I blow out a short sigh and settle into the uncomfortable chair. I clear my mind, close my eyes, do what I can to ignore the aches and pains from my latest beating.

I won't know whether this is possible until I try.

Jamison or Perch—or even Willard—will return at any moment. If I am going to make this attempt at communication, it has to be now, while I am still coherent enough to keep my thoughts clear.

I know your minds, little ones.

But is that truly the case? It was only the female before, daughter of Daiyna and Luther, with whom I shared the momentary link. *Where are we going?* the little one's mind asked. *Home*, I projected the thought back to her. Am I perceiving Tucker's journey through her mind alone? If so, I should focus on directing my thoughts to the female now.

We share this special link between us, and it does not matter how far away from me you have gone. I feel your presence as though you never left me.

I wait in the silence, not expecting anything in return but hoping for some kind of signal, some change in our telepathic link that will let me know the transmission has been received. Either the little one hears my thoughts, or I am talking to myself inside my own head.

Who is there with you? I ask.

I feel a sudden shiver, a tremble—not from cold or fear, but from newly awakened awareness, a soul stirring from a deep sleep.

Where are we? asks the mind of the little one, the female, curious but not afraid. *Where are you?*

I start forward, jerking against my restraints. The sensation is strong, an energy pressing into my own consciousness through this metaphysical conduit. *Are you in danger?* I want to ask. But what do these young ones know of danger? They have been sealed inside chambers from the moment of their conception and now are contained in those portable incubation pods strapped to Tucker; their environment would be no different. They know nothing of the outside world: its fears, pains, and horrors.

You are with our friend, Tucker. He is taking you home—

Home? But we are already here.

I nod, keeping my eyes closed. I can understand why she would think that. *Yes. And he is taking you to—*

How to explain? The little ones have parents that are not even aware of their existence.

There are others here, in addition to Tucker, the young female's thoughts come through.

Again I nod, taking a quick breath to steady my nerves. *How many? Can you see—?* I stop myself.

See?

Too late. I take a moment to berate my own foolishness for using a word unknown to the little one. It describes a sense she cannot understand.

Yes. It is what you are doing now. You see Tucker. You know he is there with you. I pause. *Can you see the others as well?*

Another trembling sensation courses through the link we share. I strain to remain present, in the moment.

Yes, but they do not see me.

And do they see Tucker?

Yes. They rumble at him.

I understand this approximation, a word that holds meaning for an unborn consciousness trapped in amniotic fluid. The others with Tucker now, *rumbling* at him, are speaking to him. They can *see* him in the same way I can see this little one: they are able to communicate with one another. But no one present is able to share a telepathic link; no one else is able to communicate with her in the same way I can.

Tucker may have arrived at Luther's camp. From what I remember, there wasn't anyone in his group who shared my special mutation and its abilities. This little one and I could be the only two of our kind.

Can you—? I want to ask her to read their thoughts, these people who rumble at Tucker. But how can I explain *thoughts?* Or even a *mind?* Better to stick with what is working already: approximations. *They cannot see you the way I can, these others that are with Tucker. But can you see them?*

Yes.

This is good, very good. *And can you see the—?* Words? What are they to a neonate? *Can you see what is behind the rumbling?* The thoughts behind their words?

I hope my meaning comes through clear enough.

They are not content.

My head jerks back; my eyes twitch beneath their lids. This is a new presence now linked to my mind, one that has been silent up to this point: the male, son of Shechara and Samson.

Not content, I echo his thought.

They are agitated. Unhappy.

Such a vocabulary. But is he truly using words to communicate with me? Or is it my mind, translating whatever synaptic signals they transmit into words I can comprehend? *Agitated* and *unhappy*—are these the feelings of a male child ready to be released from an incubation chamber, emotions he can easily understand?

The others that Tucker has encountered could be agitated because he caught them unaware. Likely, due to his special mutation and penchant for appearing without warning. Or are they trigger-happy UW troops, uncertain of their orders? I doubt they were prepped to meet an invisible man.

What else do you see? I ask the little ones, my heart surging now as heavy boots tread along the steel catwalk outside my room.

Confusion. They do not know who we are.

I frown at that. Luther would remember Tucker—

The bolt on the door slides back. It is not Jamison or Willard who enters, but Perch with his bolt cutters in hand and a hungry look on his face.

"Wakey wakey." He chuckles.

I shut my eyes, struggling to keep the link open with the little ones for as long as possible before the torture begins anew. I have to know they are safe.

Through the metaphysical conduit, I hear a sudden noise, one that brings the *rumbles* of conversation to a halt.

A gunshot.

My eyes widen.

Perch grins down at me, liking the reaction. He licks his teeth.

7. BISHOP

18 MONTHS AFTER ALL-CLEAR

Wedged between Sinclair and Harris in the backseat of the solar jeep, I bounce along with the rest of the team as Morley takes us across the rough terrain, tearing through the barren Wastes as fast as the vehicle can manage. No doubt sending up a plume of dust in our wake visible to any of the hostiles we hope to outrun on our course due east.

Destination: Eden. Some kind of subterranean city, by the sound of it. Tough to imagine.

Visually, I remain closed off from my surroundings, thanks to the malfunctioning HUD in my helmet. But I can hear well enough, and Granger was able to make contact with Captain Mutegi aboard the *Argonaus*. The entire team was given access to further instructions originally intended for my eyes only.

"I don't like the idea of you going in blind," Mutegi said, the irony of his words lost on no one. "The more you all know, the better."

We're not here just to make contact with the last bastion of survivors from D-Day. We've also been tasked with convincing these survivors—led by an engineer by the name of Arthur Willard—to give up their newborn children for testing. If Harris and Sinclair find them to be healthy, contaminant-free specimens of humankind, Mutegi will send in a second chopper from the fleet. Not a moment beforehand.

I don't blame him, considering what happened to the first one.

"Still no sign of 'em," Granger's voice comes through on comms, and the others in the jeep murmur affirmatively, accustomed to his periodic updates even as they each keep their own watch. But I appreciate it, as Granger has to see for the both of us now.

We managed to scavenge an impressive arsenal from the dead hostiles: two high-powered rifles with long-range infrared scopes in addition to three military-issued daggers. All with the same UW insignia, plain to see.

We agreed they probably weren't from Eden.

"That's what we'd look like without our suits," Morley said as we piled into the solar-powered jeep. He hadn't been able to shift his gaze from the mutilated corpses we were leaving behind.

"So it would appear," Harris said, deep in thought.

"They were ours," Morley persisted. "UW troops."

"Not for a long while, by the looks of 'em." Granger cursed. "The bastards."

"We can't just leave them here like this." Morley stood beside the jeep, reluctant to take his place behind the wheel.

There is no spite in my tone, only a grim acceptance of the bizarre new reality we face, when I say, "What do you suggest we do? Bury them? Say a few words?"

"It's the least we could do," Morley said. "After all they've suffered."

"Do not allow your emotions to interfere with what must be done," Sinclair said, but even she seemed to have softened a few of her sharp edges. "We must leave this place before other hostiles return. By all appearances, these men have not been *men* for some time. The others like them may be out of their minds, for all we know. Lunatic cannibals who will not think twice about gunning us down and feeding on us—despite whatever soldier's brotherhood you think you share with them."

Morley cursed. "Leaving them to rot in the sun? It isn't right."

"Not much about this mission is," I said. "But we'll see it through. And then we'll go home to our loved ones." I paused. "So get your ass behind the wheel, soldier, and drive us the hell out of here."

Morley obeyed orders without grumbling, but his reckless driving ever since has made it clear that he's pissed off. I don't mind the excessive speeds. As long as the hot-headed weapons officer keeps both hands on the wheel, he can't threaten to shoot anybody again. But as Morley takes us sailing through the air over a dusty rise only to crash onto all four tires, testing the limits of the suspension, I realize the man could easily kill us all if he isn't careful.

I can understand Morley's sentiments. Those UW troops were sent to a diseased continent. Nuclear waste, a land ravaged by warfare—that's what they were told to expect. They would have been prepared for pockets of radiation and bioweapon residue; they would have avoided confined spaces, stayed out in the open —even as their genetic makeup was altered by whatever mutagens remained trapped in the dust at their feet.

Somehow, the soldiers had been transformed into those fanged, oozing creatures that Harris inspected firsthand. No way they could have known what they were in for.

Just like us. I crack open one eye to see the flashing OFFLINE message stating the obvious inside my helmet. No change.

"To think...*Children*," Harris breaks from his reverie as Morley takes us over a low outcropping of rock that sends the right side of the jeep lurching upward. "I had nearly given up hope!"

"Yeah. Kind of resigned myself to us humans dying out as a species, y'know?" Granger chuckles drily. "Hey, it happened to the dinosaurs. They had their time, and you don't see many of them running around loose anymore."

"Or any member of the animal kingdom, for that matter,"

Sinclair offers. Then she pauses. "But we don't know if this Arthur Willard fellow can be trusted."

"Don't get our hopes up, right?" Granger says. "That should be your motto. But c'mon, why would this guy lie to the UW?"

"Would you choose to live on this continent—or under it, as the case appears to be—if you knew Eurasia was waiting across the Pacific?" she counters.

"What are you saying? You think he just wants out? There aren't really any kids? There's no way the UW would fall for something like that."

"We're here, aren't we?" Morley speaks up for the first time since he started driving.

"There must be some credence to his claims, some proof of life. Otherwise, our government would not take him seriously," Sinclair allows. "But to have dozens of incubation chambers operational and just as many fetuses viable in a twenty-year-old fallout bunker? Highly unlikely."

"So what, then? He's stacking the deck in his favor?" Granger sniffs. "He's got maybe a couple babies, if that?"

"Even two would be more than we'd ever thought possible," Harris murmurs. "One male, one female—"

"Adam and Eve all over again," Morley interrupts.

"The UW would be willing to send us through anything, hell or high water, in order to retrieve them. Our exalted government officials have grown desperate as of late."

"What do you mean, Doc?" Granger says. "You know something we don't?"

I'm sure he does. In recent years, the politicians and medical community have been working hand in glove, and lately it seems the genetic engineering firms are getting in on the same action—whatever it is—in a big way.

"I am not at liberty to say. But I can tell you this much: the United World government has not resigned itself to dying out as a species. Not by a long shot."

Now it's clear why the good doctor was assigned to this

mission. More than a standard-issue medic, Harris is someone the UW governors can trust to see their interests carried through, fully to term.

"So you could say we're their last hope. They've got a whole lot riding on what we're doing here."

"Don't let it go to your head, Granger," I warn. "We're expendable. Easily replaceable. Don't forget that."

Harris grunts uncomfortably in response. "Not the best way to keep up morale, Sergeant."

"He's right," Morley says. I can imagine him tightening his grip on the wheel. Wringing it. "If they cared about us at all, they'd send in air support. Not cut us loose. But it's what they do. Same as they did to those poor souls we found. Left them here to rot."

"We're on our own," I reiterate. "Period. We shouldn't expect any help from Mutegi and the fleet. But if we do our job right—make it to Eden and bring back what they want us to—then we'll be welcomed as heroes. More importantly, we'll be allowed to go home. I don't know about the rest of you, but that's all I want."

Granger chuckles. "You heard the man, Doc. Let's git 'er done. *Hoo-rah!*"

No one echoes his spirited cry. Sinclair releases a petulant sigh, of course.

Quiet for a few moments, Harris gathers his thoughts. "What we're doing here is of the utmost importance. The future of our species may very well depend on it. You do realize the weight of the matter, Sergeant."

"The sergeant sees himself as our escort, not as the savior of humankind," Sinclair interjects.

"You're inside my head now?" Sitting between the two of them is getting to be a bit much. "We've got a job to do—"

"But that's all it is to you: a mission," Harris says. "I don't get the feeling you are fully invested in it, now that we know more of the details. Speaking for myself, I am completely awestruck by this turn of events. Meeting the remaining survivors on this continent would have been momentous enough, but to learn that these people actually have...*children*. It's far beyond anything I could have imagined."

I nod, but the gesture goes unnoticed behind the black tinted polymer of my helmet. Rivulets of perspiration stream down my face.

"Perhaps it is different for you," Harris says. "Having children of your own. Being one of the last couples to conceive. How old are they now?"

"Young." Was the doctor given access to my personal file?

"Of course. You are very fortunate."

I am. I'm out here in the fresh air. Meanwhile my wife, daughter, and son are distinguished guests of the Eurasian prison system.

"We count our blessings," I return with a helping of irony in my tone.

Harris chuckles, trying unnecessarily to smooth things over between us. "As should we all, Sergeant. I know that more than anything, you wish to return safe and sound to your family when this mission is over. But I want to invite you to look at the bigger picture here—"

"I get it, Doc." I have to cut short the incessant patronizing. I'm still the team leader, despite my visual setback. "Our mission is important. What we're doing here—meeting an enclave of survivors who are still able to reproduce. It's going to change the world as we know it. None of that is lost on me."

"By no means did I intend any—" Harris sounds taken aback. A nice act.

"But the tactics have changed," I continue. "We're up against armed hostiles, and we're out in the middle of a foreign land, completely on our own. So forgive me if saving the world is no longer my top priority. I'm too busy planning how the hell we're going to make it out of here alive."

Neither Harris nor Sinclair has a cute comeback to that. Only Granger chuckles in the silence.

"Still no sign of 'em," he announces, surveying our surroundings.

"They're out there," Morley says under his breath. "I can feel it."

"Yeah?" Granger says. "More voodoo mumbo-jumbo?"

"If they were anywhere in range, their life signs would be registering on our heads-up displays," Sinclair says irritably.

"Well, look who's read the owner's manual cover to cover," Granger quips.

"There was no cover. It was digital."

I smirk at that. The woman's sense of humor is about as robust as a chemistry book. I have a hard time imagining what kind of family is waiting for her back home, if any. Are they also being held by the government to ensure her wholehearted commitment to orders? Somehow I doubt it. The UW must have found some other incentive to keep her on board for this suicide mission.

During the remaining hours of daylight, Morley takes us as far as the solar-powered jeep will carry us, running well after sundown on reserve power. According to Granger, the headlights cut a wide swath of white out of the pitch black up to a hundred meters ahead of us. Plenty to see by. But eventually Morley starts to slow down. The power drain on the solar cells has reached substantial levels, and as the hours creep toward midnight, the jeep decelerates to a crawl, the headlights dimming, flickering, then going out completely.

"Describe the terrain," I order as Morley squeezes every drop of juice out of the batteries.

"A whole lot of black," Granger says.

"There is a large outcropping of rock forty-five degrees to the southwest," Sinclair says. "I suggest we find cover there for the night."

I nod, my face now visible—as are the faces of my team. My helmet tinting decided all of a sudden to clear automatically like everybody else's. And the flashing OFFLINE message is gone, along with the blinding static. So finally, I can see again. Night means a welcome twenty-degree drop in my suit's internal temperature. As far as my O2 is concerned, I can't detect any change in the quality of my air; but rationing it remains a priority, right behind *Don't lose it in front of your team.*

"We'll stop here." I reach forward to tap Morley on the shoulder, but it's more of a heavy slap in this unwieldy suit.

"How're you doing in there, Captain?" A frown of what appears to be genuine concern creases Granger's brow. "Still got enough air?"

I nod, pointing toward the rocks. "Everybody out. We'll make camp there. Granger, you've got first watch."

"Thanks, Captain." That look of concern is quickly replaced by one of sullen exhaustion.

I clap him on the back as I stand, fighting the hazard suit for every centimeter of movement. "Better than a court-martial, you've got to agree."

Granger glances up with sudden recollection. He did disobey a direct order after our chopper crashed. "Yes, sir."

I half-smile. "Don't plan on it being a solo mission. I'm staying up with you." *Can't imagine sleeping here, anyway.* "Four eyes are better than two."

Sinclair places a hand on my arm. "Do you think that's wise, Sergeant?" she says. "Your life support system could fail at any moment. If you were asleep, immobile, you would consume far less oxygen than—"

"I'm fine. My HUD is offline, that's all. Everything else appears to be functioning normally. I'll run out of O2 the same time as the rest of you." I give her a wink. "Get some sleep. That's an order. We've got another long stretch ahead of us tomorrow."

She turns away without another word, climbing out of the jeep to join Harris and Granger as they shuffle stiffly toward our campsite. Only Morley remains with the vehicle, popping the hood to take a good, long look at the solar batteries underneath.

"How are they?" I drop down from the jeep's rear, my boots landing with puffs of dust that rise like white mist in the moonlight. I can't help but think back to the film I saw in school as a kid, that scene from the first lunar landing. *One small step for man...*

"Should be good to go once they're all charged up."

"How long should that take?" I approach his side.

"As soon as the sun rises, they'll start charging. And they'll continue to do so while we're en route." He glances up at the moon. "A pity they're outdated."

I frown. "When's their expiration date?"

"Not an issue. They'll run fine unless they're damaged. But if the jeep was this year's model, we would be able to continue our journey under moonlight. The newer power cells are hypersensitive, able to capture all the energy they need to run a vehicle this size."

"Any way we could overhaul these batteries to do the same?" I gesture vaguely at the complicated apparatus under the hood.

"I'm not your engineer." Morley shrugs. "We would probably need to replace the solar panels as well. But if Granger had the right tools, perhaps." He bares his teeth in a tight grin, but his features fall suddenly as a frame pops up on his HUD, flaring red. "Movement, Sergeant."

I don't have to ask. The weapons officer is pointing the direction we came from. It can mean only one thing: we were followed.

"How many?" I peer into the moonlit dark but can't see a thing beyond the range of my unaugmented vision.

"Two figures, four and a half kilometers away."

"They must've doubled back and gotten behind us somehow." There would be others moving into position to surround us. "Granger, do you copy?"

"Hear you loud and clear, Captain." At the campsite, Granger, Harris, and Sinclair have formed a circle, facing outward with rifles at the ready, scanning the landscape on all sides. "Only the two of them so far, that I can see. On foot."

"Moving at a steady clip," Harris says. "Straight for us."

I grip the handgun I took from Morley. "Find cover. No shooting until you hear otherwise from me."

"All due respect, Sergeant," Morley says, "but with your HUD offline, I don't think you—"

"We have our orders," Sinclair's voice interjects.

"Everybody spread out." I nudge Morley. "You're with me. I want to hear everything you're seeing as you see it." I crouch beside the jeep's grill, grimacing as I force the hazard suit to comply with my movements. "Start talking."

Morley drops heavily onto one knee. "How about some firepower, sir?"

"Leave that to me."

"What sort of weapons officer am I unarmed?"

I glance at him. "Prove you can keep a level head, then you can take your pick from our limited arsenal."

Morley's nostrils flare as he exhales. "Yes, sir." He blinks, focusing on the HUD frame tracking the two incoming figures. "They're armed, both of them. Same UW-issued assault rifles we found on those hostiles—dead soldiers."

Why on foot? There were two other jeeps when that freak sandstorm ripped across the hillside. Are they still out there, keeping their distance? If so, Morley's HUD should be picking them up. What kind of range does it have? It can't be more than five kilometers, or he would have registered these intruders sooner.

"Based on their current velocity, they should reach us in less than thirty minutes." Morley faces me. "But why should we wait? I say we bring the battle to them!"

"That sort of talk will keep your holster empty, soldier."

"We outnumber them two to one—"

"Try again." I give him a sidelong glance. "I doubt our doctor or science officer practice much on the firing range."

"If we surround them—"

"We have no idea who they are or what they want. As far as

we know, they could be advance scouts sent from Eden to tail us." Unlikely, but the point is that we're situationally in the dark here. "We stay put for now."

Granger clears his throat. "Understood, Captain. We're digging in."

I turn to check their position and at first can't locate the half-sized engineer or the other two members of my team. Then I catch a glint of moonlight against one of their helmets, bobbing slightly. They're hiding behind the rocks, jagged like dinosaur teeth in stark relief against the black sky.

"Keep your heads down over there," I warn. One well-aimed round, and triple-polymer or not, those helmets will crack, exposing them to the contaminated air. Or they'll end up in the same situation as me, without a HUD.

"They're not in hazard suits," Harris notes, staring west. "They're moving much too fast for that."

"Rules out Eden. They would know better than to come out here unprotected," Morley says.

"Look at what they're wearing instead," the doctor continues. "They appear much better-dressed than those sun-charred souls we found earlier. Such cloaks would shield them well."

"A separate tribe, perhaps?" Sinclair suggests.

"Cut the chatter," I order. They can discuss the continent's de-evolved sociology at a later date. Right now, I need the channel clear to hear everything Morley is seeing. "Have they altered course?"

"Still heading straight for us, following the trail we left," Morley says. "No night vision equipment, no breathing apparatuses."

Fully exposed to the elements, the contaminants—these infected strangers are fearless.

"Three kilometers and closing," Morley adds, facing me. "Orders?"

"Unchanged."

I ignore the impatient look on my weapons officer's face.

While I'd never admit it to anyone, part of me wonders if that strange, other-worldly presence will make another appearance—the *spirit of the earth* that manifested itself as my daughter, then as my wife. I'm sure it was responsible for killing off those three hostiles. The way their corpses were scattered across the ground and broken to pieces—no human force could manage something like that.

Will that *spirit* intervene again? And if it doesn't, could that mean the two unidentified figures closing in are not a threat?

You are here for a purpose, James Bishop. We cannot allow you to come to harm, the spirit told me. No idea what it means, but I like the sound of it. Always good to have backup.

So I wait. Am I putting my entire team in danger, trusting the word of an entity I can't comprehend? Should I tell the others about it?

They'll think I landed on my head when I fell out of that chopper.

"Hold on." Morley adjusts his position, frowning through the red frame glowing on his face shield. He blinks. "It looks like... They're making camp."

Granger's incredulous voice comes through: "What the hell?" He steps out from cover. "They're calling it a night?"

"Must have no idea we're watching them," Morley says.

"Keeping their distance." I nod, sizing up the situation. "They know we're here, but we're not going anywhere. Not until morning."

Harris and Sinclair follow Granger, the three of them converging on the jeep.

"So now what?" Granger slings his rifle over one shoulder by the strap and spreads his boots in an overconfident stance. "I don't know about the rest of you, but if they start cooking up some grub, I just might have to go over and make their acquaintance."

"And if they decide to cook *you*?" Morley says.

"Not enough meat on him," Sinclair dismisses the idea.

"Only muscle. You like muscle?" Granger starts toward her.

I hold up a hand, and they quiet down. Granger is right about one thing: food's a scarce commodity. All of our ration packs went down in flames with the chopper. If these two strangers have food with them, and if they're not the cannibals Morley thinks they are, then digging in for the night and going hungry might not be the best course of action. I can go without eating; I was trained for it. But the other members of my team are a different breed. Soon their appetites and survival instincts will be at odds, and I can only imagine the recklessness that may ensue.

"Either they don't see us as a threat, or they can't see us at all," Morley remarks, gazing into the distance. "Making camp out in the open like that. It's brazen, that's what it is."

What are they waiting for? Are they under orders to observe but not interfere?

"Report," I remind Morley.

"Looks like they've got a full spread of standard-issue protein and hydro-packs. No meat. Guess we can forget about them being cannibal freaks." His boots shuffle forward a step, stirring up dust.

"How about you send me in for a little recon, Cap?" Granger says. "My belly would sure be in your debt."

Harris chuckles sympathetically. Sinclair remains stoic and silent.

"What's the plan, boss?" Morley says, fingering his empty holster.

"We've got time," I tell him. "We're not going anywhere until sunrise. For the moment, it appears our friends are doing the same. Granger and I will take first watch. If we decide to backtrack and make their acquaintance, you'll know about it. But for now, get some rest if you can." I can't imagine anybody sleeping in these suits with the clock on our O2 supply running down, but they might as well try. "Shift change in two hours."

Harris and Sinclair nod, returning to the outcropping of rock where they drop awkwardly into seated positions and lean back, rifles across their laps. Still sulky over his unarmed status, Morley is reluctant to join them. But he follows eventually. I already have him in mind for the next shift.

I'll rotate them to join me one at a time until sunup. Sinclair will be last. Maybe by then, I'll be able to nod off a little. I can't imagine spending five minutes alone with her, let alone a two-hour night watch.

"We'll use the jeep as cover," I tell Granger. We move into position, fighting our suits into submission as we crouch in front of the jeep's grill. "In case our stalkers decide it's time for a little target practice."

"Don't see how they can be carrying Stingers hidden in the stuff they're wearing, but I guess it's possible."

"Any weapons out in plain sight?"

Granger gazes unblinking through the glowing heads-up display. "If I had to guess, judging by the bulges, I'd say automatic rifles. Can't really tell—" He curses abruptly, muttering to himself, "Stupid." Then he clears his throat. "Identify weapons," he says in the authoritative tone he reserves for HUD voice commands.

A full display spreads across the face shield of his helmet as an assortment of daggers, short swords, handguns, rifles, and an array of small explosives are recognized by the HUD system and tagged, each delineated from its point of origin on the two figures: a hip, shoulder, or leg holster, a makeshift scabbard across the back. Granger releases a low whistle at the sight.

"Well now..." He clears his throat. "You want the good news first or the bad?"

"They're armed to the teeth."

"You could say that. But on the bright side, I don't see any RPG's. And I'd be willing to bet we're well out of range. Ain't nobody I've ever heard of who could chuck a grenade over fifty meters."

"Rethinking your plans for making first contact?"

Granger grunts. "I've lost my appetite." He shakes his head

and glances over at me. "But I don't get it. They could wipe us out easy. Toss a few grenades on approach and take out our jeep, then one lays down cover fire while the other advances. Trade off until they've got us flanked. We wouldn't stand a chance."

I raise an eyebrow. "Good thing you're on our side." I squint into the distance. "They must be under orders to stay put." That's the only explanation. Otherwise, Granger's description of events would have already occurred.

"Like us." Granger smirks. "Orders is orders."

Harris and Sinclair come on the channel then, both with abrupt cries of alarm. I jerk against my suit, forcing it to turn back toward the outcropping of rock so I can see what's happening, just as Morley lumbers off with a rifle.

The one he snatched from Harris.

"Wait here to be slaughtered in your sleep!" Morley growls, charging as fast as the hazard suit will allow, heading west. "I'm taking the fight to them. If you've got any backbone left, you're welcome to join me."

I struggle to my feet. "Stand down, soldier," I order, keeping my voice even. "Make an about-face before you do something you'll regret."

Morley doesn't look back. "Go to hell!"

8. TUCKER

17 MONTHS AFTER ALL-CLEAR

Carrying the incubation pods through the intense heat of day and bone-aching cold of night hasn't been the hardest part of my journey across this scorched earth. Fussing over the pods' settings and hoping the little ones are getting enough nutrients is worrisome but not intolerable. Neither is watching my shadow during the day, hoping no band of marauding mutos catches sight of it.

Nope, for me, the worst part is the silence. The loneliness. Endless days with no one to talk to. Nights I curl up in a cave or behind some sizeable rocks, unable to share anyone's warmth. Not that I ever had much to share back in Eden, but that isn't the point. Out here, I'm always alone, with only my thoughts to keep me company—whether I want them or not.

It reminds me of a time I'd rather forget. Locked out of the Sector 30 bunker.

For the good of the many...

Sometimes I speak to the little female strapped across my chest in her canister or the male slung over my shoulder. But I know better than to think they will—or even can—talk back to me. They're not even born yet, after all.

So it's with a great deal of excitement jittering through my nerves that I call out to the first human being I've seen in weeks.

"Hello there!" I wave broadly. My shadow mirrors my movements, elongated and distorted like a dark spirit mocking me. For the moment, I don't care that I'm an invisible freak, just a shadow scurrying across the sand with a voice but no body to go along with it. The figure above me on the hillside, half-hidden in a makeshift outpost constructed of shale, is obviously no muto. That makes my heart glad. "Hello! Boy, am I glad to see—"

"Hold it right there!" The figure snatches up his rifle and brings the stock to his cheek, pointing the muzzle in my general vicinity. "Identify yourself!"

I keep both hands in the air. My shadow mimics me. "Hey now, no reason to get—"

"Identify yourself. Now!" The fellow looks agitated. Clutching his rifle and readjusting his hold on it, cowering behind the barricade where he commands a good view of the surrounding area, he seems either new on the job or inexperienced with first contact. Or, more likely, he's never met an invisible man before. I can't fault him for that. Far as I know, I'm one of a kind. "Don't you take another step!"

I sniff and shuffle my feet. "Hey-uh, is Luther around? Maybe Milton or Daiyna?"

"Who are you?"

I could ask him the same thing. Under all that sand-colored fabric he's wearing, it's impossible to see what the fellow looks like. But I'm positive he wasn't with Luther and company when they were in Eden, back when Willard and Perch tried to reverse their mutations and make them human again.

The first-edition variety of human, that is.

"How about you tell Luther I'm here? My name's Tucker. He'll remember me."

"Why can't I see you?"

I shrug. So does my shadow. "Maybe you should get your eyes checked."

"I could shoot you down right where you stand. So you'd better answer me!"

Is he really as trigger-happy as he looks? I sure hope not. "Okay. By all appearances, I can see you're not one of those muto-types. You know what I mean. Nasty-smelling, flesh-eating—"

"I'm no daemon."

"Right. One of those. And neither am I, obviously. So that makes us both on the same team here, don't you think?"

"I'm not *invisible*." The sentry clears his throat—an abrupt, nervous tic. "So I'm pretty sure we're not on the *same team*." He pauses, staring through his black goggles at my shadow. "Are you a UW scout, sent inland to spy on us? Wearing some kind of invisibility cloak with light-refracting technology? Government-issued, I'll bet."

I laugh out loud.

"Something funny?" demands the sentry.

"It's just—I mean, think about it. If this was UW-issued, don't you think they would have eliminated the shadow glitch?" I wave my arms around to make my point. "Isn't it more believable that I'm like you? Maybe just a bit more on the extreme end of things?"

"What do you mean?"

"I'll lay it all out on the table for you, son. This ain't some sort of high-tech gizmo that's making me unseen by the naked eye. Not even close. I got like this from breathing the air out here, getting all this godawful dust into my lungs. It changed me." I pause. "And seeing how you're not wearing some sort of O2 apparatus, I'd wager it's changed you, too." I take a gamble and shuffle forward.

"I said not another step!"

I throw down my arms with impatience. "If you had any idea how many kilometers I've walked or what I'm carrying here, just to find myself graced by your warm welcome—"

"How do you know Luther?"

Now we're getting someplace. I almost smile, but the expression is lost in translation. "How many of you are there now?" Enough to have a sentry posted at the perimeter of their camp.

Are there others stationed nearby? Are they aiming their guns at me, too?

"*I'm* asking the questions here." He readjusts his aim for the umpteenth time.

"There were only five when I last saw them: Luther, Daiyna, Milton, and two others, both augmented with mechanical implants and limbs, courtesy of our doctor."

"You're from Eden..." The sentry can't hide the awe in his voice.

I shrug. "Afraid so." Willard's underground refuge wouldn't have the best reputation among these folks, I imagine.

"Why have you traveled out here, disguised like that?"

"Honestly? To meet you folks and—" I turn to glance over my shoulder. Two other sentries have crept up behind me, uncanny in their ability to move with absolute silence. Must be their *gift*.

They've got me surrounded. And I'm not liking it.

"What's he got there?" one of them barks, gesturing toward my shadow on the ground. My profile makes it clear that I'm carrying something bulky across my chest and my back.

"Howdy," I greet the newcomers with a friendly salute.

"Get on your knees. Do it now!"

I hold out my hands. "Hey, you don't understand. I'm unarmed. These—" I reach for the incubation pod strapped across my shoulders.

"Don't even think about it." The sentry at my eight o'clock steps forward, the muzzle of his assault rifle trained on the area where he thinks my head might be. Good guess. "I said kneel! Hands up, where we can see them." He catches himself. "Put your hands behind your damn head!"

"Alright, it's all right," I mutter. "Just calm down."

"We're calm, pal. Dead calm. You wouldn't want to see us when we're not calm. It's *you* who should watch yourself."

I drop first to one knee, then both, careful not to jostle the little ones I'm carrying. I keep my hands up in the air, their respective shadows clear to see. The last thing I want is to set off one of these self-important trigger fingers. All it would take is a single round, and either of the incubation canisters could be irreparably damaged. Not to mention myself in the process.

"She always said they'd come after us," says the hillside sentry, now descending with cascades of sand. Did he summon the others, somehow? Maybe they share a form of telepathy, like Margo.

"How many from Eden are with you?" The eight o'clock sentry advances another step. It won't be long before he tries poking me in the back, clinking his rifle against the young male's pod. "C'mon, speak up!"

"I don't want to disappoint you, because it sure seems like you're itching for trouble." I shrug again. "But I'm it. There's nobody else."

They curse at that, muttering to each other. Why strung so tight? What's been going on out here?

"You can't expect us to believe you came all this way on foot—and alone—"

"Yet here I am."

They confer among themselves for a moment. The sentry from the hillside grumbles, "We should just take him to see Luther."

"Best idea I've heard all day," I agree.

"First we find out what he's carrying," says Eight O'Clock. "We don't want an invisible suicide bomber walking into the Homeplace."

I don't like the sound of that—them touching the pods or thinking I'm some kind of rebel, like those *Patriots* back before D-Day. Margo doesn't want anybody but Luther and Daiyna touching the incubation units. Not this crew, that's for sure.

"Listen." I hold out a hand. They watch my shadow on the baked earth. "What I've got here, it's meant for Luther. Sensitive cargo—"

The two behind me close in, shouting orders and kicking where they assume the backs of my legs should be. One boot makes contact, and I groan, tipping sideways with sudden pain shooting through my hamstring. I try to make them understand I'm no threat, that what I'm carrying isn't dangerous in any way. It's fragile and has to be handled with care. The hillside sentry fires his rifle into the air, a short burst to silence me.

"You shut your mouth and do as you're told. I don't care who you are or why you're here. We're taking whatever you're carrying. Got it?"

I nod, biting my lip. Margo sure didn't prepare me for such a hostile welcome. The mutos are one thing; I know what to expect with them. But this?

One of the men shoulders his weapon and reaches out a tentative hand toward me, gloved fingers grasping through the air. Judging by the shadow and the angle of the sun, he eventually makes contact, his hand landing heavily on my shoulder and throwing me forward a bit.

"What the hell?" The other two sentries jump back a step, seeing something they can't quite believe.

"What?" The sentry with his hand on me frowns, unsure of himself all of a sudden. His buddies curse a string of foul obscenities. "What is it?"

"They can't see you," I tell him. "You're like me now."

He jerks his hand back and reappears, darting glances from his buddies to his own torso.

"I'll be damned," says the hillside sentry. He whistles, shaking his head slowly.

"If I didn't just see that with my own two eyes..." Eight O'Clock trails off.

"What are you talking about?"

"You vanished, man. Into thin air, soon as you touched him."

"What? No, I could see my—"

"I can see myself just fine," I explain. "It's other folks, everybody else, who thinks I'm the invisible man."

"What did we tell you? Shut the hell up!" Hillside jams the butt of his rifle into what he thinks is my throat. I flinch to avoid having an eyeball ruptured.

"I'm not touching him again. What if I don't come back the next time?"

"You think it's *catching*?" snickers Eight O'Clock.

"How the hell should I know?"

He curses, keeping his distance. They argue among themselves for a bit, but in the end, it's decided that I'll remove both of the objects from my person myself, and I'll set them on the ground in front of Hillside. I explain that, as soon as these objects leave my grasp, they will become visible. They nod mutely.

I make one more attempt at convincing them to summon Luther, but they'll have none of it, threatening to break my nose instead. I've got to calm them down. I can't have men like this, all amped up and prone to violence, welcoming these little ones into the world. But what other choice do I have?

Carefully, I unbuckle the incubation pod strapped to my chest and place it on the cracked earth. My hands linger on the chamber door. Inside, through a liquid haze of artificial amniotic fluid, the female floats contentedly, eyes closed, thumb tucked away in lips that have yet to utter their first cry of alarm.

"Step back," says Hillside, watching my shadow. "Don't you try anything."

They're so sure it's a bomb. What will they think when they see this tiny angel?

I do as I'm told. I withdraw my hands from the canister and step back, waiting for the inevitable confusion to ensue, the questions. Namely, why is Eden sending babies out into the barren wasteland?

What happens next isn't even on my radar.

"What the hell?" says Hillside.

"You said we'd be able to see—" says Eight O'Clock.

"Why can't we?" says the third sentry.

"What have you done?" Hillside demands.

Their voices merge as one, and they advance on me with weapons at the ready. I stare at the pod and frown. It's no longer in contact with any portion of my body. It should be completely visible to them now. That's how this works!

"Wait. You're telling me you can't see it?" I say.

"Quit playing games. Turn it off—whatever invisible shield you've got protecting that thing."

I shake my head, extending open hands. "I have no idea why you can't see it." Are they trying to pull one over on me? Why? "I touch something, it disappears as long as I'm in contact with it. I let go, and it's visible again. This has never happened before..."

"You saying there's something wrong with our eyesight?" Eight O'Clock says.

Hillside scowls at the pod's shadow. Then he draws back his boot and gives it a solid kick. The metallic thud rings loud enough to cover my horrified gasp.

"Don't do that again." My voice is low and steady. The status lights on the pod continue to blink at regular intervals. The little one's vital signs remain normal. Sure, the canister was designed to withstand getting jostled around a bit, but I don't want to see its limits tested.

Hillside aims his rifle at the pod's shadow. The muzzle stares through the transparent chamber door, right into the face of the little female. "Turn off the shield."

"You don't understand—!" I plead with them.

The female's eyes open. Instantly, the incubation pod becomes visible to the three sentries. Dumbstruck, they freeze in place, goggles transfixed on the chamber door. One by one, they shoulder their weapons in slow motion, as if they're mesmerized, in some sort of trance. Boots shuffling through the dust, they gather around the canister like it's a holy shrine, and they're pilgrims. But they haven't known until this moment what it was they've been seeking.

"It's a—" Hillside says, his tense frame relaxing.

"Yeah. It sure is," says Eight O'Clock.

"I'll be damned," the third sentry says, shaking his head. "There's a *baby* in there."

"You don't say." Hillside chuckles and gives his buddy a shove. His goggles glance at me. "So, you're carrying a couple of newborns?"

"Unborns," I correct. I remain kneeling in the dust. "They've yet to breathe anything but that oxygenated fluid in there."

"Eden's sending us babies now." Eight O'Clock curses in disbelief. "Can't say I ever saw that coming."

"It's precious cargo I've got here, no doubt about it. Both pods, they're meant to be taken straight to Luther." I gesture with my shadow hand. "Mind if I get up now?"

"Go ahead." Hillside points in my general direction. "Take off the other one. We'll make sure Luther gets them both, safe and sound."

I hesitate, fingering the strap buckled across my chest. After carrying these little ones for the past few weeks, it's safe to say I've grown attached to them—both physically and emotionally. In my mind, this isn't how I envisioned the end of my journey. Handing them over to complete strangers?

I imagined walking right up to Luther and Daiyna and the others and saying something like, "Hey, remember me?" Then I'd hand over the little ones in their canisters. And maybe I'd say, "I guess this is what you get when you go mixing gametes around in test tubes." Something like that, a bit of humor to go with what was sure to be a whole lot of surprise.

I never planned to stick around for their artificial births. But I wanted to be there for the introductions.

"C'mon, take it off." Hillside motions with his hand for me to speed things up. The rifle remains slung back on his shoulder—for now. "We can't be out in the open here much longer. Daemons might catch a whiff of us."

He means the mutos. Reaching over my shoulder to steady the incubation pod, I unfasten the strap and carefully remove the canister. "I can carry this one," I offer, reluctant to let it go. "Wouldn't be any trouble."

"Set it down beside the first one." Hillside's goggles stare at me without expression.

Biting my lip, I nod and obey the sentry's command, cursing myself inwardly as I do so. This isn't right. It's not what Margo would've wanted.

"That's it? Just the two?" Eight O'Clock says.

I nod, placing the male's pod on the ground next to the female's. For a moment, it seems like she's looking up at me with some kind of warning in her eyes. But that can't be possible. A newborn isn't able to focus on much, so how could an *unborn* register anything visually through all that fluid?

The canister materializes as I withdraw my hands. I stand over the two little ones, my shadow falling across them both.

"Better check him." Eight O'Clock nods at the third sentry. "Pat him down."

"I'm not going anywhere near him. *You* check."

"Coward."

"Hey, there's more than enough weird abilities going around lately. The last thing I need is to pick up another one. Invisibility? No thanks!"

"So you *do* think it's catching." Eight O'Clock laughs.

With an impatient curse, Hillside levels his rifle with my midsection. "Move away from the pods. Keep your hands up."

I frown as I take a tentative step back. My heart thuds hard at the sight of the weapon and the two incubation canisters lying exposed, out in the open. I'm still close enough to throw myself on top of them if shots start flying. I'd do anything to keep them safe, even if it means sacrificing myself.

I didn't realize that until just now.

"Check him. We don't want any surprises." Hillside gestures at the third sentry, who seems to know better than to argue with him. A pecking order is obviously in effect.

I raise my arms. "I'm not your enemy. I've tried to make that clear."

"I recommend you shut it for the time being," the sentry mutters, slapping at the air around me until he makes contact.

"Hot damn!" Eight O'Clock hoots. "There he goes again!"

Just like before, the sentry vanishes as soon as he comes into contact with my jumpsuit-clad body.

"What's it feel like to be the invisible man?" he hisses into my ear as he smacks my arms and torso in a rushed manner. "Hidden from the world?"

I shake my head. "I'm kind of used to it by this point. But you don't have to be afraid, son. If it was catching, you'd have already gotten it by now. That's how it works, seems to me. You take a big gulp of this air—"

"I'm not afraid," he whispers. Then loud and clear: "Well, look here!" He tugs a 9mm semiautomatic from my belt and steps back, reappearing in an instant.

Eight O'Clock aims his rifle at me. "He's been armed this whole time."

"Just a precaution, boys," I do my best to reassure them. "You can't blame me. There's plenty of mutos—*daemons* all around these parts."

"That's all you found?" Hillside's tone sounds oddly flat.

The third sentry shrugs and nods, checking the clip. Then he flinches as Hillside pulls the trigger on his rifle. The shot explodes, hitting me in the chest and throwing me over backward like I've been kicked by a horse.

"What the hell?" shouts the third sentry, goggles splattered with my blood.

"Pick them up." Hillside points at the incubation pods and shoulders his weapon, climbing up the hill toward his deserted post. "We're going to the Homeplace."

Without a word, Eight O'Clock follows orders, shouldering his weapon and stooping to retrieve the canister. The third sentry remains rooted, 9mm gripped in one hand, his spattered goggles darting from my shadow to Hillside's retreating form.

"We're just gonna *leave* him?"

"Get the other one," Eight O'Clock grunts, hefting the male's incubation pod to his chest, bearing the burden like an unwieldy sack of potatoes. Amniotic fluid sloshes around inside as he nearly loses his grip.

"We can't do this!"

Mid-stride, Hillside says over his shoulder, "Look east. Then tell me what we can't do."

The third sentry turns to find a billowing dust cloud on the horizon. It can mean only one thing.

"They followed his tracks," Eight O'Clock says hoarsely. "He's led them straight to us!"

Halfway up the steep incline, Hillside says, "They'll smell his blood before they smell us. He'll buy us some time. But we need to pick up the pace, boys."

Eight O'Clock doesn't need to be told twice. Clutching the pod to his chest, he scales the shifting sand on the hillside at full tilt, his legs a blur of speed.

I watch him go and nod to myself. They are indeed gifted, just as I supposed.

"Damn bastard," the third sentry mutters, giving my shadow another glance before stooping to retrieve the female's canister.

I cough and clutch at the bleeding hole in the right side of my chest. At close range, the high-powered rifle should have killed me. But the round went straight through, only taking enough flesh and bone to leave a bloody mess.

"You'll look out for them, won't you? Both of them." I grimace, falling back to the ground. The grey sky above is all I can see. "They're in your charge now." There's so much more to be said, but I don't have the strength. *Tell Luther and Daiyna there's plenty more just like 'em back in Eden. You need to get your people together, and you've got to go back for them. Because if you don't, the UW will take them all.* "Keep them safe," is all I manage to say.

The sentry pauses. He weighs the 9mm in his hand and glances at my shadow. Then he tosses the weapon into the dust, hefts the incubation canister to his chest, and starts up the hillside after his companions, scaling the shifting sand with incredible speed and agility.

When the gun landed with a puff of dust at my side, for a split second I considered rolling over, grabbing the weapon, and squeezing off three headshots. That would serve the sentries right for leaving me as muto bait. But with my bleeding wound and all, my aim wouldn't be the best, and I can't risk a round accidentally hitting the little ones.

If Hillside was right and the approaching dust cloud signals the arrival of a roving muto pack, then the unborns better get out of here as fast as possible. They appear to be in capable hands.

Capable, but misled. Who gave them standing orders to fire on an unarmed man?

I curse and clench my teeth as a wave of dizziness sweeps over me. Maybe they're right, leaving me to bleed out like this. It gives them the time they need to put as much distance as possible between them and the mutos. The freaks will sniff out my blood and see my shadow. Invisible or not, I'll provide the meal they crave. How will they react to seeing their pals disappear once they start digging through my juicy insides? Should be entertaining.

But I have no intention of making things easy for them. I grab the gun and check the clip: eight rounds. Plus another two clips stashed in pockets the sentry failed to check. I need to climb to higher ground, up to that shale outpost. A good vantage point.

I curse my shadow. I curse my blood, staining the hard-packed earth, drooling out of me visibly as soon as it leaves my shoulder.

"Some guys never get a break," I grunt, straining to rise. The sky goes black for a split-second, and I shake my head sharply. I can't pass out, no matter how bad the pain gets.

No way am I getting eaten in my sleep.

I squeeze the handgun's grip. Tears sting my eyes. "Sorry, Margo," I whisper. "I've failed you in a big way."

I sniff, blink until my vision clears. Then I roll onto my side, nearly crying out as I force myself to sit up. My right arm, right shoulder and corresponding chest muscles are absolutely useless.

And they hurt like hell. But the pain keeps me conscious, in the moment. No telling how long that will last. Soon I'll go numb and lose consciousness. Not yet.

I've got something else to do first.

I cock the gun and stare at the dust cloud as it approaches, looming larger and more malevolent with every meter it gains. The closer it comes, the clearer I hear the hum of those solar-powered jeeps the cannibal freaks are so fond of. Already I can make out three vehicles, distinct black blurs heading toward me at top speed, following the tracks left by an unlucky invisible man.

I curse again and spit into the dust. I rest the gun on my lap and retrieve the spare clips, keeping them close by. I won't be going down without a fight. I'll take as many of their sorry carcasses with me as I can. Hell, maybe every last one of them. Now wouldn't that be something?

"Come and get it, you rotten bastards."

9. CAIN

18 MONTHS AFTER ALL-CLEAR

When I dream of Gaia, I see her in white sheer fabric that billows in the sea breeze. She strides barefoot across the ashen sand under a full moon's light, her long hair tossed playfully by the wind as she casts an inviting glance over her shoulder. She beckons me to follow with eyes that burn into my very soul. I would go wherever she leads me, even to the end of the world.

She glides inland across kilometers of barren earth, into the lowlands and through the valleys, climbing scorched hillsides strewn with rock, covered in shale. She never tires, and neither do I, miraculously, following close and rarely missing a step. Together, mother and son, we climb toward the yawning mouth of a cave where men and women garbed in loose fabric, with black goggles dangling around their necks, have gathered to hear the words of a man I recognize with loathing.

"This is their Homeplace," Gaia whispers into my ear, drawing me beside her and pointing toward the cave. "Now you will know it when you see it."

I nod, refusing to voice the reservations I feel. But she already knows my thoughts. My fears.

"There is something else you must do first." She takes my face in her cold hands and stares into my eyes, her look so direct, so full of incredible power, that I cannot bear to meet her gaze for longer than a moment. Yet in this dream, I am unable to look away, and her eyes ignite a fire that burns me from the inside—

I awake with a start, sitting upright and wide-eyed, naked in the dark.

"Ready now?" Lady Victoria eyes me from the opposite side of the bed. "I thought you would never wake up."

"You have that effect on me." Our recent lovemaking is impossible to forget—the first time a weapon of any kind has been involved. She had to make sure I wouldn't send my guards after the exiled Lemuel, and holding her knife to her own throat did the trick.

It did not get in the way at all as I reclaimed her loins.

"I'll take that as a compliment." She winks at me as she fingers the blade of her dagger. "You certainly enjoyed yourself."

"Always." I regard her figure with an appreciative eye.

She reaches out a hand, beckoning me to her bosom. I come close, caressing her protruding abdomen as I do so, fingering the minor incision she made earlier with the tip of her blade. The blood has already dried.

"Does this mean I'm forgiven?" she says.

"Hardly." In a single movement, I have the dagger out of her hand and my elbow jammed against her throat, pinning her down on the pillow. I have to chuckle at the surprised look on her face. "Did you honestly think I couldn't take this from you whenever I chose?" I toss the weapon across the room where it clatters against the wall.

"Why not sooner?" she chokes out.

I grin down at her. "I was enjoying the show."

"You didn't think I would do it."

"End your life? Or the child's?" I shake my head, the coarse braid sweeping across my broad shoulders. "Not while you still have me to ravish you."

She almost smiles.

Whatever feelings I once had for her are no more. They evaporated the moment I saw her with the runt Lemuel. She is a tool in my hand now, nothing more. Should she continue to prove useful, then perhaps I will allow her to be the mother of my child. If not, then I will cut the infant out of her and give it to one of my other wives to raise. They have proven themselves faithful and above reproach.

I remove my forearm but keep a hand on her neck, my thumb on the quick pulse of her jugular.

"I am ready," I tell her.

She blinks up at me. Then she reaches with both hands and cups them over my ears, pressing her fingertips against my temples. In turn, I cover her eyes with my hand. So joined, we share the same vision and hearing even as these senses are projected kilometers away. It is a melding of gifts we first discovered while making love months ago.

It has served my purposes very well since then.

"Where are they?" I murmur, staring vacantly across the room as our shared sense of sight travels across boundless stretches of unknown, untraveled desert.

"They have kept their distance," she answers.

For a moment, our vision rests on two men clad in hooded cloaks, camped a kilometer beyond a group of five figures in heavy protective suits waiting for their solar jeep to recharge. Then our shared vision veers off-course abruptly, shifting kilometers away to focus on a lone figure stumbling awkwardly through the dead of night, casting furtive glances in every direction. Scared and alone. Exiled.

"Focus, woman." My hand tightens on her throat.

"He will not survive out there." She clenches her jaw. "Lemuel's blood is on your hands!"

"And yours could be as well, whore." I shake her until our vision returns to my two cloaked men. "Now give them this message: Take the UW scouts, dead or alive. Move in now."

Victoria frowns as I loosen my grip on her. Of course she would wonder about this sudden change in tactics. Until now, my two warriors have been told only to follow the UW scouts. Keep their distance, and do not engage.

Nevertheless, she does as she is told.

"Move in on target," she relays my order, using her gift from Gaia to speak telepathically across the distance between them. To their ears, it would sound as if she is whispering to a lover. "Take them. Dead or alive."

"And bring their bodies back to me." I nod as she sends the message.

Then we watch. It is as though Victoria and I hover behind and above the two cloaked men as they shoulder their weapons and prepare to close the distance between them and their quarry. I am reminded of the films I watched in the Sector 15 bunker so many years ago. Our current perspective is much like a camera angle used to film battle sequences. All I need is some popped corn.

I almost smile. A protein or vitamineral pack will have to suffice.

"Now what?" Victoria shifts uncomfortably, but her hands remain on my ears. The child in her womb no doubt has something to say about her remaining in one position for too long—pressing against her bladder when she least expects it. Will she relieve herself right here as a way to get back at me?

I scowl as our vision jitters in and out of focus. "What's wrong now?"

"Nothing."

Our view sharpens into crystal clarity. We watch as an unidentified figure charges through the night, straight for my two tribesmen.

"Who's this?" Victoria's attention no longer wavers.

"One of the UW scouts."

"What's he doing?"

My frame tightens as I notice what the UW soldier carries: an assault rifle, the goblyns' weapon of choice.

"They're *armed*?" Victoria says in disbelief. "But you said—"

"My men are armed as well." Nevertheless I grit my teeth, unsure about this turn of events. "Tell them to fire at will."

She nods, relaying the command. But my warriors seem confused. "They don't see him. He must not be in range."

"Tell them to prepare for attack—"

"They don't hear anyone approaching."

I curse under my breath. "Gaia help them then," I mutter, already planning ahead, deciding who I will send after the UW scouts once these two incompetents fail me.

I can only watch as the UW soldier closes the gap, lumbering awkwardly in his unwieldy armored suit, hurling himself forward. A man on a mission, but one who will soon tire from the exertion.

"Tell them to find cover. Do not engage." Time for a new tactic, now that an automatic weapon and combat armor are in the picture. "Repeat: Do not engage. Observe target from cover." No reason for them to be slaughtered outright.

Victoria sends the command twice for good measure. "They have him outnumbered and outflanked," she says. "They would easily subdue—"

"A trained, armed man encased in reinforced Kevlar? With four others right behind him? The last thing our men should do right now is engage."

"So we fall back."

Interesting. She seems to have a vested interest in this endeavor.

"We wait. And we watch." I want to gauge this soldier's fatigue level once he reaches his destination. How difficult is it to move in that suit? I also want to be certain he is acting alone. It makes no sense, but at present he appears to be making a solo attack.

"Our men have taken cover." Victoria points, taking her right hand from my ear briefly to do so. In our shared vision, I see her hand with its index finger extended.

For a moment, I am deaf in that ear, unable to hear the night winds whisking through the sands where my two warriors hide themselves. An odd sensation, even as I hear the hull of the ship creaking around me, cooling with the night. It is strange to feel as though I am in two places at once.

Her hand returns to my ear just as the UW soldier stumbles across the level stretch of sand where my men stood moments before. Swinging the muzzle of his rifle to and fro, he wavers, unsteady on his feet.

"Where are you hiding, you sons of bitches?" he demands, out of breath. He sprays rounds into the air with no targets in sight.

Victoria and I cringe instinctively. For a moment we feel exposed, but the fool is only wasting ammo. And we are beyond his reach.

"Show yourselves! Why are you following us? Who are you?" The soldier takes a moment to catch his breath, nearly doubling over with the effort. "C'mon, man! What are you —*cowards?*"

I groan at that. It is never wise to question a warrior's courage.

One of my men emerges, rising like a phantom from where he buried himself in the sand, unseen and unheard.

"Do not engage!" I repeat the order, but even as Victoria relays it, I recognize the futility.

"That's Markus," she says. All the explanation needed.

The UW soldier staggers backward in his cumbersome suit at the warrior's sudden appearance and now trains his weapon on him, the red laser sight jittering across Markus's wide chest.

"Where's Vincent?" Victoria scans the scene before us for any sign of the second tribesman.

"Still in hiding—for now," I mutter. Thanks be to Gaia, at least one of them has the sense to follow orders and keep a lid on his pride.

"Put your hands where I can see them!" the soldier barks.

Markus stands with his arms out to the sides, staring down the armed UW scout, and seemingly with no weapons of his own. But I know better. Both Markus and Vincent carry an impressive array of weaponry, from daggers and short swords to handguns, rifles, and explosives, all hidden by the folds of their cloaks.

The soldier soon realizes it as well. I notice the display on his face shield flash red as it catalogs every weapon in an instant.

"Drop your weapons! Do it now!" He tightens his grip on the rifle. "I'm warning you, this gun's got a real hair trigger."

Markus's direct stare never wavers as he reaches carefully with both hands to remove his weapons one at a time and drop them to the sand with puffs of dust, white in the moonlight. I become aware of my own breathing in the moment, even as I notice Victoria holding her own.

"Good." The soldier nods, but Markus is nowhere near finished. "Now tell me who you are. Where are you from?"

"The coast," Markus says in a rich baritone. He doesn't sound nervous in the least.

"Why are you following us?" The soldier takes a step toward him. "And where's your partner?"

Markus nods over his shoulder. "Taking a leak. He'll be back." Guns and blades lie scattered around his boots. Only the explosives remain in hiding.

"Those too." The soldier gestures with his rifle muzzle at the pockets in Markus's cloak.

"You don't miss much." There is actual humor in the warrior's tone.

"No. I don't."

"Then you've probably noticed I'm not wearing any sort of breathing apparatus." Markus fishes into his pockets, and each hand reappears with a frag grenade in it. He thumbs the detonators, activating them.

"What the hell?" I can only stare.

The soldier does the same, wide-eyed as he stumbles backward.

"You do realize the air is fine out here, don't you?" A tight grin spreads across Markus's sharp features.

"What're you playing at, man?" Real fear tightens the soldier's voice. "Shut those things down!"

Markus frowns, regarding the explosives with curiosity. "I don't think they work that way..."

"So what, then?" The soldier knows better than to think he can outrun the blast—not in his suit. "What happens next?"

"You drop your weapon."

"Yeah, right." The soldier curses. The laser sight remains on Markus. "You don't expect me to believe you're gonna blow yourself—"

"My orders are to take you dead or alive. The particulars are up to me."

"Either way, I need him in one piece," I grumble. "Not blown to bits!"

Victoria frowns at that, but she doesn't ask me why. And I am glad of it. The last thing I want is to explain how Gaia tasked me with starting a war between the Sectors' survivors and the UW. Staking the body of this soldier and his comrades along the shoreline in clear view of the UW ships will be a surefire way to get their attention.

"The hinges," she murmurs, bringing me back to the moment. "You see?" She points, and I see what she means. At the joints, while not providing the best mobility, the hazard suit's heavy Kevlar is missing. Instead, there appears to be a dense mesh material of some kind. "A blade should slip through easily enough."

Has she been looking for a weakness in the suit all this time? I can't help being impressed. But then again, there is a reason why I chose her as a wife.

I nod. "Tell them we've found Achilles' heel."

No sooner has Victoria relayed the message than Vincent springs upward from the sand behind the soldier. As Markus advances with the explosives held outward like a peace offering, Vincent's blade gleams in the moonlight, puncturing the back of the soldier's knee joint before he has time to whirl around and face his new adversary. The soldier cries out, trigger finger contracting spastically as he throws up his arms in alarm and agony, bursts of automatic fire puncturing the night. Then he crumples awkwardly to the ground, cursing and pounding his fists.

Markus deactivates the grenades and pockets them, moving quickly to confiscate the UW scout's only weapon. "Nice work."

Vincent nods as he wipes his machete clean before sheathing it over his shoulder. "You didn't do so bad yourself."

The soldier writhes, grappling with his injured leg, bleeding profusely in spurts of crimson across the earth.

I scowl. "Tell them to stop the bleeding. Otherwise, they'll leave a trail straight back to us."

Victoria relays the message.

"Have them bring him to me."

"And the others?" She scans the distance. No sign of them on approach. "I have a feeling they will be close behind this one."

"As do I." Of course they would have heard the shots fired.

Markus does his best to hold the soldier still, but he fights a losing battle, finding the heavy arms of the suit difficult to restrain, much less the legs.

"We've got to get him out of that thing," Vincent says. "No way to apply pressure to his wound with him still inside it."

Markus curses. "We can't carry him like this, that's for sure."

Vincent faces the soldier through the transparent helmet. "You like it in there?"

The soldier spits foul curses and insults, eyes bulging, teeth flashing against his dark skin.

"Thought as much." Vincent reaches for the helmet's locking clamps.

"What the hell are you doing?" The soldier swings his arms, fighting to keep the two warriors at bay.

"Hold him!"

Markus moves to intercept the flailing limbs. "You sure this is a good idea?"

Vincent has one of the clamps pried free. Four others remain. "Cain said dead or alive."

Markus smirks at that.

"No—you can't! You—!" the soldier shrieks, reaching an octave usually reserved for small boys. Or men missing their testicles.

"The air's just fine out here, boss." Vincent pries open two more clamps.

"Y-you're *infected*!"

"Hear that?" Markus turns to Vincent and shakes his head. "He thinks we're sick."

"Do we look sick to you?" Vincent chuckles.

Markus slaps the side of the soldier's helmet. "Must not have seen any goblyns yet."

The soldier stops moving. "You can't do this to me. Please—!"

"Gaia is the All-Merciful One." Vincent unlatches the remaining clamps and jerks the helmet upward, tossing it aside. "Me? Not so much."

The soldier took one last gulp of processed air, and now he holds it as if his life depends on it—life as he knew it, anyway. Markus clocks the soldier across the jaw with a solid left hook, whipping the man's head to the side with a gust of expelled air.

"May Gaia do with you as she will," Vincent says.

"He's out cold," Victoria observes.

"Easier to carry." I watch as the two tribesmen set about removing the hazard suit from the UW scout's limp body. "But they must hurry."

Victoria reminds Markus and Vincent, and they both nod as if she spoke into their ears simultaneously. "Do you think Gaia will bless this one?" She looks down at the soldier's slack-jawed face with what could be mistaken for concern.

He won't live long enough for it to be a possibility. Fortunately for me, this link I share with my fourth wife does not include the merging of our thoughts. Otherwise, Victoria would already know what I have planned for this man.

"More than likely, his true nature will be revealed." I adhere to the catechism I teach the tribes, that which I have learned from Gaia herself.

"Then he is to become a goblyn." She nods gravely. "It will be the first time."

I frown. "How's that?"

She faces me, her expression difficult to read. Does she challenge me yet again? Or is it the catechism itself that she disdains? "No one has seen a man turn into a goblyn before."

True enough. After All-Clear when we emerged from the bunkers and began our journey to the coast, inhaling the air Gaia used both to bless and to curse in equal measure, there were goblyn packs already roving across the barren terrain in their solar jeeps, seeking victims to devour. When Gaia first appeared to me, visiting in the dead of night as I sat on a windswept dune facing the brackish sea, staring at the blockade of ships in the distance, I had just become aware of my far-sight ability. Blinking, staring, unable to believe I could focus on the lettering alongside the *Argonaus* without the aid of binoculars, I suddenly noticed her presence beside me.

"Hello, Cain." In all her glory, Gaia stood on the dune and radiated an unearthly glow. "You have been blessed. Come, walk with me. I have much to tell you."

As if in a dream, I followed after her, learning with every step the way of things—the catechism I have taught to my people ever since.

"They are on the move." Victoria returns me to the present.

I peer eastward for the telltale signs of the UW scouts' advance—glints of moonlight in their face shields, dust stirred in their wake. But there is neither. I see only Markus and Vincent with the wounded soldier tossed over one shoulder, the man's knee bound with healing salve, the rest of him stripped to his underclothes. They head west.

"There," she points, and I see them then, my far-sight zooming to focus in this shared vision. Four figures in environmental suits, each armed with either an assault rifle or a handgun, approach on foot. They left their jeep behind. It will be at least a kilometer before they reach the ground stained by their comrade's blood.

"Tell them to hurry." Once Markus and Vincent use their gift of speed, the UW scouts will be left in the dust. "I'll meet them outside."

I take hold of Victoria's wrists and remove her hands from my face, breaking our link. I step out of the shared vision, returning to the here and now: sitting naked beside her in the massive king-sized bed. I watch her in the dark, my grasp on her arms lingering as my gaze drifts along her swollen abdomen. I almost stretch out a hand toward where my child ripens, waiting to be born.

Victoria's eyes remain closed, her lips moving silently as she bids the tribesmen to return home as fast as possible. I briefly consider having another go between the sheets before taking my leave. But I think better of it, getting up from the bed to gather my clothes and pull them on.

Will she keep an eye on the young Lemuel, abandoned in the desert? Undoubtedly.

I savor the thought of her watching him die.

"No need to get dressed." I half-turn as I reach for the wheel on the room's door.

Victoria's eyelids open reluctantly, her gaze rising to focus on me as if I am an intruder on her thoughts. But then a seductive smile spreads across her lips as her hand drifts down her thigh. "I will be here waiting, my husband."

Lady Victoria's appetites are as insatiable as my own. It will be a shame to end her, once my child greets the world.

I throw open the door and let it clang shut behind me.

The corridors of the ship are quiet, empty. Odd for this time of night. My people are usually wide awake, having taken their rest during the heat of the day. We are a nocturnal breed, and the lifestyle suits us well.

We didn't carry any of the hydration suits out of the bunker, the ones with face shields tinted to protect us from the sun. Traveling to the coast, we hid ourselves during daylight and made our long treks by night. The habit afforded relief from the dangerous rays of the sun, and it also spared us from goblyn raids. By and large, the creatures are a diurnal lot. They often attack in the early evenings, but by dead of night, when only a sliver of moon lights their path, they are nowhere to be seen.

Some say that every night they crawl back into the hell-holes from which they sprung. I do not know what becomes of them under cloak of darkness.

Gaia has yet to tell me.

I find her waiting outside, forty meters beyond our compound with its fence of rusted sheet metal and barbed wire. She stands on the same dune where I found her earlier, when she summoned me from the gathering.

"It is quiet tonight." She reaches out an alabaster hand, long-fingered and slender. "Where are your people, my son?"

I kneel in the shifting sand and take her hand, pressing its cool flesh to my brow. "They are otherwise occupied, Mother."

"Are they not your concern?"

I have greater concerns now. I know she will be pleased. "We have one of the United World scouts. Two of my strongest warriors are bringing him here as we speak."

"Is that so?"

I cannot read her expression. Does she already know what happens before it occurs? Of course she does. Gaia knows all things.

"You will need every one of your warriors when the United World accepts your invitation to battle. You do not intend to fight their armies alone, I trust." She withdraws her hand from my grasp and places it on the back of my head.

"Once there is war, my people will rally to my side, as they have in many a battle against the goblyns." For a moment, I recall Lemuel and the thirty-odd heads he has added to the compound wall, staked in plain sight to rot under the sun. Only his fighting skills will be missed.

"You do not wish them to see the war instigated. You wish to spare them from this." She speaks as if I am a misled child in need of correction. "Your concern is a noble one."

Is it? I do not know; I cannot figure out my motives right now. But as I take a moment, it becomes clear that I am acting out of self-interest. When war comes to our continent, I do not want the tribes and their battle-weary chieftains to know it was my doing. In case things go horribly awry—

But that is fear rearing its ugly head. Not faith.

"I trust you with all that I am. When the UW soldier arrives, I will do as you ask. When the sun rises, his body will be the first thing the crew of the *Argonaus* sees in the light of day."

She nods, caressing the back of my head with the tenderness of a doting mother. "You must draw them ashore. For it is only here, on your home soil, that you will be able to defeat them. They will never leave you alone, otherwise." She inhales a deep breath of the cool sea breeze. "Imagine, my son: the coast cleared entirely of their ships."

I can imagine it. I want it more than anything.

"Yes, Mother." My voice is hoarse with emotion.

Men approach, climbing the dune's leeward side from the east, heading straight for the compound. I recognize them instantly and rise to stand as they approach, passing through the space where Gaia stood only a moment before.

"Lord Cain!" Markus attempts to salute, nearly dropping the unconscious body of the UW scout in the process.

"You made good time." I narrow my gaze.

"Gaia be praised," Vincent says, saluting as well.

"Drop him," I order. They do so without question. "Round up a dozen more of our best warriors and go back for the other UW scouts. Leave now."

They nod and follow my orders without question, sprinting toward the compound with their Gaia-given speed, vanishing from my sight in an instant. I make sure they are gone before I grab hold of the unconscious soldier's ankle and drag him through the sand toward shore. There I find two three-meter lengths of rebar, sharpened to cruel points at each end. I frown, wondering where they came from. But then I nod to myself.

Gaia provides all that we ever need, does she not?

"She's thought of everything," I muse, impaling the soldier through the chest.

His eyes open wide as a ragged wheeze escapes his lungs. I lean toward him, watching the shock, rage, and confusion fade while his life slips away.

Pounding the rebar through flesh and crunching bone, straight into the damp sand beneath, I mount the man's body on the two iron bars. I cross them to form an X and drive the rebar deep into the earth to withstand the push and pull of the tides.

Then I step back to survey my bloody handiwork.

"Gaia be praised," I breathe.

PART III
RESCUE

10. MARGO

18 MONTHS AFTER ALL-CLEAR

The Hummer rocks, lurching as it climbs another series of rock-strewn hills. I cling to the steering wheel, grateful for the automatic transmission. I wouldn't want to stall while shifting between gears on such a steep grade. The collared mutant beside me groans and digs its sharp fingernails—claws, really—into the padded dashboard to counter the violent motion of the vehicle. The creature reeks like death warmed over, and constant waves of nausea swim through my insides.

"Let's hope we're getting close." I grimace and gun the accelerator. Rocks spit upward in the vehicle's wake.

The mutant doesn't respond. I am fairly certain these creatures no longer comprehend human speech. But it does turn toward me at the sound of my voice and stare. The bulbous yellow eyes ooze the same fluid that drips from its other facial orifices—a gaping skull's nose without any cartilage and a slack-jawed mouth, lips chapped beyond recognition, teeth sharpened to fangs—all the better for tearing into human carcasses. The fluid reeks worse than bile, and it has taken me more than a day to barely tolerate the foul stench in these close quarters.

"I've got to be sure nothing happens to you while you're out there, my fair lady," Willard said before I left Eden. "I'd escort you myself...but you know how it is. I don't make a habit of going topside."

We were sitting in Willard's quarters, with Perch and Jamison reclining on the couches and the captain of Eden leaning against the mantle on the fireplace like a 19th-century gentleman. All he lacked was a pipe and smoking jacket—anything would have been an improvement over his blue camouflage.

Unlike before, when we discussed the unborn children incubating in Eden's lowest levels, I wasn't their welcome guest this time. I was their prisoner, collared like one of the mutants and shackled hand and foot. Guards flanked me on either side.

"She's in no condition to travel," Jamison argued with a scowl.

He was probably right. After weeks of torture at Perch's practiced hands, my appearance had deteriorated to what it was before, back when I'd been collared like one of Willard's dogs. Long after it became clear that I was involved in Tucker's absence, Perch continued to terrorize me. Even though there was no more information to be gained from the process, no new knowledge to extract from me, he'd enjoyed himself—committing unspeakable acts in that room.

But unlike over a year ago, when I'd been a groveling, sniveling creature living at Willard's beck and call, I was now able to stand tall before them—as tall as I could, considering the bruises and reset bones. I knew more than I would ever tell them. Before Willard's men put the shock collar on me, I'd been in constant communication with the unborn female in Tucker's care. I knew the two incubation pods had reached their destination and were now with their rightful parents. As for Tucker, his current whereabouts were unknown.

That sound of gunfire I'd heard concerned me.

"She's tougher than she looks," Perch said, giving my haggard features a glance. "Believe me."

If it had not been for the collar locked around my throat, I would have planted the thought in his mind that his genitals were on fire. I almost smiled at the thought of it.

"She'll be fine." Willard looked at me with uncertainty in his eyes. "We'll be in constant communication with you, thanks to Jamison's new..." He snapped his fingers with a sudden mental lapse.

"Relays," Jamison said.

"That's right. Relays." Willard's eyes bulged with enthusiasm. "Up to now, we haven't been able to send the dogs long-range. Their collars would lose connectivity, and the freaks would run off, thinking they were free." He chuckled. "They had no idea about our little safety feature."

"Damned heads exploded!" Perch said with a snicker. "So don't you get any ideas, little lady."

Imagining his genitals exploding instead helped me to maintain my composure.

"You're not stupid. Those mutos, on the other hand, have barely a brain between 'em." Willard cleared his throat, smoothed his mustache—nervous ticks familiar to me. What did he have to be anxious about? "But that safety feature's still in full effect." He gestured at my steel collar, blinking with an array of remote-controlled features that included a camera to broadcast everything I saw as well as enough voltage to stop me in my tracks. It also had the added benefit of dampening my mind-reading and thought-planting abilities. "Your head will definitely burst if you go out of range without planting Jamison's relays. And we wouldn't want that to happen, now would we?"

I frowned, vaguely curious. What were these *relays* they kept mentioning?

Jamison spoke up, rising to retrieve what looked like a spear from behind the couch. "This is what we're talking about. It's basically an iron stake outfitted with the necessary equipment to receive our remote signal and carry it another five or ten kilometers, depending on weather conditions. Unfortunately, that's as far as we can go for now. But you keep planting one of these at regular intervals along the way, and we'll stay in range, no matter how far you travel."

"Which is where, exactly?" I almost didn't recognize my own voice, it was so hoarse.

Jamison deferred to Willard and set the relay down on the carpeted floor.

"You're going to meet our guests," Willard said. "The UW team. They've had a...little trouble with their chopper, apparently, thanks to our wild muto friends out there. The five-man team is hoofing it the rest of the way in their hazard suits. The captain of the *Argonaus* is concerned they won't have enough O2 to get them all the way here." He paused. "They should be less than five hundred kilometers from Eden by now. Due southwest."

I nodded, silent for a moment. "So I'll need a hundred of these relays to keep my head from exploding, is that it?"

"Well now, she can count." Perch smirked.

"We've got them all packed up in the back of the Hummer you'll be driving." Jamison seemed eager to answer. "As long as you plant one every five kilometers or so, we'll be able to keep in contact with you," he repeated himself, meeting my gaze briefly before looking away.

I faced Willard, my shackles clinking. "You want me to run a shuttle service."

His grin was tight, stretching his gaunt face. "You'll bring them back here, and we'll continue our negotiations with the United World government. We may have lost out on the chopper, but we haven't lost our bargaining chips."

"The children," I said.

"We've got what they want. Soon as their people see it firsthand, we'll have 'em right where we want 'em."

"But don't even think about joining your sand freak friends once you're out there," Perch growled. "You deviate from the course we set for you, even half a klick, and that pretty little head of yours goes to pieces."

I did my best to ignore him. "Explain to me again why you're sending one of your dogs on this little joyride? I doubt the UW team will like being greeted by such a thing."

The collar would require someone with a finger hovering over the muto's voltage control to ensure the creature didn't eat one of my limbs while I wasn't looking.

"If we could go with you, we would," Jamison said.

"Speak for yourself," Perch grunted, shifting on the couch to expel some gas. A real charmer.

"Jamison's working on the suits we'll need once we eventually make our exodus from Eden." Willard turned toward him. "How's that project coming along, by the way?"

Jamison nodded. "I need more time to—"

"There you have it." Willard clapped his hands together and rubbed them quickly. "So we're sending one of the dogs with you instead. But don't worry. The thing is completely tame with Perch at the controls. He'll be camped out in the control center and will make sure the dumb muto behaves itself. And if you run into any trouble out there with the wild mutos, we'll sic this one on 'em. Get a little muto-on-muto action going."

"We could sell tickets." Perch grinned. "I'm sure the boys would go for it. Haven't seen us a good fight in—"

"We'll be watching the whole time, Margo," Jamison interrupted. "Through your camera. You won't be alone out there."

I nodded, understanding I had no choice in the matter—as long as I wanted to keep my head. "No special suit for me, then."

"You're already a sand freak." Perch cursed. "What good would it do?"

Jamison ignored him. "A standard-issue jumpsuit is the best we can offer. The windows in your vehicle are tinted, so you won't need to wear the face shield while you're driving. But be sure to put it on if you step outside during daylight."

"Don't want the sun to mess up that gorgeous face of yours." Perch guffawed.

The jumpsuit they had for me was not impermeable to the *demon dust* that Willard was so afraid of, a toxic, mutagen-carrying agent that turned anyone who breathed the stuff into a *sand freak*—his pet term for anyone with superhuman abilities. So far, none of the other men in Eden had displayed mutations like my telepathy or Tucker's invisibility, and Willard planned to keep it that way. Jamison's current project was to create environmental suits to safeguard against all external air and dust, with enough O2 to see the men of Eden out of their sealed, underground refuge and up to the surface. A chopper would then take them off this diseased continent and into the domed, sterile world of Eurasia on the Mediterranean Sea, the last bastion for all-natural humankind.

Willard's dream come true.

"No suit for the muto, obviously." Willard chuckled. "Even God himself wouldn't be able to reverse what's been done to that thing."

Sitting now in the Hummer with the creature beside me, I glance at it intermittently to find the protruding eyes either staring straight ahead or focused on me, the drooling fangs gaping. Willard was probably right. There is no hope for these mutants. They carry no memory of being human. All they know are animal urges and the primal need to feed.

"You still there?" I dip my chin toward the mic on my collar.

"Another kilometer until your next relay point. We hear you fine." Jamison sounds exhausted. He's been in the Eden control center from the moment I drove out through the tunnel, and he's been on watch ever since, unwilling to leave Perch in charge. For now, Jamison keeps tabs on me while Perch supervises the mutant riding shotgun. "Everything all right?"

I glance at the muto. "He's looking...hungry."

Jamison curses under his breath, followed by what sounds like a short scuffle on his side of things, and ending with a string of curses from Perch and a short burst of electricity shot through the mutant's collar. It stiffens and jerks away from me, returning its bulbous-eyed gaze to the terrain before us.

"Jackass nodded off," Jamison mutters, followed by another string of foul obscenities from Perch.

"You sound tired yourself," I tell him. "You should get some rest."

"Don't worry about me. You're the one out there...with that muto. I'm not going anywhere until you meet up with the UW crew."

"You'd better not be drinking anything."

He chuckles softly. "Coffee, lots of it. But I'm wearing a jumpsuit like yours to avoid restroom breaks." It was designed to recycle urine into the cooling element.

"The wonders of modern engineering."

I reach the peak of the hill and nose the Hummer over to the other side, approaching a short plateau. A valley of ash meets my gaze, the same unaltered moonscape stretching on for endless kilometers in every direction.

"Still no sign of them." I lean forward, scanning from left to right.

"You won't reach their position until after dark, I'm afraid. You've got another hundred kilometers to go."

I glance into the rearview mirror at the pile of relay rods in the back of the vehicle. Less than fifty remain. "I'll stop here and plant another relay. This is the highest geographical feature in my line of sight. Might provide better reception from here on out."

"Don't want to lose your head, after all," Perch cuts in, commandeering Jamison's microphone.

"Good idea," Jamison says after another scuffle between them. "How many rods do you have left—exactly?"

"I'll take a look." I ease the vehicle forward another meter and set the parking brake. "Stay," I tell the mutant. This time, it doesn't turn at the sound of my voice. I shove open my door and step out, stretching my arms and back in the waning light of day as my boots crunch across the gravel.

"You should have thirty, at least," Jamison reminds me.

I reach for the rear hatch and tug it open, surveying the pile. "We're good."

Gunshots echo from the valley below. I reel at the sound, my heart pounding.

"What was that?" Jamison demands, alarmed.

"Shots fired." I slam the rear door and dash back to my seat. "Is this thing bulletproof?"

"Everything but the tires."

"Good to know." I pull my door shut and stare out through the tinted windshield at the valley floor. Two solar-powered jeeps, each carrying a full complement of gun-toting mutants, kick up plumes of dust in their wake. "You're seeing this?"

"Yeah." Silence.

"Would've been nice of you to send some weapons along."

"That damn muto is your weapon," Perch says, back on the line.

"Those things get close, you open its door, and we'll take care of matters from this end," Jamison says.

"A remote-controlled killing machine?"

"Something like that." Jamison sounds wearier than ever.

"They've spotted me." Dread sinks down into my stomach. My hands grip the steering wheel. "I could try to outrun them. Their solar batteries won't last long into the night."

"Lead them straight to the UW team, you mean? I don't think so." Perch curses. "Besides, we didn't pack enough fuel for you to go burning it up in some high-speed chase."

Jamison takes the comm. "That's a last resort, Margo. First we'll see how much damage the dog can do."

"He's outnumbered—eight to one." I watch as the jeeps tear up the hillside, straight for me. Have they already encountered the UW crew? Pried them out of their hazard suits and feasted on their insides?

"Leave that to us," Jamison says. "You stay put and hope they're not smart enough to blow out your tires."

"Then you'll be in a *real* pickle." Perch chuckles.

The jeeps advance at full speed, gravel flying up behind them, two mutos seated in the front of each vehicle and two standing in the back, holding onto the roll bar and aiming their assault rifles single-handedly at the Hummer. They squeeze off a volley of shots that rake across the hood, sparking as the rounds are deflected by the vehicle's armored plating.

I cringe as bullets plow into the windshield. How much abuse can the reinforced glass take before it caves in?

I glance at the muto beside me. It stares at the scene outside with what looks like keen interest. Does it recognize these mutants as others of its kind? They look so different to me, so well-fed in contrast to my emaciated travel companion.

"How close are they now?"

I frown at Jamison's question. Isn't he seeing everything I'm seeing? "Twenty meters and closing." I flinch at another barrage of weapons fire.

"Release the hound!" Perch roars.

"He's unarmed. They'll tear him to pieces." Do I hear concern for this hideous, foul-smelling creature in my voice?

"Just wait," Jamison says. "Unlock the door, and we'll take things from there."

I watch the mutant as it grunts quietly to itself. The jeeps outside skid to a halt a few meters in front of the Hummer, and a cloud of dust sweeps over us. I bite my lip and hesitate just a second before hitting the passenger side's door lock on my armrest. The dog's collar flares red, and the mutant jerks to attention, turning toward the door. It swings open automatically and then closes behind him, locking into place.

Outside, the wild mutos have already disembarked from their vehicles, grunting and snorting at one another, their heads jerking spastically. Automatic rifles at the ready, they stare with oozing yellow eyes fixed on my windshield—almost as if they can see straight through the black tinting.

Maybe they can, I realize with a sick chill.

Eight of them approach, muscular in build, their skin charred and blistered where it has been exposed to the sun. Where it is covered, they wear some sort of hide stitched together as clothing, a leather unlike anything I've seen before.

"Human flesh," Perch says as though he's the one reading *my* thoughts. "Quite the fashion statement, don't you think?"

"Focus," Jamison says.

I sink lower in my seat. My hands remain on the steering wheel, and my right boot hovers over the gas pedal. I will run them down if I have to, if the collared dog proves to be no match for these superior specimens.

Moving jerkily, like an automaton from half a century ago, the collared muto staggers toward the mutant pack. They surround him, for the moment losing all interest in the vehicle where I hold my breath and watch.

The wild mutos sniff at the dog, poke him with the muzzles of their assault rifles, nudge him back and forth between them. For his part, the collared muto allows their curious groping without so much as a twitch, holding himself erect and not turning his head to stare back at them. I notice his eyes, pulsating in a frenzy. Is he frightened?

One from the pack prods the shock collar with its gnarled, clawed fingers, grunting with interest.

"Get ready," Jamison says, but I don't know if he means me or Perch.

The wild mutos close in, reaching for the collar's blinking lights, clawing at each other to get their hands on the device. They fall on one another, onto the dog, reaching violently and elbowing their way closer.

"Now," Jamison says.

"Hell yeah." Perch chuckles.

I don't know what to expect. Will the collared mutant suddenly go berserk in some sort of remote-controlled killing spree, ripping these unsuspecting creatures limb from limb in a fountain-spray of blood before they can get off a single shot?

Apparently not.

One moment, the mutos are all over the dog, pawing at his blinking collar like it's something more valuable than gold. The next instant, the dog is rigid, head thrown back and arms extended, clawing the air and shrieking a guttural roar as a burst of high voltage issues forth from the collar, passing from his body to anything in contact with him. The other mutants close by are instantly as paralyzed as he is, jerking upright and screaming as the current blasts through them. Only two on the perimeter of the throng remain unaffected. Thrown back by the initial shock, they hit the ground and shake their heads sharply, growling at one another in confusion, slow to return to their feet.

I keep my eye on them. "Six neutralized. Two remain unharmed," I report. I bite my lip as the two unaffected mutos turn their full attention on the Hummer.

Silence on the comm. Disconcerting, to say the least.

"There should be a flare gun in the glove box," Jamison offers. "You could use it—"

"Just run them over," Perch says. "I'm giving the rest of 'em all the juice I've got. Heads should start exploding any second now."

Lovely. I reach for the compartment below the dashboard on the passenger's side. There is an operations manual with the large UW Motors logo on the cover. Beneath it, a flare gun sits unloaded with no cartridges nearby.

"Try the rear hatch," Jamison says, watching my efforts through the camera in my collar.

With a curse, I check the parking brake to be sure it's set, then crawl onto the backseat and over it, reaching for the utility compartment next to the relay rods. Meanwhile, the dog and its six paralyzed friends continue to strain spastically against the electrical current coursing through them, and the two other mutos stagger toward the Hummer with harsh barking noises between them, sounding more excited the closer they come.

The hatch on the compartment pops open at my touch. Inside

I find an adjustable wrench, a multitool, spares for the roof's supplemental solar panels...but no flares.

"Try the other side," Jamison says, referring to the compartment above the opposite wheel well.

I slide along the rear seat and extend my arm toward the hatch just as a volley of rounds rake along the vehicle's side. I fall back, flinching at the close-range thuds.

"What the hell are you afraid of?" Perch scoffs. "No way they'll pierce that armor."

It isn't the armor that concerns me as I note small fractures along the side windows. Blowing out a quick breath, I dive forward, over the backseat, and pop the second utility compartment. Among what looks like tire-changing equipment, I locate one unused flare cartridge.

Better than nothing. I slide it into the empty gun and snap the muzzle into ready position.

Outside, the collared dog's head bursts with a sickening pop and a splash of blood and cranial matter. The body remains standing, remote-controlled by Perch, as the voltage continues to hold the other six mutos in its agonizing grip.

"Take out one of them," Jamison says, referring to the pair at my window.

"Unless you can get 'em to line up for you," Perch says.

A stupid remark. The flare will burrow into one target and set it aflame, allowing the other one to blow out my tires and leave me stranded here. It's what I fear most.

That, and having my own head explode.

"What are you waiting for?" Jamison sounds stressed, even though he's safe and sound far away from here. What does he have to be worried about?

The two mutos pound the ends of their assault rifles against the Hummer. The reinforced glass repels their blows with hollow-sounding bumps.

"Roll down that window and let 'em have it!" Perch urges.

"Go for a headshot." He chuckles eagerly. It's all fun and games to him.

"You should have sent me with a real weapon," I mutter.

"We did," Perch counters, probably meaning the expired dog.

"A lot of good he'll be now."

"Just wait and see. We've got it under control."

I doubt that. By all indications, they're flying by the seats of their pants, strategizing moment to moment with no clear plan of action.

Unlike me. I know better than to think I can stay here much longer. There is no telling how long the dog's collar will keep the other mutos incapacitated, and it's only a matter of time before the pair assaulting this vehicle manages to get inside.

I have one flare.

And plenty of relay rods.

Sucking down a quick breath, I crawl into the rear cargo hold and kick the hatch release. Immediately, the two mutos stagger around toward the back as the door opens. The first one gets a flare in the face, recoiling and shrieking as it sparks and sizzles. He drops his weapon and claws at the blossoming flare, falling back on his partner, forcing him aside and giving me the split second I need to grab one of the relays and lunge out of the vehicle with the rod poised like a javelin.

The muto with the rifle shoves his writhing pal to the ground and squeezes off a few rounds that ping off the back of the vehicle and pierce the faux-leather interior. I duck at the same time, hurling the rod as hard as I can. The sharp end, designed to be planted deep into the hard-packed earth, impales the muto's midsection, doubling him over with a hoarse scream. He looks surprised more than anything else. But he doesn't let go of his weapon, even as he staggers under the impact with one hand on the rod skewering his abdomen.

I drop to the ground as the creature lets loose another volley of shots, badly aimed but wild enough to be dangerous. I retrieve the fallen assault rifle from the flare-faced muto and take quick aim, squeezing the trigger and holding it there until the magazine empties. I don't realize my eyes are closed until the weapon clicks in my hands.

Once my eyelids open, I see the relay rod quivering erect from the motionless muto, covered in its own blood, punctured by thirty-odd rounds.

Perch curses in appreciation of my handiwork.

The other muto also lies still, its face a smoldering mass of scorched flesh. Despite my medical training, I feel a sudden urge to vomit, which I do my best to restrain. Even so, bile burns my throat.

Gritting my teeth, I step toward the skewered muto's corpse and enter the rod's planting code. After a moment's verification, the relay rod sinks completely into the ground, straight through the creature's bullet-ridden body.

I pick up its loaded rifle and then climb up into the Hummer without a glance back. As my insides threaten to rebel, the rear hatch automatically shuts behind me, locking me inside where, for the moment, I'm safe.

"Good work, Margo." Jamison sounds relieved. And impressed.

I don't reply. Setting the weapon on the empty passenger seat, I climb behind the wheel and gun the engine, veering sharply around the headless high-voltage square dance that has lost none of its fervor.

"What do you think you're doing?" Perch demands. "Don't you leave that dog—"

"It's no good to me now. I'm staying on mission. Keep those other mutos occupied as long as you can."

"He's just pissed that you're leaving his camera behind," Jamison mutters. "Ignore him."

"I plan to," I agree—and instantly regret doing so. A sudden shock nearly sends me into convulsions.

"What the hell?" Jamison shouts on the comm.

"Damn bitch should learn her place!" Perch counters.

I swallow, struggling to stay in the moment. The vehicle skids lengthwise down the embankment as I fight the wheel for control.

Jamison adds a few choice words for emphasis. "Margo, I'm sorry. That won't happen again."

It had better not. The next time, I might end up flipping the vehicle.

"Are you all right?" Jamison sounds concerned.

The Hummer jostles me as it hits the valley floor, but I hold on, in complete control now as a level stretch of terrain opens before me. "Fine."

I glance at the passenger seat and the weapon it holds.

I could end it all right now with a bullet to the brainpan. Refuse to be Willard's remote-controlled limo driver. How long does he plan to keep me alive, anyway? Until the infants are delivered to the UW?

Over my dead body.

They belong with their rightful parents. Tucker has found Luther and his people, I'm sure of it. So it's only a matter of time before they mobilize and move on Eden to reclaim what belongs to them.

But will they? I haven't considered that possibility.

If only I could pry off this damned collar, I would know exactly where the little male and female ended up. I could communicate with them, tell them I'm on my way.

Instead, I follow the course set for me by Jamison, always here in spirit when I briefly lose my way. "Three degrees west by southwest," he says.

I correct the steering wheel and settle back in the seat for a long drive, shoving my thoughts far from my mind. Night falls abruptly, and the Hummer's high beams knife through the dark. I stare unblinking at the whitewashed terrain before me, instead seeing the host of incubation chambers housed deep in Eden's concrete sublevels. Dozens of them with no hope of survival if not for my medical expertise. None of the men in Eden have a clue how to care for them. I am their only hope, and Willard knows it.

So much for pushing my thoughts aside.

For the moment, I table the idea of blowing my own head off, robbing Perch of the satisfaction of pressing the button himself. I set my mind on autopilot as the ambient temperature drops significantly and the internal environmental system starts filling the vehicle with warm air. I focus on not focusing on anything at all. Jamison will guide me true. I am just their remote-controlled chauffeur, after all. No mental strain required.

"You'll need to pick up the pace, Margo," Jamison says at length, his voice clipped.

I have no idea how much time has passed. It can't have been long; I haven't planted the next relay rod yet. "Trouble?"

"You could say that. The UW team is under attack."

11. BISHOP

18 MONTHS AFTER ALL-CLEAR

The tracks beside Morley's discarded hazard suit make no sense. Morley's boot prints simply end—as do those of the two hostiles that took him.

"You said they disappeared...but this is insane." I shiver inside my suit. The temperature plunged as soon as the sun went down, but up to now, the insulation has done a decent job of containing my body heat.

"Guess they really did vanish. I thought it was just a glitch in my HUD." Granger surveys the bloodstained ground beside me. "Speaking of which, how're you holding up in there, Captain? Your O2 still good?"

The oxygen levels are fine, as far as I can tell, but we're all getting low. It's the cold that worries me. I clench my teeth to keep from chattering. "How far will the temp drop?"

Harris steps forward with the ambient readings displayed on his helmet's face shield. "I'm afraid this is the warmest it'll be until sunrise. Thermal energy readings are declining as residual heat loss increases. Give it an hour, and it'll be close to freezing out here."

"Way to cheer him up," Granger mutters.

"He is merely stating facts," Sinclair interjects, her face expressionless in the moonlight. "Allow me to follow up with an observation: We have no way of knowing where our weapons officer was taken. There are no tracks to speak of. It would make the most sense to proceed—"

"We don't leave anybody behind." I turn away from her to scan the ground the old-fashioned way: with my eyes.

"Even insubordinates?" Harris raises an eyebrow.

"Them too." I trace the last set of boot prints to a pair of twin streaks across the sand, as if the hostiles' feet suddenly became runners on a sled of some kind. But that can't be. Nobody said anything about seeing a sledge. I follow the streaks across the ground until they, too, end, dissolving into untouched terrain.

"What can possibly be gained by staring at the ground, Sergeant?"

I glance at Sinclair. "Head back to the jeep if you want. I'm not going anywhere until I figure out what happened here."

"According to my HUD, they disappeared completely: on radar one second, off the next. You think maybe they've got some kind of matter transportation device?" Granger looks dead serious. "You know, like maybe they were able to…*beam* themselves out of here? And they took our guy with them?"

"Ridiculous," Sinclair says. "That technology does not exist even in Eurasia, the most advanced city in human history. How would these hostiles manage such a thing?"

"We've got tracks that vanish into thin air. What else could explain it?" Granger faces her with his chin jutting upward.

She releases a weary sigh. "Have you considered a hovercraft of some sort? One with runners built for travel across the sand?" She points at the streaks on the ground where I stand. "Which are then retracted once the vehicle reaches full escape velocity."

I nod. It makes sense—except for the fact that nobody mentioned seeing any kind of hovering vehicle on their heads-up displays.

"Hovercraft. Huh." Granger sounds like he's intrigued by the thought. "Maybe outfitted with cloaking tech?"

"Possible," Sinclair allows.

"Regardless, we have a mission to complete, do we not?" Harris holds out empty gloved hands. Morley took his rifle, and it's nowhere in sight. "I say we go back to the jeep, get a little sleep, and prepare to—"

"Nobody's stopping you." I face west, the desolation glowing under frosty moonlight.

"You're not seriously considering going after him?" Sinclair steps forward.

I turn to Granger. "Get the *Argonaus* on comms. See if Mutegi will send in support now."

"And if he doesn't?" Harris sounds incredulous as Granger brings up the communications module on his HUD. "You would sacrifice our mission for the sake of *one man*? When the future of humankind is at stake here? We must go to Eden and see those fetuses! Nothing else matters." His eyes bulge, his teeth clenched. "Nothing!"

I stare him down. This mission is the only thing standing between me and seeing my wife and kids again. There's nothing in my orders about bringing back every member of my team in one piece. Just make contact with Eden. That's it.

Do the job and get out alive.

"Got him," Granger says.

"Captain Mutegi." I face the holographic projection on Granger's face shield and do my best to salute, despite the cumbersome hazard suit.

"Sergeant Bishop. We were about to contact your team." The captain's features are drawn tight. On edge.

"Sir?"

"There's been a...situation. You'd best clear out of there as fast as you can. We've tracked movement headed your way—and judging by the heat signatures, they're moving at some godawful speeds."

Harris has already started backpedaling. "What did I tell you?" he hisses as if he already knows what's coming.

I glance westward. I've got a feeling that's where any trouble will originate. "How many, sir?"

"Two dozen, at least. Armed and dangerous, covering ground like nobody's business. You get back to your vehicle and get the hell out of there. Do your damnedest to stay ahead of them."

"And our man?"

Mutegi pauses. "Sergeant, your man is dead. I'm sorry. That's a whole other issue we're contending with on this end. But rest assured, I'm pushing hard against my superiors for permission to allocate the help you need. For now, Eden is sending a transport to pick you up. You get that jeep of yours to run on fumes if you have to, but you head north by northeast. That's where you'll meet them. *Argonaus* out."

The hologram dims, revealing Granger's wide-eyed expression behind it, pale in the moonlight.

"Move out," I order.

The debate is over. It's back to lumbering along as fast as our bulky suits will allow. The only plus side: movement keeps me warm. Somewhat.

"We should've asked about that hovercraft," Granger huffs.

"Why would they take our man only to kill him?" Harris sounds honestly perplexed. "It makes no sense at all. Wouldn't they have made a demand of some kind? Ransom, perhaps?"

"If these hostiles are the same as those creatures we came upon earlier," Sinclair says, not sounding winded in the least as she strides ahead of us, leading the way. "They could have taken him to feast upon."

"And now that they know how good we taste..." Granger coughs.

I nod. "They've scrambled a full-on hunting party."

At the same instant, all three of my team members' helmets chime a warning signal.

"Movement detected." Sinclair half-turns toward me. The upper right quadrant of her face shield shows thermal images of our pursuers. "Five kilometers out and closing, Sergeant."

"Mutegi wasn't kidding." Granger struggles to keep up despite his short legs. "They've got to be on hovercrafts or something—they're moving so *fast!*"

"Five minutes, at this rate. That's all we have until they overtake us." Harris curses, always the optimist. "We can't outrun them."

"How many?" I keep my tone level.

"More than twenty distinct heat signatures, sir," Sinclair says evenly.

"Some of that heat's gotta be from their hovercrafts, right?" Granger sounds hopeful.

"The heat readings are organic," Sinclair says. "No vehicles detected."

No one responds. As unlikely as it sounds, this is reality: people moving at superhuman speeds.

"So we're outnumbered five to one." Granger curses. "We could've handled better odds—say, three to one. But five? I don't know, Captain. What do you think?"

I almost grin at the half-sized engineer's bravado. "I think we need to get back to that jeep."

"We're on a mission that will change the world—*save* the world—and the *Argonaus* can't be bothered with providing us any air support?" Harris complains.

"Mutegi's working on it. You heard him," Granger says.

"Two kilometers and closing," Sinclair reports for my benefit. I appreciate the gesture, if not the news itself. "One kilometer to the jeep."

"Damn it!" Harris shrieks, stomping his boots. "We're not going to make it!"

"Don't you quit on me, Doc." I tug his arm with a rough jerk. "Think of all those little babies waiting for you. All those medical journals with your bio and image in 3D. C'mon, you owe it to your readers to keep *moving*."

"They're going to kill us, just like they—!"

"Pull yourself together." I would slug him a hard right hook if his helmet wasn't in the way. "Stay on mission. You're alive, I'm alive. You can fall apart later, but right now you're running as fast as you can. Got it?"

Breathing heavily, Harris nods with a stolid air of defeat. Yet he keeps moving.

"Hey, don't you think these suits should've been rigged with a turbo mode or something?" Granger breaks the tension.

"Turbo?" Sinclair eyes him with disdain as he struggles to keep pace beside her. "Yes, that would be quite convenient, now wouldn't it?"

"Hell yeah!" He clears his throat. "Turbo," he says, using that solemn tone he reserves for voice commands.

"You can't be serious," she says.

"Why not? Has anybody else even tried?"

"It was not in the operations manual."

"Like you read the whole thing." His sidelong glance becomes an open stare. "No kidding. You did?"

"There is no high-speed mode, I can assure you."

Granger frowns. "Well, what if it's a hidden feature?"

"You've lost me," she says.

"Turbo. Turbo! *Turbo.*" He alters his inflection slightly, but always with the same result: nothing. "Jetpack! Rocket launcher!" Still nothing.

"Can't fault him for trying," I tell the doctor as we press forward.

Harris nods and then stops abruptly, planting his boots into the sand. "I can see them," he whispers, rotating on his heel until the HUD rearview becomes a full frontal view of the west. He stares at the approaching figures moving in a convergent blur of speed, and he curses hoarsely in disbelief.

Reaching the jeep is out of the question. We're just not fast enough.

"Ready weapons," I order, raising the only one I have—the handgun I took from Morley. It's like waving a twig at an advancing herd of angry beasts. I have to fight against the overwhelming sense of futility. "This is it, folks."

Granger and Sinclair halt and do an about-face, fumbling with their assault rifles.

"Conserve your ammunition," I tell them.

"So many..." Harris says in a hushed voice. "How is it even possible—moving so fast? Could it be...that we are witnessing a new stage in human evolution?"

"Back to back. Get into position." I can't help recalling the bloodstained earth Morley left behind. "Don't fire until I say so."

"It has been an honor, Sergeant." Surprisingly, there is no reproach in Sinclair's voice as she and Granger take their positions behind me.

"Right back at you." I stare as the blurs of speed solidify into human forms all around us. Tall, muscular figures in hooded cloaks with an array of assault rifles, handguns, and blades.

"Ain't over till it's over," Granger mutters.

"Stay in the middle, Doc." I nudge the unarmed doctor behind my back toward Granger and Sinclair. "If one of us has to survive this, it's you."

"Thank you," Harris says absently.

The hostiles surrounding us are entirely unlike the creatures we saw before. These are fellow humans, not sun-charred monsters—but these people have the ability to run faster than humanly possible. So they're more than human.

The silence runs on as I glance from one superhuman to the next, noting their lack of breathing apparatuses or face shields. They stare back at us with unguarded fascination. Yet no one speaks.

I clear my throat, lowering the muzzle of my handgun slightly. It points toward the kneecap of a superhuman who doesn't seem to mind. Can the guy move fast enough to dodge a bullet? That would explain his total lack of concern—seemingly shared by all of them.

"Who's your leader?" I demand, my voice emanating loud and clear inside my helmet, my breath fogging the cold face shield.

The superhumans don't respond.

"They can't hear you, Captain," Granger says on internal comms.

Right. My fractured helmet strikes again. For some reason, I continue to hear ambient noises fine, but I have no way to activate the external speaker.

"Want me to interpret?" Granger offers.

"Go ahead." I nudge him, and he repeats my question.

Silence. The superhumans' breath comes out in short bursts that float like mist before dispersing.

"I am Markus." One of them steps forward and bows slightly, his gaze never leaving me. He holds no weapon in sight, but Granger's HUD has already lit up, identifying small explosives in his pockets.

"I am Vincent," says another one, striding forward to stand beside the man named Markus. Vincent sweeps aside his cloak as he bows, revealing blades of various sizes sheathed across his leather-clad abdomen. "We have been sent to find you. We hope you will come with us without any…ugliness." He extends open hands.

Can these be the same men who took Morley? Hard to believe, considering their curious, almost childlike interest in my team.

"We're on a peaceful mission." I push Granger's rifle muzzle down a few degrees. No need to shoulder the weapon. Not yet. "But we'll defend ourselves if necessary."

"Got that right," Granger mutters, aiming at Vincent's boots. Then he remembers to repeat what I just said.

"An understandable reaction," Markus says. "Your comrade felt the same way."

"Is that why you killed him?" My grip tightens on the handgun as Granger relays my question.

The hooded faces around us look surprised, then seem to take offense.

"We did no such thing." Markus's gaze narrows haughtily. "We captured him. Pacified him—"

"We saw the blood."

"He resisted," Vincent says. "We defended ourselves. Your man was alive when we delivered him to Lord Cain. He may have expired due to complications afterward, but we did not kill him."

"Complications." My jaw clenches. "The air would be bad enough. Did you think of that before you pried him out of his suit?" I nudge Granger, and he repeats what I said, word for word.

"There is nothing wrong with our air." Vincent inhales deeply, nostrils flared, and exhales a loud, contented sigh. "You see?"

Harris pushes his way out of the huddle protecting him, breaking free of Granger and Sinclair, neither of whom offer much resistance.

"You must realize how different you are from us. Your ability to travel at such great speeds, to breathe this air that is toxic to our kind..." Harris's voice falls near a whisper. The superhumans incline their heads and focus their dark eyes on him. "You have evolved far beyond the capabilities of *homo sapiens* as a species. I have to wonder, are there other...*abilities* you possess besides this amazing speed?"

Markus holds up a hand to halt any further questions. "Lord Cain will explain these things to you. He has asked that we bring you to meet him, without delay." He reaches for my handgun. "So, if you would kindly hand over your weapons, we'll be on our way."

I raise the muzzle, aiming between the tall superhuman's eyes. "We're headed the other direction. Place called Eden. Ever hear of it?"

Just as Granger finishes relaying the message, Harris cuts in, "Sergeant Bishop, put down your weapon. Can't you see they mean us no harm?"

I don't lower my gun.

"I would listen to your man there, *Sergeant*." Markus holds his ground despite the gun barrel level with his forehead.

"You might be fast enough to take my gun, but I doubt you're fast enough to dodge a bullet. Otherwise you would've tried already." I keep my aim steady and wait for Granger to finish echoing me. The ring of superhumans tenses, ready to spring into action. "You can tell this *Lord Cain* of yours that we decline his invitation and must be on our way. We have a date with Eden, and we're already late."

Vincent smiles—a strange reaction in the moment. Hands on his hips, blades plain to see across his broad chest, he says, "Wouldn't you like to taste our air, Sergeant?"

"You're making them agitated," Harris grumbles at me before stepping closer to the superhumans, seeming to dare them to lay hold of him. "We mean you no harm. We come in peace. I for one would very much like to meet your Lord Cain. Please, take me to him."

"Well, that's more like it," Vincent announces, half-turning to his men. They chuckle and nod.

"Get your ass back here, Doc," I order on comms.

"This is the opportunity of a lifetime." Harris extends his arms as if to embrace new friends. "We have so much to learn from these people. UW Command has no *idea* they exist!"

"What about Eden?" Granger frowns.

"It's not going anywhere." Harris smiles broadly.

"Neither are you," I seethe. "Get back here, or I'll shoot you myself."

"Such a violent lot." Vincent shakes his head. He must have read my lips. "It's no wonder you think your man is dead. Violence breeds only more violence."

"Let us be on our way, and there will be no trouble. You have my word." I nod. So does Granger.

Markus crosses his brawny arms. "And what good is the word

of a United World soldier? Your people destroyed this continent —not to mention the rest of the world."

Vincent pats him on the shoulder. "We're wasting time here. Lady Victoria says Cain grows impatient. We are to act now."

"No communications equipment, yet they receive orders from their superiors in real-time..." Harris muses aloud.

"Fire at the first one to make a move," I order on comms.

Sinclair and Granger respond with curt nods, their rifles checked and at the ready.

Markus raises an eyebrow. "Get ready to dodge a few bullets, men!"

The circle of superhumans releases a chorus of wild shouts as Markus dashes forward, blurring out of focus with incredible speed. My gun is wrenched aside, but I hold on tight and squeeze off every round until the clip empties. Spurts of blood drift through the air; I know my shots found targets, but with the indistinct haze of motion all around me, I can't be certain who I hit.

Assault rifles briefly spit fire on my right and left, courtesy of Sinclair and Granger before they're disarmed and thrown to the ground.

The next thing I know, I'm on my back as well, pinned to the sand.

"Damn it!" Granger lashes out against the two superhumans who restrain him.

So he's fine.

"Sinclair, report."

"I'm here, Sergeant. We're all right."

"No thanks to *you!*" Harris is disgruntled. No surprise there. "Let me up, please. I am no threat. None of us are, now that you have disarmed us so spectacularly." He does his best to placate our captors. "It was a wonder to behold, in point of fact. To see you *move* like that!"

Vincent no longer smiles. He holds a polished machete that gleams in the moonlight. "Get them out of those suits."

Harris's obsequious tone takes an about-face. "Hold on now—don't be hasty. You have already subdued us. There is no conceivable way we would pose a problem for you, so there is no need to remove our suits. They are for our protection, you see. We are from a domed city on the Mediterranean Sea, and we breathe only air that has been purified—"

"Your suits are heavy." Markus shrugs. "They'll slow us down."

"Does your Lord Cain want us brought back to him dead or alive?" Harris demands.

"He wasn't too specific on that point," Vincent admits, smirking at the stunned look on the doctor's face. "Go on." He gestures to his men. "Open them up."

We thrash wildly, doing all we can to delay the inevitable.

"Sergeant!" Harris shrieks.

"Turbo!" Granger screams, a last-ditch attempt. "Force! Power! Thrust!"

I take a different tack. Despite my cumbersome suit, I jab a hand between the arms that restrain me and seize the hilt of a superhuman's blade. Slipping it free of its sheath, I proceed to slice and hack away at every superhuman body part in range, aiming first for the hands that try to dislodge my helmet clamps. Blood sprays across my face shield, combining with the fog from my breath to make me just about as blind as I was after my crash-landing.

"Subdue him!" Markus roars over the screams of his men, a chorus of pain that intensifies as both Granger and Sinclair follow my lead, snatching blades and going to work. "Subdue them all!"

Shots ring out, fired into the air. I gain a little breathing room and wipe at my face shield with one gloved hand while swinging the blade in violent arcs with the other. I meet no resistance. The superhumans are wisely keeping their distance now.

Between the streaks on my face shield, I see the one named Vincent advancing on Sinclair from behind. I lunge forward with all the strength I can muster to intercept, my blood-stained blade at the ready.

"No!" Harris cries.

Vincent plunges his machete into the gap behind Sinclair's left knee and quickly withdraws his weapon, leaving her leg to buckle. Too stunned to utter more than a harsh gasp, she topples to the sand, clutching at the blood flow with her gloved hands.

"Tell your people to lay down their weapons," Vincent says.

"I'm unarmed!" Harris makes it known, throwing up both his hands.

I glance down at Sinclair as she struggles awkwardly to stop the bleeding. I point at Harris. "Take his suit off first."

The good doctor turns a slack-jawed face toward me.

"You can be our guinea pig, Doc. If the air checks out, we've got nothing to be afraid of." I lower my blade and look at Granger. "Tell them."

He nods and repeats everything I said.

Markus scowls. "You will stop resisting us, or we will forcibly pacify you—as we have already done with your woman."

Despite her wound, Sinclair is visibly chafed at being referred to that way.

"Pacify my ass," Granger snarls, his own bloody blade gripped tight. "You want to dance? Let's dance!"

Vincent smirks. "You wouldn't survive my first strike."

"Let's all take a deep breath here and settle things like reasonable human beings—and highly evolved human beings." Harris steps between them. The superhumans maintain a tight perimeter, ignoring the lacerations they received, now blossoming in wet patches under the moonlight. "It's clear we are not getting anywhere like this, so why don't I make a proposition?" He pauses, waiting for an invitation from the superhumans to continue.

"You waste your breath, old man," Markus says. "Lord Cain has spoken, and we follow his command." He gestures to his men, and they move like the wind.

Granger hits the ground first, screaming and lashing out with his borrowed weapon. But his retaliation doesn't last long. First a blade punctures the joint at his elbow, and the weapon in his hand drops to the ground with a puff of dust. Then he lies still, groaning.

I'm next. But I drop the blade and don't fight back. I need to conserve my strength for when they decide to remove my suit. I'll have to deal with whatever violent changes overcome me at that point. I trust—without knowing why—that these superhumans will be true to their word. That if I don't retaliate, they won't harm me.

Ironic, considering they're prepared to remove my only protection from this toxic environment.

"Finally, you see reason." Harris nods.

A pair of superhumans take hold of my helmet. They start unlatching it.

"My O2's almost out anyway."

"You are a brave man, Sergeant," Markus observes. "Your comrade was squealing like an infant by this point."

"We're not scared." Granger favors his injured arm as another pair of superhumans work on removing his helmet, struggling with the remaining clamps. "But *you* should be. Who knows what kind of mutant freaks you'll have on your hands once we catch a whiff of your air."

Markus chuckles. "We'll put you down, if need be."

"Dead or alive," I remind the engineer. "We're wanted men, ol' buddy."

Granger curses.

I take a quick breath and hold it as the final clamps release. My helmet lifts free, exposing my face to the chill of the night.

Will I ever see my family again?

"Breathe it in, Sergeant," Markus says. "Our air flows from Gaia herself, permeating all that it touches. There is no way for you to—"

He's interrupted by a new player on the scene: an engine

roaring through the dark with headlights on full blast, as blinding as the sun in all its glory. I shield my eyes with one hand and recognize the vehicle—a black, armored Hummer. It must have been running on silent mode until now, revving as it skids to a halt a few meters away.

Who sits behind the wheel? Impossible to tell behind those tinted windows. A fanged mutant? Someone from Eden? Or a survivor from some other enclave the UW knows nothing about?

"Looks like our ride's here." Granger smacks the superhuman's hands away from his helmet and slaps the clamps shut. "Sorry fellas, but we've gotta go."

Markus and Vincent have our assault rifles at the ready. They order their men to do the same, taking aim at the intruder. Ignoring me and my crew for the moment, they fire volley after volley into the vehicle's exterior, the shots deflecting with sparks of light.

I grunt as I latch my helmet back into place and release the air I've been holding. A little light-headed, I gulp down whatever O2 my suit still has to offer and roll onto all fours. Then I heave myself upright. "Can you move?"

"Go, Sergeant." Sinclair sits in a pool of her own blood. "I would only slow you down, I'm afraid."

"You kidding? Why do you think we brought this guy along?" Granger holds his bloody arm out to Harris. "Work your magic, Doc!"

A stunned look is plastered across the good doctor's face. His eyes dart from the vehicle to the superhumans, and he squints at the bursts of weapons fire illuminating them in the night.

"How about it?" Granger urges.

Harris nods, blinking, unable to ignore the cacophony around us. "Of course—but my medkit, it's back at the jeep."

I glance at the Hummer taking fire from all sides. The resilient vehicle continues to withstand the abuse without a single window broken. How many are inside? Are they armed? What are they waiting for?

"Can you stand?" I step beside Sinclair.

"With help." She nods.

"We won't get far," Harris says. "Do you have a plan, Sergeant?"

"Their ammo will run out before long, and when it does—"

As if on cue, the superhumans pause to reload with mags fished from deep pockets in their cloaks. The vehicle lurches forward suddenly, driving a few of the shooters back.

"The tires!" Markus shouts. "Go for the tires!"

A fresh barrage erupts. I curse as the vehicle's tires blow out beneath it, sinking into the sand. The superhumans cheer like cavemen subduing a mighty dinosaur—

Until a sudden sandstorm descends on them from above without warning, whirling violently and whipping the rifles out of their hands, dispersing the superhumans, driving them into the night screaming something about *demons* as they disappear in blurs of speed.

I blink, unable to believe my eyes as the form of a man materializes out of the whirlwind. The storm dissipates as abruptly as it arrived, leaving everything eerily still.

"We don't have much time." The man approaches us at an easy stride, caked in dust and wiping the stuff from his black goggles. "They'll be back."

12. TUCKER

17 MONTHS AFTER ALL-CLEAR

Thinking back on it now, the particulars are a little fuzzy. Maybe it had something to do with the pain of being shot or the fear of getting eaten alive. Either way, I'm grateful for it. Kind of dulled the sharp edges around what was sure to be the stuff of nightmares—for the final few minutes of my life, anyway.

I'd dealt with the mutos plenty before, so I knew what to expect from their kind. I knew where I stood with them. They were hunters; I was prey. But up to now, I was able to stick to the shadows and the cover of nightfall as I went about doing Willard's bidding. More often than not, that involved fastening fancy shock collars onto every muto I could find. They never saw me coming, and by the time they realized what I'd done, I was already well out of range. If I was real quiet, I could slip off into the dark without being noticed.

Not the case when you've been shot and left for dead in the middle of sun-scorched earth. Invisible man or not, you bleed. You leave a trail of crimson across the hard-baked ground when you crawl over to a patch of shade behind a boulder. You curse your shadow that only makes itself known in direct sunlight, oddly enough. As if that's fair in any way. You grab hold of the gun they've left you—those sons of bitches who made off with your precious cargo and shot you for your troubles.

"Keep them safe," I told that third sentry, parting words between the two of us. Last words, I figured at the time.

Lying here now in this cool, dark cave on a padded cot, in the quiet with only my thoughts and recollections to keep me company—and the sting of the healing salve doing its job on my wounds—it's all I can do to keep my mind from straying back to those godawful moments.

The mutos in their jeeps made a beeline straight for me. By the time I got myself into the shade, I knew there was no point in hiding. The mutant freaks had already spotted my blood. But I hoped to take out as many of them as I could before they started tearing into me, chewing on my intestines like sausage links.

I've got a good imagination. Always have. But I didn't appreciate it much once I started visualizing the feeding frenzy about to ensue.

Crouched low behind the rock, handgun at the ready, spare clips good to go, I grit my teeth against the pain, cursing myself in silence to remain conscious as the sunbaked terrain swam around me. I couldn't pass out. Not that I wanted to be fully conscious when the mutos started their bloody feast, but I did want a fighting chance. And if there happened to be an extra round left over when things started turning south, I'd have the option of sealing my own fate—with a gun muzzle up tight against the roof of my mouth and a split second between the trigger pull and the hole out the back of my head.

The jeeps skidded to a halt less than twenty meters away, and I heard the mutos snorting, growling and cavorting as their ragged boots hit the ground running. Despite their lack of nasal appendages, the creatures had a keen sense of smell—something I'd learned all too well in previous encounters.

The first one to reach me had only a moment to notice where the blood trail ended in a small pool, having cascaded down the side of the granite behind my back. I raised the 9mm and squeezed off two rounds. The muto's head whipped back as blood and brain matter exploded out the back of its skull, and the body went limp in midair.

I considered grabbing the creature's weapon, a UW-issued assault rifle, but there was no time. The others were already upon me. I didn't count rounds or targets. I just aimed and fired, one headshot after another, picking them off as they approached with their weapons at the ready, aimed in my general vicinity.

I wince now at the memory of the muto with the death grip on his rifle, how when my first shot plowed through his left eye with a burst of yellow pus and blood, the creature's trigger finger jerked back and froze there, spraying bullets like rain. They pocked the ground with little geysers of dust and raced in a line, straight for my outstretched leg. I was too weak to move anything but my shooting hand by that point, leaning there against the boulder with my head back, drenched in sweat and blood—most of it my own. I howled in agony as a dozen rounds ripped into my leg.

The mutos seemed taken aback at the primal sounds coming from the shade, and they halted their approach for the moment, staring bug-eyed and slobbering.

"Yeah, you know me," I managed to rasp at length, my throat raw. "The invisible man. I've collared hundreds of your pals." Through blurred vision, I saw them crowd around me, six or seven of the horrors, snorting and staring with their lidless eyes, unable to blink even if they wanted to. "C'mon now. Have at it. What are you waiting for?" My words slurred at that point. I knew I wouldn't be ending things on my own terms. I didn't have the strength. "Ain't you hungry?"

They jostled against one another in excitement. Their exposed nasal cavities twitched and snorted sharply, some kind of preliminary reaction. Then their fangs came at me, teeth that had once been human but were sharpened to points, perfect for biting and tearing into flesh. They didn't care that I was covered in a cold sweat and going into mild convulsions—either from blood-loss or fear, tough to tell which. They were hungry for meat, pretty much always on the brink of starvation, by the looks of them. Beggars couldn't be choosers.

Neither could cannibal freaks, apparently.

I seized up, fists clenched, muscles tight. I remember feeling the teeth like two dozen needles piercing into my arm all at once—like getting a flu shot back when I was a kid, but twenty times worse. And that was only one bite. I screamed out, banging the back of my head against granite as three more fastened their jaws onto me. My invisibility had posed no problem for them at all.

I look down at my arm now, bare and glistening in the greenish light of the glowsticks mounted on the cave walls around me. My skin is covered in healing salve. Almost every square centimeter of my body is lathered in the stuff. From the warm, prickling sensation, I can tell it's working its magic.

I don't bother trying to move. I tried before when I first woke up in this strange place, and it was nothing doing. Maybe they gave me some kind of paralytic to keep me still while the medicinal gel did its work. I sure was a bloody mess out there by the time they found me.

The details of my rescue are unclear. I remember the biting, and I figured that would be my last memory—the awful sensation of fangs and claws tearing, releasing spurts of blood and revealing the juicy organs underneath. More horrific than anything I could have ever dreamed up.

Then a blast of sand and dust washed over us, choking me mid-scream and alarming the mutos something fierce. The sounds they made with their blood-drooling mouths in no way resembled human speech, but I thought I recognized a tone of terrified familiarity with the sudden sandstorm. Or maybe I was hallucinating. Either way, once the dust began to swirl around me like a whirlwind, driving the mutos back, shrieking and fleeing to their jeeps, I coughed and allowed a smile to stretch across my face as I cracked an eye open to take a peek at the afterlife.

What I saw instead was the form of a man descending out of the dust cloud as if it had been his chariot or something equally biblical, a man covered from head to boots in the cotton sandcloth of a desert nomad. The black UW-issued goggles strapped over his eyes were directed straight at me as he walked on the air —or so it seemed.

That was one of the fuzzier details, I have to admit.

Grin intact, I started losing consciousness at that point, but not before an oddly familiar voice said "Gotcha" as strong arms encircled me.

But that couldn't be right. For one thing, the voice that seemed so familiar at the time holds no meaning for me now, yet I really doubt that a complete stranger would have walked right up to my half-eaten invisible body and given it a great, big hug. Would've been a bloody mess.

Regardless, when I awoke who-knows-how-many hours later, I found myself in here, and I knew right away where I was. Not because I'd ever been here before, and nobody told me where *here* was—I've yet to see a living soul—but I used the process of elimination to figure it out.

There were three options I could think of, but only one made any sense.

First off, this might have been some kind of cave the mutos called home sweet home. But that couldn't be. For one thing, Whirlwind Man wouldn't have rescued me from the mutant freaks only to give me right back to them. And for another, those yellow bug-eyes of theirs can see perfectly well in the dark, so they wouldn't have any use for these glowsticks posted along the walls.

The second possibility: this was a UW encampment. The UW team Willard was expecting could have met with some difficulty once they'd set foot on this continent, and they might have decided to hole-up in here while they waited for backup. But that didn't make sense either, because Whirlwind Man wasn't wearing a UW uniform.

So it had to be door number three. This was Luther's *Homeplace* those sentries had mentioned before carrying off the two incubation pods. One of them must have let it slip that they'd left me to die—maybe the guy who dropped the 9mm—and Luther sent one of his best and brightest sand freaks to go after me and bring me back as fast as he could. Then they laid me out and lathered me up, and I've been lying here ever since, dozing on and off in this peaceful, cool, quiet cave.

A coffin of earth and rock from which I might rise from the dead, if I'm so lucky.

Am I sure this is Luther's Homeplace? Of course not. But if I was a betting man, and if there was anything of value to wager—maybe a few hydropacks—I'd be willing to bet it's Luther who took me in. His people always seemed like a good lot.

Except for those sentries. I'll have to ask Luther about that bunch, when the time's right.

Maybe it has something to do with Daiyna. She might have ordered them to shoot me on sight and leave me out there.

I can't help but feel a twinge of guilt at the memory of double-crossing her the way I did. In the city ruins above Eden, I promised I was leading her to her friends. But in point of fact, I was just trying to get on Willard's good side, so he'd let poor ol' Tucker back into Eden's fold as a bona fide member of the team instead of a retriever—the only one of Willard's men allowed topside.

Once upon a time, I took in a few lungfuls of air on the surface. I found myself locked out of the bunker due to some awful snafu and had to fend for myself. The best thing about being stranded in a trade sector: plenty of everything I'd ever need, right there for the taking. Buried under piles of rubble, but that was to be expected after an apocalypse of nuclear and biochemical proportions.

Thanks to the UW military mixing massive amounts of atomic energy with nerve-altering bioweapons, and thanks to the residue somehow surviving in the dust of the earth, I was changed into an invisible man. And when I finally found a way into Eden through the city's abandoned sewer system, I soon realized that none of my old pals were able to see me.

So, of course, I had to have a little fun with them—after I got over the shock of the whole thing.

I became the Ghost of Eden, haunting Willard on a regular basis until my shenanigans were found out. That's when they collared me with one of Perch's latest inventions: a remote-controller wired for video transmission and able to give quite the shock-load whenever you disobeyed Perch's orders.

Perch. Now there's one gent who personifies the term *bad apple*. I've got no clue what happened in the man's past to make him the way he is, but he's rotten all the way to his core.

Like that sentry who shot me. Daiyna's idea of vengeance? Is she in charge of the sentries? Did she warn them about an invisible man—one who can't be trusted, no matter what?

I glance down at my slick skin, seeming to glow in the dark. *Probably serves me right.* How many wounds are healing underneath the salve? Enough to even the score between me and Daiyna? A man can hope.

Heavy clunking sounds head toward me through the darkness. I strain my head forward but can barely lift it.

"Good. You're awake," a deep voice rumbles, reaching the side of my cot. "Now maybe we can get some answers out of you."

I recognize the voice along with the steel arms and legs of the massive man looming over me. "I remember you." I fight to swallow what feels like a wad of sandpaper lodged in my throat.

The big man's broad, bearded face drops closer to me and grins. "I'm not an easy one to forget."

I cough, rasping, "You're Samson—Luther's—"

"Cyborg. Right." He rises, returning to the shadows. "That's me."

I would have said *friend*. "How did I—?"

"There are plenty of questions going around right now, believe me. Enough to sink a battleship. Namely, what the hell were you doing with a couple of babies? And where'd they even come from?"

"Are they all right?"

"They're fine. Lucky for you, our numbers have increased a bit since the last time our paths crossed. We happened to pick up a couple folks with medical training along the way. Here." He fishes a hydropack from the satchel he wears slung across his chest and tears it open with a rough tug. One of his metal hands lifts the back of my head while the other squeezes some of the H2O substitute past my parched lips. "Take it easy. Last thing we need is that invisible belly of yours exploding."

I blink to indicate I understand the warning and down half the pack before coming up for air. "Thanks. Much better now." I can already feel the fluid healing the insides of my throat the same way the salve is working to fix my outsides.

Samson keeps the hydropack nearby, withdrawing his hand from my head as his gaze wanders across my wounds. Oddly enough, he seems to be looking right at me.

"Are you able to—I mean—" I sniff awkwardly. "Can you *see* me?"

"Afraid so," Samson mutters without pause. "Those daemons sure gave you the business. Don't know how the hell you lived long enough for Milton to find you."

That's who it was—the Whirlwind Man. I remember Milton and his incredible speed. There was even talk that he could fly like a superhero or something. "So I'm not invisible anymore?" Do I dare to hope?

"Sorry, pal. That hasn't changed." Samson blows out a sigh. "Seems like the spirits have their own way of doing things. They gave me superhuman strength, but your people decided to hack off my arms and legs. These robo-limbs are something else, don't get me wrong, but they're nothing like the set I had before." He pauses. "Here's the thing, though: the spirits weren't thrilled with what happened, so they blessed me with this night-vision ability—I don't know what else to call it. So yeah, I can see you just fine where our medics smeared your injuries with healing gel. It gives off a heat signature I can pick up, clear as day." He chuckles, low thunder deep in his chest.

Blessed? What the hell is he talking about?

"You've been checking up on me, I take it."

Samson shrugs large shoulders of flesh and bone. "Luther's orders. He's had me guarding you from the moment you arrived. You don't need me to tell you: Eden and its people aren't the most popular among our ranks."

"Daiyna..." My voice trails off. I don't know what more to say.

Samson frowns in the light of the glowsticks. "Yeah." He clears his throat, half-turning away. "Luther will want to know you're awake. So you just stay put for now. I'll be back."

I nod—glad my neck decides to cooperate. Maybe the rest of my muscles will soon follow suit. "I'm not goin' anywhere."

Samson clunks away on his robot legs. He's much better at walking than he was the last time I saw him in Eden, wobbly and nearly tipping over with every step.

I close my eyes. Of course these people would hate Eden. Anyone hurt by Perch and Willard in their sadistic experiments is bound to hold a grudge. But will their tune change once they realize whose children are in those incubation pods? Their own kids—Luther and Daiyna, Samson and that other girl, the one whose eyes were taken out. Sure, they weren't given a whole lot of say in the matter, but those two babies are theirs.

Not to mention the whole batch back in Eden.

If she still harbors ill feelings toward me, Daiyna won't believe a word I say. I betrayed her trust once upon a time, and she didn't strike me as the forgiving kind. Can I blame her? At the time, I'd been looking out for myself for so long, it hadn't even crossed my mind to be concerned about somebody else.

Yet here I am, risking my life for a couple of unborns floating around in tanks. Why have I made this journey? To save humankind? From what I've heard second or third-hand from Margo, that's pretty much the shape of things.

Over twenty years ago, when the United World government put down the Sector Rebellion, they used high-yield nuclear weapons that changed the face of the entire North American continent. The rebels had already done their part by releasing all manner of illegal biochemical and neurochemical weapons. Apparently, the twain should have never met.

The aftermath? All you've got to do is look around this godforsaken continent. Not a single living thing in sight. Those of us still alive only survived because of the bunkers the UW prepared for the best and brightest or those with the best genes—the engineers, the trade workers, the medical experts, the breeders.

The UW crushed the rebellion, but at what cost?

According to Margo (via Willard, via the Chancellor of the UW herself—a woman named Persephone-something), while the bunkers held their precious human cargo secure for decades, things on the surface deteriorated rapidly. The desolation of North America somehow spread through weather systems, killing all life on the surface of the earth. Eurasia, a domed city on the banks of the Mediterranean Sea, became the last bastion for humankind to escape the toxic air, ash, and nuclear winter. Millions stormed the gates for protection but were turned back. Eurasia hadn't been built to sustain more than three million citizens and was already straining at the seams.

Those inside the glass walls watched while millions on the outside froze to death. But all was not well for the Eurasians. Thousands inside the dome became ill, having ingested biotoxins unawares, and sicknesses the likes of which they'd never seen before spread among the populace like wildfire. Thousands died in the first month. Then tens of thousands. The population was decimated. The dead were ejected from the dome into the sea with the rest of the city's waste. Citizens avoided Eurasia's transparent walls, unable to bear the horrors lying outside.

Years passed. The nuclear winter eventually ended, and ash cleared from the atmosphere. The sun came out to shine upon a scarred, lifeless world. And the remaining citizens of the United World found themselves just as barren, unable to conceive their next generation. A lingering effect of some toxin released by the rebels? Nobody knew for sure.

Their only hope of survival as a species: the breeders from the North American Sectors, huddled deep in their bunkers with no contact from the outside world—or what remained of it. The bunker doors would open automatically at All-Clear, set twenty years after D-Day. *Destruction Day*, I've heard it called—a little on-the-nose.

But the UW grew impatient.

Tests confirmed the air was fine, so they sent in swarms of recovery teams early, troops that landed on the continent en masse to check each bunker and see if there was some way they could rig the steel doors to open sooner than scheduled. The male and female breeders were the priority; their bunkers were separate, and they had to be brought together as soon as possible. They had to get busy if humankind was going to have a chance at being fruitful and repopulating this wasted earth.

The rest is history. All of it is, I guess.

The UW had no idea what they were sending their troops into. Hundreds and hundreds of them turned into the mutant freaks that still roam around in their government-issued jeeps with their government-issued weapons and seemingly inexhaustible supply of government-issued ammunition. Months passed, and the UW made contact with good ol' Captain Willard of the Eden Guard via that shortwave radio I found in the ruins above Eden. Willard clued-in the Eurasians that their so-called saviors, the breeders from Sectors 50 and 51, weren't exactly *human* anymore. They'd become freaks of nature with abnormal abilities—definitely not the all-natural children of God the UW was hoping would spawn the next generation of humankind.

But all was not lost, Willard assured them. And so began his plan to harvest eggs and sperm from his captive sand freaks—Luther and company. In a controlled environment beneath the surface, free of any contaminants from the outside air, he would join them together, ushering in a new generation on this broken planet. Or Margo would, actually. She was the brains behind the whole operation.

All very humanitarian, right? Wrong. This was Captain Arthur Willard, after all. He taught me firsthand what it means to look out for *numero uno* when he locked me outside the bunker and left me to die.

Willard was always paranoid about the air on the surface, convinced there had to be something unnatural in the dust. Everybody else in the bunker was skeptical until a few of the scouts came back and turned into fanged, clawed freaks. They would have torn him limb from limb if he hadn't put them down like the rabid animals they were.

Sand freaks. Mutants. The same kind of folks who now have me in their cave. Not monsters like the flesh-eating mutos outside, but just as un-human. And I'm one of them.

Back to the question that took me down memory lane in the first place: why did I risk everything to come all the way out here? Easy answer: more than anything else in my sorry excuse for a life, I want to spite Arthur Willard. Finding the folks who hate that bastard as much as I do, getting them riled up about their young, maybe inspiring them to return to Eden and give Willard his comeuppance—well, that sounds like the best revenge to me.

Besides, us freaks gotta stick together.

I know better than to think Margo or I will be included in Eden's direct flight to Eurasia. Of course Perch and Willard will leave us behind to rot—and to take care of the collared mutos. Can't forget about them.

"Be sure to feed the dogs now, Tucker," Willard will say. "They can get mighty ornery when they're hungry!"

"You still awake?" Samson's voice returns with the sound of his mechanical legs.

"If I wasn't, I would be now." I sniff, arching my head forward.

"They're on their way—Luther and Daiyna," Samson says. "Might want to brace yourself."

I don't know what to make of that. I try to push against the cot with my arms, but they're still too numb to respond. "Got a blanket or something? I'm feeling a bit exposed here."

"Can't give you anything to wear yet. It'll mess up the healing salve."

Right. Wouldn't want that. "How's...that girl with the eyes?"

"Shechara's keeping watch over the babies. I'm looking forward to hearing all about them, by the way." He crosses his arms and shakes his massive head in either wonder or consternation.

Hushed tones echo along the earthen chamber with sure-footed strides and the soft rustle of clothing. I haven't heard much of Luther's voice before, but I recognize Daiyna's right away. No chance I'd ever forget it.

"How is our patient faring?" Luther steps into the green glow and surveys the cot before him, his eyes unfocused. He looks older than the last time I saw him. More grey, more wrinkles. The past months have been rough on him, by all appearances. But he still exudes an inner strength to match his stolid bearing.

"Speak up, man," Samson mutters.

I clear my throat and sniff—a self-conscious tick I couldn't quit if I tried. "Hey. Thanks for taking me in like this. I would've been a goner out there."

"I'm glad Milton found you in time." Luther glances over his shoulder toward Daiyna, who remains in the shadows. "You've made quite a long journey, and on foot no less." He frowns slightly, focusing his gaze on the pillow where my head lies. Maybe he can see the depression in the fabric. "How did you know where to find us, Tucker?"

I nod to myself, remembering the dust devil that barreled toward me down the middle of that street, the voice of my mother's as clear as if she was standing right behind me, whispering into my ear. Like having her dear, departed spirit talk to me from beyond the grave.

"Does Willard know where we are?" Luther persists.

"No." I shake my head. "No idea. And Margo's gonna keep it that way. I'm sure ol' Perch will give her hell for it, but she's gone through twelve rounds with him before. Besides, all she knows is that I went west. No exact coordinates or anything." I release a weak chuckle. "Hell, I was surprised when I ran into your sentries out there. Thought I had a lot farther to go, truth be told."

Luther's frown deepens. "Yes. About them..." He pauses, and the silence is heavy. "I cannot tell you how sorry I am for what they did to you."

"Yeah, well, maybe we're even now." I peer into the shadows, hoping to catch a better glimpse of Daiyna. "I probably had it coming."

A quiet curse erupts from the darkness behind Luther, but he continues, uninterrupted, "And those...canisters you were carrying—"

"Right." I suddenly feel overwhelmed by how much I have to tell them.

"They're ours." Daiyna steps into the light, and she's a vision of beauty. No longer the bald, stubble-headed woman she was before. Now thick, dark hair drapes her face like velvet curtains. Thanks to the healing salve on my invisible skin, she's able to see me with her night-vision, and she stares me down. There's a hard look in her eyes, daring me to contradict her. "Created in Eden. From what they took out of us."

I sniff. Nod. "Yeah."

Samson curses under his breath. Luther closes his eyes for a moment. The news doesn't seem to come as a complete shock. More like an anticipated fear-become-reality.

"So what do you expect us to do with them?" Daiyna demands.

13. MARGO

18 MONTHS AFTER ALL-CLEAR

I cower in my seat, curled into a fetal position, covering my head as an unrelenting barrage of bullets plows into the Hummer from all sides. The hostiles have the vehicle surrounded, and there seems to be no end to their ammunition. They're not mutos, that much is clear. They move with the superhuman speed and agility of Luther's friend Milton. Large men, well-built, their jaws set with a grim determination.

When it becomes clear their rounds won't be able to puncture the vehicle's exterior, one of the men shouts for his comrades to aim for the tires.

I curse, fists clenched as the vehicle rocks wildly, then hits the ground on its underbelly.

"What was that?" Jamison's voice demands from my collar.

"They shot out the tires." *I'm stuck out here.* "We're not going anywhere."

There won't be a way to transport the UW personnel back to Eden now. Willard is going to have to wait for the next envoy. By the looks of this crew—two wounded severely and another low on oxygen—they don't have long to live. Why haven't these hostiles killed them already?

"Are you in immediate danger?" Jamison sounds concerned.

"Don't even think of sending our last Hummer," I warn.

"Hadn't crossed our minds," Perch sneers, commandeering the line. "I'm thinking we'll use you as an old-fashioned suicide bomber. That collar you're wearing packs a real wallop. Are those hostiles still within five meters of the vehicle?"

Jamison curses. "Margo, that's not going to happen."

I bite my lip. The cacophony outside is deafening, like fireworks going off at close range. They're determined to break through the armored hull, no matter how long it takes.

"How many of them would you be able to immobilize?" I ask.

"Immobilize nothing. They'll be blown to pieces." Perch chuckles. "And so will you."

"Stay the hell off my line," Jamison says gruffly. "Margo, Perch has no control over your collar. I'm not letting anything happen to you."

I appreciate the sentiment, but Perch has Jamison beat by at least a hundred pounds of fat and muscle. If the beast so desires, he could easily overpower the well-meaning Jamison at any moment. He already has once before, sending a jolt of electricity through my system that felt strong enough to stop my heart.

"Sit tight, and we'll try to get back in touch with Captain Mutegi. If he gets approval to send in a chopper, I'll make sure you're on it."

These hostiles would blow a helicopter out of the sky. I part my lips to tell him as much when a sudden gust of gale-force wind kicks up outside, colliding with the Hummer and skidding it sideways across the hard-packed earth.

I risk a glance out the window and can only stare.

What appears to be a hurricane of dust and sand whips around the vehicle, keeping me in its calm center. Screaming, the hostiles are forcibly disarmed by the power of the wind and thrown to the ground. A few struggle to their feet only to be knocked down again, grimacing in the sandstorm and shouting at one another over the roar. I cannot make out their words, but it's clear they are terrified.

Have they experienced this bizarre, unnatural phenomenon before?

One of their leaders, a man who carries blades strapped across his leather-clad chest, gives a signal, and the men vanish, running faster than humanly possible. One moment they're crouching low, digging their fingers into the cracked earth and holding on for their lives. The next moment, they're gone in blurs of speed, leaving their weapons scattered across the ground.

That's when the strangest thing happens: from out of the whirlwind steps the figure of a man. As the dust settles, he says something to the UW personnel rising cautiously to their feet. Then he turns to face my vehicle, and I recognize him instantly.

There is only one among us who can move that fast, able to create quite the dust devil and make the hostiles look like slugs in comparison.

By all appearances, Milton has gotten faster over the past months.

"What is it? What do you see?" Jamison's voice demands as silence descends on the scene. Only my eyes peek out the side window. I'll have to sit upright for the camera on my collar to give him a full view.

"I don't know." I don't move.

"Give us a better angle."

Milton approaches. He removes his dust-caked goggles and unwraps the sandcloth from his face. Behind him, the UW people struggle to their feet, two of them bleeding—one from his arm, the other from her leg wound. They collect as many fallen weapons as they can carry.

"Up a little higher," Jamison says.

The windows are tinted black. Milton can't see me.

"They're all gone..." I murmur.

"What?" Perch is back on comms. "How the hell—?"

"Some kind of freak sandstorm. It came without warning, drove off the hostiles." I bite my lip for a moment. "But the UW crew appears to be fine, more or less. Two are injured."

"What are you waiting for? Haul your ass out there and start administering some first aid. Mutegi won't be happy if he hears you let his people bleed out."

A knock pounds against my window, knuckles rapping twice. Then Milton's voice: "Hey-uh, open up."

"Go ahead, Margo," Jamison says on the comm. "Get everybody inside the Hummer, and wait it out. You'll be safe in there while we send for help."

"Hello?" Milton knocks again.

What will Perch and Jamison do when they see him? Blow my collar then and there, just to eliminate him? They can't be that stupid. The UW personnel are well within the kill zone now, staggering toward my dilapidated vehicle in their heavy hazard suits. But the men of Eden hate Milton with a vengeance. He made them all look like fools when he escaped all those months ago, moving so fast they were frozen in their boots, powerless to stop him as he disarmed them, knocked them out, and piled them on top of each other like rag dolls. Perch in particular would do anything to wipe Milton off the face of the earth, once and for all.

And if he were to find out that Milton has actually become *faster*—

"C'mon, open up. We've got wounded out here," Milton says.

"That could be their team leader, Margo. His name is—" Jamison pauses, probably to consult his notes. Of course he wouldn't recognize Milton's voice. "Sergeant James Bishop, United World marines. A good soldier with a clean record. A family man, looks like. I know you've been through a lot, and I know you're afraid, but this man is not dangerous."

"Open the damn door!" Perch bellows in the background.

I curse him silently and reach for the manual release lever. With a whir, the internal mechanism unlocks the door, and it drifts upward. Milton ducks under, extending his hand to me. Fortunately for him, he isn't more than a dark silhouette against moonlight in the collar-cam's eye. But it's clear he wears no hazard suit.

"Who the hell—?" Perch demands.

"Hey!" Milton grins at me. "I remember you."

I try swallowing the lump clogging my throat and reach cautiously for his outstretched hand. He notices my collar, and his smile fades.

"They've got you wearing one of those again?" He frowns.

"Margo, who is this man?" Jamison says in alarm.

"I'll tell you who he is!" Perch lapses into obscenities. "He's one of those sand freaks—the fast one!"

"I'm sorry," I tell Milton. My muscles tense, waiting for the inevitable blast that will blow us all away in bloody pieces.

Will we feel anything? Or will it happen too fast?

He shrugs. Then, in a flash, he grabs my collar and breaks it off my neck. Throwing it to the ground, he crushes it beneath the sole of his boot. All in the span of a split-second.

"Better now?" His boyish grin returns.

I stare at him with my hand gingerly touching my throat. It feels naked, exposed. "You've gotten stronger, as well," is all I can think to say.

"I guess." He regards the broken steel band for a moment, watching the red pinpoint of light fade out as the signal with Eden is lost. "You've got a medkit in there, I hope."

"Yes—of course." I pop open the passenger dashboard compartment and retrieve two plastic white boxes with red crosses on them.

"Looks like a couple of these people are hurt pretty bad."

"I'll see what I can do." I climb out of the vehicle.

"I don't know how much you'll be able to help, dressed the way they are." He gestures at their bulky suits and helmets.

"They fear our air." I walk past him.

He follows me as I approach the first member of the UW team, a well-built man with grey stubble along his jawline and a clear face shield on his helmet. Unlike the others, there are no lights from a functioning heads-up display. The man's unguarded wonder is plain to see as he stares first at Milton, then me. He nudges the short, stocky member of his team, the one with a wounded arm, who speaks up.

"You're from Eden?" he says.

"She is." Milton points. "I'm not."

"You…" The man clears his throat, but no words emerge.

"I can fly." Milton shrugs. "Weird, right?"

The man nods, but nothing registers in his eyes. His mind has no frame of reference to make sense of recent events. A dust storm drove away a score of heavily armed hostiles, and Milton—wearing no protective suit or breathing apparatus—descended from the whirlwind, stepping out of it as one would have a carriage to the cobblestone streets of 19th century London. It is too incredible to be believed, even though he saw it with his own eyes.

"The air—you're able to breathe it…just fine?" An older man in another hazard suit approaches me. "You see this, Sergeant? It's remarkable!"

"Which one of you is in charge here?" I don't wait for an answer, moving between the men as they turn to face me. I make straight for the injured woman, unsure what good I will be able to do. She and the short fellow were both cut with a blade of some sort. Apparently, there are vulnerable spots in their armored suits. The designers hadn't expected them to go up against sword-wielding desert warriors.

The man with the malfunctioning HUD pats his chest plate, but it's the short one who speaks for him again, "This is Sergeant James Bishop, ma'am. United World Marines. His helmet's on the fritz, so I'm acting as translator. Name's Granger."

"Margo." I look Bishop over. How much oxygen remains in his suit? He's doing a good job at hiding it, but he is frightened, as any man would be in a similar situation. I don't have to be a telepath to notice. But his fear has nothing to do with his O2 levels or the armed hostiles who are sure to return in greater numbers. He's terrified of one thing only: not being allowed to return home.

"We were hoping Eden would send more than—"

"One woman?" I glance back at Granger as I kneel beside the woman on the ground. She's lost plenty of blood, but there is no way her femoral artery was pierced at this angle.

"I'm sure they could've spared a few more personnel."

"Not on the surface." I shake my head. "The men of Eden refuse to breathe the air. Something you have in common."

Bishop's worried gaze focuses on his crewmate's suit at the site of the puncture.

"This suit no longer serves any purpose—other than impeding the care she needs." I make eye contact with the tall woman and keep my tone matter-of-fact. She stares unblinking from behind her face shield. "If you would like me to save your life, it will have to come off."

The woman appears to have frozen. When she eventually speaks, her voice is a choked whisper. "Will it be a life worth saving?"

Granger takes a knee beside her. "Hey now. It won't be all bad. I'm in the same boat you are, remember. Hell, we might get some cool mutant superpowers or something. Did you get a load of this guy?" He nods toward Milton.

"Or we'll end up like those creatures we found," the woman retorts.

Milton clears his throat. "Don't worry about that. You guys are under the spirits' protection. Just let Margo do her thing, and you'll be fine. I promise."

"Spirits?" The older man steps toward Milton with keen interest. "Did I hear you correctly, young man?"

"Yeah—the spirits of the earth." Milton nods as if it's common knowledge. "You know, from all the animals that were blown up on D-Day."

The old man blinks, lips parted for words that never make an appearance. He half-turns toward Sergeant Bishop, but his eyes are still fixed on Milton like he's some sort of science experiment gone awry. "You hear that, Sergeant? Not even a quarter century has passed…and already a primitive religious structure has sprung forth among the survivors. How incredible!"

Bishop dismisses him to assist the wounded. He watches as the older man shuffles off, muttering to himself, before he turns his attention fully on Milton.

"If you're not from Eden, then what are you doing out here?" Granger asks.

"That's a long story, and we don't have a lot of time. Like I said, Cain's boys frighten easily—they're a real superstitious bunch—but they'll be back." Milton beckons to Bishop as he surveys the Hummer's tires. "How about you lend me a hand, and we'll get this thing back in order? Those bastards sure did give it the works."

Bishop nods and approaches the vehicle.

Milton kicks at what remains of the right rear tire. "Grew up in a trade sector, so I know my way around the parts of almost anything. Putting them all together, though? That's beyond my job description." He drops to one knee and runs his gloved hand across the flabby tread, sliding toward the hub. "With InstaGoo, anything's possible!" He half-grins at the sergeant. "Trade sector humor," he explains.

"You're a survivor. From which sector?" Granger asks.

"Good ol' 43." Then he mutters, "There's got to be a repair kit inside…" He climbs into the passenger side.

"Try the rear compartment," I call, knowing what he's up to without looking. His thoughts are loud enough to be my own.

"Thanks." He rummages around.

My hands pause for a moment as I work to help the stoic UW woman out of her hazard suit. Meanwhile, I project my mind outward in a single pulse of extra-sensory perception, and my efforts do not go unrewarded. Almost immediately, the thoughts of the young female, offspring of Luther and Daiyna, connect with my own. The little one seems confused but unharmed, unable to understand where I've been all this time.

A sense of impending danger comes through our link, along with visceral fear.

I blink, returning my focus to the woman's suit. I will have to reconnect with the young one at the next opportunity, whenever that is. For now, it's enough to know she is safe—and the male, as well. They are both all right despite a danger which, strangely enough, does not seem to be directed toward them. I am glad of that.

But what about Tucker? Is he still with them?

I glance back at Milton as he clambers into the back of the vehicle. Should I probe his mind for answers?

"I do not require your help," the UW woman snaps at her short crewmate.

"Hate to break it to you, but you're leaking like a sieve here." Granger, despite his own injury, is doing all he can to assist—perhaps a little too eagerly.

"You're no better off yourself." The older man reaches for the short fellow's bleeding arm. "Dr. Jefferson Harris, ma'am." He extends his gloved hand.

I grasp it briefly and return to the woman's stubborn suit before realizing: "Dr. Harris...I read your work. All of it—in the bunker." I blink up at him.

Harris is obviously pleased with his living-legend status. "Glad they gave you kids some adequate reading material while you were down there. Although, of course, most of it was outdated halfway through your internment." He chuckles dryly. "Couldn't be helped, I suppose. All that concrete made it impossible for wireless transfer."

"Your work on genetics and artificial insemination—your case studies—" I could go on.

"Fascinating, I'm sure," the injured woman interjects with a pained gasp. "But if you're going to expose me to the elements, then hadn't we better get on with it?" She sounds resigned to her fate.

"Isn't there some way we could portion off the suit at the site of the injury?" Harris suggests. "There's really no need to remove the entire thing, is there?"

"I'm sorry, Doctor. Her air supply was compromised as soon as the puncture was made."

"Damned design flaw," Harris mutters.

"After I treat the wound, we need to get her into the vehicle where it's warm, let her rest. She could go into shock at any moment."

"They will be back..." The injured woman glances westward into the night.

"Captain's working on that with the superhero." Granger lets out a low whistle. "Did you see that, Doc? The way he came out of the air? Holy crap!"

"Your suit should come off as well," Harris tells him, surveying his injury. "There's no way to get at it with this armor in the way."

"What the hell, go ahead and pry me out. Guess we'll be your guinea pigs. You can monitor what happens to us and publish your findings." Granger gives me a sidelong glance. "Say, what's your superpower, ma'am?"

I ignore him as I strain against the woman's suit with very little help from her; she is too weak to lend much of a hand. The upper portion comes off like pieces of shell from a beetle's back, revealing a white, skin-tight bodysuit the woman wears underneath.

"Come now, as one doctor to another." Harris begins to remove Granger's suit in like manner. "Why were you the only member of Eden sent out to meet us? And how did this flying superhuman know exactly where to find you?" He pauses. "Could it be that you share some sort of advanced telepathic ability?"

Instead of answering, I project an intense burst of fear into his mind that the hostiles are returning at this very moment—skimming across the sand in blurs of speed.

"We must hurry." The good doctor doubles his efforts.

Granger winces and groans at the lack of any bedside manner whatsoever, but he does what he can to help the process with his functional arm.

I glance at Milton and Bishop. They have located the repair kit and are jacking up one of the front wheel wells to remove the deflated tire. With Milton's speed, they are sure to be done in a matter of minutes.

But how much time do we have before the hostiles return?

I project my mind westward, searching for any signs of life, expecting to find hundreds of them surging this way. But instead I find only one. That's strange enough, but what makes it even more perplexing: the lone figure is being watched by someone with telepathic abilities equal to or greater than my own.

I draw back into myself, hopefully before I'm detected, as I work the suit free of the injured woman's legs. Who is that solitary figure stumbling through the night, filled with fear and despair? Who watches over him?

Harris has removed the upper torso of Granger's suit, freeing both arms. He applies the healing salve from my medkit. "I'd like to say we've come up with something better in the past twenty years, but honestly, nothing beats this gel in a pinch. It guards against infection while regenerating cellular activity, providing a secondary layer of skin and stimulating renewed tissue growth. Rather a genius creation, I must say."

"Doctor, in case I'm mistaken, weren't you the one who invented it?"

Harris grins broadly at me. "Why yes, of course. Just testing your memory, that's all. Had to make sure your bunker database was up to snuff."

"Damn, it burns!" Granger complains. Already his bleeding has stopped due to the biogel, which seems to glow faintly—an amber luminescence on his arm, surrounding his elbow like a cast.

"That means it's doing its job." Harris glances at me. "Could you use a hand?"

I nod. "Please take all of the weapons to the Hummer. Once the tires are back in working order, we'll need to leave quickly."

The doctor appears flustered for a moment. I declined the assistance of an exalted man of medicine?

"Very well." He stalks away in his clumsy suit with Granger at his heels.

"He doesn't think much of himself," the injured woman says with a raised eyebrow. Then she winces as I apply gobs of the healing salve to her leg. She's lucky, despite her wound. A little higher and the blade would have severed her hamstring.

"So I've noticed." I ease off before applying more of the gel. "But it's not every day you meet a living legend in your field."

"You are a doctor, then."

"Nuclear engineer." I shrug. "But I'm the only one in Eden who took any medical courses while we were in the bunker." *The only one still alive, anyway.* "So I'm the only doctor they've got."

"You're doing a fine job." She pauses. "What is your name?"

"Margo." I keep my eyes on my work.

"Sinclair," the woman replies. "Elaine."

"Let's get you on your feet, Elaine. You must be freezing."

We approach the Hummer. I have both arms around the woman, helping her make every step. Milton and the sergeant have already succeeded in reinflating the two front tires. The air pressure appears to be holding—only they're not filling the tires with air. Instead, it's some kind of expanding foam from a large aerosol can that seals punctures from the inside and turns into a gas after a few seconds, filling each tire completely.

"Don't know why the Edenites didn't use this stuff to begin with." Milton grunts, working with the sergeant to remove a deflated rear tire. "As long as this goo-gas is inside, any additional punctures will be resealed immediately. Just in case those trigger-happy goons decide to have another go at it."

Bishop knocks a gloved fist against the vehicle's scarred black hull to show that the armor plating is holding up fine.

I can't tell how much air remains in his O2 reserves, but his helmet is close to shattering. So far, it has not been completely compromised, but it won't take much to break what remains of the cracked polymer, fragile as a damaged eggshell.

Harris and Granger each carry an armload of weapons to the vehicle. The stocky fellow's injury is already on the mend.

My mind wanders as we wait for Milton and the sergeant to finish their work. Small talk is attempted, then abandoned to the cold silence of the night. No one brings up the most important question: Where will we go once the vehicle is up and running?

I doubt that Milton intervened just so we could head back to Eden. If my plan was carried out successfully, then Luther's people know their children are to be used as bargaining chips to get Willard and his pals off this continent. Luther would have sent Milton to intercept the UW team and bring them to him, to convince them that these children are as *special* as their parents.

They will not be welcome in a world where such differences are not tolerated.

But are the little ones *special*? I have to assume so. How else have I been able to communicate with them telepathically? The female, in particular, seems to have an ability that will no doubt rival my own someday.

"How soon will I know?" Elaine asks me quietly. Unlike Granger, she opted to keep her helmet on until the battery runs out—perhaps to stay in communication with Sergeant Bishop on internal comms. But without her suit, she is breathing our air. "That I've been...changed?"

"It depends on how much of the dust has been absorbed into your system." I pause. "Before it became clear that my neurological pathways were altered, I'd been out on the surface multiple times with scouting parties, breathing in the air. Our bunker commander, Arthur Willard, made us promise to wear oxygen masks. He was paranoid that there was some kind of toxin in the dust and ash, residue from the blast zones. He ended up being right about that."

The woman nods. "So it will happen...whenever it happens."

There's no point in sugarcoating the matter. "It could be days—weeks even, before you notice anything out of the ordinary." I glance back at the vehicle to find only one rear tire in need of repair. They are making good time.

"Was he correct about you?" The woman keeps her voice low. "The doctor?"

"A lucky guess," I admit. It's good to have my ability back, thanks to Milton snapping that shock collar off my neck.

Elaine stares at me in unguarded amazement. "Then you know what I'm thinking before—"

"—you even put it into words? Yes." I don't feel comfortable under this woman's microscope. There are more important matters at hand.

Harris notices the two of us speaking in hushed tones. "So, tell me about the fetuses down in that *Eden* of yours. I assume you're the one in charge of monitoring their growth and development?" He ignores Elaine, turning his full attention on me. "How are they progressing?"

I face him as Milton and the sergeant fill the last tire. Unfortunately, this is the only time during the repair work when Milton can't use his high-speed abilities; he has to wait for the foam to work its magic. It's unclear how much of the substance remains in that can.

"They are developing within expected parameters," I answer.

He laughs at that. "Details, you must give me details. We're talking about the last best hope for humankind here. I've been in the dark until just recently, and I still have no idea how many there are, what the gender ratio is, how close to term they are, what sort of arrangements have been made to facilitate their artificial births..." He shakes his head and closes his eyes briefly, holding up a hand. "Forgive me. I sound like a frantic mother."

"It's understandable, Dr. Harris. It seems that one thing after another is keeping you from your mission."

"You're damned right. First those deformed hostiles who blew us out of the sky, then that second variety who wanted to remove our suits and drag us to their leader—some *Lord Cain* person..."

I frown at the name. I have never heard it before, and yet instantly, an awareness grips me that I am being watched—all of us are. Somehow, I recognize the disembodied sentience as the same that was watching over that solitary figure languishing eastward through the night.

Cain is coming for you.

The words resonate in my mind. Someone is projecting thoughts into my consciousness that are not my own. It's not like the two-way communication I share with the little female; this is one-sided, from a completely unknown source. Whether benevolent or malevolent, I cannot tell. As Dr. Harris continues to ramble, half the time making demands, half the time apologizing for himself, I turn inward to focus on these thoughts and their source:

Cain will destroy you. It is the will of Gaia, Mother of the Earth, whom he serves with his whole heart. She has blessed us with all manner of supernatural gifts, and she demands only our love and obedience in return. A brief pause. *Cain loves her more than he loves me. He despises me now, even as I bear his child.*

I blink, unable to believe what I'm hearing. *Who are you?* I project with no clear target in mind.

The thoughts continue uninterrupted, surging in a torrent: *You will die, unless you do as I say. As powerful and omnipotent as Gaia pretends to be, she cannot be in all places at once. So she does not know that I speak to you now, even as she and my husband plot to overthrow the United World. He forgets, you see, that I know his thoughts. We are much alike, you and I. Whoever you are...*

And whoever you are, I return.

Cain uses me to see into the distance. Without me, he is blind. His men have returned, telling him of a vengeful demon, an evil spirit incarnate who thwarted his plans to retrieve the United World scouts. He now tries to convince them that Gaia is stronger than their fears, and he will send them emboldened, and in greater numbers, after you. But he will not go with them. Instead, he will return to me in this bed we share, and we will link our bodies and our minds. We will watch your slaughter as if we are standing in the distance.

"Why tell me this?" I murmur aloud before realizing I've done so.

"How's that?" Harris looks perturbed by my interruption as he continues to spout off.

But you can help me, the pregnant woman's thoughts continue. *Or rather, you can help someone I love. You have seen him already, stumbling through the darkness. His name is Lemuel, and he is my lover, my own, whom I share with no one. Cain banished him into the dead of night. He has nowhere to go. When the sun rises, the goblyns will tear him asunder and devour his flesh.*

Goblyns. Daemons. Mutos. Every enclave on this continent seems to have a pet name for the monstrosities.

Please, go to him. You know where he is; you saw it. Tell him Victoria sent you, and he will trust you.

I frown. This is not part of the plan. There is so much more at stake than—

Do this for me, and I will lead Cain's men off course. They will not find you. I am their eyes, and I will choose to look elsewhere. When Cain discovers that I have deceived him and sent his men in the wrong direction, there will be hell to pay. But my Lemuel will be safe. There is one last pause in the transmission. *I am watching you. Save his life, or lose your own. I leave the choice to you.*

I sway, suddenly unsteady on my feet as the mental link breaks and the presence in my mind departs. Harris braces my shoulder with his gloved hand.

"Forgive me. You've suffered a great ordeal coming out here. We all have," he says. "I'm sure I can wait until we arrive in Eden to have all of my questions—"

"We're not going to Eden." The thought escapes my lips, and

on its tail comes the sudden awareness of a mass of predators headed our way. I jerk my head westward, peering into the dark with the light of my extrasensory perception. The superhuman hostiles have doubled in number. "They will be here in a matter of minutes."

Did Victoria lie to me? Has she already sent the warriors straight to their prey? Or are they merely retracing their own route of retreat from earlier?

"Good to go!" Milton calls from the vehicle's rear. The sergeant nods in agreement.

The battle-scarred Hummer now sits on four tires strong enough to hold its weight. I beckon to the UW personnel to follow as I dash to the driver's side.

"Luther wants to see them." Milton holds my door open. "Before they go to Eden."

"I know. But I have to make a stop first." I help Elaine into the backseat, followed by Granger. The sergeant and Dr. Harris load the weapons they collected into the rear hatch.

"Want me to run some interference?" Milton glances west.

"You've endangered yourself enough for one night. Go back to your people and tell them we will be there shortly." I give his shoulder a gentle push. "Go on now."

Elaine speaks up, "Where are you planning to take us, exactly?"

"Do what you gotta do." Milton shuts the door after me. "I will too."

I grip the wheel and rev the engine, looking into the rearview at the pair seated behind me, shivering in their thermal bodysuits. "I'm sure you're both cold—"

"Freezing," Granger says, "but you haven't answered the lady's question."

"I don't—"

"You can't expect us to play dumb here. We're toast, and we know it. We've tasted of your forbidden fruit, and the UW won't want us back inside Eurasia now. Neither will your friends in

Eden. We're mutants in the making, right?" He clears his throat. "So where can people like us get a bite to eat around here?"

I almost smile at his devil-may-care attitude—until I see movement on the horizon less than a kilometer away, figures running with plumes of dust sky-rocketing into the moonlight behind them.

14. BISHOP

18 MONTHS AFTER ALL-CLEAR

Harris and I throw ourselves into the rear compartment of the Hummer, rifles and bladed weapons clattering against the armored plating on our hazard suits. The rear hatch closes automatically, and Margo guns it, sending sand and gravel pinging upward in our wake. The flying man, Milton, takes to the sky—but not to escape the situation. Instead, he tears straight toward the hostiles at an angle that sends a wall of ash and dust upward behind him, concealing our vehicle's escape route.

Except Margo hasn't altered course. The vehicle is heading west, following Milton.

"Turn us around, ma'am," I holler, struggling against my suit, fighting the knees to bend so my boots can brace against the rear hatch. The doctor and I jostle around like unsorted luggage. "We're going the wrong way!"

She can't hear me. *Damn helmet!*

"She's not taking us to Eden," Harris says, his tone wary.

I swivel to stare him down. "Where then?"

The doctor shakes his head.

"I believe she knows what she's doing, Sergeant." Sinclair turns in her seat to face me. "Saving our lives appears to be her main objective at the moment."

"By taking us to the enemy?"

Harris curses. "Sinclair, you're in no condition to know what the hell is going on."

"Meaning?" She raises an eyebrow.

"You're one of *them*," the good doctor hisses, his gloved hand pointing at the driver and then upward, referring to the flying mutant above. "You've got us outnumbered now. The sergeant and I are at your mercy!"

"Can it," I order. "Any more talk like that, I'll relieve you of duty."

"You haven't the authority—" Harris sputters, wide-eyed.

"Keep your head on straight, Doctor." I face Sinclair. "Where is she taking us?" She shakes her head. No idea. "Push comes to shove, we're commandeering this vehicle. You got me?"

Sinclair warns, "Careful, Sergeant. She knows your thoughts."

I look up to find the driver's dark eyes on me in the rearview mirror. Not creepy at all.

"Please, tell us where we're going," Harris demands.

Margo remains silent. Then with her eyes darting between the mirror and the uneven, whitewashed moonscape ahead, she says, "We're picking up someone who needs our help. Then we'll find cover until morning."

"You're taking us straight into harm's way!" Harris shouts.

My gloved hand falls flat against his face shield, quieting him for the moment.

"Ma'am, can you hear me?" I test the waters. If it's true that she's a telepath, then she doesn't have to be on our comms, and my soundproof helmet won't be an issue.

"Yes."

"Alright then. It's not as though we don't have cause for concern here. Those men coming for us—they're not *human*."

"I'll try not to take that personally, Sergeant." Margo whips the wheel expertly around an outcropping of rock, and the vehicle pitches sideways. "Rest assured, we're not in this alone."

"The flying man? They'll shoot him out of the sky. He caught them by surprise the last time. They'll be gunning for him now." I pause. "Unless he's bulletproof."

"Not that I know of," Margo says. "But he's not the help I was referring to."

I cough. The air in my helmet is getting thin; I can taste the difference. *Not now!* I cough again, my throat tightening, burning.

"Sergeant?" Harris faces me as my arms drop like dead weight.

"His oxygen is depleted," Margo says. "You'll have to swap out the O2 supply. Quickly."

Harris looks aghast. It wouldn't be from his suit, that much is clear. He turns to the pair in the backseat, both in their thermals. "Where are your suits?"

"Left 'em behind," Granger says. He frowns at me and takes a deep breath of the ambient air. "Really, Captain, it ain't that bad. I don't feel any different, honest to God."

"Check the emergency compartment in the rear," Margo says. "There should be a breather or two in there."

Harris scrambles to pop open the compartment. Three breathing apparatuses hang on hooks inside. "This is not a sealed environment, Sergeant. You will need to take one deep breath before I disconnect your helmet and affix this breather to your face. Do you understand?"

I choke but nod, unsure there's enough oxygen left for a deep breath. I start fumbling with my helmet clamps, prepared to remove the cracked polymer. In my mind, all I see are the faces of my wife and children. If this doesn't work, if I become infected in the process, I will never see them again. The UW authorities will never allow me to step inside Eurasia.

But if I suffocate here, the end result will be the same.

My gloved fingers move with clumsy trepidation, unable to function correctly. This is fear—an old enemy I thought I beat into submission long ago—rearing its wicked head.

"Help me," Harris barks at Granger. "We don't have much time."

Granger turns around in his seat to lend a hand. Sinclair moves to join them. The Hummer hits a deep rut and rocks at an awkward angle, throwing them off-target. Margo casts an apology over her shoulder.

A hermetically sealed interior with its own air supply would be ideal right now, but we'll have to make do.

"Ready," Harris says.

I'm about as ready as I'll ever be, and barely conscious. Both Granger and Sinclair are there to lend my spastic fingers assistance.

"On three—"

"You mean on it, or right before?" Granger frowns. "One, two, *three*—or one, two, then three?"

"*Now*," Sinclair says, and they lift the cracked helmet off me.

The breather slips over my nose and mouth, guided by the doctor's steady hands. I grit my teeth, grimacing as my lungs cling to the last iota of air I was able to suck out of my depleted oxygen supply. My body lurches, fighting for breath.

Harris curses suddenly. The breather is in place, but the helmet's docking clamps are not aligned properly as it slides back down over my head. "We can't start the flow of oxygen until these clamps are fastened tight!"

I fight the panic surging within me. I'm going to suffocate with a breather ready to go. So close, yet so far.

I grapple with the rim of my helmet, fighting to push it away—an irrational response. On some level, my body must know there's breathable air inside the vehicle, and its quality doesn't matter right now. My mind knows better, however, and I don't retaliate when Harris and Granger swat my hands out of the way.

I'm shaking. The fear is winning.

Then a voice enters the maelstrom of my mind, and I know exactly where it comes from. I stare into the rearview mirror with wide, bloodshot eyes.

I know you're afraid, Sergeant, Margo says, mind-to-mind. *They have taken your family from you, and you can't bear the thought of never seeing them again.*

How is this possible? I freeze. *Have I already been changed? Am I like you now?*

Not to worry. Then she says out loud, "Try to relax. Your people are taking care of you."

Despite all evidence to the contrary, I feel no reason to be afraid. An overwhelming sense of calm sweeps over me instead, making me feel light-headed—or that could be due to hypoxia.

From you? My eyes remain fixed on the rearview. Margo nods in response, returning her gaze to the terrain ahead. She's filled me with a sense of peace. Amazing. Indescribable. Tears burn my eyes and a couple spill out, streaking my face.

Granger slaps the side of my helmet. "Breathe, dammit!"

They've clamped it back into place and activated the breather now that it's housed inside. I gulp down the air, inhaling oxygen deep into my lungs, coughing until my breathing settles into a steady rhythm.

"Thanks," I rasp, glancing at each of them in turn. "I owe you." I squeeze Granger's shoulder.

"Hey, we've gotta keep our fearless leader in one piece, don't we?"

"Are the hostiles in pursuit?"

"They are not following us, Sergeant," Margo reports. "For the moment, they don't appear to know where we are."

"They'll find our tracks in no time," Harris grumbles, always the optimist.

"Don't think so, Doc." Granger glances outside and jerks a thumb back toward the ground behind us. "That guy's covering our trail."

I swivel to look out the rear window. Sure enough, Milton is sweeping side to side through the air, whipping up the sand in our wake.

"That'll buy us some time," I allow. "But you still haven't told us where we're going."

Margo nods. "We're here."

The Hummer skids to an abrupt halt, throwing its passengers forward. I strain to see where we are, but thick clouds of dust hover outside, obscuring my view.

Harris gives the voice command "Life signs," and instantly his face shield lights up with a thermal image of a lone figure standing stock-still twenty meters ahead of us, out of the headlights' range. "Who the hell is that?"

I watch Margo. She sits as if in a trance, her hands loose on the steering wheel as she stares straight ahead. The engine idles.

"I don't like this one bit," Harris mutters. "It's another one of them—dressed just like those superhumans we're trying to escape!"

"Our numbers keep growing, don't they Doc?" Granger smirks at him. "Sure you don't want to come over to the winning team? The air's great." He inhales deeply.

"Cut the chatter." I watch as Milton touches down in the glow of our headlights. Removing his dust-covered goggles, he glances over his shoulder at Margo behind the windshield and nods with some sort of unspoken understanding between them.

"Now what's he doing?" Harris demands. "You had better do something about this, Sergeant. The situation is gravely out of hand."

Milton approaches the stranger with hands out to the sides in an unthreatening posture, taking slow, deliberate steps.

"He's armed." Harris's HUD has already cataloged the stranger's array of weapons, similar in variety to the hostiles we encountered earlier.

"So what? Our guy's faster than a bullet, right?" Granger grins.

The stranger stumbles backward, away from Milton, smaller in frame and nearly overcome with exhaustion by the looks of him. His hands don't go to his weapons. He doesn't appear to feel threatened by the situation, just wary.

"What are they saying?" There must be a setting on a functional helmet that can pinpoint and receive distant audio signatures.

"He's young, maybe twenty. Milton is doing his best to convince him we are his friends, that we're here to help him." Harris pauses, glancing at the silent woman in the driver's seat. "I cannot be certain, but it appears that Margo may be speaking through Milton. He's telling the young man we've been sent by someone named Victoria, that we're here to help him, that he can trust us. But this is *not* our mission." Harris struggles against the pile of weapons, turning around to kick against the rear hatch. "Get that damned door open! If you won't put a stop to this, Sergeant, then I—"

"Stand down," I order. "You're not going anywhere."

"You're through giving me orders, Bishop. It's clear that you're unfit for duty, so as ranking medical officer, I hereby relieve you of command!"

Margo glances into the rearview. She focuses her gaze on the emotional man writhing like a toddler in the throes of a mean temper tantrum. "Dr. Harris, I can see you're concerned. You don't understand what's going on—"

"Damned right! I demand an explanation."

She pauses before continuing, "This young man has been exiled by his people—the same people we're doing our best to avoid. He has no one to help him out here, and without us, he is sure to die."

"He's not our concern!"

"We need every ally we can get," I argue.

"The enemy of our enemy is our friend?" Sinclair suggests.

Something like that.

"They're shaking hands," Granger observes as Milton and the youth step into the headlights' glare. "That's gotta be good, right?"

Judging by the young guy's body language, he doesn't fully trust Milton or the idling vehicle full of strangers, spewing exhaust into the frosty moonlight. But his options are limited.

Unafraid, he carries himself with the confidence of a man who's won his share of fights.

Milton faces the windshield, squinting and raising a hand to shield his eyes. He gives Margo a thumbs-up.

"He should be disarmed immediately," Harris grabs one of the assault rifles beside him and holds it ready.

While his attention is elsewhere, I reach over nonchalantly and flip on the weapon's safety. The last thing we need is the good doctor killing one of us by accident. Or intentionally.

Margo hits the release lever on her door and steps outside. "Lemuel?" Her tone is friendly, inviting.

The fellow perks up at the sound of his name. How'd she know it? He's got a tall, solid frame he'll grow into someday. I can't help but think of my own Emmanuel and the man he will grow up to be. I hope I'm there to see it.

I hope we're not wasting precious time here.

"Will you come with us?" Margo extends a hand toward him. "Victoria sent us to find you."

"If he blows her head off, we're screwed, Sergeant," Harris says on comms. "I don't know about you, but I have no idea how to drive one of these old gas guzzlers."

"Cool it, Doc. That's your final warning."

"Victoria?" Lemuel says in a guarded tone.

"Yes," Margo answers. "She is worried. She...does not approve of how your Lord Cain treated you."

"He's not my lord." The youth draws himself up to his fullest height. "I'm my own man."

Granger chuckles to himself. "I think I like this kid."

"He certainly is sure of himself," Sinclair allows.

"You're welcome to join us, but the choice is yours, of course," Margo says.

He thinks for a moment. "You got any food?"

"If you like protein packs, we've got plenty where we're headed," Milton says.

"Hallelujah!" Granger can't contain his excitement. His stomach growls as if on cue.

Lemuel's bony shoulders shift upward and drop. "I could probably eat a goblyn, I'm so hungry." He packed every weapon he could carry, but he didn't bring anything to eat? He must have left in a real hurry.

Margo resumes her position at the wheel as Lemuel tentatively climbs in beside her. Milton lingers at her door.

"If you've got everything under control here, I'll go ahead and let them know you're on your way." He looks eastward. "Another hour or so until dawn. You'll make it by first light."

Margo nods, revving the engine as Milton steps back and waves. Then with the greatest of ease, he takes to the sky. I won't be getting over that trick anytime soon. Lemuel cranes his neck to watch as Milton disappears into the night.

"Gaia has indeed blessed him," he murmurs, awestruck.

"Tell me about Gaia," Margo says. "Is she a member of your bunker?"

Lemuel frowns. "You don't know Gaia? How can that be?"

Harris looks ready to interrupt with something irate or belligerent, but I seize his weapon and pin him against the rear hatch, staring him down. The vehicle crosses a rough patch of terrain, rocking and lurching. No one seems to notice our commotion.

"We need to learn all that we can here, Doc," I tell him. "We're still on mission, make no mistake. But we're not running the show right now. We'll leave that to the folks busy saving our asses. So why don't you do your profession a service and start taking notes. Seems to me you've sure as hell forgotten what you were preaching earlier."

"That was before I knew they wanted to kill us!" Harris's eyes bulge.

"Observe now, report later. As soon as the opportunity arises, I'll let Mutegi know what's going on. Until then, we sit tight. Got it?"

Harris nods reluctantly. "Glad to see you back on track, Sergeant. I had my doubts."

I would have rather knocked him out cold. But the way things stand, I can only hope Harris will take it down a notch and pay close attention to what's going on.

"You're the United World scouts from the *Argonaus*." Lemuel turns in his seat to face Sinclair and Granger. "Cain said you would be coming."

"Tell us about him—your leader?" Margo focuses his attention on what we need to know. She's good about it, keeping that friendly, curious tone intact, the kind that inflates a young man's pride and makes him eager to share.

Her telepathic abilities might also be in play.

"Cain thinks he's Gaia's chosen one, just because he's the only person she speaks to," Lemuel says. "He's the biggest and the strongest, and he throws his weight around all the time."

"He's a bully," Margo observes.

"And he's got more wives than anybody—*four*. Can you believe that?"

"No, I—" She appears flustered for the first time during their interchange.

"He's got them all with child, even Victoria—his fourth wife. She isn't much older than me. Hell, we grew up together in the bunker!"

"They're able to reproduce," Harris whispers on comms, gripping my arm.

"You guys get in trouble or something?" Lemuel looks at me.

"They were in a hurry," Sinclair explains. "They didn't have time to find a seat."

Lemuel nods, assessing my threat level.

"That's our team leader and our doctor." Granger points at each of us in turn. "I'm the engineer on this expedition, and she's our science officer. We had one more, but we lost—"

"Do you have a designation, Lemuel?" Sinclair interjects. Best not to mention our weapons officer's demise.

"A rank or something, you mean?" He frowns. "No. We're not military."

"Yet they're armed to the teeth," Harris says on internal comms. "And notice he said *we*—he still identifies with the group that exiled him. That could pose a problem later on, should we cross paths with that hunting party."

"I'm a warrior. Staked thirty-four goblyns all by myself." Lemuel's chin rises with pride as he speaks. "I would've gotten my own wife next year, but Cain would have taken her for himself first. He does that, you know. He's the only one with any seed to sow."

"The alpha male," Harris comments.

"You and Victoria are close," Margo continues. "Will she leave Cain to join you?"

The youth shakes his head, eyes downcast. "Cain won't let her live, once she's had his baby." He faces Margo with sudden hope in his voice. "But he does need her, you know. She's his eyes and ears out here. She can send her mind long-distance. That's how she contacted you, right?" He watches Margo nod. "So you're like her, then. You have the gift of far-thought?"

Margo glances at me in the rearview before she replies, "I was able to hear her thoughts as if they were my own. She guided us to you."

Lemuel nods, his eyes distant. "Yeah, that's what she said." He gestures at the vehicle, changing the topic. "Somehow I don't think you're part of Luther's nomads. They don't have a single set of wheels to their name."

First Cain, now Luther—tribal leaders of some kind? And who is this Gaia the kid mentioned? Some sort of queen over them all?

"Where do you think I'm from?" Margo almost smiles.

He shrugs. "Eden, probably." He stares hard at the terrain ahead.

"Good guess. What do you know about Eden?"

"Not much. Only that you still live under the ground. You didn't come up to the surface with the rest of us after All-Clear." He pauses. "Cain says you rejected Gaia's blessing and have been cursed because of it, that you can never leave your bunker. But that can't be right. You've obviously been blessed, so that makes him dead wrong."

Harris nudges me. "They see their mutations as part of a religious *blessing* from some higher power."

I flash back to when I crash-landed out of the chopper. Hearing the voice of my daughter, followed by the voice of my wife. Gale-force winds thrashing those mutant creatures to death. Was that the intervention of a powerful spirit-being? Is that who this *Gaia* is?

"Only two of us remain." Margo again makes eye contact with me in the rearview mirror, confirming that I'm listening. "There were more in Eden, many others, but our leader had them all exterminated—anyone who showed signs of being different. My friend and I, we are the last of them."

"Your leader sounds like a real monster," Lemuel says. "What's his name?"

Again, Margo's eyes focus on me. "Arthur Willard."

Harris squeezes my arm but says nothing. Of course I recognize the name.

"Your friend—you don't mean the flying man. He's from Luther's tribe, I think."

She nods. "My friend's name is Tucker. He is already there, where we're headed."

"Luther's *cave*?" Disdain runs thick in Lemuel's tone.

"Milton said you would be welcome—"

"I don't doubt it." A derisive laugh. "Luther has been trying to get our people to join him for months now. If I'm going there, I must truly be in exile."

"You don't like the guy," Granger observes.

Lemuel turns to face him. "Luther and his people are infidels. They're blessed with the same gifts and abilities as my people, yet they refuse to worship Gaia for all she's done. Instead, they choose to follow a false god who doesn't even show his face to his followers."

"This is incredible," Harris whispers, "to see this sort of religious fervor resurrect itself after a century of post-religious advancements throughout society worldwide. It's as if they have gone back to the Dark Ages!"

I nod absently, tuning out the doctor well enough.

"You've seen this Gaia then?" Margo glances at Lemuel.

He pauses. "She appears only to Cain. Our chieftain among chieftains." The phrase sounds bitter on his tongue. "He's the mediator between us mortals and our divine mother."

"Then how do you know she's even real?" Granger voices the obvious question. "I mean, if your head honcho is the only guy seeing her, couldn't he just be...I don't know. Making her up to keep himself in charge?"

The kid frowns at his ignorance. "Gaia has blessed us with all that we have. We would not be able to live as we do without her. Besides, Victoria has told me that she senses our mother's presence hovering over the earth. She knows Gaia's light."

Margo seems willing to accept that at face value, for the time being. "Did she tell Cain that these ambassadors from the United World would arrive?"

Interesting term: *ambassadors*. Not soldiers or scouts. The word she chose implies a mission of peace, which, in all honesty, was why we were sent here in the first place. We hadn't counted on being blown out of the sky by heavily armed creatures suffering from massive deformities, or hunted by high-speed superhumans. First contact was our primary mission—as well as saving the future of humankind. But after all we've experienced, it's painfully naïve to think that when we arrive in Eden, the transfer of the fetuses will be a peaceful transaction.

Lemuel lowers his voice, but it's unclear why. "Cain said they were looking for trouble and that Gaia had used the goblyns to... shoot them down from the sky."

"Goblyns—a fitting name for those creatures," Harris comments. "The mythology here is fascinating!"

Granger chuckles again. "We didn't come looking for any trouble, kid. But we sure as hell found it!"

"It found us, rather," Sinclair corrects him.

"Your leader believes that Gaia is opposed to the UW presence here, and he has stirred up his people against them? All because a few well-armed mutants decided to fire a missile at their helicopter?" Margo frowns at the logic of it. Or lack thereof. "Couldn't it be just as likely that the creatures were hungry and hunting for their next meal?"

"They're always hungry," Lemuel agrees. "But Gaia made them do it. Why wouldn't she use them to serve her will? They are hers to do with as she pleases. As are we all."

"She made them," Margo clarifies.

"Of course. Just as she made us as we are." He glances back at my team. "Those who have pure hearts are blessed with amazing abilities, while those with evil inside them are changed for the worse. We were transformed after All-Clear, but the goblyns were deformed." He shrugs again. "Gaia moves in mysterious ways. They are not our own."

Granger has paled noticeably. "Now let me get this straight…" He leans forward, gripping the back of Lemuel's seat as Margo takes us through another patch of rugged terrain. "There's a fifty-fifty chance here? We might end up like you two." He gestures at Margo and the youth. "Or just as likely, we could turn into something like those freaks that shot us down?"

Lemuel nods. "Gaia alone decides your fate."

"How-how long? Until I know?"

Sinclair scoffs, half to herself. "Don't be a fool." She reaches to draw Granger back into his seat, but he brushes her hand aside. More and more, they're acting like an old married couple.

Lemuel looks Granger over. "Were you wearing a helmet like theirs until only recently? With your own air supply?"

Granger's nod is a quick jerk.

"It may take a while, then. Perhaps weeks."

Granger curses and falls back into his seat. "So I'm a freakin' time bomb."

"You don't honestly believe any of this," Sinclair says quietly to him. "It's religious babble created to explain the inexplicable." She faces Lemuel and speaks up, "Are there scientists among your people?"

He shakes his head. "We're all from the labor sectors. But that was before my time. I was born in the bunker."

"They allowed your mother to become pregnant?"

"She already was before we were sealed inside, the story goes. Cain said it would be all right, and nobody questioned him at the time. They still don't."

Margo's eyes flick to the rearview, and again I hear her thoughts enter my mind as if they are my own: *Cain could be Lemuel's father.*

I nod to show I received the transmission. Makes sense. Males in labor sectors were sterilized, back in the day. But this Cain fellow with his four wives has a fully functional seed sack. And so would Lemuel, unless he was neutered at birth while they were living underground. Regardless, it doesn't matter that Cain exiled the kid; if Lemuel is the man's son, there's no telling what may happen in our near future.

Blood ties run deep.

Harris nudges me. "Family relation, do you think? Could this young fellow be a prince among his people, and all this *exile* business nothing but an elaborate ruse?"

Was Margo's thought-transmission sent on a scatter pattern? Had the doctor picked up some of it, or had he come up with this idea all on his own?

"Is there some reason why his people haven't found us yet?" I ask Margo. "Cain doesn't sound like the kind of guy they'd want to disappoint."

She relays my question.

"Victoria won't let them find us," Lemuel says. "She's guiding them in the opposite direction until we have reached our destination."

Margo nods as if confirming the news. Has she heard the same from Victoria herself?

"By then, it will be daylight," Lemuel continues. "They will return to the Shipyard—unless they feel like dealing with the goblyns."

"The Shipyard," Margo continues to pry information out of him. "Is that the name of your people's settlement?"

For the first time, Lemuel smiles. He's enjoying himself, being the center of attention, having us hang on his every word. "You'd have to see it to believe it. We live in these overturned ships—big ocean liners, some of them. They protect us from the sun during the day, and there's plenty of food stores and water to be had, protein and hydropacks. The Shipyard is our home, thanks to whatever storm blew those vessels ashore."

"Gaia has provided well for you." Margo sounds like she's bought into the kid's belief system. "Does she also protect you from the goblyns?"

Lemuel shakes his head. "Gaia helps those who help themselves. That's what Cain has taught us. She provided us with all the weapons we'd ever need. One of the ships had holds full of guns. So we are able to match the goblyns round for round when they attack. And we have a wall of barbed steel that surrounds our compound with sentries always on duty." His pride swells as he shares, "I have mounted enough goblyn heads along the wall to rival any warrior in my tribe."

"Captain Mutegi must be warned of this," Harris whispers. "There are two factions of well-armed mutants on this continent, and we haven't even seen Luther's cave dwellers yet. But if that flying man is any indication, they will be a force to reckon with. And what of Eden? How well armed are they? We have no idea!"

"It's not as bad as it sounds," I argue.

"No. It's *worse!*"

I shake my head. "You're not paying attention, Doc. Margo is getting Lemuel to tell us everything we need to know. Namely, that none of these armed groups are working together. If they were, then maybe the UW would have some trouble on their hands."

"*Our* hands, Sergeant. We're all alone here!"

"For now, we don't tell Mutegi anything. He won't send in air support if he thinks it'll be shot down again. We bank on the fact that while these groups are fighting among themselves, they'll never have the strength necessary to pose a threat to the UW. Meanwhile, we pick the strongest team, and we gain their trust. We ride them all the way to the end of a successful mission." For the thousandth time, images of my wife and kids flash before my eyes. "We go home happy."

Harris nods. "And what about this Gaia woman? Apparently, she holds the power in this young fellow's tribe. She is spoken of as a *goddess*."

"You think she exists?"

The doctor frowns pensively. "I'll believe it when I see it. But for such a religion to have sprouted up from nothing in a matter of months, and for these people to follow Gaia so devoutly, there must be someone who offers them answers when needed most. Whether she is still alive is another matter. This Lord Cain may be filling in the blanks at present, carrying on the mythology in her absence, if you understand my meaning."

I have a hard time believing that Gaia, whoever she is, and the presence I encountered are one and the same. They're nothing alike. For one thing, this Gaia is being credited with downing our chopper, while the strange voice that spoke to me in the Wastes protected me from the deformed mutants, guiding me to safety while it killed them. Why would Gaia want to destroy me and save me at the same time?

Could it be that Cain is using the Gaia myth for his own purposes? Not an uncommon practice among the power-hungry doing all they can to hold their position of power. If so, then the true Gaia may be nothing like her reputation.

"Will you go back to your people, do you think? Once all of this blows over?" Margo asks Lemuel.

"Not while Cain lives." His reply is quick and forceful. "I won't live another day under his tyranny."

He jumps in his seat. Something outside has startled him.

Margo slams hard on the brakes, throwing us forward. Milton stands in the white glare of the headlights. He faces us with an outstretched palm, silently halting our progress.

"What the devil is this?" Harris demands.

Milton jogs over to Margo's window. She depresses a pad on her armrest, and the pane of thick tinted glass retracts into her door.

"Don't go any farther," he warns, rubbing his gloved hands together in the cold. "Not this way. Things aren't looking so good up ahead."

Margo frowns, her dark eyes flitting to the rearview and back to Milton. "They've cut us off." She knows Milton's thoughts and repeats them out loud. "They knew where we were going, all along."

Milton nods. "They're quick, I'll give them that. They beat us to the Homeplace, and they're not letting anybody in or out. Luther's trying to negotiate with them, but it's not going all that well." He looks at the young man beside her. "Your people are a damned stubborn bunch, kid."

Lemuel nods, but there's no arrogance in the gesture. "They have Gaia on their side."

PART IV
NEGOTIATION

15. CAIN

18 MONTHS AFTER ALL-CLEAR

I have reached the end of my patience. Killing Victoria outright and being done with her is still an option on the table, but she is my eyes, after all. Without her, I would not be able to see what I am now seeing—or *not* seeing, as the case appears to be.

"Gaia-dammit woman, how could you lose them?" I growl, low and menacing, as I clutch her wrists.

"There is one among them with a gift...like my own. She may be using it against me to misdirect us, to blind me from their true course."

I glare at her for a moment before returning her slender hands to my temples, restoring my view of the warriors I sent after the UW scouts and their meddling rescuers. Luther's flying man would have been bad enough, but there is also a black armored vehicle impervious to bullets that we must contend with. Undoubtedly, it came from Eden.

"If I did not know better, my lady, I would think you didn't want me to find them." I press my thumb against her jugular and feel its strong, throbbing pulse. "But you would not risk your life for these strangers..."

"We will find them," Victoria says without pause, reclining naked beside me in the bed. My far-sight combined with her telepathic abilities creates the virtual reality we share; flesh against flesh keeps the connection strong. "But we may have to look…farther."

I gesture toward my men who grow more frustrated with every dead end they face. They stomp their feet against the cold night, having returned to the location where the flying man frightened them off. But there is no vehicle and no tracks; only half of the weapons they discarded earlier during their retreat remain.

"They grow more impatient by the minute." As do I.

Victoria guides them eastward from there, certain the United World scouts went that direction. Toward Eden.

"We can send them northward as well—or split them up to cover more ground," she suggests.

"Enough time has been wasted. There is less than an hour before sunrise. They shouldn't have to deal with the goblyns after hunting in vain all night." I shake my head as I watch Vincent do his best to rally the men. "Send them to Luther."

Victoria blinks at me in stunned silence.

"Don't give me that look, woman. Luther has been pestering us for months now. It's high time we returned the favor and paid him a visit."

"With over a score of armed warriors? You really think that would be wise?"

"You live to obey." I narrow my gaze. "Don't question me."

She never backs down. I once appreciated that personality trait in her. "Our people have always lived at peace with—"

"We are not going there to start any trouble with them, only to head off the UW scouts if that's their destination. Luther will understand. He is a reasonable man." I pause, musing half to myself, "He can't possibly be in league with them."

Victoria shifts her weight. "I wouldn't know where to begin looking. I have no idea where Luther's people are."

Can it be that she's led the warriors astray on purpose? Is she stalling now?

"Send them to the mountains. Luther and his nomads hide among the rocks—like frightened squirrels."

She shakes her head. "There are hundreds of caves in those mountains. Do you honestly expect our men to search every last one of them?"

"Ye of little faith," I chide her. "Do you forget that we have Gaia on our side? Truly, woman, I sometimes wonder whether you are one of the faithful." My upper lip curls back into a sneer. "If you have passed infidel blood on to my child, I will slay you both in this very bed!"

"Gaia helps those who help themselves, my lord," she is quick to recite the catechism. "She is not to be summoned at our every whim."

I regard her for a moment in silence. The woman appears to be sincere. "We follow the will of Gaia by hunting down these United World spies invading our land. She will bless our efforts, once we stop chasing our tails and do what must be done." I clench my jaw, and the muscle twitches like a snake. "She told me this moment would come, that we would join forces with Luther's people to rid this continent of the UW."

"They may not see it that way, my lord," she cautions me, her voice low. "They do not follow Gaia's ways. Sending warriors to their hiding place—"

"It is up to you to make matters clear to Vincent and Markus. Tell them to keep the men on a tight leash. Luther's infidels are not to be attacked, verbally or physically. They are to be treated as allies until we have possession of the UW scouts."

"And then?"

Luther would know better than to think his people are any match for mine.

"They will let our men go without incident." I point at my disgruntled warriors. "Now tell them where they must go, and tell them why. But most importantly, tell them Gaia will lead them. She will direct us to Luther's cave. I will see her guide us by her light."

I can see plainly that young Victoria does not agree with this course of action, but she knows better than to disobey me. At Vincent's word, the men tighten their belts and adjust their weapons; then, in a blur of speed, they are off, racing across moonlit sands like ghosts on the wind. Hovering above them as a camera would have in an old Hollywood epic, our ethereal point of view follows.

Do I envy them? Do I wish I could be the one leading the warriors instead of Vincent? At times, perhaps. But whenever Gaia calls me to her, to behold her in all her glorious light, knowing that I am the only one among my people graced by her presence, all other desires pale in comparison.

Crossing kilometers as if they are only paces across the Shipyard, my warriors head straight for mountains jutting awkwardly out of the terrain as though shoved there against their will. In all likelihood, they were. The cataclysmic blasts of D-Day's bombs destroyed the Old World and all life upon it. Valleys rose upward and mountains were laid low. Topography shifted, rendering the old maps from the bunkers useless. This is literally a new world, a North American continent totally unlike its predecessor.

The UW has no business being here after what they did to this land. We have long since grown tired of their presence—that naval blockade floating out at sea, those ugly grey ships and their pretentious military presuming to keep everyone from going in or out, as if the continent were diseased.

To the unenlightened, perhaps it is. But they are ignorant of the truth.

This is a land of blessing. It is here that Gaia has chosen to reveal herself. She has chosen me and my people to be *her* people. The UW with their domed city across the sea and their filtered air have rejected Gaia's blessings, and such irreverent disregard is not to be tolerated indefinitely.

They will soon learn the consequences of their arrogance.

"Gaia will show us the way?" Victoria's tone leaves room for doubt.

I focus on the terrain ahead as we rush through the night sky, flying above my warriors. The mountains loom before them, twenty kilometers away. But considering the speed of these men, they will reach the foothills in a matter of minutes.

"She will guide us to their cave. It is her will that we work with Luther and his people." Why am I repeating myself? Who am I trying to convince?

"Working with him is different from sending armed men to his front door."

I curse under my breath. "Luther is no fool. He will know the weapons they carry are not meant for him—as long as our warriors are not provoked."

"And if they are?"

"Luther would not risk the lives of his people for UW spies."

"Will you threaten him? If he decides to protect them?"

"If he goes against the will of Gaia, he will be punished." I clench my fists.

"But you said it was Gaia's will for the two of you to work together against your common enemy." She never backs down in the face of my temper. "Will she be pleased if you start trouble with Luther and his nomads?"

"They involved themselves in this situation when that flying man interfered."

"He saved the lives of those scouts. You were going to kill them." She watches me closely, unafraid. "Or am I wrong about that?"

"I do the will of Gaia."

Victoria nods to herself. "Then she will show us Luther's Homeplace. And there will be no violence between our people and his, because we follow the will of our mother."

Do I detect irony in her tone? I let it slide. Instead I focus on the foothills before me, crags and cliff sides, for signs of human habitation—trails blazed along the ridges, caves that yawn black in the predawn darkness. There are plenty of openings in the rock, numerous places where Luther could have tucked his tribe away, high above the marauding bands of goblyns hungry for their next kill.

I scan the rocks and slopes before me with a keen awareness for heat signatures, the pulsing beats that would come from a human heart.

"Vincent is concerned, my lord," Victoria says presently. "The men are exposed. The higher ground surrounding them makes them easy targets."

"Tell him to trust Gaia." I scan my field of vision from left to right. "And to trust me."

Victoria shakes her head. "It's Luther's infidels the men distrust, afraid they will gun them down without a fair fight."

"That is not Luther's way. He is a man of peace."

There: two—no, three heartbeats. Quivering rapidly in the night, each hidden behind large outcroppings of rock along a low ridge. No more than thirty meters up the steep grade and spaced ten meters apart. Wise of Luther to have sentries posted.

I point them out, unseen by the naked eye. "Have Vincent speak to them, explain why we are here. We come in peace. Emphasize we will not raise our weapons against them."

"Are the three sentries armed?" She peers into the darkness, locating the mind of each one.

"We must assume so."

"Gaia didn't tell you?" She raises an eyebrow.

I should slap her for such insolence. "We haven't much time, my lady."

She relays the message to Vincent, who steps forward from the pack with his empty hands out to the sides.

"Friends! We come in peace," he calls up to the sentries. "You have no reason to fear us. We have never sought to harm your people. We are much alike, sharing many of the same gifts. And we share the same enemies." He pauses, looking up along the ridge for any sign of movement. He could be speaking to the mountain itself, by all appearances.

Then a narrow cascade of sand shuffles down the hillside and a voice demands from above, "Who are you? Why are you here?" The guards remain hidden, but they adjust their position, no doubt lining up the sights of their weapons with the men below.

"We come from the coast, fifty kilometers west of you. We are the people of Lord Cain, whom your leader is well acquainted with. Please let him know we are here with a message."

A few moments of silence drag on before the voice returns.

"Very well. Lay down your weapons if you truly come in peace."

Vincent's hands remain floating in the air at his sides. "Unfortunately, we cannot comply. Our weapons are not intended for you. There are dangerous people headed this way in an armored vehicle, and we are here to meet them."

"Who's coming?" calls down another of the sentries, located just south of the first voice.

"They are from the United World." Vincent pivots to face the second voice. "They seek our destruction, both yours and ours. For now, they have sent only a handful of spies into our land, but more will follow in greater numbers. And when they come, we will be overwhelmed by their strength." He pauses. "We must stop them now before it is too late."

"And your message...for Luther?" the first sentry speaks up again.

Vincent nods amiably. "We request his permission to act without any interference. We must apprehend these enemy spies and take them with us back to Lord Cain, to be done with as Gaia wills."

"What if Luther refuses to give you this permission?" The third sentry speaks up for the first time, a woman's voice.

Vincent faces the dark hillside where her voice originated. "Then we would ask to speak to him directly. Either way, we wait for you to pass along our message. But we ask that you make haste, as there is little time before the spies arrive."

"How do you know they'll come *here*?"

"They have nowhere else to go," Vincent says simply.

Voices whisper along the ridge before another stream of sand and gravel tumbles downward in the wake of a retreating shadowy form.

"Now we wait," I mutter. "We'll see how deep a sleeper Luther is."

Victoria regards me for a moment. "You haven't slept at all."

"I will sleep soundly once these UW bastards are dealt with." I smirk, recalling the blade she held not so long ago. I plan to sleep alone.

"And what will be done with them?"

An image of the soldier I staked into the hard-packed shore passes through my mind's eye. The man's corpse will be plain to see by the *Argonaus* and its crew. And Gaia-willing, there will be four more bodies to add to my message for the United World government. I will drench the sand crimson with it: They are not welcome here.

"You will reap the whirlwind…"

I frown at Victoria's hoarse voice, the look of horror she casts upon me, as if she's seen everything in my mind. Did the images somehow transfer through this link we share?

"Focus." I grip her by the throat. "My use for you is dwindling, woman."

We turn our inward gaze to the dark hillside where a figure descends the steep grade, followed by a massive figure whose arms and legs gleam in the moonlight like a robot from an old film. Luther and his pet cyborg, Samson the bodyguard. Both appear to be unarmed. They make their way down with caution, familiar with the shifting sand and ash at their feet, tumbling in rivulets beneath every step.

"With whom am I speaking?" Luther's voice echoes off the ridge above him. He halts halfway down.

"I am Vincent. I come seeking—"

"I know why you are here." Luther gives him a direct look, not intimidated by the warrior. "Are you in communication with Cain?"

For the first time, Vincent seems unsure of the situation. "Yes, I—"

"Then he and I will speak directly to one another through you. Is that understood?" Luther's tone leaves no room for misinterpretation, asserting instant control over the situation.

"Very well," Vincent says.

"Tell him it's just a power play," I say to Victoria, who relays the message. "We could overwhelm these nomads easily. But for now we will play along."

Vincent nods to no one in particular, hearing Victoria's thoughts. "Lord Cain agrees to…speak through me."

A change seems to have come over Luther since the last time he showed up at the Shipyard gates. "Tell him clearly, in no uncertain terms, that the United World team is under my protection. As long as Milton is with them, he will be their escort. He will bring them here, and I will discuss concerns that affect us all. They will remain here while I wait for Cain to arrive in person. At that time, he will participate in the dialogue I have started with the UW representatives. Now relay this message to Cain, exactly as I have said it."

"No need," Vincent says with a disdainful smile. "He can see and hear all that we say. In real time."

Luther clenches his jaw. "What does he say to these terms?"

Vincent pauses, listening again. "Lord Cain says there is no reason for this matter to involve you. The UW spies have attacked our people, not yours, and we seek only to repay the wrong they have wrought—"

"That's not what I heard," rumbles the cyborg, taking his place beside Luther and folding his steel arms across his massive chest.

"Do you also intend to speak directly to Lord Cain?" Vincent's tone makes it clear the half-machine is unwelcome in this conversation.

"Nope," Samson said. "But he should know we recognize a load of crap when we hear it."

I mutter a few curses. Vincent chooses not to pass those choice words along to his audience.

"When Milton came upon the scene, you were attempting to strip the UW soldiers of their oxygen supply, and you had already injured two of their team." Luther's gaze focuses on the blades sheathed across Vincent's torso. "They were cut. One in the leg. Another in the arm."

How does he know this? "Their presence alone is an attack upon our people, both his and mine!" I shout. "They are not here for our welfare. Their intent is far from benign."

Victoria relays the message, and Vincent voices it to Luther.

"I seem to remember telling you why they were venturing inland," Luther says.

"For the children..." Vincent replies, puzzlement spreading across his features before he catches himself. Of course this is news to him.

"We have something they lack: the ability to reproduce," Luther continues. "The destruction they wrought upon our continent had an unexpected side effect on the rest of the world."

"Came back to bite 'em in the ass," Samson mutters.

"They're sterile. That's what you're saying." Vincent tilts his head to one side at this revelation. "So they are coming to take what is ours. Well, if that isn't an attack on our people, I do not know what is. We have to stop them."

Luther holds up a hand. "Now is not the time. We can use them, once we have convinced them to help us. We can't risk turning them against us. Not so soon."

"What do you mean?" Vincent softens my exact words: "What the hell are you talking about?"

"You are expecting children in your settlement, correct?"

"Of course," Vincent replies.

Luther already knows this. All four of my wives are with child, and I also planted my seed in the fertile wombs of half a dozen other men's wives. I alone hold that right, being my bunker's alpha male—now the only one with virile seed to be found in the Shipyard.

"And you all have been exposed to the dust on the surface?"

"We have breathed this air since All-Clear," Vincent says. "Gaia has blessed us for it."

"But the United World does not see *blessings* as such," Luther cautions. "They see us as subhuman freaks of nature. Any children you bear will be viewed in the same way."

Vincent raises his chin. "We are Gaia's chosen people. Let the UW call us what they will. It means nothing."

Luther pauses, collecting his thoughts. "They will exterminate all of us once they have what they came for. Your people as well as ours."

"Gaia would not allow such a thing!"

"*Gaia* again," Samson grumbles, but Luther silences him with a glance. The cyborg exhales loudly through his nostrils.

"We are immaterial to them. They have bombed other settlements since All-Clear, obliterating them. On our journey west from Eden, we passed through many scorched ruins bearing signs of recent ballistic missile attacks. The UW doesn't see our kind as human beings. All they want are the unborn children growing inside incubation chambers deep in Eden's sublevels. My children. Samson's."

I narrow my gaze. "He is saying the UW doesn't want any of my offspring, only his own. Is that it?" Victoria relays the message, but Vincent appears uncomfortable sharing it.

"Your children will be exposed to the elements when they are born. Your wives breathe the air while your young grow within them. Willard has convinced the United World government that the fetuses protected within Eden's walls have not been contaminated."

"These children in Eden—how can they possibly be yours?"

Luther's shoulders sink. "When we were captured by Willard almost a year ago, he experimented on us. Samson and myself, as well as two women. Their ova were extracted, and multiple sperm samples were taken from us—against our will."

"Not as much fun as it sounds," Samson adds. "Believe me."

"That was when they…robbed you of your gifts?"

Luther nods. "They amputated Samson's powerful arms and legs. Tore out my claws. Removed Shechara's eyes. All the gifts bestowed upon us by our Creator via the spirits of—"

"We haven't come to listen to your heresy," Vincent interrupts. "Only to ask that you do not interfere with our interception of the UW team. Nothing else concerns us."

"And all that we ask," Luther reiterates, "is that you allow us the time necessary to talk with these soldiers, to convince them to help us get our children out of Eden."

I frown, glancing at Victoria. "Why would the UW ever agree to *help* them? They're here to take the children for themselves!"

Victoria relays this to Vincent.

"It may seem counterintuitive," Luther replies, "but we have reason to believe this team of UW personnel may be willing to see things differently. Two of them no longer wear their protective suits. They should begin to notice changes in their physiology within a matter of days. During that time, we will keep them here with us, and we will show them the two incubation pods that were smuggled out of Eden—"

"What?" This is the first I've heard of it. "When did this occur?"

"We have reason to believe," Luther continues, "that the woman driving that armored vehicle has defected from Eden. She sent two of our unborn children to us a few weeks ago via a gifted courier, one who is able to make himself invisible to the naked eye. We will show them to the UW doctor and allow him to run certain tests on them."

"What will these tests prove?"

"The United World government has yet to ascertain that these children are one hundred percent human, unaffected by our gifts."

I shake my head. "This changes nothing."

"You have not met Arthur Willard," Luther says. "He is not planning to simply hand over these unborn children. They are little more than a means of leverage for him, to be used as he sees fit. He won't think twice about exterminating them if things don't go his way. He only wants to leave this continent." Luther pauses at the gravity of the situation. "Willard is an unpredictable man, and he may very well destroy the tenuous relations he's established with the UW."

"But if he is able to bargain with them, then what?"

The crease in Luther's brow relaxes for the first time. "The children will be safe, free from Eden. Our people can join forces to take them away and then, together, we'll protect our shores from the United World's retaliation. We won't be alone in this. The spirits of the earth will be with us, of course."

More heresy! To Victoria, I growl, "Our warriors should kill these infidels—a holy slaughter in the name of Gaia our one true mother!"

She watches me. "I doubt you'd want me to share those sentiments, my lord."

"Their children do not concern us!"

Or do they? If the fetuses in Eden truly are the UW's only hope for the future, then to destroy every last one would be a surefire way to bring the United World to its knees. While my descendants continue to reproduce in greater numbers and multiply in the decades to come, the people of Eurasia will die out as a species—if Eden's incubators are out of the picture.

Mass abortion would lead to their mass extinction.

Victoria cringes back from me without breaking our physical link. There is no denying that she has read my thoughts, and they repulse her.

"Has Cain nothing more to say?" Luther glances at the warriors behind Vincent who shuffle their feet, impatient and agitated. Samson adjusts his stance, prepared to throw himself in front of Luther the moment any shooting starts. "I know our peoples do not share the same beliefs, but we are discussing our very survival. If we do not work together, we will be no match for the UW troops when they pour upon your shores."

Vincent nods at length. "Gaia has told us the same," he relays my words. "She desires that we join forces with you and your people." He pauses a moment to let that sink in. "So we will do as you ask. Lord Cain will arrive the day after tomorrow, along with every fighting man and woman from our tribes. Until then, our warriors here will not interfere with you or the UW spies. We ask only that you provide us with shelter from the sun in the interim. Providing that you have the space available."

Luther's eyes appear to glisten in the moonlight. "Of course. We have more than enough room for you." He opens his arms wide in a broad gesture of welcome. Samson, on the other hand, stares down at my people, speechless. Perhaps he did not foresee such a peaceful outcome, and he is disappointed there will be no fighting. "You look hungry. Join us inside, please."

I cannot help but sneer at the look on Luther's face, as eager as one whose fervent prayers have finally been answered. He's begged for months to have our people join together as one. Now he will have his way.

And I will play along until we reach Eden. Then my warriors will be given their orders: Find the incubation units and disable them. Every last one.

Victoria pulls away from me, breaking our link and shattering my view of the warriors climbing the foothills to meet Luther and Samson. I scowl in the dim light of the bedchamber as she gathers her clothing and pulls it on, covering her nakedness in haste.

"I am not through with you." I grab hold of her wrist as she rises from the bed.

She casts a cold gaze upon me. "But I am through with you, Cain. I will not be party to what you have planned. It is pure *evil*."

I scoff, pretending she can't possibly know what I am planning. "Luther and I finally decide to bury the hatchet, and you—"

"Don't you dare try to deceive me." She wrenches her arm free. If anything, she has only grown stronger during her pregnancy. "I know your thoughts as if they are my own. They disgust me. *You* disgust me."

"You would dare speak to me like this? After all I have done for you? I made you my *wife*, for Gaia's sake!" An honor in and of itself.

"You will bring the full wrath of the United World down upon us. How can this be what Gaia wants? You killed one of their soldiers, and now you want to slay innocent children?" She draws back toward the door, her face rippling with revulsion. "What have you become?" She grabs for the wheel on the door and spins it with one downward stroke.

I am on my feet in a split-second, slamming the door shut with a resounding clang as soon as she heaves it open. I stiff-arm it in place, the muscles in my arm tightening against her futile efforts. I take her throat in one hand and squeeze until her eyes bulge, straining bloodshot in their sockets.

But she does not struggle. She stares right back at me.

"Kill me," she rasps. "Kill us both. I don't want this child of ours to see the world you'll make for him."

A male child. This is good news—if true. "How do I know it is even mine?" I spit into her face.

"You don't." Her gaze holds a scornful smile.

I slam the back of her head against the door and catch her limp body in my arms as she drops, unconscious. With a low curse, I carry her to the bed and toss her onto her back like a corpse on a funeral pyre. Then I get dressed, making sure to retrieve the knife she threatened to use on herself. After a quick survey of the room for any other weapons, I prepare to leave.

Yet I linger, my hand resting on the door as I glance back at the bed. Here Lady Victoria will remain locked inside until I return, whenever that may be. I will take every fighting man and woman among the tribes with me to Luther's Homeplace. By the time Victoria is able to summon any of the other pregnant women or older ones left behind in order to spread her lies about my plans, my warriors and I will already be well on our way to Eden. With Luther's people and the UW spies.

One big happy family.

I bolt the door shut behind me and stride the length of the corridor toward the nearest exterior hatch.

"Lord Cain!" salutes the young sentry waiting outside.

"Summon the chieftains." I leave the hatch to swing shut and draw in a deep breath of cool night air. Starlit heavens soar above with pinpricks of light in the deep black, but they will be visible for only a few hours more. Dawn approaches. "Have each of them bring their strongest warriors, fully armed."

"Yes, my lord—but our fastest warriors have already—"

"Did you hear me say the *fastest*?" Of course they are already gone, led by Vincent and Markus. All who remain are without the blessing of superhuman speed. "I said the *strongest*. We have a long journey ahead of us."

"Yes, m'lord."

"Arm yourself while you're at it. You and the other guards will be joining us."

He stares mutely for a moment. "Y-yes, Lord Cain."

"Go then!" I roar.

I watch the fool scurry off to obey. Then I close my eyes for a moment in the calm before the storm. I recall Gaia's face, the moment when I knelt before her with my head bowed. She lifted my chin to meet her powerful gaze, too beautiful for mere words.

"May we honor you this day," I whisper.

The sun will rise, and I will brave the scorched kilometers of open terrain with my warriors. The marauding goblyns will no doubt be surprised by the sight of the Shipyard's inhabitants outside their walls. The slobbering wretches will move quickly to intercept. But Gaia will protect her people. I have no doubt.

May your will be done.

16. MILTON

18 MONTHS AFTER ALL-CLEAR

Maybe halting Margo dead in her tracks was a bit premature, but seeing all those hard-assed warrior-types heading straight for the Homeplace raised my hackles just a bit. It didn't bode well, that's for sure.

Shows how much I know.

Floating a hundred meters or so above them now, I nod and give Luther a double thumbs-up, whether or not he can see the gesture from the ground. You've got to hand it to the guy; there's something almost supernatural about the way he plays peacemaker. It's like a calling for him.

In the Homeplace, he's kept the peace between the Edenhaters and the rest of the brood. But we're all on the same side, more or less. These well-armed warriors from the coast? Another matter entirely. They serve their own fake god, for crying out loud, and they're fiercely devoted to her. Yet somehow Luther managed to talk them down, and now they're climbing the foothills toward the caves, invited inside by Luther himself.

Go figure.

Once the last of the warriors has entered the Homeplace, I plunge from the night sky like a falling meteorite or something less sparkly and land sure-footed on the hillside with just a couple extra steps to balance myself. I tug my goggles up onto my forehead and clear my throat quietly.

Samson whirls around to face me. "You'll stop doing that one of these days," he grumbles. "Sneaky devil."

"Sorry." I take my life in my hands every time I show up behind the big guy without any warning. One swing of his mighty steel arm and my head could go flying, leaving the rest of me behind. Risky, sure. But so much fun. "Everything okay here?"

Samson glances at the muscle-men invading the caves of the Homeplace, the sweat on their exposed skin glistening in the green light of glowsticks mounted along the earthen walls inside.

"What do you think?" His voice rumbles like a small earthquake in his broad chest. "We're sleeping with the enemy. I hope Luther knows what he's doing."

So do I. "I should tell Margo to keep her distance, find some shelter until things settle down."

Samson shakes his head, running a hand down his beard. Then he gives it a pensive tug. "Luther wants to speak with those UW folks before Cain arrives. He's hoping to sway them over to our side, convince them Willard and the Edenites are not to be trusted. Those babies they've got won't be safe until they're here with us."

"You think they'll go for it—the UW crew, I mean?"

Samson narrows his gaze. "You've met them. How do they strike you?"

"They're doing their best to keep it together, I think. They've seen things here they never could've imagined. Two of them are going to start noticing a change in themselves pretty soon. Their protective suits were compromised, cut open by that guy with the swords—the one doing all the talking earlier."

"Which two?"

I shrug. "Not their leader—a sergeant in the United World Marines named Bishop. Good guy, I think. Level-headed. Unlike their doctor, who's kind of an emotional wreck. Both of their suits seem to be functioning. It's the two support personnel, a man and woman. Don't know their names or anything."

Samson nods, waiting for me to go on. Over the past few months, he's gotten used to the weird way I dispense with information.

"Oh, and they picked up a kid along the way. His name's Lemuel—from Cain's bunch. Exiled, he said, sent out into the desert to die for his sins. Real Old Testament, y'know?" I chuckle lamely.

Samson frowns. "They have one of Cain's people with them?"

"Margo was in communication with his girlfriend. Something like that. I didn't get the whole story."

"And you left them out there with this *Lemuel?*"

"Uh..." Suddenly it doesn't seem like the best idea. "I had to make sure everything was okay here—"

"Mission accomplished, Flyboy. Now haul your ass back over there and make sure we haven't invited wolves into our fold for no reason. If those UW people are already dead—"

"He's just a kid, man. Scared crapless, by the looks of him."

Samson raises one of his mechanical fingers skyward. "Get going. And pray to the Creator they're all right, or you'll have some explaining to do when you get back. You've never seen Luther angry, have you? No? Well, you're in for a real treat."

I back away. "Okay, okay. But you're wrong about this kid. I can feel it."

"I hope so—for the sake of his escorts." Without another word, he turns away to stomp down the earthen corridor into the network of caves beyond.

Muttering inventive insults about the *tin man* under my breath, I take to the skies, feeling the ice-cold rush of air dig into my eyes before I remember to readjust the goggles. I aim my trajectory back toward the armored Hummer five kilometers west. Glancing over my shoulder, I see the sky on the eastern horizon begin to evolve from star-punctured black into a deep indigo above the mountain range in the distance. Dawn's on the way.

And, with it, the regularly scheduled dangers of daily life on this continent. Sure, Margo's vehicle stood up pretty well against automatic weapons fire, but a close-range blast from a daemon's RPG is something else entirely. Detonated under the vehicle's belly, it would bloom from the ground upward in a pillar of fire eating straight through the steel and cooking everyone alive inside.

Not a pleasant thought.

I find them right where I left them, parked behind an outcropping of rock with the engine off. I didn't know how long they'd have to wait for me to return, so conserving fuel seemed like a good idea. Judging by the extent of the vehicle's damage, the solar cells along the roof are no longer able to provide auxiliary power—even in direct sunlight.

Dropping from the sky, I stick my landing like a pro a few meters away from the dark headlights. *If Julia could see me now...* I can't help recalling my first flying lesson with the spirit of the earth taking the form of my long-lost love. Landing without crashing involved a steep learning curve at the time.

The spirit has always appeared to me as Julia, and at first it bothered me a bit, knowing she was nothing more than a projection of my own memories—filtered through a supernatural intelligence I can't even begin to understand. But over the past few months, I've actually grown to think of her as *being* Julia—just a different version of her. *Julia 2.0* or something. She never appears to me in the guise of anyone else, so the name's stuck. She kind of likes it, I think. It gives us a connection; we belong to each other.

Or I'm losing my mind again. Always a possibility, and always something I wake up fearing. I came close, once—possessed by an evil spirit. Hard to believe, but true.

Before D-Day, back when the United World had the North American Sectors running so smoothly, producing everything the rest of the world needed overseas so they could live in the lap of luxury, there had been no such thing as *good* or *evil*. The whole concept of moral purity versus depravity was relative, depending on the belief system you subscribed to.

Not anymore. Here, on this desolate continent, there's good, and there's evil. The benevolent spirits of the earth—manifesting themselves to me as Julia—wish us well, having bestowed upon us certain abilities that make living in this harsh environment tolerable. Super-speed, night-vision, far-sight. Flight. The abilities themselves are derived from the animal kingdom—something I've never fully comprehended—since the spirits themselves originated from those billions upon billions of creatures annihilated on D-Day.

I don't really understand that, either.

But there are also malevolent spirits of the earth who roam freely about, intent on further destruction—ultimately, extermination of the human remnant on earth. Somehow, these evil spirits are also from the animal kingdom. And when they appear to me, they manifest themselves as my psychotic bunker commander from all those years ago: Jackson. The man I killed with my bare hands...then dragged into the storeroom to lie beside all the other rotting corpses, men and women Jackson forced me to execute after a fabricated food shortage.

Julia lay among them.

The driver's side door of the Hummer swings open, and Margo steps out. "All clear," she says. Her look is direct, meeting my gaze and holding it.

"You read my mind." I wink, striding toward her. "You're not going to believe this, but Luther invited Cain's whole bunch over for dinner, and you're the guests of honor." I duck to glance inside the vehicle and give the kid up front a salute. Lemuel looks away, unimpressed. The UW crew appears to be alive and un-slaughtered, so Samson's concerns were groundless. "Whenever you want to get moving again..."

She nods, glancing eastward. "I'm not sure about this, Milton." She lowers her voice. "Cain wants these people dead."

"It's not how I thought things would play out either, I'll give you that."

"Is Luther sure he's doing the right thing?"

Her eyes are earnest, and even before I reply, I can tell she won't believe me. There's a great deal of uncertainty in my mind, courtesy of Samson and my own doubts about the situation.

"Luther knows what he's doing. I mean, he's kept us all alive since we escaped from Eden, and he's been doing a great job of collecting and uniting the survivors we've come across since then. He wouldn't jeopardize what he's worked so hard to build over the past few months, I'll tell you that much."

She shakes her head. "His people are not unified. That could pose a problem."

How could she know that? She's never been to the Homeplace. She has no clue how things are going there.

"What do you mean?"

Her facial features sag. She looks defeated before she's even begun to fight. "There are two factions among your people: those who want nothing to do with the United World and who would go back to Eden and destroy them if given the chance, and those who do not embrace their new abilities and would return to Eden to have them surgically removed, if possible. Then there are those like Luther and you, caught in the middle. Seeking peace."

"You got all that from my subconscious?"

"You are an open book, Milton. You fear for Luther and his people. You can't help it."

"*My* people. I'm one of them now."

She nods. "So you say. But you don't identify with them completely."

"Hey-uh…" the short UW fellow calls out from the backseat, leaning forward. "Are we getting this show back on the road? Guy's gotta eat!"

I take a step back. "You should go. Just make sure you—"

"I will." She climbs into her seat.

"Of course you will." She already knew what I was going to say: look out for Lemuel. We have no idea how his people will react to seeing him riding with the enemy. "I'll follow and keep a lookout ahead of you."

She gives me another direct look that makes me feel naked before her. "Thank you, Milton." With a weak attempt at a smile, she shuts the door and fires up the engine. The headlights flare white, blasting through the early morning darkness.

I raise a hand to shield my eyes and slide my goggles into place. As I do, I see her standing behind the vehicle. She looks out of place there, having appeared without warning like a ghost, glowing red in the taillights. My heart skips a beat at the sight of her.

She always has this effect on me.

"Julia." I want to run to her and gather her into my arms, but it's like I'm in a dream, and my legs turned to stone when I wasn't looking.

She smiles at me but waits until the vehicle has taken off before she approaches. I know I should follow the Hummer, soaring above, keeping an eye out for any unforeseen dangers. But as Julia melts into my embrace, there's nowhere else I'd ever want to be.

"It's been so long," I whisper. Weeks since our last meeting—maybe longer. I can't be sure. She nuzzles my chest, squeezing me tight without a word. "Where have you been?" I always ask her this.

She comes and goes with no understanding of the time that elapses in between. If it's true that she somehow represents the spirits of all the animals who once lived without fear of humankind, then it's also true that she's not a tame spirit.

No one could hope to contain her.

"I've been watching you," she says.

"Where?" I glance about, but there's no higher ground.

"You've missed me." She gazes upward with emerald eyes that

seem to glow in the dark. Wisps of her golden hair undulate in the frigid breeze.

"You know I have." I kiss her forehead, her skin warm and soft against my chapped lips. "Where do you go, when you disappear for so long?"

She shrugs as if it makes no difference. "Here and there. This is a large continent, you know. It takes a while to get from one end to the other."

"Not for you." I squeeze her against me. "What do you do out there all by yourself?"

A mischievous gleam shines in her eyes. "I'm never alone, Milton. There are many of my kind here. Not all of them are as social as I am. Most of them are shy around humans."

"Other spirits." The Hummer's engine is almost out of earshot now. "Like Jackson?"

"Yes." Her smile dims. "But he no longer spends much time in that guise."

Glad to hear it. Almost a year ago, the evil spirits of the earth tried to convince me to blow Eden's nuclear reactor. At the time, I was almost swayed by Jackson's persuasive arguments; but, thankfully, Julia's love intervened. Maybe it was only an ethereal remnant of the loyalty and devotion pets showed their trusted owners back in the day, but I prefer to believe it's love.

Because I love her, now more than ever before—even when she was alive.

"Is he still up to no good?"

"He hasn't changed in that regard," she says quietly, her gaze pensive.

I watch her for a moment. "What is it, Julia? He hasn't gone back on his word, has he?"

She shakes her head. "He is not a man, that his promise would be mutable. He will never attack you or your people again." She pauses. "Not directly."

I don't like the sound of that. "So he's bending the rules now, in other words."

She bites her lip, looking as human as Julia ever did. "He has influenced the survivors who live on the coast. Cain and his people—they worship him without knowing who or what he truly is. He has deceived them all, and his deception could lead to the ruin of all that you've fought for these past months."

I glance eastward, but the Hummer is nowhere in sight. "I have to stop them. If they're headed into a trap—"

"No. Luther and Bishop must meet. So much depends on it."

"I don't understand." I feel lost all of a sudden, and I never feel that way around her. "I've got to do something. I just don't have a clue what it is."

Her grip tightens on my arm. "Come with me, then."

"Where?"

"To the coast. You can stem the tide, before it's too late." She must be speaking in metaphor, because I seldom understand her when she does.

"I can't leave them."

"They will be fine. For now, the greatest danger lies on your western shore. Cain has committed a violent act against a member of the UW team. He has taken a life, and for this atrocity the UW will unleash its full vengeance upon the people of Cain's Shipyard."

I frown. "But...Cain is headed out here, to the Homeplace. Won't he take his people with him?"

"Not all of them. He will take the strongest and leave the rest —the old, the weak, as well as his pregnant wives. They will be at the mercy of the UW when they land on shore."

I back away from her. None of this sounds right. "He's as protective of his people as Luther is—maybe even more so. There's no way he would abandon—"

"Jackson has clouded his mind, Milton. Cain has become overwhelmed by *evil*." She shakes her head at the limitations of human speech. "There is no other word for it that you would understand. His heart is consumed by darkness. Jackson will use him to destroy all of you!"

I back away another step. "I can't go and help his people when I should be protecting my own—from *him*."

Tears glisten in Julia's eyes. "All of them are your people, Milton. Can't you see that? You must protect them from themselves."

"Why me?" I'm being pulled in three directions at once. I'm only one man—gifted with superhuman abilities, sure, but I'm limited to being in one place at a time. I can't possibly protect Luther and his people, Margo and the UW team, as well as Cain's abandoned followers. "Can't you help those people? Why does it have to be me?"

"You have faced him before," she says. "He cannot touch you. He has sworn it, and so it must be."

"Jackson?"

"He manifests himself to Cain as *Gaia*, mother of the earth. But to you, he would appear as you remember him."

Not a pleasant thought.

"Gaia, huh?" I frown at that. "Some kind of goddess?"

Jackson never was a drag queen, as far as I know. But I have to remember it's not really Jackson, just as the woman before me isn't really Julia. They're spirits physically manifesting themselves so I can interact with them. As bizarre as that is.

She takes my hands in hers. "Will you come with me? We haven't much time. But if we hurry, you can return to your people before Cain and his entourage arrive. He is not nearly as fleet of foot as the warriors he sent ahead."

Everything about this is so sudden: her appearance after weeks of being absent, the news about Jackson/Gaia, and now this plea for me to intervene—to rescue Cain's people from an impending onslaught of UW troops. Why do I have to be the one to save the day?

The truth is, no matter how heroic my deeds may seem to others, they never come close to changing the way I see myself. I can't do anything to make up for the past. I'll never find sweet redemption after what I did in the bunker so long ago.

I was a killer. Saving lives now won't change that.

But looking into Julia's eyes makes anything seem possible. She loves me, this strange spirit I can never hope to understand. She believes in me. And during these recurring moments of indecision and low self-esteem, her trust is all I need to make up my mind.

"All right," I say. "Let's go."

We take to the skies together, hand in hand, the golden aura of dawn's approach warming our backs and casting the landscape before us in stark relief against storm clouds gathering over the brackish sea. The air, chilled by the night, rushes over us and whips Julia's hair back from her brow like a glittering mane. She smiles at me, and I wink at her behind my dusty goggles. She doesn't wear any, doesn't need them, barely blinking in the cold that would have shivered my eyeballs in their sockets.

Without a word, she points out the mass of figures moving below, heading east. Cain and his people—it has to be. I bank left and hurl myself upward in a steeper trajectory. The last thing I need is a bullet in the gut from an overzealous member of Cain's tribe. Julia matches my course and speed. Together we pass over the remaining kilometers of sand and ash until we reach rolling mounds and windswept dunes. Eventually they flatten to welcome the poisoned, frothing ocean waves that break onto shore.

Julia points again, this time at a lone figure standing on the seashore a couple hundred meters to the south of Cain's Shipyard, beyond a hill of grey sand and scattered debris. I give her a thumbs-up to show I understand, and we make our descent, dropping to the sand within fifty meters of where the man stands, oddly out of place.

"Impressive," Julia remarks after my landing. Of course she remembers my fledgling attempts that would send me flailing across the ground like a broken bird.

"Lots of practice." Barely an extra step this time before I've regained my balance. I turn my attention to the figure before us, a man who appears to be reclining at an odd angle on a pair of iron poles sunk deep into the wet sand. Has he fallen asleep out here? "Who's this?"

Her expression clouds. "Come and see."

She leads me to the corpse—for that's what it is, the body of a man staked into the ground, two rods crossing through his flesh to form a large X. Judging by his thermal bodysuit, he was a member of the UW team.

I can't help wincing at the sight. I've seen more than my share of death—been the cause of a lot of it—but what happened to this man was brutal. It shows no respect for his dignity, much less his life.

"Did Jackson—?"

"He cannot harm your kind in this way." She shakes her head. "He can only influence those he's deceived to do such things for him."

"Cain."

Julia's silence is confirmation enough.

"What the hell is he thinking? Does he want all-out war?" I turn toward the sea where the *Argonaus* sits in the distance.

They will have already seen this man's body. They've probably recorded images to send back to their superiors in Eurasia and are now awaiting orders. It doesn't take much imagination to guess what those orders will be: terminate all hostiles with extreme prejudice.

But from what I've observed—hovering above the bridge of the *Argonaus* in the dead of night and listening in on conversations among the senior officers—Captain Mutegi is a far cry from the hot-headed, bloodthirsty military stereotype popularized by the Sector rebels decades ago. The same goes for the members of the UW team I've met. Either the United World military has grown softer and hopefully wiser over the years, or these people are exceptions to the rule. Regardless, Mutegi seems to have a level head on his shoulders, and he won't act rashly at the sight of this heinous crime.

I hope.

"We should bury him. Now. We can't leave him out here like this. The sun—" I move to pull the body down from the iron stakes. Lengths of rebar, by the looks of them. "Anytime you feel like lending a hand..." I grunt, hugging the body.

"I'm afraid I wouldn't be much help," Julia apologizes. "I cannot interact with humans who can't see me."

"Because he's dead."

"Even if he were alive. He was not open to the spirit world as you and Daiyna are."

"How would you know that?" I frown at the mention of Daiyna's name. Just as Margo surmised, all is not well back at the Homeplace, and Daiyna has caused most of the discord, from what I can tell. "Were you with them—the crew, before Margo found them?"

Julia nods. "This one was full of anger and fear." She holds an open hand toward the dead man. "There was no way for me to reach him. He died acting rashly. If I didn't know better, I would say Jackson had influenced him, too."

I turn my attention to the iron rods planted into the sand. The body won't be going anywhere until they're dug up. I'm not about to desecrate the man's remains in order to tear him free.

"What about the woman and the other men—their leader, Bishop?"

"The sergeant is the only one among them open to my presence."

"You revealed yourself to him?" I feel a bitter surge of jealousy. I don't like it, but I can't help it. Gritting my teeth, I dig at the damp, hard-packed sand around the rebar with my hands. "How'd he take it?"

"He could not see. Something was wrong with his helmet. But he heard me, though he could not believe what he was hearing." She sounds amused.

"What did you do? Show up as his girlfriend or something?"

"His daughter. And then his wife."

I can feel her eyes on me as I busy myself with the sand.

"The man is motivated by love. He wishes only to see his family again." She pauses. "The team was attacked by daemons. I had to intervene."

"You must really think they're important, these UW people."

"The United World government does not own James Bishop. They are using him. If he were to become an ally—"

"Why are you so interested?" I stop digging and look up at her. My heart's beating as fast as it does during flight. "Why the hell do you care about any of this—about *us*? What are we to you?"

She blinks at me as her brow creases. "Milton—"

I stand, abandoning the corpse. "Show me." I advance on her. "Show me what you looked like to him."

"Milton, it doesn't work like that. You know—"

"I said show me." I grip her by the forearms. She doesn't struggle.

"Why are you—?"

"Do it now!"

"Or what?" Jackson's voice behind me sends an oily chill up the back of my neck. "You'll kill her all over again?"

I release Julia and whirl with fists clenched to face this specter from my past. But I have no words as I stare up at the large bearded man. So I return to the sand instead.

"What are you doing with that thing?" Jackson smirks at the corpse.

"Cleaning up after you," Julia says.

"Hey, I didn't do this. I gave Milton's people my word. No more interfering."

I remain silent, digging both hands with renewed vigor. Part of me almost believes if I ignore Jackson, he'll go away. But most of me knows better.

"Where's your dress?" I mutter without looking up.

Jackson chuckles drily. "You've been telling tales out of school, my dear."

"Only the truth," Julia replies.

"As you see it."

"You have set yourself up as an object of their worship—"

"I've given them *hope*," he counters.

"Like this?" I gesture at the dead body. "You know what it will bring."

Jackson smiles coldly. "Your kind knows only destruction. If you remember, I gave you the choice to end their misery, once and for all. But you chose *life*." He laughs, and there is no mirth in his tone—only malice. "Let's see what your species does with it!"

"You want them to destroy themselves," Julia says.

"I want them to do what comes naturally. They had their time on this earth, and they squandered it. They destroyed us all, everything we ever knew. They should have exterminated themselves in the process." He folds his brawny arms and shrugs. "I'm just allowing them to fulfill their destiny."

"Through deceit." She's never backed down from him, and she isn't now. "You manipulate them and lie to them, pretending to have powers you've never possessed. If you manifested yourself in a form more in keeping with your goals—"

"You'd have me show up as what? A *devil*?"

"If the hoof fits."

I've got the iron bars free of the hard-packed sand, and I give the skewered body a slight push, sending it over backward where it falls with a puff of dust. I tug out each of the bloodstained rods, pulling them free of the corpse and sending them skidding across the sand.

"So nothing's really changed." I don't look at either one of them. "After all we went through before, everything you put me through. We're right back where we started. You want us to live." I nod toward Julia as I dig with my hands, enlarging the pit to make room for the soldier's body. "And you want us to die—only you're not acting against us *directly* this time around." I glance up at Jackson with contempt. "You're pitting us against each other instead. So that in the end, none of us will survive." I shake my head at the insanity of it.

Julia kneels beside me. "You have changed immensely, Milton. Just think back to the person you were a year ago, and compare that to the man you are now. You have earned Luther's complete trust. He sends you to scout for your people, and he makes decisions that affect all of their lives based on your word alone. Just last night, you saved every member of that United World team—"

"A reprieve." Jackson scoffs. "Their days are numbered."

"If you have your way," Julia allows. "But Milton has stopped you before. He will do it again."

The weight of her expectations sits squarely on my shoulders.

"Maybe he doesn't want to be your *messiah*. Have you ever considered that? It's just as likely he'll crumble under the pressure, and everything will go exactly as I've planned." Jackson nods with complete confidence. "The humans used to play a game of strategy called chess. What you're doing is planning your tactics around a single piece, pinning all your hopes for humankind on Milton, a fractured soul. But I've already looked ahead, three or four moves down the line, and there's no chance you're going to beat me. Because I've learned my lesson, and I don't have my entire strategy based on a single man or woman. This time, I'm coming from all angles: Cain's people, Eden, the dissention in Luther's own camp." He shakes his head. "You won't be able to stop me."

For once, he doesn't sound arrogant. He's merely stating the facts. Nothing Julia can say will change matters. It only makes sense that this time around, he would have planned for every contingency.

"You will be stopped," she says without reservation. "They don't want what you want. Cain's people, Luther's, the UW—even the daemons you made to feed on human flesh. Not one of them wants to die. They have the same survival instinct ingrained in them as we do."

Jackson shrugs. "And blinded by their survival instincts, they will annihilate each other. It has happened before. It will happen again."

The ash and sand at his feet suddenly open like a mouth ready to consume him. Laughing like a maniac, he drops into the earth as two slobbering daemons charge through the space where he stood just a moment ago. They seem to have appeared out of the air itself. Bulbous yellow eyes straining against lidless sockets, they fall upon me with daggers raised, knocking me over, all three of us tumbling with a cloud of ash into the pit I was digging.

Julia cries out in alarm, but there's no reason she should be frightened for me. Even caught off guard, I'm too fast for these creatures.

In a split-second or two, I use the first daemon's blade on the second, then return the favor, slitting their throats to release the thick, foul-smelling sludge that passes for their blood. I leave them twitching in the pit and climb out, wiping my hands on my dusty trousers.

"Well, that was unexpected."

"Are you all right?" Julia says.

I hold out a hand to halt her advance. "Fine."

"Milton—"

"You're right. I've changed. I've had a lot of time to think about things while you've been gone, and I've realized something. We don't need any spirits of the earth. Jackson—whatever he really is—or you, either." I shake my head, unable to meet her gaze. She looks too much like Julia, and right now she's grief-stricken. "Thanks for the superhuman abilities and everything. They really do come in handy. But we can take it from here. We don't need your guidance anymore."

I drag the lifeless daemons out of the pit and kneel to resume digging. Another meter or so should be deep enough to bury the mutilated soldier.

"If this is what you want..." Julia already sounds distant.

As does the report of heavy artillery—after the dune beside me explodes on impact. I reel to look back at the *Argonaus* as another shell plows into the beach, sending sand and ash sky high. A sudden alarm wails from Cain's compound on the north side of the dunes, and a ragged voice screams at me through the smoke.

"You there! Come inside. You don't want to die alone!"

17. TUCKER

18 MONTHS AFTER ALL-CLEAR

It's no secret that Daiyna wants me dead—along with everybody else from Eden. And from the sound of things, she's got more than a few supporters on her side of the fence. Luther did well assigning Samson the mighty cyborg as my personal bodyguard.

"Any chance I can get this stuff off me?" I gesture at my limbs protruding from the sand-colored tunic he gave me to wear. A filmy residue from the healing salve remains on my skin.

"Your chances of staying alive are better as long as I can see you," Samson rumbles. He arrived at my bedside moments before to escort me to some meeting in the Homeplace's great cavern. That's how everybody refers to these caves, high up the side of a west-facing mountain ridge: the *Homeplace*. "Hurry up. Luther wants you there when the team arrives."

I can't help grimacing as I pull off the cloak from around my shoulders. The great cavern is close to the exterior, and this time of day, heat wafts in from the desert on dry winds. So I won't need an extra layer. I take a moment to look over the scars healing along my abdomen and the gunshot I took to the chest, thanks to that trigger-happy sentry. Come to find out, the fellow is a card-carrying member of Daiyna's Eden-hating faction. No surprise there.

At the time, lying out under the sun and bleeding out, I was prepared to die; but Luther and company managed to bring me back from the brink of death, and I owe them big for my new lease on life.

As far as I'm concerned, I died that day—shot point-blank and served up as *Muto Lunch Special #3*. So whatever Samson tells me to do, I'll do it. They've been good to me here, and truth be told, I like it. Back in Eden, Willard never would have made room for someone like me in the upper ranks of his organization. But here? I can see myself being useful to Luther, and once I've earned their trust—hell, maybe even Daiyna's and her bunch, to boot—I'll go through a whole swarm of mutos to help out however I can.

"This way." Samson leads me down the earthen corridor where green glowsticks mounted along the walls give the space an eerie light. "Stay close."

I nod and sniff, shuffling after the big cyborg. "So, I hear we've got a bunch of unexpected guests now. From the coast, is that right?"

"Who told you that?"

I shrug. "I hear things." They've kept me in a private alcove during my recovery, but I'm privy to snatches of conversation between the folks who tend to me, passing each other in shifts so there's always somebody watching over me. Luther's orders, I'm guessing. "Am I right in assuming these folks aren't exactly your allies?"

Samson keeps his gaze fixed ahead of us. "You'd do well to mind your own business."

"Good advice." I do my best to keep up with his long strides, metal legs clunking along through dark patches between the glowsticks. "Will Daiyna be at this meeting?"

Samson grunts something that sounds affirmative.

"Any chance she's found it in her heart to forgive me?"

"Nope. Why else would you need me by your side?"

Good point. "So this team of people with Margo, they're really from the UW?" No response from Samson. I let out a low whistle. "Isn't that something? I mean, the rest of the world is still out there, just living their lives day to day. No flesh-eating mutants to contend with, no superfreaks like you and me. No offense."

Another grunt from the cyborg.

"How's it strike you? The reason they're here, I mean." I sniff and run the back of my hand across my nose. My skin smells like the healing salve has seeped down deep into my pores. Only a good long shower would clean me up—something I sure as hell won't find outside of Eden. "To claim your kids, right?"

Samson halts, half-turning with a serious look of menace on his broad, bearded face. "Remember that advice I gave you?"

"Mind my own business? Right. Got it." I raise both hands in surrender and wait until Samson resumes walking. Then I continue, "Never was sure whose babies they were, those two I carried through the desert. Who belonged to which parents, I mean. Not that it really mattered. I just had to make sure they got to where they needed to go. That's all Margo wanted. Guess I'm still curious, though."

The cyborg's shoulders of flesh, thick with knotted muscle, seem to sink, as if Samson has relinquished his hold on something. Without turning around to face me, he slows his pace. "We're grateful for what you did, Tucker."

"So yours is—"

"The boy." Samson's voice is grim. He picks up his pace. "And plenty more are still in Eden."

I hurry to follow and am about to apologize for sticking my nose where it doesn't belong when Daiyna appears, blocking Samson's path. A younger woman of slighter stature stands beside her. The girl's eyes don't look exactly natural, more like something you'd find on a robot. So that would make her Shechara, and her artificial eyes Margo's doing. Just like Samson's limbs, they were an attempt to make up for Perch's sadistic butchery.

"Where are you taking him?" Daiyna demands, glancing at me with a scowl.

I stare back at her.

"Luther wants him there when the team shows up." Samson's frame is nearly wide enough to impede my view of the two women.

"I don't think so." Daiyna crosses her well-toned arms. It's a standoff, even though she's obviously no match for the cyborg. "He has no business listening in on our decisions. Take him back to his bed and restrain him. Or I will."

I don't like the sound of that. But I know better than to say anything.

Samson grumbles deep in his chest. "Daiyna, if it wasn't for him, those two babies we've got wouldn't—"

"If it wasn't for *him*..." She leaves it unsaid, clenching her fists down at her sides.

I know all too well what she was about to say. If I hadn't betrayed her trust, she never would have been captured by Willard in Eden, never would've been forced to go under the knife. There's plenty of blame to go around, but I know full well that I carry the lion's share.

Shechara puts a hand gently on Daiyna's arm. "I will keep an eye on him." The mechatronic orbs in her eye sockets twitch as she speaks, focusing on me.

"It's not like he's invisible for the three of us." Samson half-turns to allow her a full view. "Not with that salve making him look like a ghosty."

Shechara nods. Daiyna curses under her breath. "If he tries to escape, I'll put an arrow in him myself."

They talk about me as if I'm not even here.

"He'd have to get past me." Samson sends a look my way that says, *Are we clear on that?*

"Where the hell would I go?" I can't help blurting out. "I'd rather not face those mutos out there again, thank you very much. Not in this condition." I gesture at my tunic and the wounds underneath in various stages of the healing process.

"I don't want to hear another word out of him." Daiyna points in my direction but holds Samson's gaze. There's fire in her eyes. "And that goes double during the council meeting. He says anything in there, I'll hold you personally responsible." Her finger presses into Samson's chest.

"You've got me quaking in my mechanical legs." He grins amiably.

Shechara urges Daiyna away by the arm. "Let's go find our seats."

Daiyna allows herself to be escorted away, but she gives Samson a final withering look. He's in no hurry as he resumes his trek up the passageway after them.

"I meant what I said." I sniff, following. "There's no place else I'd rather be. I'm grateful to you all for taking me in like this."

Samson exhales loudly. "Yeah, well, she meant what she said, too. So if I was you, I'd zip the lip once the meeting starts. She might aim for you and shoot me by mistake."

"Understood." I'm guessing he plans to stick by my side. And I'm glad of it.

We turn and enter a wide cavern, more or less circular in shape, with plenty of glowsticks mounted along the perimeter. Large stones have been arranged as seats to make the place look like an indoor amphitheater, roomy enough to fit a hundred or more. Luther stands in the center of the space and confers with two armed sentries dressed like those fellows I encountered. They wear sand-colored cotton garb and carry automatic rifles slung back on their shoulders by thick straps. UW-issued weaponry, by all appearances. No doubt snatched off dead mutos.

Luther looks up as Samson approaches. Kind of difficult to miss him with all the clanking parts. Luther raises a hand in greeting, and I return the gesture, forgetting Luther can't see me. I lower my hand at a low grunt from Samson. The cyborg gives a slight nod toward where Daiyna and Shechara sit in the front row.

Daiyna stares unblinking in my direction, her eyes full of unguarded hate.

"I hear you're healing well," Luther welcomes me with an outstretched hand in my general direction, having dismissed the two sentries. They jog out of the cavern, keeping their eyes to themselves. "I'm glad."

I meet his firm handshake, and gasps erupt from those who've already gathered. It isn't every day they see their leader vanish before their eyes. But Luther reappears just as suddenly when I release his hand.

"Your medics know what they're doing," I tell him. "I'd be a goner, otherwise."

"The very least we could do, considering it was one of our men who shot you." Luther has seriously aged since I saw him last, and it's only been months. Still as well-built and sharp-eyed as ever, though. "The way you risked your life to bring those incubation pods to us... We owe you."

"How are they—the babies?" I step forward, causing Samson to shift his weight uneasily.

"No sudden moves," he cautions in a low tone.

Luther smiles, the expression genuine and full of warmth despite the sorrow lingering behind his eyes. "They are well. You will see them shortly."

"Are they out already? Born?" I guess that's still the word for it.

"Not yet." Luther glances at Samson. "That is one of the matters we'll be discussing today. Sure to lead to more heated debate—something we've been fielding a lot lately."

"Never in short supply," Samson mutters.

A diplomatic way to say the Homeplace is rampant with discord? "I'm honored to be here, even if it's just to listen in. Doubt there's much I could contribute."

"On the contrary." Luther claps me on the shoulder with a solid grip. "You are our resident expert on Eden. We will need your input when it comes time to discuss returning for the other incubation pods that remain in Eden's sublevels."

I sniff, shuffling my feet. "Maybe it's best if I just keep my yap shut for now, seeing how this is my first council meeting and all."

"As you wish." Another warm, sad-eyed smile from Luther. "We won't force you to speak. But if during our discussion you have anything to add that may help us, please don't hesitate to speak up. You're among friends here."

He squeezes my shoulder as Daiyna continues to stare daggers. *Friends?* Luther might be a bit out of touch. "I'll keep that in mind."

"We should sit down." Samson guides me away.

Instantly, Luther is swarmed by a group of people dressed as he is in the same loose cotton garb. They look irate about something. Apparently, not everything is fine and dandy here in Caveville.

How have these people lived like this for so many months? Humans weren't designed to thrive inside the earth. At least Eden has filtered air and running water and electricity, even though it, too, is separated from the surface by meters of rock.

"Does he ever get a moment's peace?" I nod toward Luther as Samson seats himself in the back row, far enough from Daiyna and Shechara and out of their eyeshot.

"Luther?" The cyborg gestures for me to sit beside him. The seat is far from ergonomic, but at least Daiyna isn't staring at me. "He's a busy man, alright. For good reason. He's kept us alive, and he's kept us together."

"I've never met anybody more at peace with life in general. How is he so calm?"

Half a grin works its way up the side of Samson's face. "Luther may not know what the future holds, but he knows who holds the future. He's put his life in the hands of the Creator, the author and finisher of reality. So he doesn't sweat the small stuff."

I'm not sure how to respond to that.

The other seats fill in as men and women of all shapes, sizes, and skin tones enter the cavern with facial expressions running the gamut from anxious to angry. They all wear the same loose garments, like a cult's uniform. Did they stumble across some sort of fabric warehouse on their journey west?

"Your numbers have grown." There were only five back when I chauffeured them out of Eden. I've counted three dozen here already.

"We grew as we headed west, meeting fellow survivors along the way."

"If Willard could see you now. I don't think he's got a clue. You guys are a real force to be reckoned with."

Samson frowns at that. "Even with our numbers, we'd be no match for Eden. Not with Willard's remote-controlled daemons. We wouldn't get close."

"But isn't that what this meeting's about? Organizing an assault on Eden to retrieve those babies?"

Samson exhales loudly and looks away, watching as more folks filter in. Luther converses with two of them while making his way toward the center of the gathering.

"We're in the middle of something big here, and nobody knows how it's going to pan out." Samson shrugs his massive shoulders. "All I know is Luther's got to get everybody on board. If he can't keep us unified—"

"He's already lost on that score."

Samson lets out a low growl.

I didn't mean to offend. "Just look around. The way people are clustering in groups, leaving plenty of room in between. Giving each other the evil eye."

I mimic their suspicious expressions and wonder what my face looks like to Samson. Gaping holes for my eyes and mouth? Probably. They didn't rub any salve on those areas.

"Can you blame them?" Samson frowns. "Your presence represents everything they'd like to forget. They've heard about

Eden, and some of them want to blow it into a crater four stories deep. They hate what it stands for. What *you* stand for."

I blink at that. "What about the UW? I can't be the only baddie on their minds."

Samson has a retort ready to go, but that's when Luther holds up both his hands in a silent gesture, the tip of each finger permanently scarred from his time in Eden. He scans the faces gathered before him. Every seat has been taken, and many stand along the periphery. The voices peter out like a faucet turned off.

"Brothers and sisters," Luther greets them. Despite their divisions, one thing is clear: these people respect him. "Thank you for gathering on such short notice. I realize there are many of you who are concerned about our recent guests—our friends from the coast." A fervent murmur runs through the crowd as heads nodded emphatically, but no one speaks up. Luther raises his hands again, and they quiet down. "I understand your anxiety, and I will not insult you by saying there is no cause for concern. Cain's people are strangers among us, and it is human nature to distrust what is unfamiliar. But you have my word: they will not harm a single one of you while they are here. It is not you they are interested in, but rather a band of travelers who are now on their way to the Homeplace."

"Who the hell is *Cain*?" I whisper to Samson.

The cyborg points a metallic digit, directing my attention back to Luther.

"As you well know, it has been my desire for some time to unite our two peoples—those of us who reside in these caves and our friends on the coast in Cain's Shipyard. Some of you have accompanied me as we've gone to visit Cain's people to encourage them to join us, to invite them here to the Homeplace." Luther rests his gaze upon Samson, and all eyes focus on the big man.

There's virtually the same expression on each of their faces: a profound respect, akin to what they show Luther. But with Samson it's different, somehow. The only thing I can compare it to brings back memories of my youth in Sector 30, playing football in secondary school. My team respected our quarterback; we'd seen him in action, and we trusted him.

Samson is this team's quarterback, and Luther is their venerable coach.

"But Cain would not accept our offer of kinship," Luther continues. "He does not believe as we do, that we are all children of the Creator. The spirits of the earth have changed us with the Creator's blessing, and it is His desire for us to be united as one family, not divided as we are."

"But they serve a false god!" a voice shouts from the back of the assembly. A few heads turn to look at who spoke while a few others nod in agreement. Most remain transfixed on their leader. Apparently, heartfelt interruptions aren't uncommon here.

"The Creator does not require belief from His creation," Luther goes on, unfazed. "We all have been given the same choice, to accept or reject His existence. I am sure some of us gathered here today do not share my beliefs. I don't expect you to. The Homeplace is welcome to all. I ask only that you respect my beliefs and those of others who see our Creator's hand where you may not."

Heads nod, voices murmur assent. I shift my weight on the rock. I'm a little uncomfortable, but it's not entirely due to the seating arrangement. Attending some kind of religious revival wasn't on my radar. I glance up at Samson and wonder if the big man counts himself among Luther's faithful—or Daiyna, even.

Somehow I doubt it. Neither of them strike me as the holy type.

"We have welcomed these men and women from Cain's tribe. They may stay with us for as long as they like. It is our hope that they would choose to dwell with us permanently." Luther pauses, sweeping the assembly with his serious gaze. "We are stronger together than we are apart. The daemons are our common enemy. Now as for the travelers on their way, I know there have been rumors circulating, and I blame no one for spreading them. But today we have time only for the truth."

"Agreed!" shouts a voice from the opposite side of the cavern.

Again, Luther does not appear perturbed by the interruption. "As we have known for some time, this continent is under quarantine by what remains of the United World Navy. Their ships patrol the coast, allowing no one to leave our shores or to land on them—not that any have tried." He pauses. "Until now."

Silence holds the cavern. Luther has their undivided attention.

"It's no secret that the children of Daiyna, Shechara, Samson, and myself are being held in Eden where they were genetically engineered." Luther nods his head under the sudden deluge of curses and booing. I shrink beside Samson. "Those children are ours, regardless of how they came into being. They belong *here*. With us."

A roar of approval erupts from the crowd.

"Mr. Tucker." Luther singles me out with a grim smile and a hand raised toward my vicinity. I nearly choke in the face of the attention focused on me from all sides, whether or not they can actually see me. "Our invisible friend brought two of the children to us, braving harsh elements and the daemons to get them here. For that, we are eternally grateful."

Hesitant applause sputters from the crowd as murmurs circulate and eyes shift. I dip my head and glance sidelong at no one in particular, hoping with everything in me that Luther won't ask me to make some kind of speech.

"Bring them." Luther's attention shifts to a pair of sentries standing in a corridor at the edge of the gathering.

With nods to Luther, they disappear for a few seconds. When they return, they carry the two canisters I brought out of Eden. I don't recognize either sentry as being a member of my welcoming committee, but none of that really matters right now. The babies are safe, and by all appearances, the pods are still sealed shut. They continue to blink, indicating that all of the incubation systems are operating and the life signs are at healthy levels—

everything Margo told me to look out for. I find myself releasing a sigh of relief I didn't know I've been holding, and inadvertently my gaze shifts toward Daiyna.

Her eyes are fixed on the two pods like they're bombs about to go off without warning. She doesn't blink. Shechara, seated beside her, places a hand on Daiyna's forearm, and she seems to break from her reverie.

"This is why they have come." Luther opens his hands toward the two unborn children before him. "The United World is dying. They cannot reproduce. The devastation they wrought upon this continent was not limited to our lands. Airborne toxins spread across the globe, rendering them sterile. Even now as they hide, sealed off within the walls of their great city, they know they are doomed." He drops his hands to his sides. "Willard hopes to use these children—"

"How many are there?" someone pipes up, and others follow suit.

"Why are they in those chambers?"

"What did Eden do to them?"

Luther holds up his hands, and the outspoken members of the audience simmer down. "We do not have an exact count, not yet. But Mr. Tucker has told us...there are more than a dozen." Audible gasps course through the assembly. Samson shifts for the first time, his metallic legs scraping against the rock beneath him. Daiyna clenches her jaw, the muscle twitching as her fierce gaze burns at Luther. "If these two are any indication of the others' condition, then we must assume they all are healthy and nearly ready to enter our world. The question is, however, which world will they be born into?" Luther pauses, and silence holds the moment. "They have never breathed our air, and as far as we know, the spirits cannot pass through steel and plexicon barriers. Like Willard and his men, deep in the bowels of Eden, these young ones are as human as we once were." Luther glances at his fingers, where Perch tore out his claws one by one with a pair of pliers. "Ungifted."

Murmurs ripple through the audience.

"But their genes are yours," a pensive voice speaks up, belonging to a grey-haired woman standing in the back of the assembly. "Your DNA was changed by the dust of the earth. By the *spirits*, that is." She glances at Luther as she corrects herself, changing her phrasing to align with his belief system. "Your offspring will have inherited those mutated genes."

She sounds like a scientist. How many different Sectors does this remnant represent?

"It is my belief that the spirits bless us with our gifts only once we have breathed the air. The dust, as you say. That was how the abilities appeared in my Sector, when we came up out of the bunker, and I have heard a similar origin story from virtually every one of you. Willard and his men avoided these physiological changes by remaining hidden deep underground. They have never breathed our air on the surface." Luther pauses. "We do not know whether these children will eventually exhibit our gifts —or *mutations*. I'm sure that is how the United World scientists would view them. Willard has offered these children—our children—to the UW in exchange for safe passage off this quarantined continent. He has promised the UW that the children are not infected. That's his term for our gifts from the spirits: *infection*."

"Always thought of it as a handy little curse, myself," I mutter under my breath.

Samson nudges me with a heavy mechatronic elbow to keep quiet.

"These children are exactly what the UW needs to survive. So they have sent a team to meet with Willard to discuss terms and to see for themselves if the children are as healthy as Willard says. Unfortunately, the daemons found the UW representatives first, and then Cain's warriors came upon them. A little worse for wear, as would be expected, the four remaining members of the UW team are now on their way here. Two of them have already been exposed to the dust of the earth. It will not be long before they begin to exhibit their gifts from the spirits. As for the other two, their protective suits remain intact."

"Are we going to set them free?" Quiet laughter follows the heckler's remark.

Luther almost smiles. "It will be their choice, of course, whether they decide to join us. Perhaps seeing what becomes of their comrades will change their minds. They have nothing to fear—not from us, and not from their gifts."

"What about Cain's warriors?" someone else speaks up, starting another onslaught of questions.

"Why are they here?"

"Where are they now?"

Luther nods. "While Cain's people and ours have never resorted to violence against one another, the same cannot be said for their interaction with the UW team. I don't know all of the details, but I can tell you that Cain desires to repay them for attacking his people."

"Bullcrap," Samson rumbles. Similar murmurs sweep through the audience.

"He sees their encroachment on this land as an act of war," Luther continues. "And he has come to believe it is in our mutual interest to join forces, in case we cannot convince the UW team to hear us out regarding the children. Cain's people are staying in a separate chamber of the Homeplace, well-fed and well-supervised. Cain himself is on the way with the remainder of his warriors, and they should arrive this afternoon."

Luther approaches the incubation canisters. Standing between them, he rests one hand on each. "The UW doctor will test them when he arrives. If they are one hundred percent human, uninfected, their genes clear of any *mutation*, then he will contact his people off-shore. If, however, these two display any trace of genetic abnormality, it will be a sure sign that the others in Eden may not be what Willard is advertising. "

"Will he kill them?" someone asks, her voice echoing in the cavern.

Luther's eyes are as somber as ever. "I would put nothing past him. Arthur Willard is a man devoid of conscience. But rest assured, we will go to Eden. We will take what is ours, every single child. This is why it's in our best interest to combine forces."

"Down with Eden!" Numerous members of the audience take up the shout, raising their fists.

I'm glad I'm invisible.

One of the multitude steps forward. "We have heard you, Luther. We respect you, and we know you have nothing but love in your heart for us. Now hear what we have to say."

The formality makes me wonder if this is standard procedure in the *Homeplace* when a dissenter wants to offer a counterargument.

"Speak, Xavier." Luther nods and steps to the side. "We will listen."

"You say we all don't share your beliefs, and you're right. There are many of us who don't believe in your *creator*, and even more of us who don't believe in your *spirits*. These mutations—" Xavier pauses to flex one arm. Bony spines jerk outward from his bicep without any signs of tissue damage. "They're not *gifts* in our eyes. And we're mighty interested in having them removed. Permanently."

Luther clenches his jaw a moment before answering, calm as ever. "The procedure I underwent...was not by choice. Nor was it for Shechara, or for Samson."

"They sawed off my damned arms and legs!" Samson bellows.

Xavier nods. He ducks his head a little, seeming to know his place before the cyborg. "We can only imagine how difficult it has been for you, and we sympathize. But because of you, because of your harrowing experience, we know these mutations are curable. In Eden there are men of science who would be able to—"

"They're butchers." Samson rises to his mechanical feet. "Look at me! You really want this to happen to you?"

Luther raises a hand. "Peace, brother. All are welcome to have their say. You will have your turn."

"Already said all I care to." Samson drops back onto his rock with a resounding clang.

Xavier pauses before continuing, "All we're saying is, can't some of us who are interested...leave the Homeplace ahead of you, before this whole thing with your babies comes to a head? We can see what the people of Eden are able to do about our mutations."

Luther winces at the word. "You want your gifts—your abilities—taken away, when even now, the United World may be preparing to land troops on our shores? When we may need to fight for our very survival?"

"But you just said—"

"I said I would try my best to reason with the UW team, hoping they will hear us out. I have hope. I believe the spirits will be on our side, that the Creator wants what is best for us. He wants us to *live*." Luther's gaze drifts across those gathered. "We are stronger together than we ever were apart. When Daiyna, Shechara, Samson, Milton, and I escaped from Eden, we were told by the spirits that we would find others like us as we traveled west. And we have. So many of you!" He holds out his arms as if to embrace them all. Many of them have tears in their eyes, maybe at the memory of those early days, struggling to survive on their own. I sure as hell know what that was like. "We must stay *together*," Luther exhorts them. "We must remain *strong*. And if the Creator has allowed the spirits of the earth to change us, then who are we to argue with His divine will?"

"But Luther," Xavier persists amid the murmurs all around him, "isn't it just as likely that what's happened to us can be explained scientifically? And if so, if there is a medical solution, then we could be fixed—"

"You call this being *fixed*?" Samson bangs his arms together, and the clang brings the assembly to attention with startled gasps.

"Brother," Luther chides him like they're siblings.

"Sorry," the big man rumbles.

"They don't know about Margo," I mutter.

Samson shoots me a glance.

"What's that?" Xavier steps toward where I sit, his face awash with genuine interest. "What did you say, Mr. Tucker?"

"He has no voice here," Daiyna speaks up for the first time. "He's an outsider."

"He is our guest," Luther corrects her gently. For a moment, it looks as though she won't back down. But after a glance across the way at Samson, she drops her gaze. "And if he has something to add to this discussion..."

I swallow. The moment I feared is finally here. Luther expects me to say something, and he's not the only one. All of them do, their eyes directed my way, some with curiosity, but most with disdain. All because I was stupid enough to mention Margo.

I clear my throat.

"Careful now," Samson advises.

I don't need to be told twice. I can feel the stares of the Eden-haters just as hot as those who want their special abilities taken away.

"Uh, well, what Samson said is true," I begin, rising to my feet regardless of whether anybody can see me. I rub my nose and sniff out of nervous habit, smelling only that healing salve. "Willard and his crew, sure, they're engineers from Sector 30, but only one of them knew anything about human genetics and cybernetic transplants." I glance at the cyborg beside me. "After what Willard's man Perch did, she kind of put Samson back together again. But that wouldn't work for everybody. I mean, look at me." I shrug. "The only reason those of you with night-vision can see me right now is because of this goop all over me. It's supposed to heal my wounds, but I'm thinking it's to let you know where I am at all times."

Chuckles circulate. Emboldened, I feel a few of my jitters subside.

"She?" Xavier frowns with curiosity, staring in my general direction. "I thought the engineers in Eden were all men."

"Now, sure. But we had men and women in equal numbers, back in the day. Willard went nuts and didn't trust the women. Killed most of them—all but Margo. She was our doctor, geneticist, you name it. Without her, none of these babies would even be alive." I gesture at the incubation pods. "She's the one who sent me away with them, and I'm pretty sure once Willard finds out it was her doing, he'll kill her too." My eyes sting unexpectedly at the thought of Margo dead. I shuffle my feet. "So if you think there's anybody back in Eden who can help you, think again. There are plenty who'd be itching to take you apart and see how you work. If you decide to head out that way, ask for Perch. He's a real friendly son-of-a-bitch."

I glance around the cavern at the blank faces. No more chuckles to be had. Feeling like I might've said too much, I drop my gaze and take my seat while murmurs roll through the assembly in waves.

Samson grunts something that might be, "Nicely done."

"Do you have anything more you'd like to share with us, Xavier?" Luther says.

Xavier glances back at his supporters. All of them look deflated, fervor lost. Xavier shakes his head and sits down.

"Very well." Luther clasps his hands together. "For now, we will table the topic of returning to Eden for the children—or for any other reason. The UW team should arrive within the hour, and with them, someone I believe Mr. Tucker will be very happy to see."

I look up again to find Luther's gaze aimed in my vicinity.

"Our friend Margo appears to be acting as their chauffeur." Luther smiles.

I can't quite believe what I just heard, even as my whole body melts with relief.

18. BISHOP

18 MONTHS AFTER ALL-CLEAR

The Hummer eases to a halt at the base of a sheer cliff. High above, a cave's mouth yawns in the early morning light.

"We're here." Margo quietly breaks the silence that's fallen on her passengers.

"Don't see anybody," Granger remarks.

"Perhaps they do not wish to be seen," Sinclair says.

"Aren't they expecting us?" Harris pipes up, his eyes wide behind the transparent polymer of his face shield. "That's what the flying man said—"

"Where is he?" Lemuel strains to peer at the sky through the windshield.

"He said he'd follow us, right?" Granger glances back at me in the cargo compartment. "I don't like the looks of this, Captain. It's got ambush written all over it."

I glance at the rearview mirror to find Margo's dark eyes on me.

They are afraid, Sergeant. You need to say something.

She's giving me orders now? What makes it worse is the delivery system, something I really can't wrap my mind around. She seems to have no difficulty entering my head whenever she wishes.

Stay calm. I focus on the sound of the air passing through my breather as I scan the mountainside's crags. I always know when I'm being watched—the short hairs on the back of my neck have a way of standing at attention. Like they're doing right now. "More than likely, they're waiting for us to make the first move."

"So they can shoot us." Harris curses under his breath.

I turn toward him, our helmets millimeters apart. "How about making first contact, Doc?"

"You cannot be serious," he replies. "I am obviously the *least* expendable member of this team. You need me to verify the health of the fetuses once we reach Eden."

"If need be, I could take over that duty," Sinclair offers.

Harris blusters unintelligibly, aghast.

I almost smile at that. Sinclair isn't just a well-trained scientist. She's a stolid soldier, handling her injury with the dignity of a battle-weary marine.

"She's right," I agree. "Push comes to shove, I'm sure she could tell us all we need to know about the infants."

"You guys deciding our next move?" Granger says.

"The good doctor has volunteered to step outside and announce our arrival," Sinclair says.

"I beg your pardon!" Harris sputters.

"We'll be right behind you." I tug the rifle free from the doctor's death grip and set it down beside my own. "We'll do this unarmed, as a sign of good faith."

"In whom, exactly? Superhumans fast enough to kill us before we can get off a shot?"

"Get out, Doc." I stare him down. "That's an order."

Margo releases the cargo compartment door, and it drifts upward automatically. Lemuel opens his door and steps outside, boots crunching across the gravel.

"Anybody home?" his youthful voice echoes against the massive cliff face.

"That kid will be the death of us!" Harris mutters.

"After you." I give him a shove that sends him sprawling awkwardly out of the vehicle.

"Looks like we're on the move, folks," Granger says. "Keep your eyes sharp."

Margo opens the side door and helps Sinclair and Granger out, one at a time. Both lean on the vehicle, showing signs of weakness from their recent blood loss—but covering it up with extra helpings of bravado.

"Anybody?" Lemuel calls, emphasizing each syllable of the word.

"Hey kid, what's your superpower?" Granger asks.

Lemuel pauses, uncertain. "My what?"

I face the ridge above, wishing yet again that my helmet was functional. But I have to work with what I've got. So I nudge Harris. "Go on. Introduce us."

While he scowls and clears his throat, probably thinking up something eloquent to say, I keep an eye on his face shield. No life signs lighting up the HUD. So either the mutant lookouts are able to cloak their body temperature and heart rate, or there's no one up there at all.

But that can't be. Those hairs on the back of my neck are on high alert.

"My name is Dr. Jefferson Harris. This is Sergeant James Bishop. We represent the interests of the United World government. Milton said you would be expecting us."

Where the hell is that flying man? Having him along right now would be helpful.

"Raise your hands," I order, and Harris quietly relays the message to my team.

"We're unarmed, as you can plainly see," the doctor adds in a louder voice.

"But that vehicle of yours holds a small arsenal." A figure garbed in loose-fitting material appears behind an outcropping of rock and holds a high-powered rifle aimed straight at Harris.

"Tell Luther we've arrived." Margo steps forward, her eyes fixed on the sentry, concentrating on him.

Is she entering his mind?

"Stay out of my head, Eden bitch!" the sentry shouts. At that moment, four others armed and dressed as he is stand up and train their weapons on my team.

Margo's boots shift backward, off balance.

"You're a real motley bunch, you know that?" sneers a female sentry with one eye behind the scope of her sniper rifle. A red pinpoint of light jitters across my armored chest. "Two of you wounded, two sealed up tight in some kind of environmental suits. An *Edenite*. And a runt from the Shipyard. He's armed, by the way. To the teeth. You forgot to mention that."

I clench my jaw. I neglected to take into account the blades the kid has strapped on under his cloak.

"Stopping here wasn't my idea." I glance at Margo, whose eyes haven't left the first sentry. Not the welcome any of us was expecting. But if they don't want us, fine. "We're late for our rendezvous with Eden anyway."

"I won't go back," Margo murmurs.

"Perhaps we've arrived at a bad time," Harris calls out with a twitchy smile, nodding and attempting to bow for some reason. "We'll just be on our way, then. Sorry to bother you—"

The first sentry chuckles. "You're not going anywhere. Not until Luther has a word with you."

The woman with the sniper rifle steps off the ledge and drops fifty meters to the gravel below like it's only a meter-long jump. She lands in an easy crouch, the laser sight on my chest expanding in diameter with her proximity.

"Follow me," she says with a self-satisfied smirk, turning to lead the way up the mountain on the east side of the cliff. "Those who can, anyway."

"Go on, Captain." Granger nods after her. "We'll be fine here. It's you this Luther fellow wants to talk with, anyhow."

I frown, turning to face Sinclair. I don't like the idea of leaving them behind, but there's no way either of them will be able to make the climb in their condition.

"He's right," she says. "We would only slow you down. The

sooner you meet with this man, the sooner we can be on our way."

"Without our chauffeur?" Harris retorts. "You heard her. She won't return to Eden. Face it. We're not going anywhere. This mission is a complete failure."

Images of my family flash before my eyes yet again. I clench my fists. The mission has to be a success, and I have to return home. There's no other option.

"We're not through, not by a long shot. You got me?" I look each member of my team in the eye, even though Harris is the only one who can hear me, now that Sinclair's helmet battery died. I gesture at the driver's seat. "Tell Granger to figure out how to drive this thing."

The good doctor reluctantly relays the message.

"How hard can it be?" The engineer shrugs with a grin. "Consider it done."

"Good. And you—" I knock on the doctor's chest plate. "Make sure those two are healing up all right. I'm not losing anybody else on this mission."

Harris looks relieved that he won't be expected to climb the mountain. "We will wait for you here, Sergeant."

I stare him down—it's becoming a habit. Then I turn to Margo, who will be acting as my translator of sorts. "Ready?"

She nods and glances at Lemuel.

"What about him?" I note the kid's hesitation.

Her reply worms its way into my head: *He has nowhere else to go.*

Putting a brave face on the situation, Lemuel starts up the hillside after the sentry.

"See you soon, Captain." Granger salutes. "Just promise me one thing."

I half-turn awkwardly to face him.

"Bring us back some grub!" He winks. "And don't go getting yourself sucked into their mutant cave cult. You already have two freaks-in-the-making right here!"

Harris doesn't look amused. Neither does Sinclair.

"Be careful, Sergeant." Her gaze drifts to the armed sentries. "We have no idea who we're dealing with."

I doubt we have from the start.

If anything, this detour from our mission might provide some answers. I can only hope. I start up the rise, already lagging behind the others. With my suit slowing me down, it becomes immediately apparent that I won't catch up anytime soon. The other sentries jeer at me with catcalls and incessant comments.

"You afraid what we've got is *catching*, Sarge?"

"You really need to wear that clunker?"

"Don't you want to be able to read minds like that *Edenite* with you? Or that kid—hey, show us what you've got, kid!"

Lemuel flips them off. I almost grin, sweating as I stumble along under the heat of the morning sun.

"Cool by five degrees," I give the voice command, but of course my suit refuses to respond. No harm in trying.

"Am I moving too fast for you?" the sentry woman calls down, already more than twenty meters ahead. Margo and Lemuel aren't far behind her. "You're not doing the UW proud, Sarge. Aren't you supposed to be a superior race or something?"

The other sentries guffaw. "That's what they want us to believe. Keeping us quarantined like animals in some kind of Preserve," says the first one. "Why are you people even here? Why's the UW suddenly interested in us?"

"Luther told us all about it in the assembly," says one of the others, holding his rifle in a noncommittal posture.

"Wasn't invited."

"Oh—right. Cuz of how you welcomed that other *Edenite*."

Margo halts in her tracks. "Who was this?"

"Word is he can make himself go invisible whenever he wants."

"He's alive..." Margo murmurs.

"Better haul ass if you want to make it to your sweet reunion," snaps the female sentry. "I see dust rising on the horizon. Cain will be here by midday, daemons permitting."

"I left those flesh-eaters that invisible guy to munch on, a few days back. Guess his meat was no good." The first sentry curses. "Now I'm pulling triple shifts. How is that fair?"

"You didn't have to shoot him," mutters one of his partners.

"We needed to get those two pods to the Homeplace. I had my priorities straight!"

I glance up at him. His muzzle hasn't strayed, still trained on me. This man shot one of Margo's friends and left him at the mercy of those deformed creatures? Is such ruthless behavior representative of Luther's crew?

"I did what I had to do," the sentry continues as if he's trying to convince himself more than anybody else. "That's what soldiers do. Ain't that right, Sarge?"

Bits of gravel and ashen shale cascade from my boots as I forge onward. "He's no soldier. Mercenary, maybe," I tell Margo.

"How do you know?" she asks.

"He's got the bearing of a soldier for hire. The way he carries himself and holds his weapon. He says he takes orders from Luther, but I've got a feeling this warm welcome was all his idea. Maybe his way of getting back at Luther for those triple shifts?"

"Possible," Margo allows.

"You two sharing secrets?" The sentry pauses. "That's rude. Maybe we should leave you alone out here, see how you fare next time the daemons attack."

"So you're here for our protection?" Margo sounds skeptical.

Smirking, the sentry raises his muzzle toward my fractured face shield. "Better believe it."

"Sir—is everything all right?" Sinclair calls out from below.

I force a tight grin, my gaze riveted on the hot-headed sentry. Slowly, I raise my hand and give Sinclair a thumbs-up.

"They're just playing a little King of the Hill." Granger's voice echoes from where he sits behind the wheel of the Hummer.

"Perhaps they should focus more on climbing the hill," Sinclair replies.

I glance down at them. Hot sweat dribbles from my brow. "Halfway there."

"You're making steady progress," Margo says. "As is your engineer."

"Has he already figured out how to drive that vehicle?"

She pauses. "He has identified the accelerator."

"Good start."

"Pick up the pace, Sarge." The sentry scowls at me. "You're falling behind."

"Just planning how to take you out." I haul myself upward with a grunt. The suit isn't getting any lighter.

"I see your mouth working, buddy, but I'm not hearing anything."

"His helmet is damaged," Margo tries to explain.

"A mute ambassador? Wow, the UW really sent their best and brightest." The sentry laughs. "Hey, you're gonna like having us around when Cain gets here. Rumor is he wants you people off this continent ASAP—dead or alive. And I'm pretty sure he prefers *dead*. What the hell did you do to piss him off, anyway?"

"It's an act of war, them stepping onto our soil." Lemuel speaks up for the first time. Not winded in the slightest, he passes the female sentry leading the climb and reaches the level sheet of rock above. Dusting himself off, he adds, "But Cain knows Gaia will protect us. Or so he says." The youth shrugs.

"You're not so sure." Margo watches him as she climbs.

"I think the goblyns do what they want, and nobody has much say about it. They shot down your helicopter because they could, not because Gaia made them do it." He's changed his tune. "And because they were hungry."

"They usually are," the first sentry mutters, spitting off the side of the cliff.

The female sentry reaches the ledge and pulls herself up and over without accepting Lemuel's hand held out to her. Is the youth suffering from a new crush? For the hundredth time, I find my thoughts drifting back to my own wife and family.

Get the job done. Get it done and go home!

She stands on the ledge above me. Not the sentry. Not Margo. My wife—Emma. Without a hazard suit, her silken hair caught by a soft breeze, a white gown clinging to the curves of her slender body. Smiling down at me, she holds out both hands, her arms bare but not blistered under the sun's scorching rays.

"Come," she says, but her voice isn't in my ears. It enters my mind. "We have much to do, you and I."

Who are you? I gasp through the breather, my heart surging in my chest. No one else seems to notice she's there.

"You know who I am. Come. We must make things right, before it's too late."

"You need to take a break, Sarge?" the sentry sneers.

I do my best to pick up the pace. *Are you Gaia?* I look up at her with that question in the forefront of my mind. She looks like a goddess.

"No." She smiles sadly. "Gaia is only an illusion."

Like you. I know she isn't really there. This isn't my wife. It's not even a hallucination. This is something else, supernatural. I recognize her essence from before, when the chopper crashed and those flesh-eaters came after me and my team. Only I wasn't able to see anything at the time. I wasn't able to see *her*. If I had, would I have managed to hold onto my sanity?

"I am no illusion," she says. "I stand here before you. Waiting for you."

Nobody else can see you. My body trembles. She looks so real, reaching for me. More than anything, I want to run to her and take her into my arms.

"Their eyes remain closed to the spirit world. They cannot see what they do not believe exists. Unlike you, James Bishop."

I've never thought of myself as a man open to anything supernatural. I'm not religious; most aren't anymore. D-Day had a way of shaking people free of their superstitions, and the citizens of Eurasia have considered themselves to be post-religious ever since the beginning, when the domes were built. But if they were presented with something like this—a spirit able to take the form of someone they love—would they become true believers in an instant?

Who are you, really? What are you? I have to know.

"Luther will tell you all about us—and what you must do to save the world."

I decide it's best to ignore that last part. *Luther can see you too?*

The spirit seems to hesitate, if that's possible. The familiar face of my wife chews on her lower lip the way she does when she's thinking something over. How can this entity do that? Is it pulling strands of memory straight from my subconscious to create this persona?

"Luther believes in our Creator. That is where his faith lies, as it should. Only the Creator is worthy of worship."

I didn't ask for a lesson in spirituality. *So he can't see you.*

She shakes her head. "As much as he wishes he could, he cannot truly believe in us. He says he does, and he may believe that is so, but it is a guilt-ridden belief. He does not think we should exist, because we do not appear in the holy writings."

We? There are more of you? What kind of crazy fantasy land is this?

She reaches for me, insistent now. "You must hurry. Luther needs to speak to you before Cain arrives. Already his dust clouds the horizon."

I curse as my gloved hand slips, but I catch myself before plummeting to the gravel below. I take a moment to collect myself, let my pulse slow down a bit. *This suit wasn't made for climbing.* My recent extracurricular activities have more than likely voided the warranty.

"You will not always be able to wear it." She is very serious now. "No one else here wears one."

"C'mon, Sarge!" the sentries resume their catcalls. "You move like an old man!"

As troublesome as it is, there's no chance I'll be taking off my suit—even if I have to breathe shallow. Seeing my family again is contingent upon remaining contamination-free.

"You assume too much of your superiors," she says. "You think they will be true to their word."

Apparently, my mind is now an open book to her.

"How do you know they are not prepared to wipe out every living thing on this continent, once and for all—you included?"

I shake my head. It's not possible. Captain Mutegi would have warned us. He's a good man, and I trust him. *You know something I don't?*

She smiles slightly. "All will become clear to you in time. But I must caution you: Do not hold too tightly to your hope of returning home. Such a dream could easily be shattered."

True enough. A single round from one of these high-powered rifles aimed at me and my cracked helmet will be done for. Say goodbye to any chance of seeing my wife and kids again. They'll become wards of the state, subject to manual labor without my government paycheck.

No way in hell I'm ever allowing that to happen. I'm finishing this mission, and I'm not getting infected. My superiors will allow me to return home. Life will be the way it's supposed to be. Nothing else matters.

"That's where you're wrong, James," the specter says in my wife's voice. "There is so much more at stake here. The future of the world depends on what happens in the next twenty-four hours. Speak to Luther. Listen to him. He only wants humankind to survive. Unified."

Humankind? From what I've seen, my team is the only group of humans on this messed-up continent. The rest of these people aren't members of the same species.

I grunt as I haul myself up over the ledge in front of my wife's bare toes. Except she's no longer there. Not that she ever was.

"Sergeant, how are you feeling?" Margo leans over me where I lie on my back, struggling to catch my breath.

I nod and give her a thumbs-up while doing my best to keep my mind clear. The less she can read, the better.

Heavy metallic clanking sounds echo from inside the cave. As I roll slowly onto my hands and knees, I catch sight of a large, muscular man lumbering toward us with mechatronic arms and legs of riveted steel. The joints and hydraulics allow for almost lifelike motion.

"Samson." Margo looks relieved at the appearance of the monstrous cyborg.

"These idiots giving you any trouble?" Samson glares at the sentries. They've lost some of their swagger in the presence of the mechanized man—clearly top dog. Luther's second-in-command?

"Tucker has been injured—" She presses past him.

"He'll be all right. We're taking good care of him." Samson's metal hand clamps her upper arm and holds her in place. She doesn't resist or wince at the pressure. Either the cyborg has incredible control of his extremities, or the woman is accustomed to pain.

"I must see him." She stares up into Samson's eyes. Reading his thoughts?

"You will. Soon as Luther has a chance to talk to you and—" He frowns, sizing me up in an instant. "You're the UW envoy?"

"Sergeant James Bishop," Margo introduces me. "The rest of the team is below. Due to his damaged helmet, I'll be acting as interpreter."

I step forward with one hand outstretched.

"And who the hell are you?" Samson leaves me hanging, instead turning all of his attention to Lemuel. The youth hangs back with his arms folded, boots near the edge of the cliff as if keeping an exit strategy open.

"This is Lemuel," Margo says.

"I've heard of you. Luther's cyborg." Somehow, both contempt and respect leak out of Lemuel's tone. "How many goblyns have you pulverized with those arms?"

"Is he with you?" Samson glances first at me. Then, thinking better of it, he rests his world-weary gaze on Margo. "Some kind of stray cat you've picked up?"

"He's been exiled from his people," she explains.

"Then a reunion's in order. Cain's bunch is here, the same crew who tried to take you out." Samson gives me a hard look. "But don't worry. I won't let them bite you." He smirks. "Wouldn't want that pretty suit of yours to get scratched or anything. That could turn your life into a real tragedy. Hell, you might end up stuck on this continent with the rest of us freaks."

"Speak for yourself." Lemuel stares openly at the cyborg's legs. "How do you hope to bed a woman with all that cold metal?"

Silence holds the moment—after a sharp intake of breath from a couple of the sentries.

"What's your gift, kid?" Samson rumbles, deep in his chest.

Lemuel frowns, looking away. "None of your business."

"Hasn't Gaia *blessed* you yet? Is that why you've been kicked out of Shiptown? Little Boy Blue's not special enough to be one of Cain's warriors?"

Lemuel curses under his breath, but that's the extent of his retaliation. Impressive, not to give in to the cyborg's goading. But was it true, what Samson said? In a land of genetic mutations, could the one abnormality among them be an all-natural, one-hundred-percent human? Was that the real reason for his exile?

"Take us to Luther." Margo glances over her shoulder at the dust drifting upward in the west. "Cain will arrive soon."

The sentries set their stoic faces in that direction, resembling statues now without another word or even a glance in my direction. I like the effect Samson's presence has on them.

Samson nods, gracing Lemuel with a withering look before stomping back toward the cave. "This way. The kid stays out here."

Lemuel looks ready to protest, but he remains silent.

"Or you can surrender your weapons." Samson shrugs his shoulders of flesh. "Your choice."

The youth shakes his head and faces west, watching the dust with an expression of doomed resignation on his face.

"Luther's just finished a town hall meeting." Samson's voice echoes in the cave as Margo and I follow. "Your friend Tucker was a big hit."

"He is healing well," she seems to echo his thoughts ahead of time.

"Yeah. He'll be good as new in a week or two."

"If he lives that long," she murmurs.

Samson pauses. "I'd appreciate it if you kept out of my head," he rumbles with half a smile. "But yeah, things are getting a little tense around here."

"Daiyna and some of the others—they want nothing short of revenge on Eden for what was done to you."

"Can you blame them?" He holds out his steel hands.

"You don't count yourself among that faction." She gazes up at the cyborg as we pass through an earthen passageway lit only by mounted glowsticks.

Samson curses under his breath. "Daiyna and Shechara are the only ones in that bunch who were actually *in* Eden. The rest of them..." He shakes his head. "Some people seem to need hatred as fuel. They pour all that hate on Eden and Willard's bunch, and that faceless enemy gives them the drive they need to live."

I listen closely, gathering as much information as I can. The benefit of having Samson as our guide: he doesn't move any faster than I do. Yet again, I wish my audio relay was functioning, that I could speak directly to these people. But having Margo along will have to suffice.

No idea how long this visit is going to take, but we've got to get back on the road—assuming Luther's people allow me to leave. I should have told Granger to get going as soon as he's able to operate that vehicle. With or without me, they need to reach Eden.

I feel a twinge of guilt at leaving them alone—a science officer, a doctor, and an engineer. Without Morley, they're at the mercy of their limited weapons training. But the good news: the back of that Hummer is packed with firepower.

"That many?" Samson says to Margo. I've lost track of the conversation between them. "Tucker mentioned a *dozen*, but I had no idea. And you—" He frowns down at her as he searches for the right words. "You were in charge of the..."

"I inseminated the eggs from Shechara and Daiyna with the sperm samples from you and Luther. So yes, I am as much to blame as Willard. Without me, we would not be in this situation. Willard could never have created the children on his own."

"He would've killed you, if you'd refused. Nobody blames you," the cyborg replies.

"There is no need to spare my feelings. I'm prepared for whatever the consequence will be. I ask only that I be allowed to check on Tucker and the incubation pods before Luther casts judgment and assigns my punishment. I will accept whatever he decides."

Samson shakes his head. "I don't make a habit of it, but in this case, I think I can speak for Luther. He doesn't blame you for any of it. There won't be any *punishment*, not for you." He clears his throat and glances back at me before lowering his voice. "Can't say the same for the Eden-haters, though. I'm supposed to watch out for you and Tucker, so don't stray off."

"Who's watching him now?"

"People you can trust." He holds her gaze, and she seems to believe him. The tension in her shoulders relaxes slightly.

I can't help feeling like I'm walking into a bear's den. There are so many factions on this continent, more than I would have thought possible. At first, it was enough of a shock to find anyone alive in these barren Wastes. But now, seeing how they're divided —not even taking into consideration the bizarre, supernatural element—I've got to wonder if humankind is doomed to repeat history.

Haven't we suffered enough death and destruction already?

Samson halts at the end of the downward-sloping passage. It branches into three corridors, each lit with the same green glowsticks mounted at intervals, staked into the walls.

"Luther's waiting for you." The cyborg's deep voice resonates as he sweeps out a steel arm to usher us into the dark alcove beyond. Farther in, the faint light of a single glowstick emanates. "I'll hang with Tucker. Find us when you're through here," he says to Margo. Then he faces me. "I don't know what your intentions are, but I've got a feeling your government didn't tell you half of what's been going on since All-Clear."

I don't respond.

Samson gives me a hard look. "What I'm saying is, keep your mind open. Luther's not your enemy. I'm sure you've got plenty of questions, whether or not your bosses want you asking them. Ask Luther. Ask him anything." He pauses. "You've stepped into another world, soldier."

Margo rests a hand on the arm of my suit. "Let's go, Sergeant." Nodding in deference to Samson, she steps into the dark.

I move to follow, the earthen opening barely wide enough for me to enter. The cyborg's eyes don't leave me.

I raise an eyebrow. *Anything else?* is the expression I'm going for.

Samson almost chuckles. "He might not admit it, but Luther could really use your help. We're...sort of in a situation here. Your team's presence has heightened the tension, if you know what I mean."

I can put some of the pieces together without all the details. It's old habit to spot an incendiary situation when I see one. I hold Samson's gaze as he towers head and shoulders above me. "I've got a mission to complete, and this detour is not going to stop me from doing what I came here to do."

"He's a man on a mission," Margo translates. Close enough.

"Understood." Samson regards me silently. "*Sergeant.*" With a full metal salute, the cyborg turns about-face and clanks off down the corridor.

I follow the sound of Margo's footsteps into the dark until the confined space opens into an alcove the size of my laundry room back home. There we find a man seated at a makeshift desk—a pair of crates, one larger and one smaller. A glowstick lies atop the bigger crate, along with torn and wrinkled computer printouts from an outdated data system.

"Welcome." He stands, enfolding Margo in a warm embrace. She stiffly allows it. "You must be Sergeant Bishop." He reaches out his hand with a smile despite the sorrow that festers in his eyes. His fingers are badly scarred. "I've been told that your external comms are on the fritz."

I nod, meeting the man's solid grip with my gloved hand.

"Sergeant Bishop says he's heard of you," Margo relays.

"Likewise." The bearded, grey-haired Luther is almost the desert leader I envisioned, only more fatigued and gaunt in appearance. For the first time since I've arrived on this hellish continent, I find myself wondering what these people eat. Probably because my own stomach is growling. "I apologize, Sergeant. I have nowhere for you to sit."

"He doesn't mind standing. In his suit, it's easier that way," Margo says.

I knock on my chest plate and glance at her. She's doing a good job of sorting through my thoughts.

Luther stares absently at the hazard suit as if he hasn't seen anything like it in a very long time. His smile dims as he meets my gaze through the face shield. "We have much to discuss."

19. MARGO

18 MONTHS AFTER ALL-CLEAR

He has aged. That's my first thought, seeing Luther for the first time after so many months. But as he embraces me, I feel his strength, despite how thin he has become—all muscle with no fat to spare. I slip into his mind before I can stop myself, and I find something I have never sensed in him before: a dark fear gnawing away like a rat burrowing in his brain.

It is something he shares with the UW sergeant. Bishop wants to see his wife and children again, but his reunion with them is contingent upon the successful completion of this mission. For Luther, the future has even more at stake. His children are in Eden, and as much as he's worked to unite the various factions of his Homeplace, they are rife with division. Add to this the arrival of Cain's people, along with Cain himself in a matter of hours, as well as the UW team's sudden appearance on the scene, and it is no wonder Luther has been unable to eat or sleep for days.

Yet he smiles as warmly as ever as he says to Sergeant Bishop, "I hope you don't mind that I get straight to the point."

"He would prefer it," I translate Bishop's thoughts, careful not to reveal anything unseemly.

"The warriors who attacked you—their leader is on his way here," Luther says.

"Cain." I nod, remembering what Lemuel said about the man.

"He doesn't seem to believe the UW representatives have come in peace."

I sense that Bishop doesn't believe it either. He knows his superiors have held back certain details when a full disclosure would have been more beneficial.

"Yes. Even if you were to tell Cain yourself, I doubt he would believe you. He sees your presence on this continent as an act of war."

Bishop nods. This isn't news to him. He's already lost one of his men to Cain's warriors.

"This *Gaia* he worships—according to him, she used those flesh-eaters to shoot us down," Bishop says within the soundproof confines of his helmet, and I repeat his words.

Luther looks mildly surprised. "I see you've been studying up on the local culture."

"He's a quick study. And we came across one of Cain's young people on the way here," I add.

"It was a little out of our way," Bishop says. "As is this detour. But I hear you've got something to say to me. So let's have it."

Luther hesitates, glancing from me to Bishop. "I would prefer that you first tell me about your mission."

"Can't do that." Bishop moves his arms as if he wants to cross them, then realizes he won't be able to do so in the hazard suit. "Classified."

"Then allow me to fill in a few details I'm sure your superiors left out. You were sent to meet with a man named Arthur Willard who lives underground, sealed off from the surface. Willard told your government that he has fetuses in incubation pods, nearly to term."

Bishop says nothing.

"Sergeant, have you stopped to consider where those children came from? Or have you been so focused on your mission...that nothing else has mattered?"

Bishop frowns slightly. "I've lost one of my men. Two of my

team are infected. And the things I've seen here…" He shakes his head. "My superiors don't have a clue what's going on."

"There would be no way for them to know that these children you've been sent to recover …were stolen from their parents."

Bishop fights to keep the surprise from showing on his face, but I see past his stoic façade. The man has a father's heart.

"There were four of us—two men, two women—captured by Willard's engineers when we stumbled upon Eden early last year. They harvested our sperm and eggs against our will."

"Willard forced me to combine the gametes, creating the test tube babies he has offered your government in return for safe passage off the continent," I explain. "Before I left Eden, Willard made it clear that he will use the children as leverage to get what he wants. If that doesn't work, he will not think twice about killing the UW team."

"We have a vested interest in what becomes of those children in Eden." Luther pauses. "For they are *our* children."

Bishop sizes up Luther for a moment. "What's to keep me from radioing my ship and telling them the fetuses are no good? That they carry contaminated genes."

"We do not know if that is the case. The children have not been exposed to the dust in the air. That is how the spirits bestow their gifts—" Luther stops himself, his eyes earnest. "But I suppose you must first be told about the spirits. Then everything else will become clear."

"If that's possible. I've seen some things that…defy all manner of reason."

I try not to interfere with their discussion, to be merely a conduit for Sergeant Bishop's side of the conversation. But I know his mind, and I want to tell Luther, *He has seen the spirits. They have come to him in the guise of his wife.*

"Milton should really be the one to tell you about them. He is the only one among us that they communicate with anymore. They spoke to Daiyna for a time, but…" Luther trails off.

I know what he was about to say: that Daiyna has surrendered to hate while planning revenge upon Eden. Darkness consumes her heart now.

"Where is Milton?" Luther asks. "Didn't he return with you?"

Bishop shakes his head and glances at me.

"He said he would join us." I can't sense Milton's thoughts anywhere nearby. "I don't know where he is."

Luther nods pensively. "He goes where the spirits lead him. We must assume they had need of him elsewhere."

He stares into empty space, and I cannot discern any thoughts; it's as if his mind has been put on pause. He is under so much pressure, and the majority of it is self-induced. More than anything, he wants to keep his people unified, even as divisions threaten to rip them apart. Is he beginning to crack beneath the strain of his burden?

Bishop clears his throat. "Seeing him *fly*—even now, saying that out loud. I guess I don't know what to think, how any kind of genetic mutation could cause something like that. I have no frame of reference."

Luther locks eyes with him, listening to my translation, his mind flaring to life as neurons fire and thoughts spring forth in words, "There is much more than natural law at work here, my friend. *Supernatural*—that's as good a way to describe it as any. The spirits of the earth have blessed us with amazing gifts. Some of us can run faster than any normal human could ever dream of. Others can leap from great heights or see through the dark as if it were bright as day—or see great distances, far beyond the boundaries of natural human sight."

"How about you?" Bishop watches as Luther absently strokes the fingers of one hand with the other. "What can you do?" There's no sarcasm in the sergeant's voice, only a guarded curiosity, which I relay.

"Before Willard's henchman mutilated my hands?" There is nothing wrong with the hands Luther holds out before him—not at first glance. But each finger is terribly scarred. "When we first came up from the ground and breathed the dust of this earth, I was blessed with a gift I couldn't understand." He turns his hands over. "I was a man of peace, yet I was given claws as long and sharp as an eagle's talons. When I'd flex my fingers, like this, they would spring outward as strong as steel, as sharp as blades. I took down many daemons..." His eyes lose focus.

Bishop frowns at the scars. "Why haven't they grown back?"

I sense that he immediately regrets asking the question. But Luther does not take offense once I share it.

"When Willard captured us in Eden, he took more from us than our sex cells. He took our gifts, as well. He wielded the power of science against the supernatural, all in the name of restoring us to our all-natural selves, created in the image of God." He pauses. "You have met Samson."

Bishop nods.

"The spirits gifted him with incredible strength. But Willard's man, Perch, amputated Samson's arms and legs to take his power from him. Shechara had her eyes taken from her. She had been the most gifted among us with far-sight. As for me, Perch tore out each of my claws by the root, one by one, with a pair of pliers. Simple but effective, as you can imagine." Luther crosses his arms, hiding both his hands for now. "But as to why they have not grown back, I honestly can't say. I wish I knew. It could be that my claws are no longer needed, and the Creator in His infinite wisdom decided to return me to the man of peace I was before. Or perhaps the spirits' gifts are given only once, and it is up to us to keep them and use them well."

"How many of you live in these caves?"

Luther smiles for the first time since he welcomed us. "We are more than fifty strong now. Every few days, another survivor or two stumbles across the Homeplace, and we welcome them into the fold."

"And everyone else here...has these *abilities*?"

"The spirits have been kind to us."

"And Cain's people—the ones who attacked my team. They've

been changed as well, after leaving their bunker at All-Clear? They have the same variety of abilities?"

"As far as we know, yes. But they worship that being called Gaia, which we have reason to believe is one of the evil spirits, masquerading as a god."

He's losing Bishop with all his talk of the supernatural. I have to direct the conversation where it needs to be: back to the children.

"The fetuses Tucker smuggled out of Eden—where are they now?" But I already know the answer, plucked from Luther's mind as he turns to face me. They are nearby, under guard.

"Would you like to see them?" His eyes are bright and eager, like a child's.

Bishop nods.

"Your doctor—he did not make the climb with you?" Luther asks.

"Internal comms are still functioning." Bishop taps his helmet. "I'll note the vitals and relay whatever details Doc Harris needs to know." He pauses as Luther positions himself to usher us out into the passageway beyond. "I meant what I said before, Luther. If the readings indicate the fetuses are abnormal in any way, you'll have saved us a trip to Eden. My superiors won't be interested in Willard's bargain. The guy sounds like a real nutjob anyway."

If he only knew the extent of Willard's insanity.

A sudden concern crops up in my mind: Why haven't I been able to sense the mind of the young female for the past few hours?

Are you still there? I reach out into the unknown. *You are not alone. I am here. We are together again.*

No response.

Is she sleeping? She has always been more receptive to my telepathy—from that first moment in the nursery when she opened her eyes and projected her thoughts into my mind. But now, there is not even an inkling that the two fetuses are here in these caves.

I am not going anywhere, I press my thoughts outward. *I will never leave you again. You can trust me.*

Will Bishop detect any genetic abnormalities in the young ones? Doubtful. He is no doctor. Luther believes that only people who breathe the dust in the air are changed by spirits, altering their genetic makeup and gifting them with supernatural abilities. Willard sees the ashen dust on the earth as a contaminant and believes all who let the particulate matter into their lungs are allowing themselves to be turned into mutant freaks of nature. That's why, as far as I know, not one of Willard's men in Eden have become infected. But these fetuses are different. They are from parents whose genes have already been affected by their contact with the surface—either blessed with supernatural gifts from spirits of the extinct animal kingdom, or infected by rapid-acting mutagens. Judging by the UW team's environmental suits, I'm inclined to believe they will side with Willard's point of view.

As the fetuses grew and developed in the nursery, deep beneath Eden, I didn't notice a single abnormality in their genetic makeup. From my work with Luther and Daiyna, Samson and Shechara—under Willard's iron-fisted supervision—including my own blood samples, I noticed certain genetic markers: decidedly mammalian, but not quite human. That much would support Luther's claims. But there were no such markers in the DNA taken from the fetuses—not in any of the twenty young ones. At the time, I saw no reason to think that would change. They would be born, I assumed, as all-natural human beings.

But then the young one's telepathy manifested itself. Would having such a superhuman ability alter her genetic makeup—or be the result of mutant genes? There is no way to tell. My tests returned inconclusive: no change whatsoever in the genetic markers.

As Luther leads us through these quiet caves, I have to wonder if any abnormalities will reveal themselves now that the fetuses' telepathic link with me is apparently broken. And if not, will my presence reactivate our shared ability?

If Willard finds out the nursery full of incubation pods is useless in his bargain with the UW, he will destroy them. All he wants is to save his own skin. Nothing will stand in his way.

But if those children could be saved...

I can't imagine returning to Eden and facing Willard, the man who nearly destroyed my life. But I know Luther's mind; he wants to rescue all of the fetuses from Eden's depths, and I will do anything I can to help him. Even if it means lying about those inconclusive test results from weeks ago.

I can make those results sound as solid as granite. As long as it means Luther will receive the UW military support he needs in order to invade Eden.

"Please leave us, my brothers." Luther nods to the pair of armed sentries standing watch in an alcove beside the two incubation pods. No one else is nearby.

Bishop's thoughts crowd my mind with questions: *How extensive are these caves? Where do the rest of Luther's people hide themselves? Where are Cain's warriors?* I try to send him a sense of peace, but my attention is divided, my focus on the young ones.

"Thank you," Luther says as the sentries leave, unable to keep their curious glances from the UW sergeant in his bulky environmental suit.

"We'll be right outside," one of them says.

Bishop hesitantly approaches the two stasis chambers. He looks like one of the ancient faithful on pilgrimage to a holy temple, presented with a golden altar to his god—known until now as only legend, but at this moment so very real.

Luther looks at me, catching my gaze.

Bishop will help us. He is a good man.

I nod, agreeing with him, hoping my telepathic intuition is right. But at the moment, I can't discern Luther's thoughts from my own. Somehow, they have become tangled together. Perhaps because we both hope for the same thing.

Bishop is staring at the incubation pods. "It's been so long..." He clears his throat. I sense his surging emotions. "We haven't seen newborns in Eurasia for years—well over a decade. These two—they're not even born yet, and they look so...They're *perfect*."

I face Bishop across the two canisters. "They are healthy." My gaze travels across the holographic display in the clear pane of plasticon providing a view of each sleeping fetus. "Nearly to term."

Bishop looks up from the chambers. "So they're ready. They could be—" He nods once in military fashion at the look on my face. "They're ready," he repeats, doing his best to sound like everything is business as usual. "Are you planning to release them soon? Allow them to be...born?" He doesn't know what other word to use. Neither do I, as I translate.

"I would have to say that depends on you." Luther gestures toward the pods with an open hand. "Contact your doctor, Sergeant. See what he says."

"Right." Bishop looks over the readouts projected on each stasis chamber. "Alright Doc, tell me what I'm looking for," he says on internal comms.

Harris replies instantly, and the two of them begin conversing, the doctor instructing the sergeant on how to monitor the vital signs of each unborn child.

Without warning, the female's eyes open, focusing on Bishop.

I hold my breath.

"Well, would you look at that..." Bishop grins, despite his best intentions to keep a straight face. He can't contain himself. "She's looking right at me!"

"It may appear that way," I'm quick to explain, whether or not it's the truth in this case. "Their eyes are not yet able to focus, and with the amniotic fluid—"

Is he safe?

The young one's thought enters my mind so abruptly, I blink against a brief wave of vertigo.

"You all right?" Bishop reaches for me.

I steady myself. "Fine. I just—I haven't eaten in a while."

"You and me both." He chuckles.

Luther speaks quietly with one of the sentries standing outside before turning back toward us. "Forgive me, I should have offered you something."

Bishop faces me. "If the others are anything like these two, then it looks like we're still headed to Eden."

I focus on the female's pod. *We can trust him.*

Luther smiles as I relay Bishop's response, obviously pleased. But his eyes have yet to relinquish their sadness. "I had hoped so."

"Don't misunderstand," Bishop says grimly. "The children will be taken by the UW. There's nothing I can do about that. I'm just the middle man here."

I can tell that he regrets this being the case. My tone shows as much.

"Better with your people than Willard's," Luther says, and if I didn't know better, I might have believed him. "I ask only that you allow us to go with you."

"Out of the question." Bishop glances at me, certain I don't plan on making the return trip. He's right about that. "Your presence would only add to what could be a volatile situation—if what you've told me about Willard is true. Besides, what's to keep you from overpowering my team once we get to Eden and taking the children yourselves?" He holds up a gloved hand to halt Luther's objection once I repeat the question. "You told me yourself. They're *yours*. It makes perfect sense that you'd want them back. But I can't allow that to happen. The future of the world depends on it."

"And where do we fit into this future?" Luther asks.

Is there any place for people like us, now that the UW knows of our existence?

Bishop looks at a loss for words. "I honestly don't know."

"This is the situation," I explain. "Willard's only goal is to get off this continent and return to the outside world. The children are merely a means to that end. If he doesn't get what he wants from you, then he will destroy them all."

Bishop doesn't believe that. He cannot fathom anyone being so selfish—or evil. "Leave him to me."

"He has you outnumbered, Sergeant. And outgunned. At least allow me to send a few of our sentries with you," Luther insists. "You don't realize the power Willard has at his disposal."

"I appreciate your concern—" Bishop begins.

"Tell him." Into Luther's mind, I project a scene from last year in Eden: of Luther and two of his friends trapped underneath the city's sublevels with hordes of flesh-eating mutants advancing on them.

Luther nods, taking a deep breath before diving in. "Willard's men themselves are well-armed and outnumber your team five to one. But in addition, Willard has *hordes* of collared daemons at his disposal. Those flesh-eaters that shot down your aircraft—Willard has managed to fit them with remote-controlled shock collars to do his bidding. You'll never leave Eden alive unless he permits it, and that's assuming you make it there in the first place. There are plenty of wild daemons between here and Eden to contend with, and their only desire is for fresh meat."

I rest a hand on the forearm of Bishop's suit. "Two of your team are injured already. Would it not be wise to allow Luther to send help with you?" I face Luther. "Do you still have the Hummer you took from Eden?"

He nods. "Samson has kept it running well."

Bishop looks at me. "You won't be our chauffeur."

I let go of his arm and turn back to the incubation pods. "I am needed here." But into his mind, I project, *When the spirits appeared to you, what did they say?*

Bishop shrugs. *To listen to Luther. And I have.*

There is a difference between hearing and listening, Sergeant, I remind him.

He paints a real bleak picture. If what he says is true, then the odds are decidedly against us.

Luther clears his throat quietly. "If you will not accept our help, will you at least contact your people off-shore for their support? Believe me when I say I only want those children to live. Yes, they are your future. But they are ours, as well."

"We both want the same thing, Sergeant," I tell him. "To rescue those babies from Eden."

Bishop raises an eyebrow. "If I'd known that's what this mission was all about, I might have brought more men." He recalls the handful of well-armed jarheads that blew up in the chopper, and I see each of their faces in his mind.

"Radio your ship," Luther says. "Don't go to Eden alone."

Bishop nods. "Our doctor's taking care of it, once he has a chance to go over the information I gave him. He'll request full support. But I'm not getting my hopes up, not after the first contact we made with those well-armed freaks out there. The UW doesn't make a habit of losing its assets, and that helicopter isn't easily replaceable. It's not like your factories are running over here anymore, churning out everything we need. We've had to make do with what we've got."

Luther nods pensively as I relay the sergeant's side of the conversation. "There is another matter."

"Cain."

"His warriors are here already—those who attacked you. And Cain himself is en route with more of his people." Luther pauses. "He will want to take you and your team by force, back to his encampment. For judgment."

"That's insane." Despite his best efforts at masking his emotions, Bishop is beginning to look a little unsure about the situation. "The UW would never stand for such a thing. If he thinks he can—"

"He does. That is not the issue." Luther's features take on a hard edge in the green light of the glowsticks. "The question is whether we allow them to take you without a fight."

"You would do that." Bishop sets his jaw. "Let them take us."

"You are free to leave whenever you like. On your own to Eden, or in captivity when Cain arrives. No one is holding you here."

Bishop narrows his gaze. "But if I allow you to join us on our mission to Eden..."

"Then we would be allies, and I would not allow Cain to take you where you do not wish to go. But you need to decide quickly, Sergeant. Cain will be here within the hour."

I see an image in Bishop's mind of dust billowing on the western horizon.

"Tell me this," he says. "Why haven't you returned to Eden for your children before now—if you've known they were there?"

The glimmer of a smile appears on Luther's lips. "Until now, we would have been outnumbered. Even with the aid of the spirits, there was no telling whether we would be able to reach Eden in time. As we've said, it would not be beneath Willard to destroy the fetuses on a whim. They have no value to him unless he can use them to get what he wants." Luther reaches out his scarred right hand. "But now we have the United World government as our ally."

Weighing the consequences, Bishop extends his gloved hand, and the two men shake. "For now. We'll see what happens when we get to Eden."

"You have my word, Sergeant. No harm will befall your team. And if the Creator wills it, perhaps I will be able to convince Cain and his warriors to join us as well in our march on Eden."

That would take a miracle, Bishop muses, the sentiment as clear as if it was spoken aloud. "We should leave now."

"As soon as Cain arrives, that will be decided."

Bishop frowns. "I'd say it's in the best interest of my team to get out of here well before Cain arrives."

"His people are already here." Luther lowers his voice. "While you remain under my protection in the Homeplace, they would not think to act against you. Set off on your own, and you would be at their mercy. But if you trust me and wait, we'll see if Cain is able to set aside our differences. It will be well worth it if we are finally able to unite our people in sight of a common goal."

Bishop glances at me. This is something else the spirit said when it appeared to him—that more than anything, Luther sees it as his purpose in life to establish unity among the continent's survivors. At least the ones who aren't flesh-eating freaks. I nod, knowing Luther's welcome extends even to the people of Eden. Tucker and I are proof of that.

"I would like to see Tucker now, if that's all right," I say as the sentries return, bearing nutrition and hydro-packs.

"Of course." Luther directs the distribution of food and water.

"Standard rations." Bishop smirks as he attaches two packs to the intake valves on the abdominal wall of his suit. "Is this what you people live on?"

I tear into my packs. "Beggars can't be choosers. In Eden, however, they eat full course meals, three times a day."

"One of the benefits of living below a trade sector," Luther says. "They have been able to find everything they need in storage, unaffected by the residue from D-Day. Willard's remote-controlled daemons carry scavenged goods from the surface down into Eden." He nods to one of the sentries. "Please escort our friend Margo to see Mr. Tucker. I believe Samson is with him."

The sentry glances at me with a thinly veiled contempt. A cursory scan of his thoughts is all it takes for me to know he is one of the Eden-hating faction, led by Daiyna. While appreciating Luther's gesture of sending an armed escort along, I kindly decline.

"That won't be necessary. I'm sure if you just point me in the right direction—"

"I insist." Concern clouds Luther's gaze. "If Cain's warriors were to see you here…"

It isn't Cain's people who unnerve me. But before I can reply, shouts echo throughout the caverns. A staccato of weapons fire erupts in the distance, beyond the mouth of the cave. Luther gestures sharply for the sentries to guard the incubation pods as Daiyna appears in the passageway outside. Pausing amid the flow of bodies rushing past her, she adjusts the automatic rifle strapped over her shoulder and fixes me with a hard look. She beckons Luther toward her.

"What's happened?" he demands.

Pandemonium owns the moment amid voices clamoring and rifles firing.

Daiyna catches her breath. "It's not good." She gives him the handgun that was tucked into her belt. "Cain's here."

Bishop stomps forward. "What the hell is going on?"

I crouch down between the two incubation pods and close my eyes. It is difficult to tell whose thoughts are whose in the cacophony around us, but I am able to discern the mind of the young female clearly enough:

We are in danger.

PART V
BLOOD

20. CAIN

18 MONTHS AFTER ALL-CLEAR

I sense their heartbeats long before we reach Luther's Homeplace. Five on the ridge above, three below, two of them wounded. As the ashen wasteland before us rises steadily into the foothills, I recognize one of the pulses immediately with my keen, Gaia-blessed sight. Its youthful anxiety is palpable.

"Lemuel is among them," I mutter.

I run as fast as my legs will carry me, my skin perspiring so much that everything I wear to protect it from the sun is already drenched. My breath comes easily, and I thank Gaia for the stamina of my warriors who keep pace with me—thirty strong, summoned from the various Shipyard tribes.

The other chieftains are too old to make such a journey—braving the goblyns and the elements. They remain behind, along with the women with child. I am the only chieftain in my prime, and while Gaia has not blessed me with the speed of my warriors who've already reached Luther's cave, I have made good time regardless. And Gaia be praised, we have yet to cross paths with a single goblyn roaming the wastelands.

After everything those UW scouts have been through—some of it at my own command—it is a wonder they have not already radioed their ship for evacuation and left this land far behind.

Will they continue on to Eden? I hope Luther convinces them to join forces and rescue his unborn children. Gaia-willing, my warriors and I will be with them.

Those infants gestating in Eden represent the UW's last hope for survival, but their kind is about to become extinct. The survival of the fittest demands it. I am now more determined than ever to see that happen, and I fully intend to have a hand in their demise.

"He hasn't shown any signs yet, has he?" The warrior at my side is named Asaph. A dark-eyed, raven-haired young man a few years older than Lemuel, he is little more than a sycophant. "One would think Gaia has passed him over!"

I nearly chuckle at that.

"Perhaps when Lemuel becomes a man, his abilities will manifest themselves," Asaph suggests.

Images flash through my mind of young Lemuel and Victoria together in the bedchamber. That was not their first time; she made that much clear.

"Exile was too good for him." I clench my jaw.

"Perhaps an *accident* might befall him during our quest?" Asaph watches me a moment as we run side by side. "Leave the matter in Gaia's hands, Lord Cain. She will take care of that miserable cur. You showed great restraint by not executing him on the spot."

How much of the story has already spread throughout the tribes? The Shipyard thrives on gossip, one of our primary entertainment sources. But I hoped my sentries would keep the matter quiet.

"What do you know of his disrespect?"

Asaph frowns pensively. He knows only enough to try and ingratiate himself with his leader. My cursory glance at his heart rate proves such to be the case. His pulse has quickened anxiously.

"Only that he disgraced the tribes by—"

"His disgrace was against me alone."

"All the more reason to punish him severely, my lord. A disgrace against our chieftain of chieftains *is* a disgrace against the tribes—against our people as a whole!"

I imagine shoving Asaph forward as he runs and driving his face into the dust. That would shut him up. Of all the warriors able to keep pace with me, it has to be this one?

"Gaia will decide whether the quality of mercy has been strained enough for young Lemuel."

Asaph nods, satisfied for the moment.

Fifty meters ahead, a large, black vehicle sits alone at the base of a cliff. I signal the group to halt. Without a word, I point to the dust-caked vehicle, the frame pocked with bullets, the windows fractured but holding. I raise three fingers before pointing westward. My warriors nod to show they understand: the three figures hiding behind the vehicle are UW scouts. I point at the top of the cliff where a jagged ridge runs crosswise, providing ample cover, and I hold up all five fingers of my left hand: five sentries at their posts.

I slip the strap of my rifle down from my shoulder; the warriors behind me do the same. Judging from the heartbeats of the three UW personnel behind that vehicle and the five sentries hidden above, our presence has already been noticed. Only a miracle from Gaia could have masked our arrival across the dusty terrain. There was no cover to be found.

So it was her will that we arrive in plain sight.

I stride forward boldly, and my warriors follow.

"Show yourselves." My booming voice echoes off the cliff side. I hold my weapon at the ready but keep the muzzle aimed at the ground. "You would have fired upon us by now if that was your intent." I pause. "We see you have one of our own among you. A young pup." I release a disgusted chuckle. "Feel free to keep him."

Lemuel's pulse races as he stands up behind an outcropping of rock high above us, struggling against a figure garbed in sand-colored cloth. They fight for possession of a rifle, its stock glinting under the sun.

Asaph takes aim.

"Hold!" I command. My people will not be the first to fire.

Surprisingly strong for one so lacking in muscle, Lemuel nearly has the rifle free. But then a woman identical in garb to his opponent advances on him from behind, the end of her weapon poised for a head strike. I savor the moment, awaiting the sound of gun metal colliding with bone. But the youth seems to have eyes in the back of his head. With an ungraceful spin kick, he drives the woman back, yanks the rifle free from his opponent, and has the muzzle trained on me before I can fully grasp what just happened.

Asaph fires.

With a burst of crimson across his chest, Lemuel jerks upward, eyes wide with surprise, arms suspended loosely. The stolen rifle falls down the sheer drop, and he follows after.

There is no time to watch the youth's body break among the rocks below. Later I can pause to regret missing the sight; for now, I must find cover.

The ridge above has come alive with weapons fire, and my warriors scramble for their lives. Moving targets are more difficult to hit, but we will not survive long out in the open. Most of us return fire, running straight for the vehicle while shooting blindly upward. From what I can see, none of my warriors have been wounded. Did Luther order his sentries not to take kill shots? I have given no such command to my men. It is only a matter of time before another death occurs.

I drop into a crouch once I reach the vehicle's rear tire. I squint up at the scorching sun through my sweat-spattered goggles. It is the hottest hour of the day; of course, Lemuel chose it to launch his idiotic scheme. He thought he could shoot me? The fool. I almost smile under my hood as I imagine telling Victoria of her young lover's demise. But perhaps she already knows, thanks to her telepathic gift.

"Who goes there?" a man's voice demands from the opposite side of the vehicle.

I gesture for my warriors to join me as rifle rounds pierce the earth like heavy rainfall, and puffs of dust plume upward. There won't be enough cover for all of us here, but it certainly beats scurrying around out in the open like frightened vermin.

A short cry pierces the air as a body tips forward from the cliff's edge. A trail of crimson streams out behind, staining the cloth garments. I grind my teeth. Luther's people will strike back with a vengeance now that one of mine has killed one of theirs.

As if on cue, three of my warriors go down face-first into the dust with rounds puncturing them through the head and the heart. The sentries on that ridge have been well-trained, and my warriors are easy targets. I curse out loud and beckon sharply for the others to join me, but they are too intent on returning fire, dropping to their knees to take aim. They too are good shots. A pair of snipers from the ridge sail downward and crash into bloody heaps below. That leaves only one more shooter above, and three other potential hostiles on the other side of this vehicle.

"Throw down your weapons," I shout at the UW personnel, and I am instantly met with a single shot fired under the vehicle. I cringe behind the tire.

"We're not going down without a fight, pal!" calls out the same voice. "Tell your people to drop their weapons, or we'll take them out one at a time!"

The shooter on the ridge has withdrawn, undoubtedly to gather reinforcements. Luther will not be pleased by the recent turn of events. I curse Lemuel for starting the whole debacle.

But perhaps this is exactly what Gaia wanted all along: for Luther's people and my people to unite under my leadership. I already have my swiftest warriors planted within Luther's Homeplace, deep behind enemy lines. I need only give the word, and they will overwhelm Luther's fighters, assuming control of the situation while they await my next order.

Everything is falling into place, after all, and they are the best-laid plans I could have possibly imagined. To think, it took the idiot Lemuel to start this chain reaction. And now the sentries, save one, have been dispatched. No one is guarding the entrance into Luther's cave.

I motion to my surviving warriors, directing them to climb the mountain and take position along the way up. They will lend a hand when my warriors inside escort all of Luther's people out.

Time for a trip, folks. That's right, we're going to Eden. Think of it as Paradise Regained. Lord Cain will be your tour guide on what promises to be a fateful journey. No, you won't need to bring anything. Leave all of your weapons, we insist. But we'll gladly make use of them, thank you very much.

With Gaia's praises on my lips for what promises to be a quick victory over these infidels, I rise to my feet and stride around the rear of the vehicle. I find three members of the United World team huddled together on the other side: a tall woman pale from blood loss, not wearing a protective suit; an older man in a functional suit with utter shock frozen on his wrinkled features; and a half-sized fellow without his environmental suit, but with almost enough muscle mass to make up for his deficient stature. Each of them is armed with a snub-nosed automatic rifle. But presented with my imposing figure, they seem to have forgotten for the moment that they have me outnumbered.

Kill them, the voice of Gaia herself whispers in my ear. *Kill them all, my son.*

It is as though her spirit flows through me, guiding my steps. I level my rifle on the short man. Two rounds at close range nearly take off his head with a backsplash of crimson splattering across his stunned compatriots—but not before he is able to squeeze off a short burst of automatic fire. Two rounds catch me in the side, and I snarl, slapping down a hand to apply pressure at the site of the wound.

I don't give the other two a chance to retaliate. Ending the woman with a single headshot, I move on to the older man, puncturing his helmet with multiple rounds that send him stuttering backward, his weapon firing at the sky in spastic bursts. He topples over limply, spraying blood. I nudge each of them with my boot to be sure they are dead.

"Long live the United World," I mutter, wincing in pain.

"Lord Cain!" Asaph approaches, out of breath. "You're wounded?"

He sounds as surprised as I am, noting the blood on my gloved hand as I stanch the flow.

"Nothing serious." Gaia would not allow anything more than a sting. I am her chosen one. This is just a reminder that, unlike her, I am mortal. I will have to be more careful.

"Look!" He points at the cave above.

Luther stands in plain sight, a ghost of the man I saw months ago. Asaph and the other remaining warriors aim their weapons up at him, but they do not fire. I shoulder my rifle by the strap and raise my free hand in greeting. The other remains casually pressed against my side.

"Luther," I call out. "We meet again."

If a sudden gust were to blow up along the cliff at that moment, Luther would fall over. He sways on his feet, staring at the broken and bloody corpses below. Words fail him. The woman beside him is garbed as he is in sand-colored cloth and head wrappings, with black goggles shielding their eyes. Expressions are impossible to read, but I can tell from the palpitations of their hearts that they are experiencing the same emotion. Something akin to shock.

"What have you...*done?*" the woman manages, her words hanging in the air.

Others from Luther's enclave swarm out onto the ledge only to stop dead in their tracks. The weapons trained on them would be enough to halt anyone without a death wish.

"We defended ourselves. That is all. We did not come here looking for trouble." I gesture broadly at the carnage. "As you can see, I have lost men as well. The first to die was one of my own."

Shot by one of my warriors—but I leave that unsaid.

Luther's voice emerges, low and steady. "My sentries were given explicit instructions not to fire upon any of you." He sounds mystified.

I shrug. "They seemed awful trigger-happy a few minutes ago."

The woman's goggles scan the scene below until they reach the black vehicle behind me. "How do you explain *that*?"

Murmurs ripple through her people as I half-turn to give the pile of UW bodies a cursory glance. "A kill or be killed situation."

"Convenient." She scoffs. "What did they do—line up for you?"

I like this one. Perhaps she will replace Victoria after the birth of my son. "When you've fought the goblyns as long as we have, you learn to make every shot count. But perhaps you've grown out of touch, perched as you are. So high and mighty."

They need to be brought down into reality.

"There can be no excuse...for what happened here," Luther begins, but he is interrupted by the appearance of a man in one of the bulky UW suits, shoving Luther's people aside as he marches toward the edge of the cliff.

I curse silently. One of them is still alive. If he is able to radio the naval blockade—

Gaia knows all. I close my eyes for a moment, releasing the anxiety that twists my bowels. There is nothing to fear. If there were, Gaia would have warned me. *All is going according to her plan...*

The UW man's helmet darkens in the sun, shielding his face from its scorching rays. He faces me and freezes in that posture without a sound, without another movement. He looks like a robot that has powered down.

"Would it help matters if I apologized, Luther?" My voice holds the moment. "Very well. I am sorry for the deaths of your people, and I deeply regret the loss of my own. This is not what I had envisioned upon arrival. Trust me on that."

"I believe," Luther says deliberately, "that you saw the arrival of the UW ambassadors as an act of war, when that was not their intention. And by your actions here, you have fulfilled your own prophecy. Now the United World government will have no other recourse but to wipe your settlement from the shores you call home. Then they will move inland, intent on destroying us all."

As if to punctuate his statement, a low thump like a sonic boom trembles in the west, and all eyes turn to look toward the horizon. But even those of us blessed with far-sight cannot see the Shipyard from so great a distance.

The UW robot raises an arm and a gloved finger to point down at me, but he says nothing. He just stands there like an ominous statue. A frail-looking woman beside him speaks up, as if translating the gesture.

"You've declared war on your own people," she says. "The *Argonaus* is shelling your settlement as we speak. They will land troops within the hour."

I grit my teeth. As long as we reach Eden before the advancing UW troops, I will hold the upper hand. "Where are my men? Markus, Vincent, and the others?"

"They are inside," Luther replies. "They are well."

"I wish to see them. To know for myself that they are *well*."

Luther shakes his head slowly. Even with his covered face and eyes, the despair in his demeanor cannot be mistaken. "After what you have done here... I told you that your people would be safe—"

"If our positions were reversed, I'm sure you would be demanding the same."

"You're in no position to make demands!" the woman beside Luther shouts.

"You are mistaken." I gesture at my well-armed warriors. "But I believe we are in agreement about one thing. Enough blood has been spilled here today."

Another low tremor rumbles in the west. I fight to control the rage burning within me at the thought of the Shipyard exploding in shards and flames, of my wives left behind, of the casualties. I clench my free hand into a fist and force myself to breathe easy, to steady my heart rate.

This is all part of Gaia's plan. She knows best.

"Bring them." Luther sends one of his people back into the cave. "The two he mentioned. Markus and Vincent—"

"*All* of them," I correct him. "I want to see every one of my warriors and whatever possessions they had on them when they arrived. I want everyone and everything accounted for."

Luther pauses a moment, staring down at me. Then he nods to his messenger, who dashes away into the cave's yawning mouth.

"If you think you're any match for United World troops, think again," says the woman standing beside the last UW scout. Is something wrong with his helmet? Why hasn't he spoken a word?

"What I've seen so far has not impressed me." I shrug. "But don't worry. I am not planning to take my people back to the coast for some kind of final reckoning. I am sure the goblyns will keep the UW busy if they're foolish enough to land on shore. And while my people who remain there are not the strongest among us, you must remember: even the weakest of us are ten times stronger than anyone who breathes filtered air."

Markus, Vincent, and every one of my warriors blessed with superhuman speed filter out onto the ridge, interspersed with Luther's people who gasp in surprise at their sudden appearance. Luther's messenger trails after them.

"No, we will not be going west anytime soon." I smile broadly, my face hidden under my hood's shadow. "The time has come, Luther. Our two peoples will be united as one, just as you have wanted for so long. We will go with you to Eden and rescue your children, to take back what is rightfully yours!"

I chuckle in the silence as Luther's people glance at one other and at my warriors, who have not lowered their weapons. He must see the writing on the wall. His people do not stand a chance against mine. Will he risk more bloodshed?

Luther's goggles remain fixed on me. "It is what I've prayed for...that our two peoples would become allies one day." His voice breaks, as though he is suddenly overcome with emotion. "We must endeavor to put this tragedy behind us...and focus all of our energy instead on what lies ahead. As we...work together to—"

"You can't be serious!" says the woman at his side.

"Of course he is," I reply. "He has no other choice. Can't you see? His dream has come true, but it will not be what he has envisioned. *I* will be the one leading our merry expedition to Eden."

"Like hell you will," she growls.

I raise my voice, echoing with authority, "Lay down your weapons. Markus, Vincent—escort Luther's people down here. They are to take nothing with them but the clothes on their backs. Collect whatever you find inside the caves—weapons, food, water. We have a long journey ahead."

"What about the cyborg?" Vincent calls down.

"Send him to me," I reply. Samson's arms are weapons that cannot be removed. Or can they?

Luther's people resist as my warriors move roughly among them.

"Tell them to cooperate, Luther, and no one will be harmed."

"You're a liar!" the woman beside Luther shouts, standing her ground. He puts a hand on her shoulder, but she shakes him off. Feisty.

"You see my men standing among you? Every one of them has been blessed with supernatural speed, which only one of your people possesses—that flying man who takes to the skies." I make a deliberate show of scanning the grey heavens above. "Where is he now, by the way? Not much of a hero, if you ask me. Forsaking you like this."

"If it is your desire to join us on our journey, then why

demand that we lay down arms?" Luther holds out his gloved hands. "We face a common enemy. Why disarm us when we could join you as allies?"

Instead of answering him, I address all of his people. "You will cooperate. Resist, and my warriors will overpower you—faster than you can blink." I nod to Markus. "They won't be returning to this place. Take anything of value that you find."

"Yes, Lord Cain." He vanishes in a blur of speed.

My people shove Luther's into a single file line to descend from the ridge where others will guide them down.

"What do you hope to achieve here?" demands the UW scout's translator.

I glance up at him, then her. "Don't you know?"

"There's no place to hide in these Wastes. The UW will find you and exterminate you."

Gaia would never allow such a thing; I know this with all my heart. She will go before us and behind, clearing the way to Eden while covering our tracks, keeping us hidden from the United World's advancing troops.

But I won't waste my breath sharing this with an infidel. Such faith can only be understood by a true believer—like Luther. Unfortunately, he has chosen to place his belief in an ancient god who turned his back on creation long ago, allowing the powers of the world to destroy every last plant and animal species that once thrived on the earth's surface, not to mention the majority of its human population.

"We want the same thing." I turn toward the empty vehicle. "To save the world!"

I have to get out of this heat. Stepping over the lifeless bodies of the three UW scouts, I reach the driver's door and try the handle. After a brief whirring sound from the mechanism inside, the door drifts upward with a blast of hot air. A vehicle such as this should be capable of cooling its interior if it has enough fuel, and if the engine is running. I tap the screen beside the steering wheel, but it remains dark. No way to tell how much fuel is in the tank.

I curse under my breath and look out the windshield. Asaph holds a ready position, weapon aimed at Luther's people as they descend from the ridge, grumbling and complaining along the way.

I beckon to the youth.

"Lord Cain!" Asaph approaches the vehicle without his aim faltering.

"Put that down." I push the rifle muzzle aside. "Vincent has things under control."

"I don't trust these people."

I slap the vehicle's roof with my gloved hand. "I need you to take a look at this machine. See if you can get it running."

Asaph nods quickly, slinging his rifle over one shoulder. He's always been good with machines. Some say it is his gift from Gaia, to understand the components of a mechanical thing by looking at the whole.

"What type of ignition?" He peeks in the open door, stepping over the bodies yet to be disposed of. "Key or voice print? Thumbprint, perhaps?"

I grit my teeth against a spasm of pain and apply more pressure against my wound. "I was hoping you would be able to tell me."

"You should have someone look at that." He frowns at my bloody hand. "Perhaps one of Luther's people—"

"Focus, Asaph."

He taps the screen on the console just as I did. No response. He shakes his head. "No key slot. It must be configured for one driver in particular."

I scowl at the bodies.

"If it was a voice print..." Asaph turns to stare through his expressionless goggles.

"Try their thumbs." I lean back against the vehicle and prepare to watch the grizzly task.

Asaph retrieves a sharp knife from beneath his cloak and sets about dismembering the limp digits. Then he tries each of them, pressing the flesh flat against various points on the console, but to no avail.

"I'm sorry, Lord Cain." Asaph discards the last thumb, and it plops into the dust.

A wasted effort anyway. I'm not thinking clearly. The UW scouts never drove this vehicle. It came upon the scene as Markus and Vincent—

"What the hell are you playing at?" an angry voice booms like low thunder, and the sound of clanking metal approaches. "Is desecrating the dead part of your idiot religion now?"

Escorted by two of my warriors, Samson stomps toward the vehicle on his mechanical legs, implants grafted to his flesh and wired to his nervous system. Head, face, and torso are covered from the sun's rays by the same loose cloth all of Luther's people wear, but Samson's limbs gleam out in the open like polished steel.

The word *Excalibur* emerges unbidden in my mind. How sharp does the cyborg keep the digits on his metal hands? Could he, on a whim, decapitate the men on either side of him in a flash of movement?

I dismiss the warriors. Only Asaph remains behind, staring at the massive cyborg.

"Could've saved you the trouble, if you'd asked." Samson swings a hand toward the discarded thumbs. "They weren't the ones driving this thing. It's not even their vehicle."

"Whose then?" I fold my brawny arms and stand to my fullest height. Even so, this half-human machine is nearly a head taller. Not something I am accustomed to.

What sounds like a grunt resonates in the cyborg's chest. "You really think I'm going to volunteer that kind of information? I still can't get over this stunt you're pulling. Suddenly you want to join forces—but only if you're the one calling the shots? And this after killing four of our people, not to mention these UW folks under Luther's protection." Samson curses. "You declare war on the United World, then you decide to enlist us against our will. You've got to be out of your freaking mind, Cain."

Asaph lunges forward, rifle at the ready. "How *dare* you speak to Lord Cain like that?"

"Call off your Chihuahua," Samson growls.

I can't help smirking under my hood. "Tell me how to start this vehicle."

Samson's goggles remain focused on Asaph's gun muzzle. "Why should I help you? Give me one good reason."

"Luther is not looking well."

"He's fine. But having you betray his trust—"

"We have a long trip ahead, hundreds of kilometers across open terrain. We'll have to brave the elements along with any roving bands of goblyns we come across. I expect to travel in this vehicle, in comfort, and I should expect you'd like to do the same. Walking cannot possibly be the most enjoyable experience for you. Not with legs like those."

"They don't bother me. I'm stronger than you are." He nods toward my injury. "Especially now."

"Thanks to your modifications, of course you are. But can you say the same about your leader? How far do you think Luther will be able to go before his legs give out on him?"

The cyborg doesn't respond.

I hold out my hands. "I am not your enemy. I am your ally now—"

"Whether we want you or not."

"Luther has desired this union for months. You have accompanied him on every visit to my settlement. Or have you forgotten?"

"You haven't wanted anything to do with us. Why the sudden change of heart?"

"Where Gaia leads, we follow."

"And she's leading you to Eden."

I nod. "There might be enough room for both you and Luther in this vehicle, if we can get it running."

"Have you asked it nicely?"

I glance at Asaph, who adjusts his grip on the rifle. The youth looks nervous in the face of this half-man, and his heart is racing. "I'll ask you one more time, Samson. Who was driving? One of your people?"

Samson shakes his head. "It was their escort. A woman from Eden. My guess, the whole ignition system was keyed to her voice before she headed west. You won't get that thing to move farther than a centimeter without her."

Markus and Vincent have lined up Luther's people in an orderly fashion at the base of the cliff. The cave cult members don't look happy, but they take their cue from Luther. When he nods, they set down their weapons without a word. Impressive, the influence he has over them.

"Point her out to me," I say. "Which one is this woman from Eden?"

Samson turns to look over the crowd. There are fifty-two of them, all shapes and sizes, male and female, aged between mid-twenties to late fifties—judging by the health of their hearts.

"Don't see her," the cyborg says. "She must've found another way out."

I bristle at the suggestion and beckon to Markus. He appears before me in a blur of speed and burst of disturbed dust, crossing thirty meters in a split-second.

"All accounted for?" I demand.

"Yes, m'lord." Markus nods. "The caverns above are vacant."

"What about an alternate exit?"

"On the east-facing ridge—yes. But no one was there. All we found was another vehicle like this one, parked halfway down the grade." He lowers his voice and steps closer to me. "Two may have eluded us—a man and woman, both from Eden. Word is, they carried a pair of infants. But there is no sign of them now."

I grind my teeth. "They will not have gotten far. Take two others and track them down."

With a nod, Markus whirls into motion, kicking up the dust behind him.

"Lose somebody?" The sound of Samson's smirk is unmistakable behind his face covering.

"Perhaps." My tone is cold. "Tell me about your other visitor from Eden—and about these two...*infants*."

21. MILTON

18 MONTHS AFTER ALL-CLEAR

My ears aren't working so good right now. I know there have to be sounds—violent earth-quaking explosions as the beach is shelled relentlessly by the *Argonaus*—but I'm hearing only low, muffled whumps. The wizened old-timer leading the way through these narrow passages of an overturned ocean liner beckons repeatedly as I jog after him. Together, we cross what was once the ceiling of an upper deck.

"You don't want to die alone!" he shouted at me after the first blast.

The United World is finally breaking its silent standoff with the inhabitants of this quarantined continent. I don't have to wonder why. I just finished burying the UW soldier that Cain staked into the earth.

Come and get us, the gruesome murder seemed to say. Is Cain out of his mind?

This way, the old fellow gestures, pressing himself flat against the wall in a spread-eagle position and urging me to do likewise beside him. I'm not sure what's going on until an incredible wave of vertigo sweeps over me. The ship rolls sideways, nearly righting itself in the sand where it took root decades ago. Judging from the violent tremors coursing through the wall, the latest blast must have taken out a sizeable chunk of the hull on the ship's west-facing side.

"How many of you are there?" I shout, hoping the older man's ears aren't shot to hell like mine.

My guide shakes his head as if to say there's no time for idle chatter. Is he one of Cain's minions left behind or some kind of squatter who moved in after Cain's people vacated the place?

More than once amidst the barrage of explosions, I've felt the overwhelming urge to take to the skies. But the thought of being downed by a short-range missile has kept me grounded. I can imagine myself plummeting to the sand, rolling like a limp-winged bird shot in flight. But on the other hand, at least I wouldn't be trapped like this, crushed inside a derelict vessel.

With a quick burst of speed, I overtake the old man and grip his arm firmly. "Where are we going?" I demand.

You're him, aren't you? say the chapped lips on the man's wrinkled face. *The flying man? Not a bird, not a plane—* He breaks off into what appears to be maniacal laughter. As if there's time for such lunacy.

"We're not safe in here!" I shake him.

We have to hurry. He pulls at me. *You've got to get them out!*

"Them who? Who are you?"

I am Justus, one of the elder chieftains. The others—

So he is from Cain's crew. But didn't they all head east toward the Homeplace? Or did Cain leave the older generation behind to fend for themselves—after posting that soldier's corpse outside? That was like pronouncing a death sentence on anyone who remained here.

Which includes me at the moment.

Please—you need to get them to safety! Stronger than his years, Justus grabs hold of my wrist and takes off at a dead run down the passage.

Another blast rocks the massive vessel. Suddenly it gives way on the seaward-facing side, leaning over at a forty-five-degree angle. Justus doesn't slow down, adjusting his trajectory to make up for the wall becoming a portion of the floor. I shoot forward, my boots barely making contact. Sweeping Justus up into my arms like an ugly damsel in distress, I shout, "Point us in the right direction!"

Justus nods, jerking his thumb toward the very end of the passage. A split-second later, we arrive at a hatch on the east-facing side of the ship. I drop Justus to his feet, and the old man gestures with both hands, miming pushing the door outward. Working together, we struggle to open it, but gravity is not our ally. Shoving with all our combined might, we eventually get the hatch to budge. Sunlight bursts inside as it falls open the rest of the way with a resounding clank.

This way! Justus grabs a hooded cloak and goggles from a peg beside the door and tugs them on, ducking his head as he leaps outside.

I follow, squinting in the sunlight, and slide my goggles into place. Justus appears to be speaking as he forges across the ashen sand. This is a central courtyard of sorts, fenced in by rusted sheet metal with barbed wire along the top and rotten daemon heads mounted on spikes.

Not very aesthetically pleasing.

"I can't hear you!" I yell, coming abreast of the old-timer so I can read his lips.

Justus grimaces. *You don't have to holler at me. I'm standing right here!*

I glance ahead of us at the hulk of an old armored battleship, capsized next to a triple-deck, barnacle-encrusted fishing boat. The crustaceans have long-since dried out, now only brittle husks of their former selves.

"Who else is here?" I pull open the head covering around my left ear.

Instead of answering, Justus leads the way to the armored vessel. Another blast hits the ocean liner behind us, and it caves inward with reverberations I feel through the ground. My exposed ear can make out a muffled version of sheering, wailing vibrations as the enormous ship folds in on itself. Shrapnel launches skyward as Justus and I duck under the overturned deck of the abandoned battleship. Justus spins the hand wheel and heaves the hatch open, gesturing for me to follow him inside.

My muscles tighten, ready to burst into super-speed or flight at the first provocation. This quasi-deafness has left me at a severe disadvantage against every unknown waiting in the dark, but I forge ahead anyhow.

If Justus wanted to ambush me, he could have done so earlier. Why wait?

The darkness inside is impenetrable at first, the stagnant air stale and smelling like sweat. Blinking, I follow the old man's shadowy form into what appears to be sleeping quarters on the ceiling of this overturned vessel. I accidentally bump my shin into a mattress and feel a body stir.

"Who's in here?" I have no idea how loud my voice is.

The sudden flame of a butane lighter flares in Justus's hand. The glow shines upward against the crags and whiskers of his wizened face. He moves his lips. *You've got to get them out of here.*

"Who—?"

The light flickers across a bunch of mattresses jammed tightly together, covering the entire ceiling/floor. Lying on a few of these makeshift beds are half a dozen very pregnant women. Exhausted-looking, undernourished, and obviously stressed out, they squint up at me and Justus with fear in their eyes. Dark shadows obscure the corners of the room.

Cain's wives. Justus shakes his head and curses. *It ain't right, none of it. What Cain did to that soldier out there, then taking off and leaving us—*

"How many of you are there?"

You're looking at it. Justus shrugs.

He waves the lighter toward the back wall where other men and women close to his age are huddled, cringing with every concussive blast from the *Argonaus*. Justus turns toward one of the women as she reaches for him. She seems to have urgent news, pointing past me.

"What?" I bend toward them.

We're missing someone. Cain's fourth wife, Victoria. Justus doesn't look happy about it.

"Did she go with him?"

Justus shakes his head. *She's too far along. If she's not here, then she's in her quarters.*

I can see it in his eyes, what he's about to ask. So I head him off. "Which way?"

I'll go with you—

"I'm faster alone."

Justus nods grimly. *She's back in that ocean liner.*

Right. The one that caved in on top of itself. There's little chance anyone would still be alive after the shelling that ship's taken. It doesn't even resemble an ocean liner anymore; it looks more like a crumpled soda can, sticking up out of the sand at the port and bow.

Down the north-facing passage from the grand ballroom, Justus says. *Fifteenth cabin on the right.* He expects Milton the Flying Man to save the day.

But what if Milton doesn't want to save the day? What if Milton wants to leave these people to their fate and get the hell out of here?

As the thought of abandoning them crosses my mind, a nauseating sense of self-loathing swims through me. Memories of my life in the bunker resurface, of being Jackson's hangman, leading everyone into the storeroom when their number came up in the lottery. Leaving their bodies to rot on the floor after All-Clear, unable to go back inside and walk past Jackson's corpse. All that blood—

"You don't have to go." Justus has me by the arm. I can hear his voice well enough that I don't have to read his lips. "I will. Start getting these people out."

"Where do you expect me to take them?" I stare at the old

man, watching as hope dims in his eyes. "Back to the Homeplace? You really think Cain wants to see you again?"

"You think he left us here to die." Justus doesn't look convinced.

"You don't?"

"We're wasting time—"

"I'll go. You just..." I glance at the others. "Get them on their feet."

I heave open the hatch and step outside, leaving it to clang shut behind me. The ground trembles as the *Argonaus* mercilessly pounds the shoreline. I cover my ears as one of the capsized ships across the sand—the fishing vessel—disintegrates on impact.

It would be so easy to leave these people, to just forget they were ever here. The UW troops will take care of them, one way or another, when they land on shore. After they obliterate Cain's Shipyard, they'll poke around for any survivors. Quarantine them. Probably feed them.

They're not my concern. They're not even my people.

I can't help remembering something Margo said before we parted company: that I don't consider myself to be part of Luther's people, either. Is that true?

I have no idea. And there's no time to wonder about it now.

I burst into high speed and enter the ocean liner, tearing down the passageway Justus led me through earlier, whipping around corners and through identical hallways, until I reach the upside-down ballroom where the ceiling/floor has collapsed, crushing the west wall. What remains of the opening to the corridor beyond leaves only enough room for me to scramble forward on hands and knees. It would be comical if there wasn't a pregnant woman trapped at the other end.

How could Cain leave them here? It makes no sense. The guy must be seriously insane.

I remember what that was like.

Not that I recall every gory detail from when I was possessed by an evil spirit of the earth, and I suppose that's for the best.

Most of those memories are still a stomach-churning blur. But if these days Jackson is impersonating a deity calling itself Gaia, and Cain serves this Gaia with all his heart, then it stands to reason that Cain could be possessed as well.

But didn't Julia say the evil spirits can't act *directly* on us anymore?

Like Jackson would ever be true to his word.

After the fact, Samson told me what I did while under the evil spirit's influence: that I almost strangled Daiyna. If the same presence is now influencing Cain's decision-making, then leaving a few of his own people to die is the least of our worries.

Cain has led his warriors straight to the Homeplace. Will he declare war on Luther's people? If the good spirits don't intervene on their behalf, there will be a bloodbath. And after the way I dismissed Julia—or the spirit who pretends to be her—it wouldn't surprise me if they decide to leave us crazy humans alone.

Maybe it would serve us right.

But it wasn't Luther or Daiyna or Samson or Shechara or any of the others who told the spirit in as many words, "We don't need you." That was Milton, the hero. They shouldn't have to suffer because of my antisocial behavior.

If Cain, possessed by evil, is now on the warpath, then Luther's people need the spirits' help more than ever before. And it'll be up to me to mend matters with the spirit world, crazy as that sounds.

As if I have a clue where to start.

For the moment, there's Cain's fourth wife to rescue. And her door is obstructed. As the ruins of the ocean liner moan and screech around me, I push and pull at the barricade. It won't give. After the last explosion, the doorframe must have caved inward, wedging the debris firmly into place. Maybe if I had Samson's strength, I might stand a chance against it. But no matter how fast I move in any direction, heaving and shoving, it won't budge.

I pound my fist against the door. No use struggling if nobody's alive on the other side.

"Anybody there?" I can't be sure, but there might've been a scuffling sound inside the cabin. "Hello?" I pound a rapid-fire beat with both fists moving in a blur of speed.

A shrill cry pierces the door, words that might be "Get me out of here!" but with more expletives involved.

Amazing, that anyone could have survived inside this wreck.

"Right." I back away from the door and duck my head to keep from banging it against the sagging ceiling. "Step back!"

Bracing for impact, I hurl myself in a burst of speed and slam against the door with my shoulder. I feel it give—my shoulder a bit more than the door, but the frame weakens.

"Again!" the woman shouts.

I ready myself for take two as a superhuman battering ram. The first attempt didn't hurt nearly as bad as I thought it would. This time, I give it all I have.

With a screech of splintering wood and screws torn from their mounts, the door implodes into the room with me on top of it. I cough and try to rise, but there's a slender, muscular woman with a protruding belly holding a knife at my throat.

"Hi there." I rotate my head just enough to wink at her. Then I leap upward in a blur of speed, wrenching the dagger from her grasp and gripping hold of her arm.

"Luther's pet," she sneers, clothed in a sweat-drenched nightgown. "The flying man?"

"Cain's wife," I counter. "Left to die?"

Deadly thunder cracks the sky outside. The vessel's fragile remains shudder around us. Another well-placed blast, and we'll go down with the rubble.

"What are you doing here?" she demands.

"Old guy sent me—Justus. Know him?"

She pulls against my hold on her. "Why aren't you with your people?" Her tone is edged with concern, oddly enough.

"I was, but..." Julia brought me here, and I'm not about to try and explain that. "I'm going back to them."

"You will take me with you." It's not a request.

"I think that's the idea. Justus wants you out of harm's way." Tentatively, I let go of her arm. "We should get a move on."

"Cain will be the death of us all." Her eyes blaze with intensity. "You have to stop him."

"First I have to get you out of here." I take her hand and turn to lead her out into the corridor, but a fresh concussive blast shakes the ocean liner. It sways, creaking and moaning like a whale in death throes. I pull the woman close, and she curses in protest, but her strength is no match for my speed. I half-carry her up the hallway, keeping my head low and holding hers down with one hand, my other arm wrapped around her, bracing her tight against me. So tight I can feel her unborn child kick. "Hang on."

She clutches onto me, her strong fingers digging in.

"Hope you're not afraid of heights."

"The sun." She winces as we move through a shaft of brilliant light piercing a wide crack in the upper deck.

"Right." We pass a set of curtains draped over a wide porthole. I tear them down and toss them over her. "This'll work for now."

"Where are you taking me?"

"To your friends—"

"Take me east. To Luther's people. They have to know what Cain is planning."

I frown. "That's kind of far."

"You're kind of fast, from what I hear."

"But—"

"Every life on this continent is in danger. If Cain succeeds, the UW will not stop until they have destroyed us, once and for all: my people, your people, the men of Eden. Even the babies."

"What do you know about them?" I look her in the eye. We're face to face now, close enough to kiss—not that I'm planning on it—as I prepare to launch us up and out of a large gap in the broken superstructure ahead.

"Cain intends to kill them."

What? But I shouldn't be surprised. If Cain is indeed possessed by an evil spirit of the earth, then of course it would persuade him to do the unthinkable. Just like not-Jackson all those months ago, wanting me to blow the nuclear reactor in Eden. Now he wants Cain to destroy the United World's last chance at a future.

"We must go now," Victoria insists. "There's no time to waste."

She's right about that. As the ocean liner crumbles around us under the impact of yet another salvo, I shoot forward and upward, spiraling into the sky high above the destruction, then rocketing eastward as fast as I can fly, pushing myself to the limit. Victoria screams, clinging to me as I struggle to maintain my trajectory with the added weight, adjusting our course to keep from angling off one way or the other and plowing into the crest of a passing hill.

"I'll take you to Luther," I shout over the rush of the wind we're creating. "Then I'll go back for the others."

I hate leaving them there like that, but the battleship they're hiding in looked solid enough—for now. I hope Sergeant Bishop will be able to contact the *Argonaus* and tell them to cease fire. It wasn't Justus, the elders, or Cain's wives who staked that corpse on the beach. Cain acted alone, albeit under the influence of evil.

"Only you can overtake them!" Victoria shouts. "Cain's fastest warriors—he will send them first to take control of Eden. They move as fast as you, but they cannot fly!"

Well, that's something in my favor. "How many are there? These super-fast warriors?"

"Twenty or more."

Dealing with them won't be easy. I remember overpowering Willard's men in Eden when Luther and Daiyna were held captive, but those soldiers were mere mortals, not the *gifted* variety. How can I possibly overpower more than twenty super-speedy warriors and get them to rethink their actions? Without a whole lot of firepower, it'll be impossible.

Not that I'm keen on the idea of shooting anybody. I've vowed never to kill again, not after what went down in my bunker way back when.

I almost wish I was never given these superhuman abilities. People rely on me too much to save the day, to go where others can't. To spy and bring back intel—that's how Luther first learned about the UW sending their people ashore. If it wasn't for my ability to fly over the *Argonaus* and eavesdrop, Luther never would have known about the scouts heading to Eden.

Maybe not such a bad thing. He never would have gone to warn Cain, and Cain never would have gotten it into his head to terminate the unborn children in Eden. A decisive blow against the UW, but a horrifying solution: to kill the only new life this continent has seen in twenty-odd years.

I can't let that happen.

Will the Julia-spirit intervene somehow—with or without me, now that I've turned my back on her kind? I'll need the spirits' help if I'm going to have a chance at stopping Cain's advance on Eden. Alone, I'll be no match for them.

When I stepped out of that whirlwind and sent them scurrying with their tails between their legs, I'd surprised them. That won't happen again. Despite whatever legends are currently circulating about the *flying man*, I'm mortal, and I'm no one to be feared. I could be disemboweled as easily as any daemon. All it would take is a sharp blade across the abdomen. And Cain's people are real fond of sharp objects.

Part of me longs for death. I deserve it, and I crave the peace and quiet it might bring. But another part of me has unfortunately reared its ugly head: the part that knows the only way I'll ever find redemption for my past is by protecting those who can't protect themselves in the present.

Maybe going after Cain's warriors is a suicide mission, but at least I'll die for a good cause. For the future.

"How much farther?" Victoria shouts, rushing air flapping the drapes against her.

"We're here." I catch sight of the Homeplace atop a sheer cliff, and I aim our trajectory straight for it.

Margo's Hummer sits below with its driver's side door open. Three bodies lie on bloodstained sand beside it. Broken bodies at the base of the cliff lie in pools of their own blood. Bodies of Cain's warriors in tattered rags lie motionlessly across the ground, facing the cliff. I take in every detail as I descend onto the ridge. I set the pregnant woman on her bare feet just inside the mouth of the cave where shadows keep the ground cool.

There are no sentries on duty. They have fallen to their deaths. Beside them, I recognize the body of that kid Margo insisted on taking along, the one exiled from Cain's enclave. Was he the cause of this slaughter?

I stumble forward a step as I survey the carnage. The bodies by the vehicle are those of the UW team. Gunned down, all three of them.

Victoria chokes as her gaze rests on Lemuel's body. She staggers backward to brace herself against the cave wall.

"So much death..." she murmurs.

"Luther? Samson?" I enter the shade and tug my goggles up onto my forehead.

My heart's racing. Where is everybody? Were they attacked by daemons? No, the freaks would've eaten the remains, and those corpses are untouched, left to roast in the sun. From their positions—Cain's people facing the ridge below, Luther's sentries lying in crumpled heaps at the base of the cliff—it looks like they fired on each other. If so, did Cain's warriors decimate the Homeplace before moving on to attack Eden? Will I find the bodies of my friends inside?

I never should have left them. I should have been here.

Silently, I curse the Julia-spirit for leading me off-course, taking me to the coast. What the hell was that all about?

"Nobody's home." I can't bring myself to delve deeper into the cave. I stare at the dark interior, lit only by the sickly green of glowsticks mounted along the walls.

"No." Victoria stands beside me, the curtains pulled around her shoulders like a cloak. Her locks of thick, golden hair spill outward around her flushed face. "She is here."

Before I can reply, Margo materializes out of the darkness, her footsteps echoing. "We meet at last." She stares at Victoria with those unnerving eyes of hers, devoid of emotion.

"You failed to protect him." Victoria's glassy eyes haven't left Lemuel's body. Her voice is thick with emotion.

"Your people killed him. There was little I could do."

I frown at their interchange. "Where's everybody else?"

"If you go farther eastward, you will see their tracks," Margo says.

"Cain is taking them with him," Victoria murmurs, as if she knows Margo's thoughts.

"So, you both..." I tap my temple.

"We share a common gift." Victoria gazes into the darkness behind Margo. "As does another one here with you."

"Who else is there?" I glance from one woman to the other.

"Tucker hid us with his ability," Margo says. "The two young ones in their incubation pods, as well as myself. Cain's warriors passed us by as they went about rounding up all of Luther's people and escorting them outside."

"So...they're alive." I can breathe easier all of a sudden.

"For now." Victoria narrows her gaze. "It is one of the infants I sense—a female. She is also able to send her thoughts into the minds of others."

"Yes," Margo says.

How is that possible? Inside its incubation chamber, the fetus would never have breathed the dust of this world. The spirits wouldn't have been able to bless her with superhuman abilities. Unless the abilities were transferred through her parents' DNA. If that's the case, and if all of the unborn children in Eden are like this one, then they'll be no different than anybody else on this continent. *Infected* by some kind of bizarre mutagen, according to the UW.

"But no one can know." Margo faces Victoria squarely.

"Who would I tell?" Victoria runs a hand over the swell of her abdomen.

Someone in the shadows clears his throat. "So-uh, are you all that's left from the coast?"

Victoria stares, eyes widening. "Who's there? Show yourself."

Tucker sniffs. "Kind of hard to do that, ma'am."

"He is...*invisible?*" Victoria blinks.

"Along with anything he touches." I face Tucker's voice. "There are others on the coast. Older folks and a few women in the...same condition."

"How many are pregnant among you?" Margo says quickly.

"It doesn't matter," Victoria replies. "The UW will destroy us all if Cain gets to Eden before we do."

I frown at that. "You're not going anywhere. I'll go."

"Me too." The sound of Tucker's feet shuffle over to my side. "Might come in handy to fly out of sight, don't you think?"

I can't argue with that, but I don't like the idea of carrying the man. Victoria's added weight was difficult enough to manage mid-flight. "Those people on the coast are sitting ducks. The UW's shelling the beach."

"We've heard it," Tucker says. "I know you won't go back to Eden, Margo, and I know you want to watch over the young ones. But you're the only person here keyed to drive that thing." He probably means the Hummer outside.

"I can stay and watch over the infants." Victoria offers. "Where are they?"

I don't trust her, Margo's thought enters my mind.

"If what she says is true, then there are a whole lot of other lives at stake," I reply, preferring that Margo use her words.

"The future of the world," Victoria says, and somehow it doesn't sound melodramatic. "You have to leave. Now."

"Most of them are on foot," Tucker tells me. "They took the other Hummer—the one I drove you out of Eden in, way back when. But they couldn't have gotten too far."

"A couple dozen of them are as fast as I am."

Tucker sniffs "Sure, there's that."

"I will drive to the coast." Margo moves out into the sunlight, drawing her hood over her head to shield her features. "Enough lives have been lost today. But if anything happens to the young ones, I will hold you personally responsible."

Victoria smiles coolly. "As would any mother."

I rest my hand on Margo's shoulder. "If it's too dangerous, you turn right back around. That thing's bulletproof, but I doubt it'll stop what the *Argonaus* is spitting out."

"I won't be able to take all of them with me." There aren't enough seats in the vehicle.

"The pregnant women, then." I bite my lip. I hate the idea of leaving anybody behind. "They're the ones…carrying the future."

Margo meets my gaze and nods. "Tomorrow's children."

I feel a hand grip my arm, and I turn to find Tucker grinning at me.

"Howdy," he says, completely visible—a sandy-haired, rugged-looking man with the build of a laborer.

"Where did he go?" Victoria sounds mystified by my disappearance.

"That's how it works," Tucker explains. "If you can see me, nobody else can see you." He rubs at his nose. "So how're we gonna do this, Milton? Want me to ride piggyback?"

"Please don't."

Without any gesture of farewell, Margo descends the ridge outside. Tucker slips his arms around my abdomen, prepared to hold on for his life.

"Take the passage on the left there, third alcove you come to,"

Tucker calls back to Victoria. "The little ones were sleeping last time I checked. If the lights are blinking, they're all good."

She nods warily, looking at the direction of his voice without anything to fix her gaze upon. "Go quickly, flying man. Do whatever you can to stop him." She pauses. "Kill him, if you must. Cain is no son of Gaia if he plans to murder the innocent."

I'm about to echo what Margo said, that there's already been enough killing today. But I have a bad feeling there will be plenty more before the day is through.

22. TUCKER

18 MONTHS AFTER ALL-CLEAR

I never would've thought I'd be scared of heights. Like every other engineer from Sector 30, I had my share of high-profile assignments early in my career, back before D-Day. One in particular, I'll never forget: an exhaust manifold on the exterior of a fifty-story skyscraper. The fool designers had planted it right on the edge of the roof. There were some strong winds that day, and the whole inspection procedure had been dicey from the start.

But nothing in my experience compares to this—hurtling through the air at breakneck speeds, tightening my white-knuckled hold on Milton with every jerky twist and turn. The last time I looked, we were well over a hundred meters above the ground. I clamped my eyes shut and have yet to open them since.

"You see 'em?" I holler, my feet dangling uselessly behind me.

"Only their dust," Milton shouts back. "One group's up ahead. They've got the Hummer, but most are on foot. Cain and Luther's people, all together. Another group is farther east."

"You want to stop?"

"The slower bunch isn't our concern. We have to stop the ones that'll reach Eden first."

"Think you can overtake 'em?"

"We'll see." The wind rips past us, as if Milton has kicked his speed into high gear.

I squeeze my eyes tight and nod. But then another thought springs into my head: what if Milton flies straight to Eden, and he and I somehow manage to commandeer the nursery, barricade ourselves inside there or something? Or better yet, lock Willard and his men in their quarters, then head down to the radio room and send that whole lot of remote-controlled mutos straight at Cain's advancing troops?

"This Cain guy, he must really have a death wish," I offer.

Milton doesn't respond. Probably takes a lot of focus to fly like a superhero.

I sniff, wishing I could scratch my nose. But that would mean letting go of Milton with one hand, and I'm not about to do that until both my feet are planted on solid ground.

"I mean, he's got to know that by killing all those babies, the UW's just going to retaliate in a big way, right? From what I've heard, the United World government is putting all its eggs in one basket with those kids."

"How do you mean?" Milton rolls a few degrees to the right, adjusting his trajectory.

"They gave up on the cloning project—at least, that's what Margo heard."

"Clones?"

"Yeah." I can't help chuckling awkwardly. "Guess they realized that's no way to go. Unless they figure out a way for the clones to reproduce themselves naturally, they'd just be making copies of copies in a couple generations. Talk about weakening the ol' gene pool, right?"

"They should've thought of that before they nuked the hell out of us."

"No doubt. But I don't think they knew what the side effects would be. They just wanted all the terrorists' germ-bombs destroyed." They took care of those, all right—incinerating any living thing the government hadn't already rounded up and sent down into a bunker.

"There they are." Milton sounds...nervous?

I crack an eye open against the rushing wind and peek below. Milton has every right to be worried. One flying man and one invisible man against that crew? There's got to be over two dozen of them, each zipping across the ground nearly as fast as Milton's flying over it. Kicking up a thick cloud of dust in their wake, Cain's speedy warriors race east, cloaks flailing behind them, blades gleaming in the sun.

Time for me to share my idea: "Hey, how about we forget this bunch and go straight to Eden instead? You know, head 'em off? Maybe talk some reason into Willard and—"

"That guy's nuts. You really think he'd listen to us?"

"We could take over Eden. Lock up Willard and his cronies and defend the nursery against those bloodthirsty savages down there. Keep 'em from getting inside."

Milton's quiet. Will he adjust his trajectory to intercept Cain's warriors? Or is he actually considering my idea?

He surges forward through the air. "Sounds like a plan, Mr. Tucker. A crazy plan, but it just might work."

"Call me Tucker. My dad was *Mr.* Tucker."

What sounds like a laugh erupts from Milton—the first sign of any personality I've seen to date. The guy seems like one of those tortured souls you always read about in old works of literature, like he's trying to get out from under his past's dark shadow.

"Long as they haven't sealed 'em up, I should have a few ways for us to get inside," I shout.

Willard didn't take kindly to my surprise visits back in the day. I'd located multiple entry points into Eden from the surface streets in the city above. Most of them involved manhole covers and underground sewage pipes, which was why Willard sometimes smelled me before I made my presence known.

"Never thought I'd be happy to see *them*," Milton says.

We've slowed to a standstill in the middle of the air. Milton can do that?

"Who? Where?" I risk a quick peek.

"There." Milton points back toward Cain's warriors, far below. "Hard to make out with all the dust they're stirring up."

A dizzying surge of vertigo overcomes me for a moment, and I have some difficulty focusing. But once I'm able to, I see the battle lines clearly drawn. On the west side are Cain's warriors, moving with flashes of light as the sun strikes their unsheathed blades in violent arcs. On the east side are two vehicles, jeeps by the looks of them, wheeling about in wild figure-eights with heavy weapons fire blasting willy-nilly.

"Mutos?"

Milton nods. "They should keep Cain's bunch busy."

"You don't think..." I adjust my grip on Milton's torso. "Another bunch of mutos might've gone after the slower-moving group?"

Milton shifts direction. "We should go back."

"Risky. One of those trigger-happy sons of bitches wings you, and those babies in Eden can kiss their rescue goodbye."

"You think we should keep moving."

I pause. "I think you should let Luther's spirits do their thing. If it's true what he says about them, then maybe they'll intervene in a pillar of dust or something. You know, blind the mutos in their tracks."

That elicits a half-hearted chuckle from the flying man. "After seeing those shells landing on the beach, the daemons don't seem half as intimidating as they used to."

"Compared to something that can blow you into a thousand pieces? Yeah. A freak that wants to eat your face off isn't really a big deal!"

"With these daemons slowing down Cain's fastest warriors, we'll have plenty of time to take over Eden and prepare for their arrival..." He shakes his head. "But I can't leave Luther to face those things alone."

"He's not alone. Have you seen Cain's people? They're like post-apocalyptic gladiators. If there's anybody who can keep your friends alive, it's them. Feel sorry for the mutos. They've scoped out the wrong prey this time."

Milton seems reluctant to turn east and resume our flight. "If I find Sergeant Bishop and have him radio his ship, then those people on the coast—"

"The babies are all that matter right now. If they're lost, then all of this'll be for nothing. Willard and his bunch just want to use 'em to buy their way off this dead continent. Cain's people want to kill 'em all to screw over the UW. You and me? We want 'em to *live*. Ain't that right?"

"We're the heroes," Milton says flatly. His expressionless goggles look west, back the way we've flown. "I just...don't know if this is the right thing to do."

He seems lost, like a weather vane with no wind to blow him in the right direction.

"Don't those spirits talk to you?" I don't necessarily believe the spirits of the earth are what Luther's people believe them to be—ghosts of every animal blown up on D-Day—but I know there's something supernatural at work on this continent. And it stands to reason Milton would be the closest to whatever spiritual entity it is, what with him being able to fly like a bird and all. "Can't you ask them what they think you should do?"

"Doesn't work that way. They show up when they have something to tell me."

I nod, adjusting my hold on him. It's more than a little uncanny hanging here in midair; I'll never get used to it, not in a million years. "When did they show up last?"

Milton turns to gaze east, toward Eden, still out of sight from this distance. We have hundreds of kilometers left to cross before we'll reach the city ruins and the skyscraper skeletons jutting upward from the ashen sand. "An hour ago, maybe longer."

"What did they say?"

"I don't know."

Sounds more like he doesn't *want* to know. "They spoke to you and you alone, and you can't remember what they said?"

"We don't need them. We can fend for ourselves."

"Unlike those babies."

Milton's grip on me tightens, and he propels himself onward with a sudden burst of speed, plowing through the rushing air like a missile. It seems like we're going faster than before, but maybe it's just the contrast between hovering in midair and rocketing through it.

He's made up his mind.

"If those daemons hurt anybody but Cain's people, I'm holding you personally responsible," Milton shouts.

Join the club. Daiyna would appreciate having Milton on her side in the Eden-hating faction.

Within minutes, the twisted, charred metal spires of the city ruins appear in the distance like long, crooked fingers clawing at the sky. Below, a few levels under the ash-smothered streets, lies the subterranean refuge of Willard's Eden Guard. Won't they be surprised to find ol' Tucker and his super-friend knocking at their door?

"You got inside once before, from what I recall," I shout over the rushing wind.

"Through the sewage tunnels, yeah. I was hoping you knew a better way."

"Head south once you reach the towers. There's a network of underground waterways, separate from the sewers. They were used to channel groundwater to the surface before D-Day."

As we approach the city ruins with their crumbling buildings and heaps of dusty rubble, I notice hundreds of dark, indistinguishable forms roaming the abandoned streets below.

"We've got company." Milton doesn't sound too happy about it.

When I left Eden, Willard and the Eden Guard were doubling their efforts with the mutos, collaring a fresh dozen every day. It helped that a large number of them called the ruins above Eden their home. With plenty of collared *dogs* already wired and remote-controlled, it was a simple matter for Perch or Jamison—

Willard's right and left-hand man, respectively—to send a dog or two out to collect new recruits.

Now, staring into the distance at so many creatures wandering out in the open, I have to wonder if there are any wild mutos left in the city.

Willard has a flesh-eating army at his disposal. I don't have a gun on me, and neither does Milton. We'll just have to trust my ability to keep us invisible and Milton's ability to get us out of a tight squeeze faster than the speed of sound.

"How many, would you say?"

Milton shakes his head. "Too many."

He brings us in lower, swooping over one of the buildings that's still somewhat intact—a three-story brick apartment house. He points at the flat stretch of concrete roof, scorched and strewn with debris. I nod, assuming he means we're going in for a landing.

Touching down like a loon across the tranquil surface of a lake, Milton's boots skid once or twice as he fights for balance. He holds onto me with one arm while swinging the other as a counterweight. Good thing we're still invisible, or the mutos below would've noticed us right off. As it is, the slow-moving horde in the street tilt back their heads and stare goggle-eyed at nothing in particular. Sure looks like they heard something.

Milton gestures to keep silent as he pries my death grip off him, keeping a firm hold of my shoulder with one hand as he does so. We've got to stay in contact in order for him to remain invisible. The last thing either of us wants is to be noticed right now.

The mutos below wear the telltale signs they're members of Willard's dog pound: shock collars adorn their scabby throats. The steel bands are cinched snugly at the base of each muto's neck, and a red pinpoint of light blinks to show it's active, transmitting video of everything it faces via a micro-camera.

I nudge Milton and point down a southbound side street. We'll have to climb to the ground, then navigate our way through throngs of mutos without being noticed. As long as we move among the freaks without bumping into any of them, we'll be fine.

All those muto feet have stirred the dust along the ground in well-trod sections of the city. The trouble will come when we cross a less popular stretch of terrain. If Jamison or Perch, monitoring the muto-cams, happens to notice our tracks leading into the underground waterways, then Milton and I will lose the element of surprise.

And considering how matters stand at present, that's our only advantage.

Milton nods, ready to follow me over the side of the building and down the rusted iron ladder along disintegrating brick. If I were a praying man, I might've said some words before placing my boot on the first rung and letting it take my full weight. I try not to imagine the ladder breaking off the wall and sending me and Milton plummeting onto a bunch of hungry mutos below.

I make my descent with one hand on Milton's ankle above me, keeping him invisible. Rung after rung without a word, we reach the street. Holding my breath, and with Milton's hand on my shoulder, I head through the mass of twitching bodies more dead than alive, staggering with no clear direction in sight. Milton follows close behind. Both of us are invisible to the creatures, but knowing that doesn't make it any less horrifying: the way these rotten-smelling freaks stare right at us as we pass, their lidless yellow eyes oozing a foul fluid that seems to be their lifeblood. I'm thankful for the head covering I wear; it cuts down on some of the stench reaching my nostrils.

I pause to point down an alley blocked by a trio of mutos swaying on their feet like drug addicts higher than cloud nine. Milton nods, his goggles tracking the freaks closest to us. Even though they can't see us, they can smell well enough. Lingering in one place for more than a second or two isn't a good idea.

Milton could have saved us a lot of trouble by flying directly to the entry point. Too bad it's not an option. The way he moves in fast-forward stirs up a whole lot of dust that would be visible on the muto-cams. Better to take it slow in enemy territory. And besides, I don't know for sure this first stop will be our ticket to Eden. If the manhole covers are sealed, we'll have to take an entirely different route—one Milton won't like at all.

He'll remember it: the underground parking structure where he and his friends first ran into Willard's crew.

We reach the manhole and crouch beside it, keeping an eye on the mutos nearby, only five meters away. They don't seem to notice any invisible trespassers; they just stare off into space. Starving, most likely. Willard likes to keep them hungry, says it makes them easier to control. Truth is, it makes them even more vicious than they are in their wild state.

I mime the need for a crowbar, something to pry the cover upward. Milton runs the fingers of his free hand around the rim. It doesn't appear to have been soldered into place. I was hoping this one would be overlooked if Willard decided to seal off the access points into Eden. This corner of the city is outside the area I normally frequent, finding all manner of goods for the Eden Guard. The poor side of town back in the day, where the government housed Sector 30's laborers.

Keeping one hand on me, Milton looks around for anything we could use as a pry bar. Nothing but debris in sight—until I spot a length of exposed rebar sticking out of some rubble. I nudge Milton and point at it with a shrug. Milton nods. It'll have to work.

But it's half a meter away from the muto closest to us.

Milton reaches for the rebar and shoves down on it, moving it a centimeter at most. He heaves it the opposite direction, bringing it back to its original position. He waits to see if the muto took notice. It's still staring up at the sky, pondering the sun.

Milton bursts into super-speed, his arm moving in a blur of motion and the rebar right along with it. I've never seen anything like this—except maybe in a cartoon when I was a kid. Then with a metallic squeal and a crunch from the surrounding concrete, Milton has the meter-long piece of rebar free.

The muto snorts and reels around to face us, its eyes twitching in their sockets as its exposed nasal cavity expands and retracts in spasms. With a grunt, the other mutos join it, staggering straight toward us. Milton grips the length of iron like a weapon, but I tug him back toward the manhole cover, and we set about trying to pry it up out of the street as fast as we can.

The mutos incline their heads and snort at each other. They heard something they couldn't see, and now they're determined to sniff it out. If anyone in the Eden control station is watching their screens, they'll be more than a little interested right about now. The way the freaks' collars are facing, they'll get a clear view of the manhole cover as it slides aside.

Miming a cameraman, I point at the mutos and gesture pushing them away. Milton seems to understand. He points at a chunk of concrete the size of a man's head, sitting next to me. He shrugs, and I have to agree. It's as good an idea as any.

Gritting my teeth at the weight of it, I heave the chunk like a shot put, past the two freaks by a good couple meters. It lands with a crumbling clatter, skidding across the dusty asphalt. Immediately, the mutos' attention whips toward it, their collar-mounted cameras pivoting right along with them.

Problem solved.

We seize the moment, gripping the makeshift crowbar hand over hand and putting our backs into it. The cover is wedged in there pretty tight, proof I haven't used this access point into Eden nearly as often as the others.

The mutos grunt, seeming to curse in their own garbled, phlegm-coated language. They've reached the piece of concrete and are kicking at it now with their tattered boots.

Milton and I heave the iron cover upward and slide it aside as quietly as we can, but the metallic rumble isn't lost on the freaks. Their heads twist to look back. Milton gives the rebar a lateral toss that sends it hurtling end over end, straight at them. It strikes one in the side of its deformed head, and the muto goes over backward, collapsing onto its buddy with plenty of gargled shrieking—pain and rage in equal measure.

"After you," I whisper.

Milton drops down the hole and clings to the ladder, releasing his hold on me as soon as he's swallowed up by the street. Glancing at the two mutos, I step down the ladder after him and slide the cover over our entry point, pressing upward with all my strength until it settles into place. Closing us in.

"Can't see a damned thing," Milton mutters, his voice carrying down the tunnel before us. "Guess we go that way."

I nod, then realize Milton can't see the gesture now that we aren't joined at the hip anymore. "That's right. There shouldn't be any sort of drop-off for a hundred meters or so. By then, our eyes will have acclimated somewhat."

I pause to look around and blink against the dark. As far as I know, there are no night vision cameras mounted down here.

"That trick with the rebar was really something." I keep my voice low as we slosh through ankle-deep water. From the smell, this is no sewer. So far, so good.

Milton almost chuckles. "Can't believe I nailed that one in the head."

"Yeah." I sniff. "But I meant before, how you got it out of the rubble."

What else is he able to do with his superhuman speed? From what I recalled of my training in Sector 30, once a thing starts moving at the speed of light, Einstein's relativity principles come into play. Maybe even time travel's possible. *That sure as hell would be something.* To be able to change the past? To keep the world from destroying itself in the first place? It boggles the mind. But then again, could one man really make much of a difference?

Milton's outstretched hand meets my chest dead-center.

Focus, Tucker. Crazy thoughts, anyway. Like when I used to think this planet wasn't even Earth anymore. Or that our struggle for survival was part of some sadistic government experiment.

"Looks like we've found that drop-off you mentioned," Milton says. "Any suggestions?"

"Remember those water slides they had when we were kids?"

Milton shakes his head. "We didn't get much rec time in the trade sectors."

"Right." One of the advantages of growing up with engineers: they were always more than happy to supply imaginative diversions for the kiddies in the neighborhood. Roller coasters, water slides, you name it. "What I'm saying is, we'll need to take a leap of faith here."

Milton peers over the edge. "Or I could float us down to the bottom."

"Yeah. Or that."

Milton steps out into open space, hovering over a drop that could be anywhere between thirty to fifty meters. He beckons. "All right. Hang on."

Here we go again. Gritting my teeth, I lunge into Milton's arms. We do indeed *float*, just as Milton said we would, and seconds later, we land in cold, knee-deep water smelling like it hasn't moved anywhere in decades.

"Where's the source?"

"Groundwater reservoirs." I let go of him and regain my balance. "Eden used to be a big fat one, back before Willard pumped out all the water into channels like this. Nobody on the surface has known about it since before D-Day."

"Straight ahead?"

"Onward and downward. We've got a few more drops ahead of us."

Each time we reach one, Milton floats us down into ever-deepening waters until we come to an airlock built of solid steel and plasticon. No access point for a key or scanner, and no viewport to see what lies on the other side.

"Dead end." Milton curses, the murky water up to his chest.

I put a hand on his shoulder. "This'll be a hoot. Trust me." I place my other hand on the round airlock door, and immediately it vanishes, giving us a clear view of the dry interior on the other side. There's a well-lit corridor where a single soldier stands dozing in blue fatigues, arms crossed over his automatic rifle. He stirs, then jolts to attention at the dull clang of my fist against the hatch. "Hey in there!"

"What the hell are you doing?" Milton whispers.

I just wink. "Hey, is that you, Ayers? Open up, for crying out loud!"

With every contact between my fist and the hatch, the components of the door dematerialize, and the sentry's eyes grow wider. He clutches his rifle at the ready.

"Who goes there?" His voice trembles. Then he scowls. "Is that you, Tucker?"

"Guilty as charged." I chuckle.

"Quit fooling around!"

"How 'bout you open up? I'm soaked out here."

Ayers steps forward cautiously as I hold the palm of my hand against the airlock, giving the sentry a clear view of the chest-high water lapping against its seemingly nonexistent surface.

"What the hell are you doing, Tucker? Captain Willard sent the dogs out looking for you." Ayers lowers his voice. "He says you're a traitor, man. You and that woman, Margo."

"I've got information for him. Would a traitor return with news that'll benefit the Eden Guard?"

Ayers steps back, reaching for the radio clipped to his shoulder.

"Don't do that," I warn. "You call it in, and I'm out of here. You'll be sitting ducks when the UW arrives."

Milton gives me an incredulous look. What about the element of surprise?

"Captain Willard is working with the UW—"

"Not anymore," I counter. "Things have gone sideways. They're on the warpath now. But I'd better give him the particulars. Take me to the captain, and I'll make sure we all get out of this alive."

Ayers' hand hasn't left the radio. "You've got a lotta nerve, thinkin' you can give me orders, Tucker. The hell with you." He switches on the radio. "Base command, come in."

"What is it, Ayers?" The voice on the other end is Jamison's, and he sounds beat.

"That bastard Tucker's decided to show his face—so to speak."

"Tucker?" Now Jamison's wide awake.

Milton pulls away, shaking his head fiercely, but I hold onto him. "Trust me," I whisper.

"Stay right where you are," Jamison orders. "I'm on my way."

Ayers frowns. "Shouldn't Captain Willard know about this?"

"The captain's in the middle of a serious talk with the Chancellor. Not to be disturbed. Hang tight, I'll be right down."

Frown intact, Ayers releases his radio. I let go of the hatch, allowing it to re-materialize.

I hope we've made the right choice by coming here. I knew better than to think an entry point into Eden wouldn't be guarded—even though I didn't tell Milton about it. But this is the access hatch closest to Jamison's station, and if there's anybody in Eden worthy of an iota of trust, it's him.

Even so, a sliver of doubt digs itself into my mind. This is our only shot, and it all depends on Willard's left-hand man.

23. BISHOP

18 MONTHS AFTER ALL-CLEAR

I wanted to radio Mutegi on the *Argonaus* as soon as I heard the low concussions in the west, but with the arrival of Cain and his warriors and the subsequent round-up, followed by this forced march into the Wastes, there wasn't time to reach Margo's vehicle—to see if Doc's helmet was salvageable. *Functional* would've been good enough.

Granger. Sinclair. Harris. My blood boils at the memory of them shot through the head and left to rot in the sun. At the first opportunity, I plan to repay Cain with three shots of my own. Two in the chest, one in the head.

My fists clench automatically.

Focus. I can't allow myself to do anything that will jeopardize my trip home. That's the priority here. Has been all along.

Sweating through every pore now, I struggle to keep up with Luther's people, herded eastward on foot by well-armed warriors while Cain and Luther ride in an armored Hummer at the front of the pack. Beside me, Samson the cyborg clanks along as fast as he can, prodded forward by impatient warriors bringing up the rear.

Technically speaking, I'm still on mission, heading straight to Eden. I alone will have to see this through without a fully functional suit, breathing through a supplemental apparatus that could give out any minute, and with no way to contact the *Argonaus*.

After the beach-shelling concludes, amphibious assault teams will roll out. They'll take control of the shore while choppers provide cover for advancing ground squads. But it will be a while before my backup arrives. And when it does, I'll have to explain the situation as best I can: The factions—Luther's group, Cain's people, and Willard's engineers. How the current march on Eden may hinder the UW's plans to obtain the fetuses Willard promised us. Whether or not the unborn children are in fact contaminated. Only Harris would have been able to tell for sure.

Looking at the people around me, I have to wonder how things will play out. No one here besides me wants the UW to get those children. Genetically, they belong to Luther and his group; what they want is obvious. But it's unclear what Cain has in mind.

Having studied tribal warlords of ages past, I know a power struggle for land dominance when I see one. If Cain ever considered Luther's enclave to be a threat, he doesn't seem to anymore. They're unarmed, shepherded along like domesticated animals. Or slaves. All that remains to be conquered is Arthur Willard's underground refuge. Did Cain forsake his own settlement on the coast in hopes of turning Willard's group out of Eden? Does Cain plan for his people and Luther's to live there together? Unlikely, since Luther's tribe was forced to lay down arms.

They'll be fodder once any shooting starts.

Cries of alarm erupt from up ahead, at the front of the pack. Shouts include the word *goblyn*—something from those bedtime stories I've read countless times to Mara and Emmanuel. Cain's warriors surge forward, leaving Luther's people unguarded in their wake.

I nudge the cyborg. "Let's make a run for it."

Thanks to him, my external audio is working again. A little glitchy, but better than nothing. Samson was able to connect one of the tools on his robo-hand with a port on my collar, run a diagnostic on that small screen along the inside of his mechatronic forearm, and then monitor the repairs to my helmet as they were happening. Couldn't fix the HUD, but I'll take what I can get.

Samson grunts, heaving himself forward with no alteration in his momentum. "Be my guest, Sarge." He whips his steel right hand upward, and a long blade flips into position where two fingers were a moment ago. "I like having Cain's bunch act as a buffer between us and the daemons."

He watches the warriors with their weapons at the ready, peering into the rising dust ahead. They don't slow their advance. The *goblyns* or *daemons* will be met head-on.

"You don't think they'll make it past those warriors?"

Samson doesn't bother to face me mid-stride. "I think Cain's about to lose more than a few of his people. Bon appétit, mutant freaks."

A cacophony of weapons fire explodes, directed into the dense cloud of billowing sand and ash engulfing us all. I've yet to see a single mutant, but there is something familiar about the dust that swirls around me—a presence I've felt before in this strange land.

Voices shout in fear and battle-hardened rage. Soon I can barely see my own gloved hand in front of my face shield. Blindly, I halt and turn around, reaching for anyone nearby. My fingers clasp onto nothing but air.

Rifle shots report from a distance, followed by screams of agony twenty paces ahead. Cain's warriors raise a war cry, and their return fire roars in a mighty barrage. I drop awkwardly to one knee and cover my cracked helmet with both arms.

Maybe it's the heat from the sun or the heat of the moment, but I'm overwhelmed with anger, a fury that burns deep in my gut and radiates outward. I've never felt so powerless, at the mercy of forces beyond my control—unarmed, alone, handicapped by a suit designed to keep me alive on this godforsaken continent. I have a mission to complete, but that's not going to happen if these freakish creatures have their way.

I want to destroy them all, turn a heat ray on them and watch them melt into the sand.

A *heat ray*? Right. I'm seriously losing it.

Then I blink at the figure approaching from out of the billowing dust. She seems to float toward me, garbed in a sheer white gown that trails behind her—like a Greek goddess from millennia ago.

My wife.

"You again," I mutter.

"You are not safe here."

"None of us are. Take a look around."

"You are needed in Eden, Sergeant."

"Damned straight. But it doesn't look like I'll be getting there anytime soon."

The vision of my wife smiles as only she can. My abdomen tightens at the familiar sight, knowing it's not her but illogically yearning for it to be. My eyes sting all of a sudden.

"We will take you."

"*We?*"

Spirits of the earth, Luther calls them. As if that makes any kind of sense. This continent is one tripped-out freak show. Maybe I've been infected, after all. That would explain these weird visions.

"It is you that Arthur Willard expects to meet. Not Milton and Tucker, who are—"

"Wait a minute. Milton's headed there now? To Eden?"

"He believes he is acting in the best interest of his people, but he may instead jeopardize the lives he is trying to protect. Willard will not listen to them. But he will listen to you."

I wince at another burst of weapons fire. Another volley of screams. Cain's warriors are not going down without a fight.

"How the hell do you plan to get me there? And what about these people? Don't you think they could use a little help?"

Her shoulders lift and fall. "We have provided cover for their retreat. Instead, they choose to remain here and fight."

"Luther's people were taken against their will—"

"You do not know them very well—the fire that burns in each of their hearts. Some wish to rescue the infants from Eden. Some wish to have their gifts removed by Eden's engineers. And some wish to destroy Eden and all that it stands for. But every one of them desires to see this journey to its end. None will turn from the path they have chosen."

I turn away from her—*it*—to peer into the wall of dust. I see movement, but no figures I recognize. The truth is, I don't owe these people anything. They're not my team. I have a mission to complete, and whatever gets me there fastest is the way to go.

"Fine. Let's move." Reaching Willard and arranging the release of those infants is all that matters. With Mutegi providing back-up, I can afford to be optimistic. "Are you going to give me wings or something?"

"We will carry you through the air."

"You can do that?"

She pauses. For the first time, she looks unsure of herself. "We believe so."

"Let me guess. You've never done it before."

"No. It would have killed anyone else."

"But not me." I frown, trying to figure this out. What makes me different? I lift one arm. "Because of the suit?"

"It will protect you from the dust. You will not smother in it." As she speaks, the swirling murk around me grows denser, the sand and flakes of ash whirling around me like a tornado. I'm standing in the eye.

"All right." I curl my gloved fingers into fists. "Let's do this."

"Try to relax." She dissolves from sight. At the same time, I feel myself float upward. I can't help reaching out to steady myself—only there's nothing to brace against or hold onto.

Blind to the battle below but able to hear every gunshot, I'm carried up into the sky like a hot air balloon in a strong gust of wind. The altitude has to be over a hundred meters, judging by the sound of weapons fire beneath me. Then without warning,

I'm hurtling through the air, surrounded by the swirling dust, flying over the scorched earth as fast as a jet.

It's as though my mind has gone into standby mode as a way of protecting my sanity. I can't think about this. I can't question it. I just have to accept it. I'm flying, carried by a giant dust devil.

Should've thought of this before now. Would've saved some travel time.

There's no way to tell how fast I'm moving, but it's obviously quicker than staggering across the barren wasteland in my hazard suit.

Suddenly my wife materializes before me, floating in midair. I do my best not to be taken aback. What is this now—the third time she's appeared? Fourth? I should be used to it. She smiles, somehow able to see my startled expression through the dark face shield.

"We will set you down at the easiest entry point into Eden. With your suit on, climbing through sewage tunnels would be difficult. So we'll avoid that."

"Thanks." I'll contact Captain Mutegi as soon as Willard shows me to his radio room.

Hey. I'm here. My team's dead, but we've got some babies...

"We are not able to penetrate manmade materials." She pauses. "So we will not be accompanying you into Eden."

I wasn't expecting her to. "Will you go back and help Luther's people?"

She smiles again. "We never left them." She laughs at my confused expression. She sounds so much like my wife. "There are many of us, and we share a telepathy of sorts. We know what each other is up to."

The part of my brain that I put on pause is now warming back to life. "Is it true what Luther says? That you gave his people their abilities?" I regret asking as soon as the words escape. I won't believe whatever she says. I can't. None of what I've seen and experienced here makes any rational sense.

She dips her head forward slowly. "In a way, yes. Our essence, endowed by our Creator, remains locked in the dust of the earth from which we were made, and to which we returned. When Luther's people—and Cain's as well, though he chooses to believe in a false god—breathed in the dust of the earth, they were changed."

"So you didn't change them. Not intentionally. It was a biochemical reaction or something."

She shrugs with a slight movement of her shoulders. "Semantics, James."

As much as she looks and acts like my Emma, the sound of my name on her lips is somehow wrong.

The whirlwind around me dissipates, and my boots touch down gently on solid ground. As I turn to take in the view, I'm overwhelmed by the magnitude of this city's destruction. The ruins extending in all directions were once a major metropolitan center, comparable to Eurasia's Dome 1. Now caked in dust, they're ancient-looking. Heaps of rubble where buildings stood before; cracked streets exhibiting signs of tectonic upheaval; twisted spires of iron and steel charred black where skyscrapers covered in mirrored glass pierced the skies long ago.

"There." She extends a slender arm and points a finger I would know as well as my own—if it was actually my wife's.

I pivot to find the substructure of a blown-out building behind me. It may have held hundreds of offices at one time, but all that remains now beneath its broken skeleton is an underground parking structure. Inside, burnt-out hulks of vehicles sit in various stalls. I note the slope of the main entry as well as the downward angle beyond. How many sublevels are there?

"So that's the way into Eden?" Surprising. There are no guards stationed anywhere outside, and not one of the collared mutants Luther mentioned before.

"This is the only way you would be able to enter while wearing that suit of yours." She glances at it with disdain.

I'm sure you'd like me to take it off, just so you can watch me turn into a freak.

I'm already halfway there, hallucinating like this. Thinking I'm talking to a physical manifestation of some kind of spirit. Enough to warrant a psych-eval at the soonest opportunity.

"Good luck, James," she says.

I turn my back on her and prepare to enter the parking garage. *Keep calm, stay in the moment.* Focus on the mission. Sure, there's plenty going on at the coast and out in the Wastes, but more than enough is going on right here, right now.

I'm finishing this. Then I'm going to see my family again. I know it, I can feel it, it's going to happen. I'm more than ready to see this through.

But I'm not ready for the emaciated mutant that stumbles out of the dark and heads straight for me, staring vacantly and gnashing its teeth. I stumble backward a step, acutely aware of how unarmed I am.

The creature halts a couple meters away as a voice barks from the blinking steel collar on its neck: "Who goes there?"

I clear my throat, forcing myself to sound in charge of the situation. Because I am. "Sergeant James Bishop. Sorry I'm late."

"Figured you were dead..." The voice sounds both amazed and annoyed. "You're the only one left, huh?"

"There were a few unexpected setbacks along the way. But I'm here now, ready to discuss terms."

"Captain Willard's already discussed the terms. He's waiting to hear back on the Chancellor's decision."

"That may very well be," I reply, as patiently as possible, "but you're not aware of the present danger those fetuses are in. I've come to warn you—"

"Danger? What the hell are you talking about?"

I don't have time for this. "To whom am I speaking?"

"The name's Perch. And you'd best watch your tone with me, soldier."

"Mr. Perch, the parents of those babies are on their way here to take them away from you."

Perch chuckles on the line. "I think we can handle a few sand freaks."

I pause. "They're bringing some friends. A lot of them, well-armed. I'm sure Arthur Willard would be interested in hearing what I have to say."

"The UW hasn't told us anything about—"

"Mutegi is sending in support, but it won't arrive before your enemies do. You won't be able to hold them off."

"And you think you can help us? One man?" He scoffs.

"I'm not here to help you. I'm here for those incubation chambers. If protecting them means aiding you in the process, then so be it."

Silence holds the line, dragging on. The gruesome mutant's fangs glisten as its oozing yellow eyes stare at me hungrily. Eventually Perch grunts something unintelligible followed by, "Head down into the parking structure, five sublevels, and wait there. We'll send a vehicle to pick you up."

"Very well."

"One more thing. You'd better be wearing a ventilator under that suit."

"Check." The breather is still working—for the moment.

The mutant jerks as if shocked by an electrical pulse. Then it shambles off aimlessly, away from me and the parking garage, out into the street. Cursing under my breath, I press forward, fighting the suit's stiffness and my own sore muscles for every step. I shake my head. All of this is too much—the mutants, the spirits, the underground bastion for uninfected humanity. Yet again, I feel like I'm losing my grip on reality.

When reality itself is unraveling, it's the sane man who fails to unravel along with it.

One foot in front of the other as I delve into the desolate parking structure, I try to convince myself I'm that much closer to the mission's end. Even so, I can't help but feel that matters are more insecure now than ever before. With Luther and Cain on the way and Mutegi's assault teams fast behind them, it's unlikely the situation will end peacefully. Add to that Willard and Chancellor Hawthorne's last-minute talks. What's that all about?

Has she promised the man something I'm not aware of? Since they can't reach me on comms, my superiors are acting without my input. Because my entire team has perished. Because they've lost confidence in my ability to see this through.

Paranoid much?

For now, I have to assume nothing's changed. I will represent the UW's interests and discuss the terms necessary to transport the fetuses out of Eden and onto the *Argonaus* as quickly and safely as possible—assuming this Willard character and Perch his guard dog cooperate. These are the men in charge of the United World's future. The hopes of the civilized world have been set squarely on their shoulders.

I wish Margo was here. Not sure exactly why I trust her, but I do, and I could really use her expertise when the time arrives to transport those incubation pods. Mutegi better be sending in another medical and science officer with the ground teams.

The dull clunking of my boots echoes throughout these lifeless sublevels as I trudge downward. The farther I descend, the more vehicles I find. I glance at the elevator shaft as I pass by, wishing the power was still on. Obviously, it hasn't been in use for over twenty years.

As I round a concrete support pillar on the fifth sublevel, the sound of tires squealing against pavement echoes from the level below. I halt and face the headlights as they approach.

The vehicle is the same make and model as Margo's, but this one is in mint condition. No dust, no bullet scars, no fractured windows. How many of these Hummers does Willard have at his disposal?

Another short squeal from the tires as the large vehicle pulls to a stop, engine idling. My face shield darkens in the headlights' glare. They flicker twice as the driver taps the high beams. I raise one hand in greeting.

The passenger side door drifts open automatically, and a stocky figure steps out: a man in blue fatigues and a black beret. He wears a transparent ventilator that covers his entire face.

"Well now, get a load of this." The man chuckles, his voice making him Perch. He wears a firearm holstered at his hip, and he carries a handheld electronic device of some sort. "No chance the demon dust will get you inside that thing!"

"It's done its job so far."

"So have you." Perch leans back on his heels, sizing me up. "Man alive. It's been a while since I've laid eyes on your kind. A true blue United World marine. Semper Fidelis or something, right?"

There's no insignia of any kind on Perch's uniform. Is it nothing more than a costume? "How close are we to Eden?"

Perch squints. "You in some kind of hurry, marine? Cuz if so, I would've thought you'd have gotten here a hell of a lot sooner."

"I'd like to see Arthur Willard as soon as possible."

For a moment Perch looks like he'll either cuss me out or beat me senseless. Then he seems to make up his mind, and he does neither. "Hop in. You won't need that suit once we're inside, but for now you'll want your own air supply."

He climbs into the passenger seat and hits the manual release for the rear door. It floats upward to receive me.

The backseat's empty. My only traveling companions are the silent driver and Perch, who doesn't seem able to stay quiet for very long.

"So you lost your whole team, huh? You must be some kind of leader, marine." He guffaws as his own door drifts back into place and locks itself with a quiet whir. "But seriously, you've got to tell me what happened with Margo. When we lost contact, we thought for sure you'd all been killed."

I grunt as I heave myself into the seat. "She's fine. We were attacked—"

"Wild mutos, yeah. We're doing what we can to round them up. Got most of 'em collared." He raises the remote. "Our own special army of freaks. But plenty are still out there, roaming around. Hope to God they can't breed."

The rear door closes automatically, and the driver takes us in a crisp three-point turn, heading back the way he came. Down two more sublevels until we reach the mouth of a tunnel that opens into the lowest level, just wide enough to squeeze the vehicle through. No option of opening any doors until we reach the other end.

"Groundwater channel." Perch points at the concrete washed white by the headlights. Only darkness beyond their range, no end in sight. "We pumped it dry and directed it elsewhere. This is our main route to the surface—not that we ever go all the way up. On occasion, we meet a straggler or two who've managed to hoof it down into the lower levels. Always spot 'em as soon as they arrive. We've got thermographic imaging monitoring the structure twenty-four seven."

"Stragglers?" I remember Luther's story of being caught by these people.

"Wild mutos, mostly, looking for fresh meat. It's uncanny how well they can smell. But we sic the dogs on 'em and get 'em collared, and they're no trouble at all after that." He clears his throat. "So where's Margo? And where the hell is that Hummer we sent with her?"

"I'll share everything I know, but I'd like to wait until I meet with Mr. Willard."

"*Captain* Willard." Perch twists in his seat to face me. "And you'll answer my questions, or maybe I'll just crack open that helmet of yours and leave you topside! How's that sound?" He grins.

The man is obviously unstable.

"I'd rather not repeat myself."

"Fair enough." Perch faces forward. "But keep in mind the fact that you're our guest, marine. And truth be told, your mission ended the moment we lost contact with Margo. You're—what's the word for it?" He snaps his gloved fingers. "*Superfluous!*" He nods. "Yeah. At this juncture, you would definitely be superfluous."

I don't have anything to prove to this lunatic. When I meet

Willard, I'll let the man in charge know what's headed his way, and we'll go from there. Regardless of whatever deal Willard is attempting to make with Chancellor Hawthorne, the UW still needs me here to act as liaison. Matters must be handled quickly and efficiently.

An intercom crackles on the dashboard. The driver taps a screen mounted on the console and says, "We have the sergeant in custody, Captain."

Custody? I keep an eye on Perch's holster.

"Bring him to my quarters," replies a low nasal voice before the intercom cuts out.

"Welcomed in style!" Perch bellows, stretching his arms. "I think you'll be impressed by our lifestyle here in Eden, marine. Captain Willard is quite the host. I'm sure you haven't eaten so good since you left Eurasia."

My stomach cramps as if on cue. Other than the protein pack Luther gave me, I haven't eaten since disembarking from the *Argonaus*. "That was Captain Willard on the line?"

"Sure was." Perch drums his thick fingers across the dashboard. "I wonder if he's heard back from the Chancellor yet. That sure might change things around here!" He laughs out loud and punches the driver's right arm. The fellow cringes, seeming to know better than to make a sound. "Holy hell, we've got the UW over a barrel, and that's no lie!"

The driver nods, keeping his eyes on the tunnel. Up ahead, the headlights reflect against what appears to be a massive hatch built into the surrounding concrete at the tunnel's end. The Hummer slows to a halt as the driver reaches toward the console.

The hatch shudders and swings slowly open. The driver didn't touch the console. His hand hovers over it, not seeming to know what to do with itself.

Perch goes for his sidearm.

"Proceed with caution," he murmurs, staring straight ahead. "Something ain't right."

The mood inside the vehicle has shifted. No one speaks as the driver eases us out of the tunnel and into a vast subterranean dome a hundred meters in circumference, as bright as day thanks to lights mounted along the concrete ceiling. I take a quick survey of my surroundings, noting the details I may need to remember later.

There are large cubicles built out from the walls with steel catwalks and ladders leading down to the main floor, upon which a myriad of crates and boxes sit plastic-wrapped in rows, like in a warehouse. Three forklifts sit empty, as if they've been abandoned mid-job. Everything is still and silent, with no one in sight.

"So much for your red carpet welcome, marine." Perch keeps his voice low and his eyes darting, semiautomatic pistol in hand. "Stop the vehicle," he orders the driver. Then he faces me, aiming the weapon at my cracked helmet. "Get out."

The hatch slams shut behind us with a resounding clang. Both Perch and the driver jump in their seats. I've got an uneasy feeling they're more confused than I am.

24. MILTON

18 MONTHS AFTER ALL-CLEAR

We watch the widescreen monitor mounted above a gas-fueled hearth in the captain's quarters. Jamison sits on the sofa with a 9mm jammed into the ribs of the man seated beside him, Arthur Willard. I stand off to one side, between the monitor and the front door leading to the catwalk outside. On the screen, one of Willard's men drives the Hummer out of the tunnel and onto Eden's main floor. There it sits idling, tinted windows too dark to see anyone inside.

"You're going to pay for this treachery," Willard grates out for the fifth or sixth time. I've lost count.

"Someday you'll thank me," Jamison says. "When you're able to see past your own ego."

"How dare you? I've given you *life*!"

"Shut it." I glare at Willard. It nauseates me just to be back in the same room with this guy. The last thing I need is to hear him whine and complain. "And keep it shut."

"Or what? You'll kill me?" Willard snickers. "No, I don't think so."

"Go ahead. Try something. If Jamison doesn't shoot you, I'll break your nose."

Willard curses, shaking his head. "You honestly think you hold the upper hand here?"

"Let me see." I count my fingers. "All of your crew's locked in their quarters, and we've got the Big Cheese of Eden at gunpoint. Yeah, I'd say so."

Willard laughs, a short explosive burst. "After that escape you pulled off a few months ago, we've drilled for contingencies such as this. Just you wait."

"He's bluffing." Jamison glances at me. "We never trained—"

"As far as *you* know." Willard's beady-eyed gaze narrows. "I could tell from the start you didn't have the guts necessary for what needed to be done."

"Killing those infants won't get you any closer to Eurasia." Jamison's neck muscles strain, his face flushing. "They're the *future*, dammit! Why can't you see that?"

"We'll see what Chancellor Hawthorne decides." Willard crosses his arms. "She'll give me what I want, or I'll start taking away what she wants. One incubation chamber at a time. You know as well as I do, sometimes the electricity can really fluctuate around here—unexpectedly."

I shake my head. "You won't be going anywhere near that nursery, trust me."

"Who said my proximity matters?" Something in Willard's wild gaze makes me uneasy. Is he only bluffing?

On the screen, the tunnel's hatch closes on its own—or appears to do so, thanks to Tucker. A tense minute or two follows. Then the vehicle's rear door floats upward, and a man in a bulky environmental suit with a tinted helmet steps out. Sergeant Bishop. He survived Cain's surprise attack on the Homeplace, but how'd he manage to get here so fast? Are Cain's warriors right behind him?

The vehicle's front doors drift open next, allowing Perch and the driver to exit. Each man has his sidearm at the ready. Perch's is trained on Bishop while the driver swings his side to side and upward, scoping out the scene.

"Turn up the volume." Willard kicks back, propping his boots on a plush corduroy ottoman. A tight smile stretches his gaunt face. "I don't want to miss any of this."

I humor him, pressing the button on the side of the monitor.

"Take off that helmet," Perch barks from Eden's main floor. "And stay right there in front of me. That's right. My own personal human shield—UW marine edition." He chuckles without any real humor in his tone. "You see anybody?"

"No one," says the driver.

Perch curses before shouting, "Where you at, Tucker boy?"

No response. Bishop releases the clamps at his collar and removes his helmet, along with the breather covering his face. His short dark hair is plastered against his scalp with perspiration, and beads of sweat stand out across his brow.

"I'm sure he's enjoying Eden's cool 22 degrees Celsius," Willard says with a snicker.

"Where is everyone?" the sergeant demands. "And why are you pointing that gun—?"

Perch grabs him by the back of his collar—a rigid metal ring where the helmet docks—and gives him a rough shake. "I'm thinking you were the distraction, marine. While we were up there fetching you, some of your cohorts snuck inside via alternate routes. So how 'bout you call them out, and we see how this goes down?"

"I don't know what you're talking about."

The driver lurches forward with a sudden cry, his sidearm disappearing into thin air as he stumbles. Blood gushes from his broken nose. "What the hell was that?"

"Tucker!" Perch roars, jamming his pistol against Bishop's temple. "Drop that weapon or I swear, this guy's muto meat!"

"Shoot him, and you're next," Tucker responds in his slow drawl.

Perch whips his gun toward the voice and fires. The shot explodes like a bomb going off in the expansive concrete dome. Bishop swings his helmet upward and clocks Perch right between the eyes. The big man staggers back but maintains his hold on Bishop's collar, dragging him along with him. Bishop stumbles awkwardly in the cumbersome suit, struggling to keep his feet beneath him. He trips over Perch as both men hit the concrete floor. Perch's weapon discharges two more rounds, the sound carrying through Willard's thick steel door as well as the monitor's speakers.

Then Perch vanishes for a second. When he reappears, his gun hand is empty.

"Get the hell off me!" Perch bellows, straining against Bishop's weight.

I look back at Willard on the sofa. "Some contingency plan you've got."

"Be patient." He grins. Not creepy at all.

"All right, Sergeant, you can get up now. I've got a bead on 'im," Tucker says, invisible to the naked eye as well as the cameras mounted in Eden's ceiling. "More than one, actually." He sniffs. "Call me Two-Gun Tucker."

Bishop looks perplexed by the whole situation as he strains to rise.

"You're gonna pay for this, you damn *freak*!" Perch roars.

"Want me to shoot you in the leg or something?" Tucker offers. "Will that shut you up?" Then to Bishop, he says, "Sergeant, you might want to take off that thing. You won't be able to climb, otherwise."

"Climb?" Bishop's eyes dart toward the nearest cubicle suspended from the side of the dome. "Up there."

"Right," Tucker says. "Willard's waiting for you, along with Milton and a new friend we've made. Well, kind of an old friend, I guess. He's joined the cause."

"*Milton?* What the hell's going on?" Perch demands. "Some kind of sand freak reunion?" Even with two guns trained on him, he remains as contemptuous as ever.

Bishop frowns, looking down at his environmental suit. "I'll need a little help with this."

"Give the man a hand," Tucker orders the driver.

Scowling and wiping his bloody nose across one sleeve, the man moves to obey without a word. Seems like he's used to people bossing him around. I remember what that was like, back in the bunker.

"So, what's your endgame here, Milton?" Willard's oily voice interrupts my thoughts.

"Already told you." My gaze doesn't leave the monitor. The question is, will Sergeant Bishop agree with it? "We're taking those babies to the Homeplace."

"Don't you think they'd be safer here? With the proper facilities?"

"With you? Not a chance."

"You misunderstand." Willard sighs.

"Just what are you getting at?" Jamison demands.

"Look around you. Eden is a subterranean fortress. Impenetrable."

"I beg to differ." Jamison nods toward me.

Willard grins again, hideous as ever. "He and his invisible friend were *allowed* entry. As was the United World sergeant down there. Didn't you find it odd that our dogs left you alone? That no one got in your way?"

I half-turn to face him. "Easy to say now that we're here. I've got a feeling you had no idea what we were up to until it was too late. You've grown complacent here in your *fortress*."

"Perhaps," Willard acknowledges. "But then again, this could be the perfect trap. For you. For your friends. For the UW troops when they arrive."

"You're saying you planned this?" I shake my head and return my attention to the screen. "Unbelievable." The man has grown even more delusional over the past months.

"What I'm saying is…you would be making a grave mistake to transport the incubation chambers out west. It would make much more sense to take over Eden and make it your new *Homeplace*. Is that Luther's name for it or yours? Sounds very…tribal."

I scowl at him. "What game are you playing, Willard?"

"Oh, you'll see. Patience is a virtue, Milton. Everything will soon become very clear."

Is he just trying to get into our heads? If so, it's working. Even Jamison looks unsure of himself, adjusting his grip on the handgun. I reach for the radio at my belt, something I borrowed off Ayers before locking him in his quarters.

"Tucker, let's get moving," I tell him. "Lock up those two and bring the sergeant up here."

On the monitor, Bishop glances toward the empty space where Tucker stands. "Milton, what's going on?" he demands. The driver has freed him from the upper portion of the bulky suit, and now his thick-muscled arms are out, clad in a white thermal bodysuit. He waves the driver off and sets about pulling his legs free himself.

"I could ask you the same thing, Sergeant. Climb up here as soon as you can." I return the radio to my belt and watch as Perch gets to his feet reluctantly, scowling like a Neanderthal under his massive brow.

"That's right," Tucker says. "You heard the man. Head on over to your quarters so I can lock you inside."

The driver moves to obey, but Perch remains rooted. "I think you've forgotten something, Tucker ol' pal."

Tucker sniffs. "I doubt it."

"Oh no, I'm sure of it." Slowly, Perch raises his left hand. It holds a remote control.

I grab my radio. "Tucker—"

"See what I've got here? Yeah? You know what this does?" Perch taunts.

"Don't let him—" I start.

"Sure." Tucker hasn't answered his radio—probably tough with both hands holding semiautomatics. But his voice is clear through the monitor. "That's what you use to call the dogs."

Perch grins and nods. "I've added a couple new features. Including power to the nursery..."

Willard chuckles on the sofa.

"With the press of a button, life support will fail down there. Oh, and this one? It controls all the locks around here." Perch gazes across the dome's interior. "Every one of those doors."

Willard is laughing out loud. Jamison looks pale.

"Shoot him, Tucker!" I shout into the radio.

"Just think how many angry Eden Guardsmen will come running. Oh, and like you said, I can also call the dogs in from the surface. As you already know, Tucker-boy, we keep them *mighty* hungry for occasions such as this."

Willard howls like a maniac, kicking his feet in the air.

"Why are you tellin' me this?" Tucker's voice is surprisingly even. "You tryin' to scare me or something?"

Perch shrugs his massive shoulders. "Just thought you'd want it. Can't keep it with me if you're planning to lock me up, right? I could make all manner of hell break loose!" He holds out the remote in the palm of his hand. "You want it or not?"

I face Jamison. "Can it do everything he said?"

His head pivots slowly. "I honestly don't know. If he's bluffing—"

"Oh, he's not," Willard wheezes hysterically. "I can assure you of that!"

"Tucker, take it," I say. "Shoot him first if you have to."

Perch laughs out loud, tossing his head back. "That's right, you go ahead and shoot an unarmed man, Tucker-boy. I'm sure that won't weigh on your conscience any."

"Stand still," Tucker says.

I grit my teeth. Part of me wants to fly down there and take the remote in a blur of speed, but another part knows better than to leave Willard alone with Jamison. Willard's not a man to be underestimated, and I don't know that I trust Jamison completely. If push comes to shove, will he keep wearing his traitor's hat? Sure, he wants what's best for the babies, but that could change when his own life's on the line.

"Careful, Tucker," I caution him—and instantly regret it.

My voice through the radio betrays Tucker's position, and

Perch moves lightning-quick, disappearing as soon as he lunges at Tucker. At the sound of the invisible scuffle, the driver charges Bishop full-tilt, knocking him down just as he frees himself entirely from the hazard suit. The two go sprawling against the vehicle, but the smaller man is no match for Bishop. A solid right hook sends him slumping to the pavement. Bishop crouches at the ready, but he doesn't seem to know what to do with himself, listening blindly as Tucker and Perch duke it out.

"Take him down, Perch!" Willard shrieks, leaning forward and watching the monitor like he can actually see what's happening. "Break his neck!"

Something cracks. A sickening crunch. Bone, if I had to guess. Silence follows.

Perch staggers back into view, his face a bloody mess. In each hand he holds a gun—his own and the driver's. The remote is tucked into his belt.

"You came here to see Captain Willard." Catching his breath, he points one weapon at Bishop. "Alright then. Get moving."

"Tucker!" I shout into the radio. My voice echoes on the monitor, coming from the floor behind Perch.

"Long live the invisible man," Perch mutters. He motions impatiently for Bishop to climb the ladder leading up to the nearest catwalk. "Move!"

My chest tightens. This is my fault. Tucker's death is on my hands.

The room sways.

"One down, two to go." Willard stretches his back.

"He was one of your men!" Jamison shouts.

Willard shakes his head. "Tucker hasn't been a *man* for a long time—or one of ours. Just a sand freak, that's all. Good riddance."

I face him. "He was a good man, you son-of-a-bitch. The only freak in this room is *you*."

Willard shrugs. "Say whatever you need to say, Milton. I'm sure it'll be some time before you get over the fact that you killed him. You and that stupid radio. Why didn't you just go down there and take the remote for yourself? Oh, that's right: because deep down, you're nothing but a *coward*. And now that the tables have turned—"

"They haven't." Jamison presses the gun against Willard's temple. "We still have you."

Willard frowns, puzzled. "But it's not *me* that you want. It's the children. Those little blobs of tissue with eyes and ears and noses, gestating down in the nursery. They've made you as soft as they are. They're your weakness." He clucks his tongue. "Never show your enemy your warm underbelly, Jamison. He just might sink a serrated dagger in there—or let a hungry muto have at it."

On the monitor, Bishop climbs the ladder while Perch follows half a dozen rungs behind, gun in hand. What was the sergeant thinking, showing up here unarmed, without any backup? I've seriously misjudged him. The guy is a fool.

A heavy knock clangs against Willard's door. Bishop and Perch stand outside.

"It appears that our esteemed UW emissary has finally arrived." Willard gestures toward the door. "Do let them in, won't you, Milton?"

I stand there for a moment, weighing my options. Seething. What choice do I have? Nobody else can die. I won't let that happen.

I unbolt the door and slide it back. As soon as it's open, Perch shoves Bishop inside.

"Well now, look who's back. And look who's gone all turncoat on us." Perch stands behind Bishop and holds a gun against the base of his skull. "Drop it, pal." Perch stares Jamison down.

Jamison falters, glancing at me.

"Wait." I hold up a hand.

"Listen, you super-freak, I've got nothing against this marine or anything—I think we've actually bonded." Perch chuckles. "But I'll blow his brains out all over if you don't step back. And I'm not gonna tell you again, Jamison!"

"I would do as he says." Willard's smile fades. "He looks

angry. You know how unpredictable Perch can be when he loses his temper. I wouldn't try anything speedy, Milton—unless you truly are faster than a bullet."

I won't risk it. Not after Tucker. "Let the sergeant go."

"Why the hell would I do that?" Perch says in disbelief. "He's the only thing keeping you from going all supersonic on us!"

The man has a point.

"Jamison tosses his gun on the floor, and I don't kill the marine. Got it?"

There's fear in Bishop's eyes. But he isn't scared of losing his own life. If what the Julia-spirit said was true, he's scared of losing his family. But those children down in the nursery and the future of the world are at stake here.

I have to get Perch's remote, no matter what.

"Not counting to three!" Perch roars. "This jarhead's dead!"

"Drop it," I tell Jamison. Reluctantly, he tosses his gun onto the carpet.

Willard reaches out his arms with a sigh of relief. Then he chops Jamison in the throat. "Stupid bastard," Willard spits as Jamison lurches forward, choking, his eyes wide. "You always were the weakest link."

He seizes hold of Jamison's head and twists it with a violent crack.

"No!" I lunge forward. Everything around me freezes as I push Willard back against the sofa with one arm and catch Jamison's limp body in the other.

"Too slow," Willard says.

I stare at Jamison, unable to believe he's dead. It happened so fast. But I'm supposed to be faster. The fastest. I should have been able to stop this.

Everything is unraveling. I can't keep it together.

"Your allies are quickly dwindling, Milton." Willard smiles. "You really don't want our UW sergeant to be next, do you?"

"The children..." I manage, my voice thick with remorse. How many more people are going to die because of me? "They're all that matter." I set Jamison's body back against the sofa cushions and close the man's eyelids. "May I have a word with the sergeant?"

"Of course!" Willard nods to Perch, who prods Bishop forward with the gun muzzle flat against his skull. "This should prove to be quite entertaining."

"Talk to your little buddy, jarhead," Perch sneers.

Bishop stands like a statue, eyeing me warily.

"In private," I clarify.

Perch laughs out loud.

Willard frowns. "No, I don't think so. Whatever you have to say, I want to hear it. Perhaps it will grant me some insight into the grand scheme you were planning to accomplish here."

"The children," I repeat.

"The UW is on their way here," Bishop says. "But they won't arrive before Cain's bunch."

"Cain?" Willard looks mildly interested.

"You haven't met him yet," I reply. "He's from the coast, and he has a couple dozen well-trained warriors as fast as I am. He's coming here to take the children from you."

"Not exactly," Bishop says. "He...wants them dead."

"Oh?" Willard glances at Perch.

"First I've heard of it," Perch growls. "Making up this stuff isn't gonna help you any."

"You'll find out for yourselves soon enough," Bishop returns.

"How do you know?" I ask.

Bishop looks uncomfortable all of a sudden. He lowers his voice. "I had a little help getting here."

I nod slowly. That explains how he arrived ahead of Luther and Cain's people. "The spirits?"

"Right." Bishop bites his lip.

Willard throws his hands into the air. "Could we be more specific, please? Unless you're both speaking in code, which I will not abide."

"The spirits of the earth." The Julia-spirit was right: there is something special about this UW marine. "They brought you here?"

"Yeah. In a...dust devil or something." Bishop avoids eye contact.

I raise my eyebrows. "That's new."

Willard curses. "So the sand freaks have their own religion now? Isn't the God of the universe good enough for you people?"

"Not the one you believe in," I reply. "You've molded him into your own image." I sound like Luther. He must be rubbing off on me.

"Move the dogs into position," Willard orders Perch. "All of them! Now!"

Without a word, Perch holsters the spare semiautomatic and retrieves the remote control. He makes a show of pressing three buttons in sequence. "They'll hold the perimeter."

"Now you're protecting the babies?" I shake my head. Hard to keep up.

"Safeguarding my investment." Willard stands and starts pacing, stroking his narrow mustache. "My deal with Chancellor Hawthorne will be null and void if there are no fetuses for the UW when they arrive."

"The UW is right here." Bishop holds out his hands. "Let's discuss terms before things get—"

Willard laughs harshly, looking the sergeant up and down in his sweat-stained bodysuit. "I don't think so. The only reason you're still alive is to keep Milton in his place." He casts me a disgusted look. "He seems to think your life's worth something."

"Mr. Willard—"

"*Captain!*" Perch roars.

Bishop doesn't blink. "Captain Willard, I understand that you've been in communication with Chancellor Hawthorne. You have to understand that the people—*sand freaks*, as you refer to them—on their way here intend to destroy your investment." He glances at me. "The ones leading the pack, anyway. I don't know what Milton was planning to do, but allow me to offer a word of advice from one military man to another."

Yeah right. Willard doesn't qualify. But Bishop has his attention.

"Go on."

"You need to lock down this place until the UW arrives, sir. You need to release your men from their quarters and get them ready for battle. Because from what I've seen of Cain and his warriors, they are very good at what they do."

I half-expected Luther and Cain's people to fight their way into Eden and barricade themselves against the UW troops. But now that Cain appears to be more of a threat than Willard, I find myself rethinking the entire situation. Maybe Bishop's right.

"What do you have to say?" Willard stares at me.

"The sergeant makes a good point. I'll have to defer to him on this."

Perch snickers, but Willard shoots him a look that quiets him down. "For the moment, I would say that keeping those incubation pods in working order is in our combined best interest. Wouldn't you agree?"

"Yes sir," Bishop replies in military fashion.

I nod, even as my insides twist in revulsion at the thought of teaming up with Arthur Willard. But Eden has to be protected from the impending onslaught where Luther, Daiyna, Samson, Shechara, and all the others, ignorant of Cain's ultimate plans, will fight alongside him and his warriors.

Will the spirits aid them? Hinder them? Will Jackson appear as Gaia, soaking up the adoration of Cain and his people, leading them to slaughter at the claws and fangs of Willard's collared daemons?

It's all too horrifying to imagine.

"A ceasefire, then." Willard extends his right hand. "We work together to fortify Eden, and we set aside our disagreements for the time being. After the UW troops arrive, we'll take another look at where we stand. Agreed?"

I glance from Willard to Bishop, who's rocking a steely-eyed gaze. Perch grins like a lunatic, enjoying the awkward silence way too much.

"Agreed." Gun literally to his head, Bishop shakes with Willard.

"Alright." I'm next to clasp Willard's clammy hand, and I feel an instant wave of regret wash over me.

"Excellent." Willard frowns at Perch, who withdraws his gun from Bishop's skull. "Get these men proper uniforms. If they're going to protect Eden from the powers of unholy darkness, then they need to look like God-fearing Eden Guardsmen!"

Perch nods. But he seems reluctant to leave. "I'll inform the men. They should know these two are on our side now." He winks at me.

I give him the finger.

"Of course," Willard says. "We wouldn't want to see our new allies downed by friendly fire, would we?"

Bishop gives me a crisp nod, and I have only a split-second to wonder what it means. Then he spins on one heel, bringing his elbow back to strike Perch full in the face. The gun discharges, blowing a hole into the ceiling. Bishop pummels Perch with close-contact blows, showing no mercy to his face and ribs, plowing elbow-knee-uppercut combinations in a well-coordinated attack pattern. Perch struggles in vain to defend himself before going down face-first with an unconscious groan. I snatch the remote from his belt.

Willard stares in wide-eyed dismay. Then he dives for Jamison's weapon.

Only he's too slow.

"Déjà vu?" I wink behind the cocked semiautomatic, aimed at Willard's left eye.

He dry-swallows, appearing out of sorts for a moment. "Same plan?" he manages.

Regardless of how much I hate him, I have to admit: the guy has some nerve.

"Same plan." Bishop nods, disarming Perch. "But we're calling the shots." He glances at me and the remote in my hand. "Time to release the hounds."

Via the dome-wide intercom in Willard's quarters, Bishop explains who he is and that Willard is alive and well. He'll remain that way as long as every man in Eden does his part to fortify their underground refuge from attack and safeguard the lives of the unborn children in the nursery below. Bishop makes matters abundantly clear: If a single incubation chamber is damaged by one of Willard's crew, that man's life will be forfeit.

Giving them just a second to think things over, I press the remote, releasing the Eden Guard from their quarters.

"We must hold Eden until the UW troops arrive. They are on our side in this conflict," Willard's voice echoes throughout the dome. "As is Sergeant Bishop, their representative, sent ahead to aid us during this time of crisis. And the man called Milton, whom many of you may remember." Willard raises his voice for the next part, "The traitors Tucker and Jamison are dead. I know you all may have some difficulty taking orders from a sand freak like Milton, but I assure you, he is here to help—"

I shut off the intercom and finish tugging on one of the spare uniforms from Willard's closet. It's a little tight, but it'll do the job. I keep an eye on the monitor, watching the men's reactions on the main floor. They don't look happy.

"Let's go." I grab Willard by the arm and hoist him to his feet. "They need to see their commander-in-chief."

"Let go of me," Willard protests.

"Good idea." Clad in Perch's uniform, Bishop unbolts Willard's door and heaves it open. Gun at the ready, he steps out onto the catwalk.

Shouts erupt from the main floor below, curses and insults hurled along with fists in the air. I shove Willard ahead of me as a human shield of sorts.

"Get your house in order," I say in a low tone.

Squinting under the glare of Eden's lights, Willard holds up both hands to quiet the mob of thirty-odd men. "Guardsman, hear me!" He almost resembles Luther, speaking to us in the Homeplace, except he's a warped mirror image. "If we are to survive this day, we must work together. You, me, Sergeant Bishop, even Milton."

"He locks us all up, Captain, and you're gonna let him join us?" shouts a fellow in back. "We say cast 'im out!"

"Cast him out! Cast him out!" the chant erupts.

"No, no!" shouts another man. "We can't. He'll go and tell his kind we're expecting them."

"Better to have him on our side," says another.

"How do we *know* he's really on our side?"

Willard glances over his shoulder at me. "Want to say anything?"

Nope. But I speak up anyway, "You've got every reason to hate me. Twice now, I've gotten the better of you—thanks to this freakish ability I have." Some of them chuckle. Maybe they're not all bad apples. "The only reason I'm here right now…is to help you."

"What do you care?" Multiple shouts echo a similar sentiment.

"You've got some unborn children downstairs. Believe it or not, you're sitting on the whole world's future. I don't know how much your captain has told you, but the United World government is very interested in receiving the incubation pods intact. While the warriors on their way here have every intention of killing those defenseless babies."

That seems to sober the men.

"Captain?" one calls up. "Is what he's saying true?"

Willard seems unwilling to respond, but Sergeant Bishop claps him on the back like they're old war buddies.

"Yes, soldier. I'm afraid so," Willard says. "We have something the UW wants very much. And we aim to hand over each fetus in one piece."

On the floor behind us, Perch moans as he starts to come to.

He'll be trouble. There's no chance he'll welcome either Bishop or me into the fold. Launching myself from the catwalk railing, I glide down to the main floor. The men of Eden stumble backward, giving me a wide berth and staring wide-eyed.

"Any of you consider Perch to be a close friend?" I scan the crowd. They glance at one another with uncertainty. "I for one think he's a dangerous hothead, and I'd like to keep him locked in his quarters until this situation blows over. That alright with you?"

A few of the men frown, but no one objects. From the catwalk above, Willard calls out the names of two guardsmen and orders them to escort Perch to his quarters—and to keep him sedated. That last part raises a few eyebrows, but I saw it was Sergeant Bishop who leaned over to give Willard quiet directions.

Eden's dictator is serving as a suitable mouthpiece.

Whether the Eden Guardsmen are all on board remains to be seen, but for now, they put their backs into sealing the hatches at each of the three tunnels leading outward from Eden's central dome. Willard leads us down to the control station where multiple monitors show the collard daemons—hundreds of them—gathering at the edge of the city where crumbling, ashen asphalt disappears into desert sands.

"You don't have to watch this," Bishop tells me. "I know they're your friends."

I look past him at Willard, seated before the control panel with his hands moving over multiple keyboards and toggles, bringing various cameras into focus.

"They've fought these creatures before." I shake my head. "The daemons won't be much of a deterrent."

"Ah, but that was before our recent modifications," Willard says with a knowing wink. "These dogs are a new breed—faster, stronger, injected with metabolic steroids and muscle-enhancing growth hormones. Your friends won't stand a chance this time, I'm afraid." He grins, quick to add, "But the babies will be quite safe, don't you fret. We've all got to have our priorities straight."

Ignoring the anxiety squeezing my abdomen, I step out of the control room. "I should check on them, make sure everything's all right down there."

Sergeant Bishop nods, folding his arms as he surveys the bank of monitors on the wall.

I break into a jog. More than anything right now, I want to run as fast as I can, to fly out of Eden and warn Luther that they're heading straight into a trap. With the genetically modified daemons on one side and the advancing UW troops on the other, it would take a miracle for my friends to survive.

A miracle—or supernatural intervention.

I curse myself for telling Julia I didn't need her. And I curse myself for Tucker's death, for Jamison's. Death follows me wherever I go.

I'm already cursed.

As I reach the nursery in the sublevel below Eden's main floor, I slow to a halt. I didn't know what to expect, but it sure as hell wasn't this. There are so many of them—incubation pods with blinking lights showing healthy vitals, lined up row upon row, sitting in an almost-holy quiet.

Overwhelmed by what's at stake here, with only the hum of the equipment around me, I close my eyes and pray. For the first time in my life.

Maybe it's to the Julia-spirit. Maybe to the Creator of the universe.

All I say is, "Please. Help us."

25. DAIYNA

18 MONTHS AFTER ALL-CLEAR

The daemons appeared without warning, riding in solar-powered vehicles and stirring up the dust in great plumes behind them. They fired their rifles at Cain's warriors in the front of the pack, and we ducked, defenseless. I've never felt more vulnerable, crowded alongside Shechara and the others, herded out from the Homeplace without a single weapon. My adrenaline surges as instinctively I feel the need to fight back.

But with empty hands, I would be running to my own death.

"How many?" I shout at Shechara.

We're side by side, but amid the weapons fire and screams of agony, it's difficult to hear anything else.

Shechara's mechatronic eyes rotate, the split orbs overlapping as they zoom to focus on the battle before us.

"Three jeeps." That seems to be standard procedure; the daemon hunting parties always ride in groups of three vehicles, each carrying four well-armed creatures. "And three more."

Over twenty daemons? And all of my people unarmed? How can we trust our lives to the fighting skills of Cain's warriors who don't care whether we live or die?

"Where's Luther?"

"He hasn't left that Hummer."

At least he'll be safe inside. From what I've seen, those vehicles from Eden are bulletproof. Will Cain remain with him? Or will he venture out into the fray?

The daemon jeeps rip side to side in a frenzy, engines roaring as their guns pump endless rounds into Cain's frontline. But the dust they kick up is thickening, and I have to wonder how accurate their shots are in this murk. No one else has Shechara's eyes that can see through the most blinding of sandstorms.

I glance back over my shoulder and curse, tightening the head covering around my nose and mouth. I can't see more than a few meters back. Both Samson and the UW sergeant are out of sight. The dust whirls about us with a life all its own.

"Daiyna." Shechara puts a hand on my arm. She senses something.

"I know." I feel it too.

And then I see the figure of my old friend Rehana, dead and gone for over a year now, stepping out of the wall of swirling dust before me.

"Good to see you, sister," Rehana says with a broad smile on her dark face. She wears no head covering, no protection.

I know it isn't really her, that it's just a manifestation generated by the spirits of the earth. But even so, it warms my heart to see Rehana like this again.

"You picked an odd time to visit."

When did I see her last? Months ago—after Milton helped us escape from Eden. The spirits appeared, telling us to travel west and find other survivors. The results spoke for themselves: instead of five, there are now over fifty of us marching to Eden.

Surrounded by Cain's fighters, led like sheep to the slaughter. Once the daemons break through the frontlines, they will fall upon us. Easy prey.

"You must not march on Eden." Rehana's smile has faded. Her eyes shine in earnest. "You will meet only death there."

I motion toward the perimeter. "We don't have much choice. Cain's people are the ones in charge right now."

"They are otherwise occupied," Rehana replies with a flicker of a smile. "And they have left you a rear exit as they've rushed to meet their adversaries. Your friend Samson is realizing this as we speak. You both must lead your people away from here."

I shake my head. "We need our weapons. We're not leaving without them." I pause. "And some of us want to go to Eden."

Rehana flickers before me like a holo-image losing cohesion.

"What's wrong?" I reach for her.

"It's been a while. You've changed," Rehana replies. "Hatred burns in your heart. The darkness there has grown—"

"If we retreat, will you cover us?"

Rehana nods. "Cain will not follow. He will have enough to keep him busy once he reaches Eden. Willard's broken souls are waiting, hundreds of them."

Broken souls—the collared daemons? I clench my fists. "What about Luther?"

"You will need to free him from that vehicle." Rehana fades from my sight, but her voice lingers for a moment. "Do not be devoured by your thirst for vengeance, Daiyna."

I grab Shechara's arm. "We have to escape—while Cain's people are fighting the daemons."

"Have the spirits spoken to you?"

I curse under my breath. "Yeah."

"But I thought they weren't doing that anymore."

"They changed their mind." I squeeze Shechara's arm. "You'll need to lead me. I can't see a thing." Shechara draws me close. "Let's find Samson."

We forge through the blinding dust storm, backtracking until we reach the large cyborg standing at the rear of the pack.

"Daiyna—that you?" Samson booms, shielding his goggles with a metal hand.

"Where's Bishop?"

He shakes his head. "You're not going to believe this, but...he kind of flew off, *Wizard of Oz* style."

The reference is lost on me.

"The spirits took him?" Shechara sounds awestruck.

"We need to get these people out of here," I say. "They're sitting ducks for any daemon that breaks through Cain's line of warriors."

"Where do you suggest we take 'em?" Samson rumbles.

"North." I nod quickly, strategizing. "As far north as we can go before the United World troops arrive. Otherwise, we'll be sandwiched between Willard's daemons and the UW."

"Alright," Samson says. "You leading the retreat, or shall I?"

"I'm going for Luther." I turn to Shechara. "Point me in the right direction, then I want you to help Samson get everyone out of here. Take any weapons you find."

"Daiyna—" she objects.

"Samson won't let anything happen to you."

"Damn straight," he says.

"But what about *you*?" Shechara's voice strains with concern.

"I have the spirits on my side, don't I?" The sarcastic edge to my voice is sharp.

I squeeze Shechara once more, then take off running in the direction she pointed. Leaping over every obstacle in my way, thanks to my superhuman agility, I head straight for where the armored vehicle should be. As I cross paths with our disoriented people in the murk, I shout for them to regroup at the rear with Samson. He'll lead them to safety. Nodding quickly, they move to obey.

Charging through the fray, I reach the Hummer, parked a few meters behind the front line where many of Cain's warriors battle hand-to-hand against the daemons. Others kneel, rifles at the ready as they return fire. The daemons in their jeeps circle haphazardly, firing volley after volley. I can't see them, but I hear the engines and the shots exploding at close range. Cain's ranks have suffered only a handful of deaths so far. They lie strewn in the dust, bleeding out.

Stray rounds ping and thud against the armored vehicle. I crouch behind it, sliding up to the rear door where I saw Luther climb in earlier. I rap twice on the window.

"Luther!"

No response. I pound my fist against the glass.

The door drifts open only a meter and halts. Inside, Cain and Luther stare back at me—along with someone else I never thought I'd see again.

Mother Lairen.

"Daiyna." Luther reaches for me, and I grip his forearm, launching myself inside. The door drops shut behind me. "Are you all right?"

"Fine." I frown at Mother Lairen—or the spirit manifesting itself as her. The malevolent variety that wants nothing more than to see the remnant of humankind destroy itself. "What's *she* doing here?"

Garbed in a flowing white gown, Mother Lairen glares at me with a contempt somehow entangled with grace. "We meet again, my child."

Cain looks thunderstruck. "You worship Gaia as well?"

Luther's hand remains on my arm. "What do you see?"

I glance from Cain to Luther. "We have to get out of here."

Cain laughs out loud. Then he grimaces, pressing a fist against his side. "We have the situation well in hand, woman. My warriors hunt the goblyns for sport. This is just a routine exercise for them. Soon we will be on our way."

Mother Lairen smirks. Luther squeezes my arm gently, watching me stare at what is, to him, the empty seat across from me.

"Daiyna, what is it?"

I lower my voice. "The spirits are here."

"I will not allow such blasphemy in Gaia's presence!" Cain bellows, louder than the weapons fire outside. "There are no *spirits*, just as there is no *creator*! There is only Gaia, our mother."

"Gaia—she's here?" Luther looks around the vehicle's interior.

"She appears to me as the leader from my bunker. If Milton were here, I'm sure he would see the man who forced him to kill everyone in his bunker. That's what the evil spirits do: appear as people from our past that we'd rather never see again."

Mother Lairen smiles coldly.

Why don't the spirits appear to Cain as someone from his past? Is his mind so warped that they can take the form of anyone they choose? Maybe he has a history of worshipping goddesses, the psycho.

Cain scowls. "Get out." His hand goes for the door release.

"Why aren't you fighting alongside your warriors, Cain?" I lean toward him. Mother Lairen chuckles quietly, covering her mouth. "You'd rather they die for you?"

"Get the hell out!" he roars. The door swings open, and wind gusts in bearing dust and ash.

"He is my chosen one, child. I could not possibly allow him to suffer harm," Mother Lairen says. Then she turns to Cain. "Shut the door, my son. I would hate for a goblyn's stray bullet to find you."

He obeys without a word.

"What is the spirit saying now?" Luther asks me.

Mother Lairen clucks her tongue. "Left out in the cold, is he? Poor little man."

Cain grins at that, casting a sidelong look of disdain in Luther's direction.

"She's leading you to your deaths," I tell him flatly. "Willard's expecting us, and the UW troops are closing in behind. We'll be caught in between and wiped out."

Cain shakes his head, as if I don't know what I'm talking about. "Gaia knows all things. She is leading us to certain victory!"

"My friend—" Luther turns to face the much larger man. "We have dealt with these spirits before. You must believe me when I say...there are certain forces at work in this world that do not want humankind to survive. They blame us for what we did to the planet, for destroying all they knew, all that they were."

"What gibberish is this?" Cain scoffs. "I have no desire to hear about your religious beliefs, Luther. I know the truth, and it has set me free from fear. You're welcome to place your trust in whatever god you choose, but I follow the one I can see. The one who speaks to me, the one who has blessed my people with superhuman gifts and protected us from danger. Not that archaic *creator* you and your people trust in." He looks straight at me. "All but one of them, it would appear."

"You just don't get it." I point at Mother Lairen. "She's no *god*. She's just a manifestation. The spirits that generate her want to see you kill your own people!"

Cain clenches his jaw. "How *dare* you speak such blasphemy in her presence?"

"Allow her to speak for herself," Luther says, though he can neither see nor hear the spirit. "Tell us, Mother Lairen—or Gaia: What is our purpose in going to Eden?"

"Gaia does not speak to infidels!" Cain's face flushes with rage.

"Apparently she does," I counter.

He glares at me. "I don't know why she speaks to you."

Mother Lairen holds up an ivory hand. "I would have assumed your purpose is obvious. To take back what is rightfully yours, and to safeguard the lives of your two peoples against men such as this Arthur Willard, and his cohorts in the United World. They brought this fight on themselves by encroaching upon your lands without permission."

She gestures for me to relay the message to Luther, while Cain merely nods with a fiery glint in his eyes. Is there something else he isn't sharing, a secret between himself and the evil spirit?

"Why do you insist on using that word, my child?" Mother Lairen stares straight at me.

"What?"

"*Evil*. I can see it in your mind, whenever you look at me. Why must such a dichotomy exist? *Good and evil.* So very primitive." She laughs. "Simply because I do not believe you will ever achieve greatness through peace, you refer to me as *evil*?"

Instead of replying, I echo her words for Luther's benefit.

"In our dealings with you before," he says, "it became clear that you did not wish for us to succeed at anything. You wanted us to die out as a species. To paraphrase what you told Milton, *The time of humankind is past.*"

Cain's brow furrows. He glances silently from Luther to Mother Lairen.

"Ah yes," she continues, "but you are not technically *human* anymore, are you?" She smiles with a warmth that threatens to overcome us all. "The United World in their self-sustaining domes across the waters are the last of their kind on this planet, as are the men hiding down in Eden. They have not been blessed with abilities that make them more than human. They are a subspecies. They are weak. And because of that, they must be exterminated."

I relay her proclamation to Luther, who doesn't appear convinced.

Mother Lairen shakes her head with what appears to be both patience and pity. "When I asked Milton to destroy the reactor in Eden, would that explosion have harmed your people?"

"Eventually," I reply. "The fallout would have been catastrophic. None of the bunkers are functional anymore. There would have been no safe place for us."

"Daiyna, I would have kept the damage contained, deep within Eden. I would not have allowed it to surface. So you see, I've never wanted to destroy your people—only the ones who have wished you harm!"

Cain nods vigorously. He likes what he's hearing.

Outside, the weapons fire has ceased, and the dust begins to clear. Two warriors approach the Hummer as one shouts, "Lord Cain!"

He lowers the tinted window at his side. "Report."

"The goblyns are vanquished. We have taken their weapons and vehicles."

"Very good. We will proceed eastward and catch up with Markus and Vincent." He moves to raise the window.

"One more thing, m'lord." The warrior clears his throat. "The others, the...*infidels*—"

"What is it?" Cain demands.

"They're...gone. They took most of the weapons we confiscated from them."

With an explosive curse, Cain throws open the door manually and surveys the scene. Luther and I climb out behind him. I give Mother Lairen a direct look. The spirit's face appears slightly perturbed by the turn of events.

"Where? They could not have gone far!" Cain bellows. His warrior points northwest where a wall of swirling dust covers our people's retreat.

"Do we go after them?" the warrior asks. "We have enough vehicles now to round them up."

Cain turns his gaze westward. He has to be thinking of the UW's advance. "There is no time. We will leave them to their fate." He locks eyes with Luther. "Will you join them?"

"Do I have a choice?" Luther says.

I place a hand on his arm. "We should be with our people."

"I will not forsake our children."

"We won't." I bow my head close to his. "But this is suicide, Luther. The spirits warned me not to go to Eden. Not now."

"Go." Cain curses, turning his back on us. "We will do your fighting for you." Shouting orders to his warriors, he climbs back into the Hummer.

"So the spirits spoke to you again?" Luther faces me. "The benevolent ones?"

I nod, watching Cain's people move out, kicking up dust in their wake. The warriors on foot hasten to keep up with the seven vehicles, leaving behind half a dozen of their fallen comrades. And all twenty-four of the daemon carcasses.

"Is your desire for revenge—?"

"As strong as ever." I glance at him. "But other things are more important now."

He nods slowly. "The children."

My eyes sting. "Our children, Luther." I kick at a rock. "How can we rescue them?"

He points at the cloud of dust swirling around our people in the distance, hiding them from view. "We'll have their help, Daiyna."

"Do you believe any of what she said—Cain's *god*? That the evil spirits want only to destroy the natural humans...not the ones like us?"

"Not a word of it. The spirits who have come to our aid—they've told both you and Milton what the evil spirits want more than anything: the end of humankind. Gifted or natural-born, we are all human. And while the evil spirits have sworn never to act against us directly, they obviously have persuaded Cain to act for them. To wield their sword."

He gestures for me to join him as he breaks into a jog toward the retreating dust storm. I keep pace with him.

"Sergeant Bishop was taken up in a whirlwind, Samson said. But where to, I have no idea."

"The spirits move in mysterious ways." Luther sounds like he might actually be smiling.

When we reach the wall of rushing dust and plunge through without incident, we find Samson leading our fellow survivors northward with no destination in sight. But the air is clear on this side, and the people are sheltered from the sun's harsh rays by the sand wall following us on our journey.

Rehana reappears as Luther sprints ahead to join Samson at the front.

"To answer your question," she says, "the United World sergeant is in Eden. So is Milton. Together, they will protect your offspring from harm."

"What about Cain's people?" Why do I care what happens to them? Do I want them to die? "Will they be slaughtered?"

"You will see for yourself." Rehana points as Luther, Samson, and Shechara approach, along with two dozen others. The rest of the troop continues to trudge northwest.

"They're looping back around to the Homeplace." Samson catches his breath. "If they're lucky, they'll miss the UW onslaught entirely."

"They will," Luther says without any doubt. "With the Creator's blessing."

I frown at the eager, well-armed group around me. "What's all this?"

"We're following Cain's war party." Luther rests a double-barreled shotgun against his shoulder.

"No chance we're leaving those babies in his hands," Samson adds.

"But the spirits said not to march—" I begin.

"We'll let Cain do the marching," Samson says. "He's going at them head-on, and he's going to meet the heaviest resistance. He's got more men—"

"And women," Shechara says, checking the clip in her semiautomatic.

"—and a lot of them are the *Milton* variety. Extremely fast. They'll cut a swath through Willard's daemons, but then they'll be surrounded and have to fight their way outward. What we'll do is drive in from the flank, pushing the freaks into Cain's onslaught as we head for that parking structure we all remember so well."

His plan is far too simplistic. "You don't think Willard will have the whole place rigged with explosives?"

Samson shrugs his massive shoulders. "Another option? We hang back, let Cain's warriors go in first and set off any booby traps. Then we follow."

Rehana tugs at my sleeve. It never ceases to amaze me how the spirits can interact with us. "Cain must not reach your young ones first. He will destroy them."

"*What?*" I face her.

"Daiyna?" Luther says.

Rehana continues, "Milton and Bishop are there to protect your offspring. When you arrive at Eden's door, your friends will usher you inside."

"How do you know they're in control of the situation?"

Rehana almost smiles. "There is a reason we selected those two men. Nothing will stand in their way. Trust me."

I frown at her. "So now you want us to go to Eden."

"Samson's right." She winks. "Cain will do the marching. You'll sneak in sideways."

Luther clears his throat. "Will the spirits be joining us?"

Rehana nods. "Tell him we will. And we'll protect the others on their way back to your Homeplace."

"You can do that—be in more than one place at a time?" I sound like a child, full of curiosity.

Rehana grins, looking more like herself than ever.

Luther strides ahead, breaking into a jog again, and the others follow.

"Guess I'll bring up the rear," Samson rumbles, struggling to keep up due to his mechanical legs. "Again."

We follow Cain's progress at a distance, keeping to the northwestern flank half a kilometer behind and growing, as Cain's warriors cut the distance in their vehicles. Luther refuses to let Samson lag too far behind. Rehana keeps stride with me, explaining the evil spirits' desire to see the unborn children in Eden destroyed. Without them, the United World has no future; they will cease to exist after their youngest generation expires, leaving the *gifted* to inherit the earth. But of course the UW would retaliate in a major way after such a heinous act, ensuring the destruction of humankind as a whole.

"What do they have against us?" I ask.

"The other spirits? They want revenge," Rehana replies.

That's something I can understand. Arthur Willard and Perch deserve slow, agonizing deaths, but right now the only urgency I feel is to save the babies in those incubation chambers. There will be time for vengeance later.

I look at the group around me, recognizing most of them. They're my like-minded friends who want nothing more than to see Eden obliterated. But I hope they'll see value in rescuing the children first.

Shechara leads the way, her cybernetic eyes able to see farther than anyone else's. Already she has spotted the city ruins, along with a massive number of daemons assembled to meet Cain's advance. She sees the frontrunners of Cain's ranks, the warriors gifted as Milton is with the ability to move faster than sound. They have already met the daemons with blades flashing, cutting a wide path through the middle of the horde. Just as Samson predicted.

"So many..." Shechara murmurs as she runs alongside Luther and me. "These daemons are stronger than any we've met before. Cain's warriors are already overwhelmed."

"They fight alone," Rehana says to me. "Cain's *goddess* will not fight with them."

Would this change his mind about Gaia? If so, perhaps he will also change his mind about destroying the incubation units. I'll never forget how Milton acted while possessed by that evil spirit. Is Cain being affected the same way?

To commit such an atrocity—it's inhuman.

Shechara continues to brief us on the battle's developments as Cain catches up with his advancing war party. The warriors in jeeps drive at the periphery, shooting as many of the daemons as they can. They have good aim, Shechara notes. Every round fired is a kill shot.

"Are Willard's daemons armed?" Luther asks.

"No." Shechara's eyes zoom in to focus. "But they are winning. Even Cain's swiftest warriors are being torn apart." She pauses. "Literally."

"We go in with guns blazing," Samson booms, perspiration

soaking his head covering and tunic. "Nobody will be expecting us."

Once we are within a kilometer of the city ruins, Luther asks Shechara to estimate the distance between us and the UW troops approaching from the west.

"I don't see the ground assault teams," she reports. "But there are more than a dozen aircraft headed this way. It looks like they're…burning the ground ahead of them as they approach."

"Hoping to avoid what happened to Bishop's chopper," Samson says. "Smart."

"Burning it with what?" I ask.

"Liquid fire." Shechara shakes her head. "I've never seen anything like it."

"Sounds like napalm," Samson replies.

We press onward. By Shechara's count, Cain has already lost nearly twenty warriors. Whatever Willard did to augment these daemons, it worked. According to Luther, they are nothing like the variety that met him, Shechara, and Samson in the tunnel leading out of Eden. When Willard trapped them, forcing them to fight for their lives, those daemons were frail and emaciated. Samson with his massive strength disemboweled most of them by hand, stacking the corpses to hold back the onslaught.

I don't see that happening this time.

"Is Cain falling back?" Luther asks.

"He's still inside his vehicle," Shechara says. "It's plowing straight into the horde. The daemons are climbing on top, trying to break in, falling on top of each other."

If we're lucky, all of them will be otherwise occupied by the time we arrive on the scene.

"Everyone ready?" Luther calls back.

We raise our weapons. I carry a spear, preferring hand-to-hand combat, but Shechara insisted that I take a handgun as well. So a semiautomatic is tucked into my belt.

"Guess you can't carry a crossbow anymore," I tell Rehana.

"We'll do our best to confuse your enemy while you slip inside. May the Creator bless your efforts."

Nothing at all like the Rehana I knew, who never believed in a higher power. But I nod to show I heard her and prepare myself for what's to come. Bloodshed, I'm sure, and plenty of it.

I've killed my fair share of daemons over the past year and a half; I don't fear them. Even this new breed doesn't frighten me. What makes me nervous is the thought of rescuing the unborn children. How will we possibly get them all out of Eden safely? And even if we do, how will we take care of them in the Homeplace with no power, no running water, no heat? Wouldn't it really be better to let the UW troops take them?

My thoughts are cut short.

The stench of fresh carnage approaches as Luther leads us at a dead run into the battle's northern flank. The daemons are raging, wild and powerful, tossing Cain's warriors through the air and overturning their jeeps. The ones on top of the Hummer rock it side to side, intending to capsize it. Their gnarled fists pound the windows, unrelenting yet unable to break the bulletproof glass.

Cain's faster warriors whip through the daemon throngs leaving splashes of black blood in their wakes, blades slashing with flashes of sunlight. The fighters armed with rifles down the daemons with headshots, leaving close to a hundred lying in pools of their own blood. But there is no end to this horde. Daemon upon daemon lunges forward with hungry snarls and yellow eyes bulging hatefully, their steel collars blinking red. I avert my gaze from a pair at the periphery as they tear a warrior's body into bloody pieces and gobble up the slick organs like they haven't eaten in weeks.

Luther has his shotgun at the ready, slamming the stock against daemon skulls in his way, saving ammunition. Samson brings up the rear, sending any daemon stupid enough to approach him flying backward through the air, cut in two. The

Rehana-spirit stirs up the dust at our feet to cover our approach, blinding the enemy to our presence until it's too late for them.

I plunge my spear through the throat of a daemon lunging my way and down it instantly. Jerking the black spearhead free, I sprint after Luther, keeping up with his advance. We race toward the parking structure where we first encountered Willard and his men.

That seems so long ago. A lot has changed since then.

By the time we reach the first sublevel, we've lost six from our group. Samson tells us he saw them fall without a chance to fire a single shot. He dispatched the daemons responsible, and the black blood drooling down both his arms is proof he did so with extreme prejudice. But there is no time to claim the dead.

The underground parking garage is as dank and silent as I remember—eerily so, with the abandoned vehicles sitting right where they were the last time we saw them. As if no time has passed. We remove our head coverings, goggles slid up onto our foreheads or left to dangle around our necks.

Sudden gunshots explode like bombs going off, echoing throughout the structure. Daemons foolish enough to follow us inside fall dead, thanks to the rear guard. Luther leads us downward until we reach a tunnel that doesn't look familiar. I remember why: I didn't get this far before. The evil spirit possessing Milton took me topside and left me in the middle of the street instead.

Clunking along behind us, Samson mutters a curse at the sight of the tunnel. He remembers it all too well.

With no daemons now to contend with, it's clear that Milton and Bishop are in charge of Eden. They must have called off Willard's *dogs* from this area once they spotted us entering the parking garage. Estimating the distance to Eden's central dome to be two or three kilometers through the tunnel, we pace ourselves, moving as a unit in a steady jog. Samson does well keeping up, lunging from one leg to the other in long, awkward strides, the clanking noise drowning out the sounds of our breathing and footsteps.

Eventually, we reach the massive steel hatch into Eden.

An intercom speaker switches on above us. I hope we don't hear Willard's nasal voice.

"Glad you guys could make it," Milton says. "Want in?"

"Yeah, and be quick about it!" Samson bellows, catching his breath.

The hatch swings open with a long, slow creak. We enter Eden's subterranean dome, lit up inside as bright as day. Milton shakes hands with Luther and hugs Shechara as the others filter inside. Once Samson is through, Willard's soldiers swing the hatch shut and lock it into place.

"You all look like you've been through the wringer." Milton's gaze lingers on Samson's arms, dripping daemon blood onto the pristine concrete floor.

"You look like you're playing for the wrong team." Samson scowls at Milton's choice of attire—an Eden Guardsman's uniform.

"Couldn't be helped." Milton shrugs.

"Are the children safe?" Luther grips Milton's arm and glances at Willard's soldiers nearby, who stare mutely.

Milton nods. "Checked them out myself. Bishop's with them now. Figured one of us should always be there, you know—Willard being an untrustworthy bastard and all."

"Where is he?" Fury reignites inside me at the sound of his name. The fetuses may be safe for now, but I know how to keep them that way. "And Perch. I want to see both of them."

"Daiyna—" Luther gives me a concerned look.

I point at him. "Don't." Tears burn my eyes, and I struggle to restrain them. "They took something from me—from *us*—" I glance at Shechara, who directs her expressionless gaze at the floor. "You can't understand, Luther. We'll never be the same." Because of what they did to us, Shechara and I will never be able to have children of our own.

Luther holds out his scarred hands. "Our children are *here*, Daiyna…"

"I have to end this." I pound a fist against my chest where hatred has raged like an inferno for so many months.

Willard's men murmur among themselves, watching me. They're armed, but they won't try to stop me. I won't let them.

"Where's Willard?" I demand. One of the Eden Guardsmen hesitantly points up toward Willard's quarters. Of course. Things have come full circle. The last time I saw him up there, he was wedged between the unconscious bodies of his men.

I start for the ladder and its adjoining catwalk.

"I'll go with you," Shechara says quietly.

I don't turn her away. Milton and Luther approach.

"We need him, Daiyna," Milton says. "He's in communication with the leader of the United World, somebody named Hawthorne. They've got a rapport going, if you can believe."

I ignore him, reaching for the rungs and pulling myself upward hand over hand.

"Daiyna, think about what you're doing," Luther admonishes from the floor below. He doesn't move to follow.

"I have. Believe me." I haven't thought about much else lately.

"Stay right where you are," Samson advises Willard's men as they shift their weapons.

"What's she doing?" one of them demands.

"Payback's a real bitch," Samson rumbles.

I'm halfway up the ladder when I notice Milton has beaten me to the catwalk. He cheated, flying.

"You're not going to stop me," I tell him. A stupid thing to say. He moves so fast, he can stop me before I even know I've started.

"You're right. I'm not."

"Then get the hell out of my way."

He takes a step back. As I reach the catwalk, he unlocks Willard's door and slides it aside. "Figured you'd need to get in." He holds up the key. But he's not smiling.

I reach for the semiautomatic tucked into my belt.

"Daiyna—" Shechara climbs up behind me.

"He's not getting off this continent." I clench my jaw.

Milton nods. I've never seen him look so grim. "I'll be right outside if you need anything," he says.

I glance down below. Everyone but Samson is following one of Willard's guardsmen, probably going to check on the incubation pods and meet with Sergeant Bishop. Samson remains behind to keep any of Willard's more foolhardy men from climbing the ladder after me. They maintain their distance, eyeing his biomechatronic arms.

I meet Milton's gaze. "Thank you."

"I once killed a man who embodied evil for me, and now I see him whenever the evil spirits manifest themselves. Jackson—I might've mentioned him to you." Milton shrugs. "Willard deserves to die. Don't get me wrong. I'm just saying, if you want him showing up all the time from here on out, go ahead and end him. If you're lucky, maybe that's the last you'll ever see of him." He pauses. "But honestly, I would let the UW have the guy. They deserve each other, don't you think?"

No. Arthur Willard deserves only one thing.

I look away. I don't give myself a chance to change my mind. With my gun at the ready, I enter the apartment and pull the trigger as soon as I see the man sitting on the sofa. He doesn't get to say a word.

I keep firing until the gun clicks empty.

EPILOGUE: HAWTHORNE

18 MONTHS AFTER ALL-CLEAR

I stand before the full-length mirror in my office and smooth back the lines around my eyes and mouth. I wear my years well, but there are always improvements to be made. Thankfully, Dr. Wong will be available tomorrow to make them.

Garbed in a tailored black dress with a fetching little vest and a tasteful string of pearls around my neck, I murmur quietly to myself as I go over my speech from memory.

A new day is dawning on Eurasia, one of great hope...

On a widescreen next to the mirror, a live vidfeed from the *Argonaus* air assault on Eden comes through on my private channel. The hoverplanes' incinerators have neutralized resistance on the ground. Apparently, there was some sort of altercation between hordes of hideous mutants and clans of survivalists. Charred bodies and scorched earth are all that lie outside the city ruins now.

Ash in the wind.

Captain Mutegi mentioned something about a bullet-scarred Hummer approaching what's left of the capsized shipyard on the coast, but that doesn't concern us. If anyone survived Mutegi's shelling along the shore, I am certain they will pose little threat to our planes and precious cargo.

What matters now is the scene playing out before me.

Arthur Willard's people are bringing the incubation chambers to meet my ground assault team holding the ruins' perimeter. The man originally in charge of the mission, John (or James? Jack? I must remind myself to find out) Bishop, did not die in the line of duty like the rest of his team, as we assumed. His wife and children were released from custody as soon as he was pronounced dead; they may even have attended his memorial. Won't it be a surprise for them when he returns to a hero's welcome?

I almost smile at the thought of it—but quickly refrain. Smiling makes additional lines fold across my cheeks.

The announcement will go live as soon as the fetuses are on board the hoverplanes headed back to the *Argonaus*.

Citizens of Eurasia, rejoice! The children are coming!

I clasp my hands together as tears well up in my eyes. This is what it feels like to be giddy with joy. I cannot wait to show the doctors and scientists these prime specimens, twenty infants just waiting to be born—all uninfected and without the infertility problem plaguing the United World populace.

These children will grow up to be Eurasians of the future...

My thoughts dissipate as I focus on the screen. The first of the incubation pods emerge out of what was once a parking substructure before D-Day. The figure carrying the pod wears loose cotton clothing, a quaint head covering wrapped around his face, and black goggles to protect his eyes from the sun. Another figure similarly clothed appears, carrying an identical incubation canister. Then another, and another, each figure moving slowly with what appears to be...reverence.

The last arrival is a cyborg. The massive figure carries two pods, one in each of its mechanical arms.

"Chancellor, are you seeing this?" says the voice of Captain Mutegi on my audiolink.

I nod, counting every pod in the arms of these faceless people standing among a myriad of blackened corpses, facing the armed UW troops but advancing no farther. All twenty are here.

"Where is Arthur Willard?" I demand. "They're—" I peer closely at the monitor. "These people aren't wearing ventilators!"

"Willard has not responded. No one inside Eden is answering our hails. Not even Sergeant Bishop." Mutegi pauses. "Please advise."

I narrow my gaze. "Who *are* they?"

One of the figures speaks up, and his voice comes through the link loud and clear:

"Representatives of the United World, welcome to what remains of the North American Sectors. We know you have traveled far to reach us, and we know why you have come." The man raises the incubation canister in his arms. "For our children."

I clench my jaw to keep it from dropping. "What is this?"

Mutegi makes no reply.

"We understand your situation, that you are unable to conceive as a consequence of your actions on D-Day," the nameless man continues. "Our Creator has blessed us with unspeakable gifts, abilities you would not understand. Not that we do ourselves." The man pauses. When he continues, his voice is thick with emotion, "We give you our children, knowing you will be able to provide them with a better life. They will not suffer the hardships we have come to expect, living on this quarantined continent. They will not know us, but we hope you will tell them about us. And if they wish, at some point in the future, to allow us to live with them in their world...we pray they will look upon us kindly."

The man falters, his shoulders trembling. Yet he maintains a secure hold on the pod.

Others in his ranks stir, but no one moves. Only the cyborg shouts, "Come and get 'em, for crying out loud. Before we change our damn minds!"

"Move in," I give the order, and Mutegi relays it to his troops.

The soldiers in armored hazard suits retrieve each of the pods and carry them to the waiting hoverplanes stirring up dust with their rotors in motion. The canisters are strapped in securely for their flight to the *Argonaus* where doctors eagerly await their arrival. I watch until the last pod is taken from that peculiar assembly of desert people.

They stand like vandalized statues.

As the planes eventually lift off and the ground assault teams turn an about-face from the city ruins to march westward, I dismiss the screen with a wave of my hand. It darkens automatically, and I return my gaze to the mirror. My eyes are glassy with the tears I restrained from ruining my makeup.

Citizens of Eurasia, rejoice...

Tapping my temple, I deactivate the audiolink and reach for the antique snuff box in my vest pocket. Inside the silver filigreed container sit a few ounces of dust, taken from what once were the North American Sectors. Gently I inhale just a pinch with my left nostril, then my right. I wipe away the remnants from my upper lip with a silk kerchief that I fold neatly and keep in the palm of my hand.

For a moment, there is only the silence of my expansive office. Intermittent shadows cross my window-wall as aerocars pass by, soaring over the city's splendor at the same altitude as its Chancellor.

Then the voices hit me in waves that roll one after another, people talking on every floor of this one-hundred-fifty-story skyscraper—the tallest in Dome 1. I hear them all, acutely aware of everything everyone is saying. I am able to tune into any conversation I wish, hopping from one to another, as long as the dust effects last. Often for minutes at a time.

As the citizens await my speech, one word repeats again and again throughout countless conversations, and it makes me smile broadly:

Children...

FROM THE PUBLISHER

Thank you for reading *Tomorrow's Children,* book two in
Spirits of the Earth.

We hope you enjoyed it as much as we enjoyed bringing it to you. We just wanted to take a moment to encourage you to review the book on Amazon and Goodreads. Every review helps further the author's reach and, ultimately, helps them continue writing fantastic books for us all to enjoy.

If you liked this book, check out the rest of our catalogue at www.aethonbooks.com. To sign up to receive a FREE collection from some of our best authors as well as updates regarding all new releases, visit www.aethonbooks.com/sign-up.

JOIN THE STREET TEAM! Get advanced copies of all our books, plus other free stuff and help us put out hit after hit.

SEARCH ON FACEBOOK:
AETHON STREET TEAM

ALSO IN THE SERIES

After the Sky
You just read: ***Tomorrow's Children***
City of Glass

Printed in Great Britain
by Amazon